Enlightened

The EVE Series
Book 2

A. L. WADDINGTON

2nd Edition

Cover Design: Greg Simanson

This is a work of fiction. Names, characters, places, brands, media, and incidents are either the product of the author's imagination or are used fictitiously. Any resemblance to similarly named places or to persons living or deceased is unintentional.

PRINT ISBN 978-1-948143-02-8
EPUB ISBN 978-1-948143-06-6

Library of Congress Control Number: 2018956556

Acknowledgments

I would like to thank Jesse James Freeman and Heather Unrue for their support, feedback, and words of encouragement. Also, lots of love for my beta reader, Abbie Unrue, whose critical eye, and love of the series provided great insight and questions to be addressed. Of course, last but certainly not least, my family, without whom I could never have followed my dreams.

For Dale Danko, I am so blessed to have you as part of my life. Your love, your strength, and your faith in this world have always set an example of the kind of person I strive to be. I love you more!

Not all who wander are lost.

~J. R. R. Tolkien

Go confidently in the direction of your dreams.

~Henry David Thoreau

PREFACE

I HAVE HEARD PEOPLE SAY BEFORE that your life can change forever in a single day. I never thought it could really be true, but that was before Jackson Chandler moved into the house across the street from mine. His mere presence literally made me dizzy and nauseous. The few times we had touched caused me to blackout and experience episodes full of strange visions of another life. Memories like from a dream.

And yet, I felt this unexplainable draw to him. I had to be near him, always. I fell in love long before I even realized that it had happened. Oddly enough, he had fallen just as hard for me too. But our love could not be explored because of the episodes.

On Halloween 2015, Jackson and I were supposed to be getting dressed up in Victorian era costumes to attend our friend Cody's party, but he ran into me on the stairs and caused me to blackout suddenly and take a horrible tumble.

Battered and bruised, I lay at the foot of his stairs seeing vivid images of myself in a beautiful white gazebo on a spring day with the man I loved. This man, whom I could not see, proposed to me with the sweetest words I had ever heard. But when I'd said yes, and he looked up at me, I was amazed to see my new boyfriend, Jackson, staring lovingly back at me.

After Jackson and his parents spent hours explaining about *EVE* (*Essence Voyager Era*), a gift that I apparently inherited from my dad's brother, Monte, I was more baffled and confused than ever before. This gift, or curse, I am not sure which, allowed me to fall asleep in one plane of existence and awaken in another, making it so I was living parallel lives. I spent half of my existence in the twenty-first century and the other half in the late nineteenth. Jackson and his family were also afflicted with the same ability.

None of it made any sense to me, nor seemed remotely possible. I could not wrap my brain around the idea that because of this *EVE* thing, every night when I fall asleep here in 2015 my soul awakens to an alternate life in 1878.

Discovering that my soul traveled along parallel planes every night aroused a sense of uneasiness in me that I cannot describe.

Even stranger was when Jackson sat next to me on the couch, closer than we had ever been before, and for the first time I felt nothing. No dizziness, no cold chills, no nausea—nothing but an amazing love for him. I reached out my hand as if to touch him, but instantly decided to take full advantage of the lack of negative side effects that I normally experienced when I am close to him and pressed my lips gently against his soft, full lips.

CHAPTER 1

Sunday, November 01, 2015

I WOKE UP AS THE SUN WAS BEGINNING to peek over the horizon. My head throbbed with visions of a large group of people sitting around a hearth, listening to a man read. Several of them I recognized. Others I didn't. Yet, strangely, I knew who they were. Stranger still was the appearance of my Uncle Monte and his family. He appeared to be very happy as he spent the evening chatting with my father and brothers.

I lay there running the events over and over in my head, trying to make some sense of it all, but I couldn't. Then suddenly, I got angry.

I jumped out of bed and quietly got myself dressed. I grabbed my winter jacket and boots and snuck out onto the sun porch. My car turned over with little noise. I turned up the heat and backed out of the driveway heading to somewhere I had never wanted to go. I knew vaguely where my uncle's grave was, in the cemetery on the other side of town, where my grandparents were buried.

I parked on the north side and sighed heavily. The early morning air was musty, thick, and cold. Even though the sun had finally come up, it never penetrated the heavy cover of clouds. There was a faint drizzle coming down, and I hoped the rain would hold off for a while.

After wandering around aimlessly for a short time, I finally stumbled across our family plots. My Uncle Monte was resting next to my grandfather, with my grandmother on the other side of her husband.

I felt so out of place. I wasn't sure exactly what I thought coming here would accomplish. I had never been there alone.

I dusted the colorful dead leaves off his headstone and stared down at the dates. I knelt in front of the headstone as large tears fell silently down my cheeks.

"Why? Why did you do this to me?" I whispered. "If you knew this thing, this *EVE* thing, was inherited, why did you leave me here to deal with it? Why aren't you here to help me?"

I sat down on the wet leaves. My shoulders slumped, and I let go of everything that had been pent up for the last several weeks.

"Why? Why aren't you here to answer my questions? There are so many things I want to ask you," I sobbed uncontrollably.

"How could you be so selfish? How could you just leave me here to figure this out on my own? I hate you! I hate you for being happy." I was so angry at the man I only had a vague memory of in this life.

I climbed to my feet and paced back and forth in front of his grave. The drizzle turned into light rain, but I couldn't feel it. Adrenaline was pumping rapidly through my body, causing me to block the cold. I could only feel the hurt and anger. I leaned against a big oak tree and bent over with my hands on my knees. My mind was racing in a thousand different directions, but still the tears wouldn't stop.

I looked back up at my uncle's headstone through my blurry vision and shook my head. "You knew there was a chance! You knew it! But you left me anyways. Why?" My screams echoed about the hollow cemetery. I slid down the tree and buried my head in my knees and wept.

It was almost noon before I arrived back home. I was soaked to the bone and suffering the worst headache I'd had since I woke up in the hospital after hitting my head on the coffee table. I jumped into the shower and let the hot water drown out my fears and sorrows.

I decided not to call Jackson. I refused to come across as pathetic or even worse, needy. I paced relentlessly around my bedroom, glancing out my bay window every two seconds to see if there was any movement inside his house across the street. There was none.

This is ridiculous!

The whole story of soul switching, drifting, or whatever it is, seemed too far-fetched to even be considered possible. But I trusted them. I believed them. I believed in him. This was everything I was trying to avoid weeks ago when Jackson first entered my world —the drama that seems to go along with having a boyfriend. But I never could have ever in my wildest dreams expected this screwed up scenario.

I sat down in my window seat and leaned my head against the cold glass. His house looked as empty as I felt. Tears welled back up in my eyes. I pulled my knees up to my chest and wrapped my arms around them. My heart was ripping in half.

"Jocelyn? Are you okay?" I looked in the direction of the voice to find my brother, Ethan, standing in the doorway with a strange look on his face.

I quickly wiped the tears off my cheeks.

"Fine. Just feeling stupid and sorry for myself. That's all."

He crossed over and sat down on the other end of the window seat.

"Jackson is downstairs. Do you want me to tell him you'll call him later?"

"He's here? Are you serious?"

"Yeah. So, what do you want me to do?"

I couldn't get my mind back to the same place it was yesterday. The morning had done a number on my nerves after fighting all night not to sleep. I was terrified of what would happen once I did.

"Tell him I will be down in a minute."

I needed to fix myself up before Jackson saw me.

Ethan headed to the door, rolling his eyes along the way. "Whatever… girls," I heard him mutter under his breath as he closed my door.

The two of them were both down in the rec-room basement watching an NFL game. Jackson was lounging on the couch wearing jeans and a long-sleeved, dark green T-shirt. His dark, wavy hair was tousled perfectly. His emerald, green eyes lit up as he laughed at something my brother had said. He looked totally at ease in my home.

"Hello, stranger." I tried to keep my voice steady as I entered the room.

"Good afternoon. I tried to call you." He smiled and kissed me on the cheek when I sat down beside him.

"I'm sorry. Somehow, I must have put my phone on silent."

"I was beginning to think you were avoiding me," he teasingly complained.

"Sorry."

Jackson placed his hand on my knee. "No big deal. I live across the street." He cocked his head slightly and curled his brow. "So, it really was a lot of trouble coming all the way over here to speak with you." He flashed me my favorite lopsided grin.

"I believe that's my cue to leave. I'm going to go call Corbin and see how he's feeling today after the party last night." Ethan laughed as he climbed up the stairs.

We sat in silence, waiting until we were sure we were alone. We held each other's gazes, stating a thousand words without ever muttering a sound. I could feel the unexplainable bond to him. My love for him was so incredibly real and strong.

"I was so worried about you. I could not sleep at all last night. I was up waiting for your call." Jackson pulled me into his arms.

"I was afraid to call you." A weak laugh escaped halfheartedly. "I wanted to, but I couldn't bring myself."

"Why?"

"I was too terrified to sleep, and I didn't want to tell you."

Jackson tightened his hold and lightly kissed me on the cheek.

"I am always here for you. You never have to be scared of anything."

"I know," I whispered. "I just don't know how I'm supposed to feel about all this. It's beyond strange."

I struggled against the tears again. I was determined not to break down in from of him.

"Trust me. I have been in your shoes." He cupped my face in his hands. "I know exactly the wide array of emotions that you are experiencing, and it does get easier with help and time."

"I feel so lost."

"You are not lost. No matter where you are, I am with you."

"Can I ask you something silly?"

"Anything."

"What happened last night?"

It had been driving me crazy. All morning, I kept wondering if what I remembered was real or not.

"What do you mean?"

"*There.* What happened *there* last night?"

"It was just a typical Sunday." Jackson shrugged his shoulders nonchalantly. "Church services. Family dinner. We have very large families. Then we listened to your brother Jonathon read by the hearth for a while. It was uneventful."

I leaned back against the sofa, trying to comprehend it all. It still didn't seem possible to me.

"You wore a dark green dress today, and your hair was curled like you had it for the party. You looked so lovely." Jackson smiled lovingly at me.

I could feel myself blushing.

"You know what is funny? You are you in both eras. You blush the same. Smile the same. Laugh the same. It is truly incredible." He slightly shook his head in awe.

"Is my personality the same?" I was so curious about this *other* me.

"Almost. I mean, you are still you. Granted, a slightly different version of you because the time periods are so different. Your grammar is much better *there*. You are more proper and lady-like. You are more restrained in your words and actions. *Here* you express yourself freely; *there* you really cannot. You also hate the fact that all your brothers have got to go or are attending college, and you are not allowed to. *Here* you seem to thrive in your thirst for knowledge."

"I can't go to college?" I was confused. "Why?"

"Your father, Patrick would never allow it. He is very old fashioned and believes that a woman's place is in running the home and tending to her husband and children."

"How provincial! Why don't I just go anyway? It's my life."

Jackson chuckled. "As much as you hate it, you would never openly disagree with him or defy his wishes. But you do sneak around and read books and newspapers behind his back."

"Really? That's funny. I hardly pay attention to the news here."

"Well, the world is changing quite rapidly, I am afraid. And *there*, I believe, the fact that your father tries to restrict your awareness only heightens your curiosity."

"It must."

"As strange as I know it seems to you, you still maintain your core personality traits."

"How can I still be me? I mean, how do you keep everything straight?"

I snuggled up onto his shoulder. He held me tightly for a few minutes before he answered. "I think maybe it would be best if you spoke with my parents, rather than me. I can tell you some things, but my family was essential in getting me through this. I was honestly terrified. The world no longer made any sense to me. I did not know what was real and what was not."

"Are your parents' home?"

My mind needed some answers, despite the terror I was feeling.

"Actually, they are expecting us." Jackson gave me a puzzled look. "Can I ask you something?"

I nodded.

"Why does your father, Shane, not like me?"

"He does. He's only afraid of me getting hurt. He found your birthday gift the night I got injured. He read the inscription."

"I understand." Jackson kissed me softly.

I snuggled up against him and allowed all the tension to flow away from me.

We joined his parents later that evening for dinner. His mother, Emily, had made a roast and all the trimmings. We gathered around their dining room table that was set with an elegance that only Emily herself could pull off. His father, Robert, stood at the head of the table, carved the roast, and served everyone their plates before settling down himself. Their proper statures still amazed me in comparison to how my family behaved.

"How was your day today, you two?" Emily asked, passing around the dinner rolls.

"Fine," Jackson replied.

I smiled and shook my head. "Does this *EVE* thing get easier?"

"Yes, with time. I do not want you to believe that now, because you are aware of it, things will all magically merge and become incredibly simple. It does not. We must consciously work at it every day. But having those around you who understand helps a great deal," Emily explained.

"We have to monitor everything we say. How we act, or react," Robert continued. "It is not like we can make a reference to anything we know of history or rather history as we know it *here*. It can get quite complicated sometimes."

"How do you mean?" I asked.

"It is not like you can make references to upcoming presidents or elections. The World Wars have not occurred yet. Science, technological advances, let alone Korea or Vietnam, the invention of the automobile…all of it. Most of your world *here* does not exist in your *other* life," Robert explained, gesturing with his hands for emphasis.

I began to understand how tricky this was going to be. "So, I have to act naïve in regard to everything?" I shrugged with a smile. "I suppose it's a good thing that history is my worst subject."

That statement at least broke the serious tone and got a laugh from all.

"It is allowing the courses of action to unfold as they may. Even though we know of the horrible events that are yet to come. Tragedies, such as Hitler, Pearl Harbor, and the Holocaust or the sinking of the Titanic and thousands of other things. We must never utter a word around anyone under no uncertain terms." Emily emphasized.

"We are not trying to scare you, Jocelyn. I am sure that it will still be some time before the barrier completely disintegrates. At least a few weeks or so. Perhaps even longer. But these are things that you must know and follow by the letter." Robert's voice mimicked Emily's.

I suddenly got very uneasy. Jackson reached across the table and placed his hand over mine with a loving expression. "I know this is a lot to comprehend. But you need to know that we will all be here for you, to help you get through it."

All I could do was stupidly nod back. I stared at the three faces looking at me and felt like I was drowning in something that I couldn't find my way out of. I placed my napkin down on the table. "I'm sorry. I am not feeling very well. Thank you so much for dinner, but I believe that I need to head home."

Jackson rose from the table while Robert and Emily exchanged puzzled looks.

"I will walk you." He placed his napkin on the table and started to push his chair under the table, but I interrupted.

"No…thank you. I will be fine. I just want to go home."

His face looked hurt, but I couldn't help it. I had to get out of there as quickly as possible.

"Please call me before you go to bed."

Jackson walked me to the front door. He reached out to hug me, but I quickly backed away from him and left before his hurt look could imprint fully in my consciousness.

I ran across the yard feeling like screaming. I threw open the front door and ran straight to the bathroom and got sick. I was so mentally exhausted. I hadn't even noticed the hysterical sobs escaping from my chest.

I climbed into my old flannel pajama bottoms and a long-sleeved thermal shirt. I lay down on my bed and closed my eyes. I wrapped my arms around my extra pillow. I was terrified to fall asleep, but my head was throbbing so badly that despite my fears, I relaxed and let sleep overcome me.

CHAPTER 2

Wednesday, November 06, 1878

THE WEEK PASSED EVER SO SLOWLY. Each night before I drifted away, I would hold onto Jackson's birthday gift, the elegant pocket watch, anxiously awaiting a world that was so incredibly foreign to anything I had ever experienced before. I longed to be the woman I was in that place. Her independence, her strength, the opportunities that lay before her were everything I had ever dreamed of. I saw glimpses of her life and the jealousy I felt towards her was unbearable. She lived in a world where she could express herself freely, receive the education she desired and had the choice to choose who she wanted to become. Nowhere in anything I have thus far witnessed did marriage or children factor into her decision-making. I envied her to the extent that I almost hated her.

I still wasn't sleeping well. I tossed and turned each night and woke every morning feeling as if sleep had never found me. Our housekeeper, Mimi, had taken to staying close by my room each night after I retired since I was now transitioning back from my imaginary world into mine with screaming hysterics. She would then rush to my bedside and hold me until the sobbing subsided and I exhausted myself out. I loved her for doing so, but also felt incredibly guilty since I knew she was already worn out by the end of the day and my antics were only making her life more difficult. However, the passion I felt for this imaginary world compelled me to continue pushing forward each night to see what else it had to show me.

I walked home from school with Elizabeth, one of my dearest friends. It was shortly after three and the sun was already falling from the sky. By five o'clock it would be dark. The days were getting increasingly shorter as winter crept up on our doorstep. The frigid air was crisp, and full of moisture. The autumn smells had all disappeared with the festival. Now, moist smog filled with musk consumed the air. The transition period between Halloween and Christmas was always filled with rain and darkness, and bouts of snow that only last a day or so. It was a lonely state of being when nature hibernated before the full grasp of the upcoming winter took its hold upon us.

We pulled our caplets tighter around us as the bitter wind whipped around our bodies. I suddenly regretted telling our houseman, Eddie, this morning that I would rather walk than have him pick me up.

"How is your beau doing?" I inquired, trying to take my mind off the cold.

"Lee is well. His career is really taking off, so he is busy until late in the evenings, but he comes by every night after dinner to spend some time with me."

"He seems like a wonderful man. I am truly happy for you."

"Are you alright?" She glanced over at me with her eyebrows wrinkled towards the center of her brow.

"Yes, of course. Why?" I was curious as to why she would ask such a question.

"You seem tired."

"Not really."

"Wedding jitters?" She gave me a coy smile and relief flooded through me.

"Yes. Most likely."

"I thought all the plans had been taken care of. What are you concerned about?"

"I let Miss Olivia wear my wedding gown when she married my brother, William."

I glanced over at her face. I could see she was truly shocked by my gesture.

"That was very thoughtful of you, but why? With your wedding so close, you will never have enough time to have another gown made."

"She needed the gown more than I. She was having such a difficult time. I knew that her wearing my gown would mean a great deal to her. She needed to feel that we were all behind her no matter what," I explained as best I could.

"You love that dress." Elizabeth commented more to herself than to me.

"True. But I love her more," I shrugged.

"What are you going to do now?"

"Can you keep a secret?"

Elizabeth nodded.

"After their wedding, Mrs. Chandler took me aside and invited me over to her house for a surprise. The next day she showed me the gown that she married Mr. Chandler in." I couldn't contain my excitement just recalling the magnificent wedding gown. "I have to tell you; it is the most amazing gown I have ever seen in my life."

"That was a very kind gesture. Is your mother all right with it?"

"I have not told her yet. We are keeping it quiet. Besides, there is no way possible that I could wear my mother's gown. She is taller and more petite than I. Plus, as close as she and Mrs. Chandler are, I am sure she will be as thrilled as I am."

"What about Jackson?"

"He has no idea either. His mother wants to surprise him."

I was practically bouncing with excitement even though I was chilled to the bone.

"You are truly lucky to be getting such an incredible mother-in-law. I am so worried about meeting Lee's family at Thanksgiving, especially his mother."

"I am sure his family is going to love you. It would be impossible for them not to." I grinned, trying to reassure her. "Also, we need to get together soon to figure out your dress for my wedding." I wanted to brighten her mood. "How about Saturday afternoon?"

"Saturday afternoon would be wonderful."

We stopped in front of my house. I opened the front gate and saw that the front door was open slightly and Jackson was waiting to welcome me home. Elizabeth hugged me briefly before departing for home herself. I rushed up the walkway and into the arms of my soon, but not soon enough, to be husband.

The intoxicating aroma of his skin flowed through me as I wrapped my arms around him. For the first time in days, I felt safe and no longer cared about the other world consuming every thought that passed through me. That other woman in my visions may have everything else in this world, but she lacked the single most important thing that I wouldn't trade for every opportunity that she had: my Jackson.

"Hello, darling. How was your day?" Jackson leaned down holding me tightly in his arms and gently kissed the top of my head.

"Better now that you are home. I have missed you so much." I rested my head against his chest and listened carefully to the steady rhythm of his heartbeat. The sound filled me instantly with comfort and security.

I took off my caplet and scarf and handed them both to Eddie. We retreated to the parlor to warm me by the hearth while our housekeeper Missy brought in some hot tea. We sat down on the lounge, and I snuggled back into Jackson's arms, letting the heat from the fire flow over me.

"So, tell me. How are you really feeling?" He gave me an odd look that told me William had informed him about what happened last Sunday evening.

"My brother has a big mouth."

"He is concerned about you, as is Mimi," Jackson added, turning my face upward with his hand so I had to look him in the eye. "Be honest. What is going on that has you waking up screaming?"

"Really, it is nothing. Simply wedding jitters." I clung to the excuse that

Elizabeth had come up with.

Jackson narrowed his eyes as he stared at my face for a few moments. "No. I do not believe that. There is something else bothering you. It has been a while, and apparently, it is getting more discerning if it is now waking you up screaming in the middle of the night. Why will you not tell me what it is?"

"It is nothing. I have an overactive imagination."

"Explain please."

"I honestly do not know how."

It was impossible to explain what his birthday gift was doing to me. *How can I possibly tell him that this ordinary trinket is causing me to have visions of a world I so desperately want to be a part of? How can I tell him that I am not waking in horror of what I am witnessing, I am screaming in horror of the fact that I am returning to this world where I feel trapped by societal rules of who I have to be?*

I gently pulled away from him and stood up, walking over to the fire. I stared down at the flames and wondered how I could possibly feel so torn between the two worlds. Especially when one, I knew, was only a figment of my overactive imagination, and the other was real.

Jackson came up behind me, wrapping his arms around my waist and rested his head down upon mine.

"You know there is nothing you cannot share with me. No matter how silly it may seem. It worries me when something is troubling you so." The sincerity of his words touched my heart, but I knew this was something I had to keep to myself.

"I know, my love." I turned to face him. His bright green eyes looked so sad, and I hated that I was the one who put that sadness there. "I promise. It is nothing for you to concern yourself with."

"Jocelyn, you can be so difficult sometimes."

He took a deep breath and let me go. He paced around the room for several paces before he stopped and confronted me again.

"You truly aggravate me when you get like this. How can I ease your pain if you refuse to be honest about what is troubling your mind?"

The harshness of his tone annoyed me. I couldn't understand why this was bothering him so much. "Jackson, if I believed this was something you could help me with then yes, I would share it with you. But this is something that I need to work through on my own. Please try and understand that." I could not think of a better way to explain it to him or ease his consciousness.

"How do you know that I cannot help you unless you let me try?"

"I just do. You must trust me. A few nightmares are nothing you need to concern yourself with," I tried to reassure him, but the look on his face told me that nothing I could say short of the entire truth was going to ease his concern.

Missy came in and announced that dinner was ready just in time to save me before the conversation became even more intense. We retreated to the dining room and joined our families around the large table. Although everyone obviously knew about my nightmares, no one mentioned the subject outright. However, their constant odd glances in my direction throughout the meal were quite unsettling.

I did my best to ignore the looks and concentrate on the conversations instead. William was discussing his classes with Jackson and Robert. He seemed excited about the upcoming break that Thanksgiving was going to give him and commented on how it was becoming increasingly difficult to spend so much time away from his new wife.

The ladies listened almost silently as the men shifted the subject to politics. My mind drifted back to the visions I had witnessed recently. I stared off into the distance, barely touching my food, thinking about walking down the crowded strange hallway of what appeared to be the school I was attending.

The other students were all dressed in a bizarre array of fashions with strange-looking accessories. The metal boxes slammed open and shut, people shouted greetings to other peers. Many talked into, or were pushing buttons on, funny looking hand-held devices. Others remained silent with weird wires from their ears that led into a pocket on their person while nodding their heads aimlessly. It was an incredible sight to see.

The three girls I had seen previously in the musty room with the iron cages came bouncing up to me as I stood beside a tall metal box that I mindlessly turned the combination on and opened. Without thought, I exchanged several books and listened intently as the tall blond-haired person rattled on about something. I got the distinct feeling she was angry about something, but I had no idea as to why.

"Jocelyn?" I vaguely heard someone call my name. "Jocelyn!" I blinked and refocused my attention back to the boring reality of the table at which I was seated.

"Jocelyn? Are you feeling all right this evening?" My father's voice rang in my ears causing me to look over in his direction.

"Excuse me. I am sorry. I guess my mind was elsewhere." I could feel the blood rushing to my face.

"What was distracting you so much?" My mother inquired.

"I was recalling the lecture from Mr. Grahame's history class today. I was thinking about the essay I need to write this evening."

"Oh. That is nice dear." she said brightly.

"We have been concerned about you lately with the reoccurring nightmares and the screaming." My father continued eyeing me.

"There is nothing to worry about. I've had a lot on my mind lately."

"Understandable. However, when it causes me to bolt upright in my bed in the middle of the night, then I believe I have a right to inquire about the problem." His tone joined his look.

"Honestly, it's nothing. I am sorry that I awakened you," I apologized.

"I am more concerned with you than my sleep, sweetheart." My father's face softened.

"Everything will be fine. I am working through some things, and they are starting to work themselves out."

After Missy brought in the tray of saucers and coffee to the front room, I excused myself from the group claiming that I still needed to work on my history essay. I was secretly grateful that Olivia was no longer attending classes and wouldn't know I was bluffing about the assignment.

Jackson followed me over to the staircase and took a seat on the second step. I stood in front of him holding his hands in mine.

"I will be so happy when this semester is finally over," I pouted.

"You only have a couple weeks more. I will be done before Thanksgiving break. Unfortunately, even though I will be home, I will be consumed with studying for the bar. I must take and pass it before Christmas and our wedding. But I do promise you, after that, I am all yours."

"I know. But it is going to be difficult having you so close and not getting to spend any time with you." I continued my playful childish pouting with a sly grin.

"You will be so occupied with the final details for the wedding with our mothers that you will not even want me around to be in your way," he laughed and pulled me down beside him.

"Probably because you will drive me insane with your comments on how things should be done." I rolled my eyes with a smirk that only made him laugh harder.

Then his expression got serious. "Are you sure everything is all right?"

"For the millionth time, yes! Everything is fine. Will you please let it go?" I shook my head in frustration. I was so sick of having to constantly reassure everyone.

"It really scared me when William told me what happened on Sunday night. I believe you gave him a good scare also. And when I got here today, Mimi told me that you had repeated episodes the last two nights as well." Jackson shifted sideways to face me. "I am very worried about you, Jocelyn. You have been acting so differently lately and are being very elusive."

"Don't be silly. Nothing has changed, including me."

"I am being serious." Jackson's tone shifted just enough to make me look back up into his eyes.

"You need to worry about finishing your classes and passing the bar. These trivial little nightmares are nothing for you to concern yourself with. I promise." I quickly leaned over and kissed him passionately before he had the opportunity to retort.

The fire within me burned hotter and brighter than ever. I entangled my fingers through his hair and pulled him closer to me. Our breathing became labored, and I could feel the stubble of his facial hair brushing against my chin with searing desire. I loved the way he smelled, tasted, held me against him with an unquenchable thirst. I knew that he was the one thing in this world I would never sacrifice for anything in her world.

Jackson gently pulled back, breathing hard. "You know we cannot get carried away," he smiled seductively. "And you need to work on that essay. I must get back to campus."

"You are going back tonight? Why not tomorrow morning?"

"Yes. I have some work that I need to complete before tomorrow also. I really should not have come out this evening, but I was worried about you."

Now I really feel bad. He was neglecting his own studies because of my night terrors.

I stood back up and pulled him up alongside me. We held each other silently for several minutes, hating this part of the evening every time it arrived.

Darkness flooded my room. The soft glow from my fireplace added a little comfort. I snuggled down beneath my covers to foster my own torment. The embers glistened off the shiny metal of the trinket that rested quietly in its little box on the table beside my bed. I closed my eyes tightly, attempting to ignore it calling out to me. I couldn't risk another night of hysterical screaming, especially with William sleeping down the hall ready to report back to Jackson. The overwhelming curiosity of what I still desired to see was almost unbearable.

I rolled over and wrapped my arms tightly around an extra pillow. I buried my face into it consciously reminding myself that for tonight, the visions were prohibited.

CHAPTER 3

I HAD SUCCESSFULLY AVOIDED JACKSON since Sunday evening. As horrible as it may seem, I'd driven myself to school the last two days. I told him Monday morning that I wanted some time alone to think about things and thankfully, he had been very respectful of that.

We had been sitting beside one another in our shared classes and lunch as well, but we hadn't talked about anything more personal than the weather forecast. He seemed hurt by my behavior, and I did feel bad about that, but I wanted a little time to figure out how I felt about everything.

I also wanted time to do a little research on my own. I browsed through numerous websites on the 1870s, the history of Chicago, and everything else I could find on that time. I wasn't sure exactly what I expected to find, but it was all so depressing and foreign. Thomas Edison hadn't even invented the light bulb until 1879! The south was still a mess from the Civil War and experiencing the final leg of the reconstruction era. Working conditions in the north were deplorable and indoor plumbing was a rarity.

The more I read, the more depressed I got. This was not exactly a happy time. I wasn't looking for moonlight and roses by any means, but certainly not dread and hopelessness.

I pushed my keyboard away and rested my head down on my desk. I wasn't sure if I wanted to cry or scream. I thought again how ignorance was truly bliss and how much I wanted to go back to a time when I'd never heard of Jackson Chandler or *EVE*. This inherited gift felt more like a curse than anything else and I wasn't even sure I believed in it.

But of course, I knew I did, as much as I didn't want to admit it, especially to myself. I knew I needed to talk to Jackson, more than just superficially, and listen to all he and his family had to share with me. I knew in my heart that they were only trying to help me during this difficult transition, and I loved them for it. I just felt so confused and overwhelmed.

Once we finished dinner, Ethan and I went outside to shoot hoops. We both wanted to practice up a little since basketball try-outs were coming up the following day after school. Despite both of us being veteran players, it was always a requirement to go through try-outs like everyone else.

The evening was cool as the temperature hung around the mid-fifties and the clear skies kept none of the day's warmth. Ethan turned on the driveway lights as we headed out the back door.

"One on one?" he asked, tossing me the ball.

"Let's warm up a bit first," I suggested, feeling a little rusty.

We shot around for a good half hour playing nearly fair ball with one another. Ethan and I had such a playful rivalry that it was so natural for us to deliberately torment and show off to one another.

My younger brother paused and held the ball for a second pretending to be out of breath.

"Can I ask you something, Jocelyn?"

"Sure," I responded, coming up behind him and knocking the ball out of his hands. I made a run for the lay-up and for once, he didn't try and block my shot but rather just stood there watching me. I paused under the backboard looking at him curiously.

"What did Jackson do to piss you off?"

"I'm not mad at him," I shrugged and began dribbling again.

Ethan placed his hands on his hips and narrowed his eyes. "Right. And I just met you yesterday." He rolled his eyes at me before stealing the ball and taking the easy shot. "You have been driving us to school all week instead of riding with him. What changed?"

"Nothing. I just don't want to get so serious. Things were moving a little too fast. I wanted to slow it down a bit."

"I thought you really liked him." He gave me an inquisitive look.

"I did. I do. But I also must think about next fall. We're probably going to end up at separate universities and a long-distance relationship is unrealistic. Don't you think?"

It was the best excuse I could think of.

"Depends on how much you like him. And who's to say you can't go to the same college?"

I stopped in my tracks and stared at him. "Did he say something to you?"

"No." He shook his head. "I thought he might, but honestly he hasn't said a word about what's going on with you two."

"Well, it's no one's business but ours."

"All right, no need to get your panties in a bunch, I was just asking," he laughed and slapped the ball out of my hands. "Oh, did I tell you I broke up with Mariah?"

"Really?" He nodded, smiling. "Wow! When?"

"Yesterday. I told her that I thought we should see other people. She got really ticked and told me she really didn't like me anyways." He smirked and made an easy three pointer.

"Good for you. You deserve someone better than that." I caught the rebound and threw the ball back up.

"Yeah, but guess who asked me out after witnessing the scene between us in the hallway?" Ethan stood still with the ball giving me a funny look.

"Who?"

"Taylor Perry."

"What! You're kidding me?" This was too much, even for her.

"Yeah," he began dribbling again. "She asked me out for Friday."

I stood still glaring at my little brother. "If you start up with her, I swear E, I will never speak to you again. She is such a skank!"

Ethan laughed, clearly enjoying himself.

"Like I would ever be that desperate. I know she only asked me out to annoy you. Do you really think I'm that stupid?"

"What did you tell her?"

"I lied and told her I was interested in someone else," he shrugged. "It was easier than stirring up more crap between you guys."

"Are you interested in someone else?" I eyed him.

"Not really." The smirk that slid across his lips informed me otherwise.

"You two gossip more than old women," Kyle announced.

We spun around to see Jenna and Kyle walking over from Jenna's house.

"So, who are you interested in Ethan?" Jenna teased.

"I said no one in particular. If you're going to eavesdrop, at least get the story right." He tossed the ball towards Kyle.

"Touchy."

Jenna playfully bumped into him catching the rebound before he could get it.

The four of us played two on two for the next hour. It felt so freeing to cut loose and act so immature. It was exactly like old times, before Jackson, before *EVE*...before my life spiraled out of my control. This was everything I needed for the last several weeks. The time to be me, confident and assured. The me who was an athlete, a friend, a sister. The me who was normal.

"Mind if I join? I could use some practice too," Jackson's cheerful voice broke off our laughter.

I rebounded the ball, smiled painfully, and tossed it to him. "Of course."

Jackson made a three pointer from the top of the key without any difficultly and ran over to guard me for the rebound. No one said a thing and we continued our game. We naturally paired up with Jenna, Kyle, and I against Ethan and Jackson. Kyle was so severely handicapped on the court that he was more of a hindrance than an asset.

Finally, the game broke up because of rain. Kyle and Jenna headed off towards Kyle's while Ethan took off for the shower leaving Jackson and I standing alone on the sun porch. I felt ashamed of my recent behavior even though I knew I needed the time and space. I truly didn't want to hurt Jackson.

I stared down at the floor, afraid to look up into his beautiful green eyes. Afraid of what I might find there if I did.

"Jocelyn, are you going to talk to me?" He gently placed his cold hand on the side of my face, bringing my eyes up to meet his.

"I'm sorry. I just needed some time."

His eyes held mine with such tenderness that I was having difficulty breathing.

"I know." His voice was gentle and full of understanding, which only made me feel worse.

I slowly backed away from him and sat down on the wicker loveseat. I patted the cushion beside me gesturing for him to join me.

"This has been a lot to process and I'm feeling a bit overwhelmed," I squeaked out in a voice that was barely audible.

"I understand." He placed his hand on my leg. "I want to help you, not make it more difficult."

"I've actually been doing a lot of research the last several days."

"Research?"

"Yes. Mainly on the Internet. I also found my sister's old history book from the college course she took last fall. It covered everything from the Civil War to the Bush administration. I was curious about the period and all that was going on then. I guess I drastically underestimated how much things were changing in the world during that time."

"I told you the world was changing fast," he smiled softly. "However, that does not change things with us."

I couldn't help but smile at the way he looked at things.

"It's so hard to read about that time of period and know what is going to happen next. All those horrible things that we could prevent."

"You must remember something else. There are true horrors occurring in the world right now and if you were looking back at reading in a text, it would be disturbing to you. But sitting here on your back porch, you know there is nothing you can do to change them. The war in Iraq, the troubles in

Afghanistan, North Korea—can you change them?"

"No." I suddenly understood what he was saying.

"I know you are feeling helpless, but you must remember that things happen for a reason. We may not always like them and wish we could make a difference, but in our situation, we cannot change history. It is too dangerous and any alterations that you make can affect the current world you are living in today."

Jackson placed his hands over mine and brought them up to his lips kissing them softly.

"I hope your parents aren't to upset with me."

"No, they understand. They are impressed with how well you are handling it all." A small smile crossed his lips.

I brought my hand up to the side of his face, tracing his cheek. He hadn't shaved in a couple of days and had a sexy shadow of growth that made him look more his true age than the eighteen years he was trying to pass for.

"I've missed you." I felt a tear well up behind my eyes realizing, as I looked at him, how lonely I'd felt for the last several days without him.

"I have missed you also." He paused, staring at me. "I love you Jocelyn, I truly do. You are my life. Always."

"I love you too, Jackson." A small smile danced across his face.

He leaned over suddenly and kissed me passionately. A fire burned deep inside me as I wrapped my fingers through his hair holding him firmly to me. I slid a little closer, but he pulled back still smiling.

"You are trouble," he chuckled.

"Maybe."

"Does this mean I can drive you to school in the morning?" he asked with my favorite lop-sided grin.

"Of course."

"Are your parents around?" He glanced at the atrium doors.

"No. They sent text messages earlier. They are both stuck at the hospital."

"I don't want your dad to get upset with me again."

"He's just being a dad," I rolled my eyes playfully. "He remembers what happened when Danny moved, and he doesn't want to see me go through all of that again next fall when college starts."

"Who's Danny?" *Damn, I'd forgotten he knew nothing of him.*

"Danny was my first serious boyfriend. I mean, we were young and grew up together. We dated for a few years. But his dad was transferred to California, and he had to move. It was hard. I didn't take it very well." I felt foolish explaining an old relationship to him.

Jackson held a slight smile across his lips. "Well, at least I got to be your first love in one of your lives."

I wrinkled my forehead and stared at him. "You have any idea how weird that sounds?" He laughed and kissed me on the forehead. "And if you're really almost twenty-two years old and already finished with college, or at least your bachelor's, then you can't honestly expect me to believe that you never dated anyone but me."

"Okay. Guilty. I dated other women when I was in high school and college in Boston."

"Anyone serious?"

"Not really. Honestly, before I knew that you possessed *EVE*, I was talking with my family about doing what your Uncle Monte did and staying solely there. I did not believe that I could handle the dual lives and relationships as well."

"So, you have had other relationships with women, *here*. What about *there*?"

I was dying to understand everything about how this worked, but the thought of him touching someone else was killing me.

"*Here* yes, but you are the only one *there*. I mean since we have grown up. I had a few crushes when we were kids."

"Can I ask you something personal?" I hated asking, but since he already knew my status after the embarrassing confession in front of his parents, I figured I had the right to know as well.

"You can ask me anything." His voice was light and cheerful. Obviously, he had no clue what was on my mind.

"How much experience with other women have you had?"

His expression immediately changed. "Jocelyn, I did go to college."

"Yes. And?"

He took a deep breath as if he was choosing his words very carefully. "Well, *there*, you and I have been together for three years. I have always been faithful to you. *Here*, or rather in Boston, yes, I have been involved with other women."

"How involved?" I asked, grinning slightly.

"What exactly are you asking me, Jocelyn? You are the only woman I have ever proposed to."

"Are you a virgin?" Jackson looked shocked by my bluntness. "You know that I am, in both places. I'm just curious if you are as well." I tried not to grin, realizing how uncomfortable my line of questioning had made him.

"I cannot believe you would ask me something like that," he blundered. "Yes. *There* I am. You and I are waiting for our wedding night."

He suddenly let go of me and leaned back against the throw pillows and stared at his hands for a few moments. I remained silent thinking perhaps I had pushed it a little too far.

"You must understand something, Jocelyn. I do know exactly what you are feeling. I did not handle it well when my barrier began to deplete. I was a freshman in college, living away from home for the first time. I was frightened. I had no clue what was happening to me. I was scared half to death to try to explain it to my parents, thinking they would have me committed. So that first semester, I drank excessively with my friends almost daily to keep the visions away. My grades were okay, but not great. When I went home for Christmas break, I had a horrible screaming episode. That was when my parents and siblings sat me down and explained everything to me. For the remainder of the break, I questioned them extensively. And when I returned to school for the spring semester, I changed my major to psychology. I took every class available on neuroscience to try and understand everything better. It helped a little. After that, I decided to study law like my father."

I looked down at the couch absorbing everything he had just admitted. I knew he hated showing any kind of weakness, but I felt better knowing I was not alone in my current feelings. I needed to know that my reactions and questions were normal. If there was such a thing.

I tried to play it off as if all he had said was no big deal. After all, we all have a past.

"So, I guess then, you are telling me you thoroughly enjoyed your first semester of college with the ladies?"

"Yes." His voice was soft, and he refused to look me in the eye.

I reached over and placed my hands over his. "Am I supposed to be upset with you for having a life when you didn't know I existed?" Jackson barely looked up at me. "Sweetheart, I'm not judging you or upset with you. What you did to handle this realization is something I would never judge you for. I'm not exactly handling it all that well myself."

"But I really regret the fact that *here*, I did not wait." He dropped his eyes again.

"You know, as silly as it sounds, I would probably judge you if you had. I'm not sure what I would think of a guy making it to twenty-two in 2015, and still being a virgin. I would probably think there was something wrong with you." I tried to laugh it off to make him feel better.

"True." He lightened up a little. "I guess it is hard for you to imagine how truly different views are held between the two worlds."

"Yes. It is." I let out a deep breath.

Jackson glanced down at his watch. "Well, as much as I hate it, I had better leave before your father comes home and discovers us alone."

"But I don't want you to leave."

"I will be right across the street if you need me. All you must do is call." He leaned over and kissed me again. "I love you," he whispered in my ear.

"I love you too."

"I will see you in the morning. Sweet dreams, my love."

I sat there alone and watched him disappear around the corner in the dark. I knew it was getting late, but I wasn't ready to call it a night. Instead, I wanted to run after him and beg him never to leave my side, tell him I was too scared to be alone, especially at night.

But of course, I headed upstairs for the shower, dreading the long hours between now and morning when I would see Jackson again and feel safe.

CHAPTER 4

Thursday, November 07, 1878

I WAS CREEPING DOWN THE STAIRS in the darkened house, trying to be as quiet as possible, knowing that everyone else was still asleep. The banister along the stairwell was glowing with tiny little white lights covered in prickly greenery. Every other pedestal was adorned with a big, red velvet bow. It was Christmas morning; I could feel it. And I was young, very young.

I stood on the steps and looked down at my attire and ran my fingers over it. It was soft and fuzzy. It was one piece, with the feet attached to the legs. It was bright red with little white snowflakes all over it. I lifted my foot and looked at the bottom of it, a strange white, bumpy fabric. There was a continuous metal clasp that ran down one leg all the way up to my neck. *What bizarre sleeping apparel.* I shook my head slightly in disbelief and realized, as my pigtails whipped around my face, that I must be very young. Perhaps five, maybe six years old.

I began my descent once again when I was almost knocked the remainder of the way down by someone, a little boy, whom I knew somehow was my little brother.

"Santa came! Santa came!" He sang out as he ran past me.

I giggled aloud at his excitement and raced to catch up with him. I noticed that he was wearing similar sleeping attire to my own, except his was a dark vibrant blue trimmed in red around his collar and cuffs. He had bright primary-colored designs of some sort printed all over it. His stubby, dark blond hair stood up in various directions as he began to climb under the enormous Christmas tree.

His voice echoed through the house. I could hear movement coming from up above as our parents began to awaken. I turned around to the sound of feet on the stairs and saw a young girl rushing into the room. She was wearing a long, light pink nightgown trimmed with lace and ruffles. Her long blonde hair draped over her shoulders in soft curls, and her feet were covered in what appeared to be ballet slippers. She was petite and graceful, and beautiful.

She pranced over and sat down amidst the array of packages beneath the tree. I hesitated a moment, caught up in the vast similarities and numerous differences between this fantasy and my everyday reality. The fireplace mantel was the same, but the accessories and stockings were different. The furniture was dated, yet not ours. Same with the draperies. However, I felt oddly at ease in this environment.

Two adults entered the room calling out a chorus of "Merry Christmas" to the three of us. We all answered in close unison. I studied their faces carefully, realizing they were a somewhat younger version of the two people that I had seen on the Indiana University campus. My eyes quickly shifted back to the little boy who was still crawling around through the gifts. He must be the younger version of the young man who had accompanied us that day. I looked closer at his eyes, and he briefly smiled over at me, noticing my gaze. Yes, I was positive he was the same person.

"Ethan, honey. Please climb out of the tree before you break something," our mother gently told him.

Her face was beautiful and kind. I couldn't take my eyes off her as the vision started to blur before me. My heart began to beat out of my chest. I could feel the uncontrollable sobs escape from me. I knew the inevitable was coming, and I was powerless to do anything to prevent it.

The morning sunlight broke through the shadows surrounding my bedroom. I was sitting upright in my bed, sweating profusely, screaming, and sobbing uncontrollably. My entire body was shaking, while my vision cleared, and I could make out the images around me. Seconds later, William came bursting into my room, rushing to my bedside.

"Jocelyn! What's wrong?" he demanded, grabbing hold of my shoulders.

I reached out for him, trying to stabilize myself. I managed to slow my breathing, holding onto my brother, feeling the safety of his arms about me. I closed my eyes and rested my head upon his shoulder. *How did this happen? I wasn't holding the pocket watch. My hands were empty!* I was sure I had denied it when I went to bed the night before.

I peeked over at my night table. There it was, lying silently in its blue velvet. Untouched!

William slowly released me, but still held onto my shoulders. "Jocelyn are you alright?"

I nodded slowly, trying to make some sense of what had happened. *How was I having visions of this other world without holding the watch?*

"What is going on with you?"

I blinked several times trying to bring my focus back to William. "It was just a nightmare. I am sorry I woke you." My breathing slowly returned to normal.

"You didn't. I was getting ready to leave for school."

It was then that I realized he was already dressed for the day.

"You have to tell me what is going on with you. This is the fourth night you have woken up screaming."

"I know." I took a deep breath and fell back against my pillows. "I can't explain it." I shook my head and looked down at my hands.

"What is frightening you so badly?"

I closed my eyes thinking how wonderful it was going to be once he got back to campus and told Jackson all about this. I knew it was only a matter of time now before Jackson would start grilling me again.

"Jocelyn, please talk to me."

I opened my eyes and stared at him for a few moments. "It's nothing you need to concern yourself with, William. Honestly."

"I do not believe you. If this was a onetime episode, I could dismiss it. But I know you well enough to know that something has been bothering you for the last couple of weeks. I know that it is progressively getting more intense." He eyed me curiously.

"You are hardly ever here. How can you make such a proclamation?" I rolled my eyes and looked back over at the trinket.

"Say what you like, but I know you too well. And I know when something is bothering you."

"You are going to be late for your first class," I stated flatly and climbed out of bed. I grabbed my robe off the back of my vanity chair and wrapped it around me. William sat there for a minute just watching me. I knew he was studying my behavior, looking for something out of the ordinary.

"All right." He stood up and walked over to my door. He turned the knob but stopped and turned back towards me.

"Jocelyn, if you feel that you cannot confide in me about whatever is going on with you, then you should confide in Jackson. I know he is very worried about you, and it would ease his mind if you would talk to him about your nightmares."

I felt purely exhausted. My body was physically drained from too many restless nights and my mind was so mentally spent that the line between the visions and my reality was becoming rapidly blurred.

I sat down in my vanity chair and slumped over; tears began pouring down my cheeks. "I know. Please, tell him that none of this has anything to do with him."

William came over slowly and knelt in front of me. He placed his hands over mine and squeezed them tenderly. I looked up into his eyes and pleaded. "Please, William. Promise me you will make sure he understands that."

"I promise," he answered in a quiet voice. "Please, tell me what is going on. I cannot leave you like this. I will not be able to concentrate on anything at school because you will consume my thoughts."

"All I want to do is sleep. I feel like I have not slept in weeks," I weakly complained. "I am so tired. I don't think I can make it to school today. Can you please explain it to Mother for me?" I leaned over and rested my head upon his shoulder that was still damp from my tears.

"Of course." William cradled me in his arms and carried me back over to my bed. He lay me down and pulled the covers back over me, tucking me in tightly.

I snuggled back into the pillows and closed my eyes. I felt William's weight on my bed as he sat down beside me. He gently brushed my hair away from my face and wiped away my tears with a handkerchief. The soft touch of his fingers running constantly through my hair was incredibly soothing. It wasn't long before I drifted off into a deep, dreamless sleep.

It was late afternoon before I opened my eyes again. Olivia was sitting in the rocker beside my bed knitting quietly when I finally got up in the silent room that was warmed by the roaring fire.

She looked up with a smile. "Feeling better?"

"Yes, much. Thank you. What time is it?" I rubbed the sleep out of my tired eyes.

Casually, Olivia reached over and lifted my birthday gift out of its velvet-lined box.

Instinctively, I reached out and screamed, "No! Don't touch it!"

But she was already holding the silver pocket watch firmly in her hand. Startled by my sudden outburst, she dropped it to the floor. She gave me a confused look then picked it up again, opening it and glancing at the time.

"It's almost four-thirty." Olivia closed the latch and set it lightly back into its box. "What is wrong? Why did you not want me to touch your watch? I was only checking the hour." Her voice was thick with innocence and confusion.

"I'm sorry." I rested back against the pillows, utterly confused as she looked at me, still puzzled by my reaction. *Why did the watch not inflict a reaction on her like it did me?* The question rang through my ears with no explanation that made any sense whatsoever. Not that any of this did.

"Where is William? Did he make it back to school?" I attempted to change the subject.

"Yes. He left shortly after you drifted off. He asked me to sit with you until you woke. He is very concerned about you." She casually began knitting again.

"I know, but it is unnecessary. I am fine. You really did not have to spend your entire day in here watching me sleep." I readjusted myself and sat back up.

"I did not mind. It gave me a chance to catch up on my reading and knitting. Besides, it is very peaceful in here away from the racket downstairs."

"What is going on downstairs?"

"Your mother and Mrs. Chandler are finalizing the menu for Thanksgiving. Apparently, we are going to have a houseful. So far, all the family is coming except for James and Rachael. I guess they are traveling to her family this year, much to your mother's dismay," she smiled coyly.

"Yes, she hates it when we are not all together on the holidays. But she has to understand that Rachael's family would also like to enjoy time with them."

"James explained that since they are going to be here for Christmas and the wedding, they really needed to spend Thanksgiving with his wife's family in St. Louis." Olivia readjusted the blanket she was knitting before she continued. "I think it is nice that they are trying to balance both families. Not like William and I must worry about that." A small scoff escaped her lips, but I knew that fact truly bothered her.

"We are going to have a great holiday season this year. We have so much to be thankful for."

I wanted to cheer her up, but I knew there was nothing I could say that was ever going to heal the wound that her parents' actions had created.

"Well, it has been interesting, that is for sure," she stated flatly.

I knew it was time to change the subject. "I suppose I should get my lazy self out of this bed sometime today."

I kicked my covers aside. I picked up my robe off the foot of my bed, where William had left it, and tied it around my waist.

"Care to join me downstairs for some dinner?"

"Of course." She placed her knitting back into her basket and headed downstairs alongside me.

Jackson's parents joined my family for dinner. I could feel their eyes closely studying me throughout the meal. They were like a second set of parents to me, and I loved them both dearly, yet somehow this evening their constant glances were making me very uncomfortable. I wondered if Jackson had mentioned my nightmares to them and if he had asked them to check in on me. It was something that I was sure he would do if he was as concerned about my behavior as William claimed he was.

Dinner passed slowly as I dodged questions and made constant reassurances.

The act was growing old and tiresome. I wanted them all to just leave me alone. I was even more confused now with this new revelation that I did not need the pocket watch to trigger an episode. Not to mention the fact that it seemingly had no effect on Olivia. I wasn't sure what was going on or if indeed I was just losing my mind.

Once we all retired to the front room, Emily came over and joined me on the lounge. I knew something had to be up since it was typically Olivia who sat beside me to hear all the news about our friends and classes from school at the end of every day.

She said nothing for a while, only small talk amongst everyone. Once Robert and my father were absorbed in their talk of some new breakthrough and my mother and Olivia were talking about pregnancies, Emily leaned in closer. "Jackson phoned us this afternoon," she started out casually.

"How is he?"

"He is greatly concerned about you." She placed her hands lightly over mine. "He says you are having night terrors that are causing you to wake up screaming."

"Only a couple of times." I looked down not wanting to meet her eyes.

"Every night since Sunday from what I hear. William told him that you had a frightening episode this morning. He mentioned he stayed with you until you finally went back to sleep, and you did not make it to your classes today." She patted my hands trying to make me look up at her.

I glanced up briefly into her beautiful motherly face and felt incredibly guilty. "My brother exaggerates. It was really nothing for him to be concerned about. I apologize for him making more of this than necessary. He should not be upsetting Jackson for no reason."

"What are you seeing?" she leaned in and whispered softly in my ear.

Her choice of words stunned me to my core. *Seeing. Not dreaming? How could she know?* My body began to quiver unconsciously as I stared blankly at her. She had confirmed that Jackson had something to do with these visions. Now I honestly believed that she was in on it as well. Was Robert also? *Do they all know what was happening to me? How could they? I haven't breathed a word about what I was experiencing.*

"They are just bad dreams. Nothing else," I squeaked out. But I knew from the expression on her face that she did not believe me.

Emily smiled slightly and patted my hands again. "I understand what you are going through, Jocelyn. I honestly do. I can help you with these visions if you will just open up to me and tell me what you are seeing."

Her soft gentle tone was comforting, but her choice of words cut through me like a hot blade.

Visions? Seeing? Help me with them?

I felt light-headed and numb to my surroundings. I could only imagine the horrified look that must be written plainly across my face. I couldn't move. There were no words to describe the terror I was feeling in the pit of my stomach. *She knows! She knows it all! But how?*

"I am sorry. I'm not feeling that well. I think I need to go upstairs. Please, excuse me." I got up quickly, and Emily followed me over to the stairs, gently grabbing my arm before I could escape.

"Jocelyn, I know that you are frightened, but we can help you understand all of this. You just need to be honest with us about what you are seeing. Please, speak to Jackson about it. Tell him the truth if you cannot tell me." Her eyes were pleading me with, but my head was spinning, and I knew if I didn't get away from her, I was going to faint.

I barely nodded and squeaked out, "Please, excuse me," before fleeing up the stairs and hiding behind my bedroom door.

I curled up in a ball under my covers, in my darkened room, determined not to fall asleep. I was terrified to my very soul, unsure of the world that was waiting anxiously for me to arrive. I knew I was losing my mind.

Emily's words rang through my ears repeatedly. I recalled Jackson's words from our day of house hunting and the autumn festival, and I was positive they were all connected. *What are they doing to me? Why?* Nothing made any sense. I knew I could not fall asleep. I had to stay awake and fight the visions of the world I was rapidly becoming so attached to.

CHAPTER 5

Thursday, November 05, 2015

I WOKE UP FEELING GROGGY. Images ran about in my head like a vivid dream that I couldn't quite shake. I closed my eyes. I could see myself walking down the stairs holding a bouquet of flowers towards Jackson at the bottom. He was standing next to the man I had seen before during the wedding episode I'd had. I realized he must be Patrick, my *other* father.

I was wearing a heavy, auburn gown with ivory lace. It was so beautiful and elegant. But so heavy. I could feel the weight of the multiple layers on my frame and the tightness of the corset underneath.

I took Jackson's arm and smiled over at Patrick, who smiled back lovingly at me. We walked forward into the front room where Robert was standing in front of the fireplace with the young man whom I recognized as William. He looked incredibly nervous, like he was going to get sick or something. I looked around and noticed an array of faces I'd seen previously along with Emily.

Jackson let go of my arm once we reached Robert and stood on the other side of William and whispered something in his ear. Then I saw Patrick and a young girl I suspected must be Olivia follow us into the room. She had her arm looped through his and looked like she was about to cry. I realized that this must be Olivia and William's wedding that Jackson had told me about.

I shot out of bed and ran towards the bathroom, barely making it before I got sick. I sat down on the floor and rested my head against the tub. This confirmation of *EVE* destroyed any notion that Jackson and his family were playing a sick joke on me. Tears of frustration released the tension that was building up in my chest.

I had to wait all day, and even through try-outs, before I could get Jackson alone to tell him about what had happened. By lunch I felt like I was ready to explode and blurt it out. I hated all this sneaking around and not being able to confide in Jenna. I did my best to remain cheerful and casual during lunch, and in-between classes, but I knew she could tell something was bothering me.

We pulled into Jackson's driveway shortly before six o'clock. Each of us was worn out from try-outs and in desperate need of a shower. I told Ethan to take a quick one and smirked at him about not using up all the hot water. It was a good excuse to get rid of him, so I could have a moment alone with Jackson.

We waited in his car until Ethan was safely across the street and heading into the house before he turned towards me with a look of deep concern on his face.

"Jocelyn, what is wrong? You have been acting funny all day."

He placed his hand over mine across the console trying to reassure me. Today, I really needed it. I was beyond freaking out at this point.

"I woke up this morning feeling really strange, like I was stuffed in a fog or something." I went on to recount the images I recalled and the faces I'd seen. All of which were still clearly etched in my memory, as if they had just taken place moments earlier.

Jackson sat there silently and listened to me ramble on without interrupting. His face was expressionless. I couldn't tell what he was thinking to save my life and it scared me. Normally I could read him well, but this was terrifying.

When I had completed my tale, he remained expressionless for a moment. Slowly, a smile slid across his shapely lips. "You are remembering things that just happened recently."

"What does that mean?"

"The barrier is coming down, or at least holes are developing in it, where you are starting to recall events that recently occurred in your life there. This is a good thing, Jocelyn. Their wedding was only a little over a week ago and you remember it perfectly." His voice was calm and soothing.

"Am I going to wake up with these memories every day?" My eyes pleaded for him to just lie to me.

"Probably. I would say yes. But this is a good thing, sweetheart. A very good sign that your mind is accepting and even embracing the events."

"It's terrifying. I feel like I don't know who I'm supposed to be."

"You are my Jocelyn." He leaned over and kissed me softly.

"How are we going to do this?"

"Do what?"

"Our upcoming wedding...our marriage...*there* and *here*? How are we going to be together as husband and wife? Share a life together? Live with one another *there*, and *here* we must act like just boyfriend and girlfriend—dating? I don't want to do that."

"I know. I am not too happy about it myself, but what else can we do?" he shrugged.

I looked down at his hands over mine. "I don't know," I replied in a low voice.

"We could get married *here* too."

I looked up at him surprised by his words. His eyebrows were slightly raised, and a smirk crossed his lips. I choked on what should have been a laugh. "Yeah, my parents would be so happy about that one."

Jackson suddenly got excited. "Of course. We should get married *here!*"

"Hello? College?" I rolled my eyes at him.

"No, seriously. Think about it, Jocelyn. We could get married next summer, and both go to school in Boston. I delayed my law school entrance a year citing family emergency, so I am already enrolled for next fall. You could apply as an undergrad, and we could live together in campus housing. It is perfect."

I sat there staring at him completely dumbfounded. "My God, you're serious, aren't you?"

"Yes! Why not?"

"I'm eighteen!"

"So?"

"So?" Wasn't it obvious?

Jackson laughed and jumped out of the CRV. "Come on!" he shouted excitedly, slamming the door, and running towards his house.

I sat there for a moment before reluctantly opening my door and sliding out of the seat. *He's lost his mind.* Yet I followed him up the walkway.

Jackson stood waiting impatiently in the front doorway. "Hurry up." He looked ready to explode with excitement, as if all his problems had been instantly solved.

We entered the kitchen to find both his parents cooking dinner together. The aroma was intoxicating. The two of them happily greeted us and Emily promptly invited me to stay for dinner.

"Yes. I'd love to. But I'm afraid I need to run home and shower first if there's time." I felt so incredibly gross and sticky from sweating so much during try-outs. I couldn't believe I was even standing here in their sterile kitchen in my present state.

"Mom, Dad, Jocelyn and I were just talking, and I think I may have a solution to this whole marriage thing." Jackson's voice was giddy with excitement.

"I'll let you explain while I go shower. I'll be back shortly." I slipped out before anyone could intercede.

The hot water was refreshing as it rained down on me. My mind was whirling in a thousand different directions. *Can he really be serious? Get married this summer?* That would certainly cause my dad to stroke out and I couldn't even fathom what my mom would have to say. Both my parents were so intent on college and graduate school I couldn't imagine either of them even considering paying for my education if I pulled a stunt like this.

Twenty minutes later I was running back across the street. Emily was putting dinner on the table when I arrived, and Robert was fixing the drinks. Jackson came downstairs a moment later with his hair still wet from his shower. He laughed at my wet hair that I had just brushed back out of my face and ran his fingers lightly through it before taking his seat.

"How have you been, Jocelyn?" Robert asked, passing me a basket full of dinner rolls.

"I'm gettin' there," I smiled.

"Jackson explained about your vision this morning," Robert began. "How do you feel about it?"

"Strange. It was weird being able to not only see it but feel it as well." I picked up a roll and quickly began buttering it.

"Did you like the dress you were wearing?"

I looked up at Emily, surprised. *What an odd thing to ask.* "Yes. It was beautiful. I loved it. But it was very heavy. I could even feel the tightness of the corset."

"I made you that dress for your birthday this year." Emily smiled happily across the table.

"Wow. You did a gorgeous job." I shook my head amazed. "But then again, you did an amazing job on the costumes you made for the party. You are incredibly talented."

"Thank you. I thought the color would go so well with your hair and eyes. And it truly did. You look so lovely in it."

"Thank you."

"Okay. Enough about the clothes," Robert laughed. "Jocelyn, our son also explained to us the idea he had about school next fall." He continued cutting his chicken. "How do you feel about that?"

"My parents would kill me," I stated flatly.

The three of them laughed casually as if that fact was no big deal at all.

"I am sure they would be surprised. But if you were still going to college and graduate school, then how could they object?" Emily asked.

"Because I'm eighteen."

"True, but if we explain to them how much we love each other."

I halfheartedly laughed at Jackson's ignorance of my parents and their views on their children's education. "Jackson, to them, we've only known each other for a couple weeks. How can I possibly explain to them that I'm going to marry you?"

"Make them understand. You can do that," he pleaded.

"I seriously doubt it. Perhaps if we decide to do this, we can wait until late spring to make the announcement."

It felt so strange having this conversation in front of Robert and Emily. I felt this was something that Jackson and I should discuss privately.

"These things take time to plan, Jocelyn. Especially if you want to have a big wedding," Emily chimed in.

"I honestly haven't given it much thought." I shrugged while all of them looked from one to another like they were shocked by my words. "What?" I asked confused.

"I guess there are a few things about your personality that are different between the two places," Robert stated. "We just need to get used to them is all. Like you, we have some adjusting to do as well. You have to remember that we think of and know you in a certain way, and *here*, well, you are somewhat different."

I thought about that for a moment. True, I was sure that there had to be some differences in my personality between the two places. As Jackson had pointed out, I was raised by two separate sets of parents with extremely different views in vastly different time periods. There had to be influences on me that would change my behavior and personality.

"We are just a little surprised. You see, you have made a huge production out of your wedding this Christmas. Plus, you have repeatedly stated that you have been dreaming of how you wanted your wedding to be since you were a little girl. So, we just assumed that the same would be true *here* as well," Emily politely explained.

"I guess *here*, I've always dreamed of going to college and grad school. I've never really given much thought to my wedding or anything like that. I figured it was years away."

"That is understandable, especially considering both your parents have advanced degrees. It is only natural that they emphasized the same for their children."

Robert nodded, but Emily still looked at me like there was something wrong with me. "Have you thought about it lately?" she inquired, looking hopeful.

"In the last hour you mean?"

Jackson and Robert both laughed, but Emily still looked concerned.

"No, dear. I mean since you found out that you and Jackson were getting married this Christmas. I am rather surprised you have not asked us any details about your wedding." She seemed almost offended.

"I'm sorry. I guess I was still trying to accept the fact that I am getting married. Not so much about the details of it," I explained.

Doesn't she get the fact that here I've only known her son a few weeks and it is a bit of a shock to discover that I am marrying this man?

"Of course. I apologize. I suppose I had not thought of it that way. We are just so used to knowing you all your life that seeing you *here* we do not really think of the differences and the shock you must be experiencing." Emily gave me a motherly smile.

We all ate silently not being sure what to say to one another. I still was trying to grasp the idea of getting married next summer and how I would even attempt to explain it to my family when Jackson broke the silence cutting into my train of thought.

"What kind of wedding would you like to have?" he asked, looking at me over his broccoli.

"What do you want?" Okay, two could play this game.

"I would like a medium sized, outdoors wedding. Something where all our friends can stand up with us."

Damn, he is good. I have to give him that.

"All right," I answered casually. "Who would you have in it?"

I could see Emily out of the corner of my eye looking happy about the turn in the conversation.

"I would ask my brother Alex to be my best man, then have Ethan, Kyle, Zak and probably Cody as well." *How has he figured this out so quickly?*

"I guess I would have Jenna, obviously. Plus, Sidney, Caitlyn, and Hilary."

"Wonderful. And Lucinda and Charlie can serve as the ring-bearer and the flower-girl," Emily added.

"Who?" I asked.

"My brother's children," Jackson explained.

"Oh, I see. And they still live in Boston, right?" He nodded.

Emily started discussing color schemes and flowers. I stared down at my plate and moved the food around. This whole idea was so beyond absurd and did not merit a discussion because I knew all hell was going to break loose when my parents caught wind of it whether it was next week or later next spring. Besides, what Jackson and his parents were failing to understand was that it wasn't just my parents' dream. It was one that I deeply shared with them.

Jackson and I curled up together with a blanket on the couch to watch the new episode of *Grey's Anatomy*. The fireplace was blazing, and I could feel the heat melting away my resistance to the prospect of getting married this summer. I loved the way his arms felt wrapped around me. I felt safe and secure with him beside me.

I couldn't imagine living only part-time with him and I knew that once I had full awareness there was no way I was going to be happy in a part-time situation. I loved this man with every fiber of my being and there would never be another who could ever come close to reaching my heart that he now owned.

I shifted enough to see his beautiful profile. I don't believe I could ever tire of gazing upon his face. I slowly traced the fullness of his lips with the tip of my finger causing a gentle smile to spread across them showing me his childish dimples.

"Are you serious about getting married this summer?" I whispered.

"Yes." His eyes softly caressed my face.

"I didn't expect the reception I got from your parents when I got here." I tried to keep my voice low. I knew his parents were in the other room.

"Would you be happy only being together on a part-time basis?"

I shook my head.

"Then can you see any other way?"

"No. I'm just scared."

"Of?"

"Of getting married so young. But honestly, I'm more scared of living without you." I took a deep breath still gazing intently at him. "I don't know how to explain it, but I know I'm supposed to spend my life with you. I love you more than I ever thought I could possibly love anyone."

He leaned down and kissed me overpoweringly causing the fire within me to reignite instantly. I wrapped my arms around his neck, pulling him closer to me. His taste, his smile, his body. All were like an addiction to me, and I was thrilled to be intoxicated by him.

He pulled away reluctantly, "You have no idea how happy it makes me to hear you say that, Jocelyn." His breath was heavy on my neck. "I love you so much. There simply are not enough words for me to express the full depth of my feelings for you."

I completely melted under his words. I moved my lips to meet him once again and allowed myself to be enveloped fully within him. He reluctantly pulled away from me and attempted to recompose himself.

"You are making this extremely difficult for me. You realize that?" He smiled brightly.

I let out a little laugh, thoroughly enjoying his torment only because I was elated that I wasn't alone in my anguish.

"Are we going to wait until we are married *here* or *there*?" I inquired with a smart-assed grin.

"I do not believe I have the willpower to wait until next summer," he laughed.

"But you haven't even proposed to me yet," I pouted.

"My goodness woman! How many proposals do you need? I thought you recalled the last one in the gazebo." His smile stretched firmly.

"I do, and it was so beautiful and romantic. It was perfect, but I am afraid that I can't recall that story for my friends and family," I complained.

"True." He looked lost in his own thoughts. "But I thought we were not going to tell anyone yet."

"We aren't."

"Good. Then I have the time to plan a proper proposal." Jackson kissed me softly on the lips and pulled back before things could get reheated again between us.

"I hate to say it, but I think it's time for me to head home before my dad comes looking for me." I knew it wouldn't be long before my dad either called or sent Ethan to drag me home.

"Soon we will not have to worry about curfews or parents. It will just be the two of us forever," said Jackson. *I loved the sound of that.*

I started to get off the couch, but he pulled me back down across his lap and wrapped his arms around my waist. "Not so fast. Who said I was willing to let you go?" He laughed and playfully kissed me on the cheek.

"You know I don't want to, but I need to before my parents send a search party out for me."

"Let them."

"Jackson, I haven't even done my calculus homework yet," I complained.

I hated that class, and I knew it was going to take me over an hour to get the assignment done. I was going to have to reread the chapter we were covering because I didn't fully understand the whole concept of differential equations.

"Why didn't you mention it earlier, I could help you with it. I am very good at calculus." He squeezed me a little tighter.

"Well, I kind of got side-tracked by all this marriage stuff next summer." That was a pure understatement. Ever since we climbed out of his CRV a few hours earlier, I had thought of nothing else.

"If you have any questions, you can call me," he offered.

"Don't say that because I'll have you on the phone half the night working on this crap," I grinned, knowing I had to get started or I would be up late.

"I don't mind at all, my love. If I did, I would not have offered."

I kissed him quickly on the cheek and stood up. This time he allowed me to.

"Keep your cell phone on because I just might call," I said, standing over him.

He got up and we walked over to the front door.

"Tell your parents goodnight for me and thank them for dinner please." I stalled my departure.

"I will." Jackson took me in his arms and held me close.

"I'll call you before I go to bed if it's not too late."

"Call anyway. No matter how late."

"All right." I tried to think of something else to bide me more time with him.

"I love you, Jocelyn," he whispered quietly in my ear.

"I love you too." I rested my head upon his chest. I held him tightly in my arms and closed my eyes listening to the sound of his strong heartbeat.

Reluctantly, I opened the front door and headed off towards my house. I hated saying good-bye to him even though I knew I would see him first thing in the morning. The hours between now and then felt like an eternity.

Chapter 6

Saturday, November 09, 1878

THE SUN WAS BLISTERING HOT and blinding. I was sitting on a bright, royal blue, smooth, hard surface that sparkled in the sunlight. Some type of boat that I had never seen before, and I knew immediately I was in the *other* place.

I was surrounded by water and there was a beach in the far-off distance. The sky was a rich blue without a cloud anywhere to be seen. Gentle waves rocked the large vessel from side to side like a gentle lullaby. It was incredibly peaceful, with the sounds of music and laughter dancing about low in the breeze.

My eyes hungrily searched for familiarity and rested upon the four other people who accompanied me on the boat. The two adults I recognized as my parents, the boy, who was perhaps twelve or thirteen years old, my brother, and the older girl, my sister. Their faces were smiling and happy as they playfully teased one another. Their words were hard to distinguish from the strange music floating through the air. They were wearing swimming attire that barely covered their bodies, as was I.

My suit was made of a soft, smooth material. I ran my fingers over it ever so slightly just to memorize the feel and texture so that I could recall it later. It was two separate pieces that scarcely covered the most intimate parts of my body. I could feel a blush rush to my cheeks and felt rather foolish since the other two females were dressed in the same fashion. My mother, however, also wore a sheer black material wrapped around her waist, but I could see her black bottoms easily through the material. Her top was tied around her back with strings of the same color. My sister's suit was very similar but was a bright purple while mine was a bright pink.

I couldn't tell what type of fabric the men's shorts were made of. It didn't look nearly as soft as our attire, but rather different. I don't know exactly how to describe it. I had never seen anything like it before and it was covered in strange designs of many colors.

I stretched out on the deck and could feel my long hair wet against my bronzed skin. My arms, legs, and stomach were more defined than I had ever seen them look before. Even my toenails were painted a bright pink color that sparkled beautifully in the sun. I was amazed with the subtle differences in my physical self from one place to the other. I felt like me yet somehow entirely different. It was odd in a comforting liberating sort of way.

I jumped and screamed as I felt the cold water hit my skin.

"Hello, Jocelyn. You're daydreaming again." My brother leaned over the side of the boat and splashed me again with water laughing aloud along with the other three.

"Sorry," I laughed and hurried out of his line of fire.

The bright sunlight and images before me began to fade slowly. I knew it was pointless to try and hold on to it once it began to blur, although it ripped my heart out to be so helpless and watch the happy family I felt so attached to disappear before my eyes.

I woke up sobbing, but not screaming. My room was empty and silent. Only the crackling of the wood in the fire broke through the silence. It was still dark outside, and I had no idea as to what hour it was. I was too terrified to check the pocket watch that still rested safely in its box on the night table.

I rolled over and pulled my covers up around my chin. I was at least thankful that I hadn't woken up screaming and no one was rushing into my room this morning. I had hidden away from everyone yesterday and missed another full day of classes, something I truly hated doing. I loved school, loved my classes. But now, I couldn't bring myself to face anyone. Yesterday, I woke up screaming nearly scaring Mimi half to death out of a deep sleep. After which I felt horrible for.

The stress of not sleeping well was obviously taking its toll on me not only mentally, but physically as well. I had large dark circles under my eyes, no appetite to speak of, and my muscles felt fatigued. It had been at least a week since I woke up feeling refreshed and energized.

All I wanted to do was sleep, yet I was terrified to do so. I was trying everything I could think of to stay awake. I was reading every book I could sneak unnoticed out of my father's library until the wee hours of the night when my brain could no longer process anything and the words on the pages were became indistinguishable from each other. Then I would try and recite various passages from course lectures to keep my mind occupied. Eventually, my efforts would prove to be fruitless, and I would collapse into a restless sleep. It wasn't fair.

I closed my eyes trying to shut out Emily's words that played continually over and over in my head. They held me baffled in a spiral of confusion and speculation. Jackson would never do anything that would put me in harm's way. I was sure of it. He loved me every bit as much as I loved him, I felt that in my soul. *But then how could he deliberately put me through something like this?*

Early signs of dawn started to break through the curtains and filled my room with its soft morning glow. I debated on whether I was going to get out of bed or simply spend another day here feeling helpless and frustrated. I knew that Jackson had gotten home last evening, but I had refused to see him, claiming that I wasn't feeling well.

In the same manner, I managed to avoid William and everyone else in the house except Mimi. However, I had invited Elizabeth over today to decide upon her dress for my wedding. Certainly, she wouldn't come by since I wasn't in school for the last two days. But then again, she may stop by just to check on me. I wasn't sure one way or the other.

I crawled out of bed and sat down at my window seat, pulling a blanket around me. It was so bitterly cold despite the roaring fire across the room. I hated the drafts the windows allowed to enter my room during the cold months. I leaned my head against the window and stared across the street at Jackson's quiet house. I could see no movement behind their curtains, and I wondered if anyone was up over there yet. What I couldn't figure out was how I was going to deal with Jackson. *Should I confront him? What would I say?* I felt as if I was accusing him of something horrible and strangely, it made me feel guilty for witnessing the visions.

An invisible force pulled me over to my bureau. I lifted out an ink well, quill and a stack of parchment. I flopped back down on my bed and took the cork out of the ink well. I dipped the quill and started scribbling all the bizarre things I had witnessed in every vision I had seen. I tried to write down all the people I had seen. I did not know names, so I jotted down their physical descriptions and characteristics of every individual I had encountered.

I tried to connect the dots between people who I knew were somehow part of my family and others who I had seen at what I believed to be school. Only the one young man appeared to be a part of both. Without even thinking I began sketching out various things I had seen—the funny clothes, the talking picture boxes. Everything that I could recall I wanted to put down on paper. Somehow by doing that it made them become real. I knew they could not be. *How could they?* But doing something so trivial eased the burden off my troubled mind and heavy heart.

I heard the clanking of pots and pans from the kitchen below as the house slowly began to awaken. Shortly thereafter I heard creaking on the stairs and the voices of my family members talking quietly as they went downstairs to have their breakfast. I could not bring myself to want to join them.

I flipped through the scattered papers tossed about my bed and the strange objects and words I had written on them. *Are they real? Could there really be a place where women are free to decide the course of their own lives? Where I could be free from the bonds that hold me to this provincial world?*

This world held everything I had always dreamed of and more. The only thing I had here was Jackson and my love for him. Of course, I loved my family, my friends—the new life that was soon to begin when I finally became Jackson's wife. *But is all that going to be enough for me? Can I really be happy just being a wife, a mother, and hosting parties like my mother? No, I honestly do not believe in my heart of hearts that it is a life I want to live. I want more. I want it all.*

I leaned back against my pillows and closed my eyes. My mind drifted off to her world and the afternoon I got to spend *there* at Indiana University. The gorgeous campus was so full of life. All the young adults rushing about, working hard, arms filled with books, getting to fulfill their dreams, and become anyone they desired. I was so jealous I almost screamed.

But can I live in a world without Jackson?

The point, however, was moot. It was all a fantasy after all. *Wasn't it?* I got up and wandered back over to the window and pulled back the curtains. The sun was shining brightly upon his house, and I could see some movement behind their front windows. I hated to think about having a life without Jackson. A life without feeling his arms around me, his lips upon mine, without being his wife and the mother of his children. *Could I honestly do that?*

I slid down into the window seat and wrapped the blanket back around me. I tried to push her world out of my mind and solely concentrate on my own. But it was impossible. My forehead dropped against the cold pane. Thank goodness I do not have to choose. Her world and mine were two entirely different entities. Mine was real, hers was not.

A lone tear ran down my cheek. I could not believe that I was getting so upset over something that was not even real. *Her world, my dreams. All wrapped up together and yet never meant to exist at the same time. As much as I dearly love Jackson and want to be his wife, I know there is so much more out there yet for me to become.*

I stayed curled up in that blanket on the window seat for the remainder of the day, seeing no one again, except Mimi. She insisted that I eat some toast and drink some chicken broth around dinner. Other than that, she was sweet enough not to pry and left me alone to wallow in my own dilemma and self-pity.

CHAPTER 7

Saturday, November 07, 2015

I GOT UP EARLY AND HEADED OUT with Jenna, Jackson, and Ethan to basketball practice. All of us had made the school teams after our final try-outs yesterday and for the next couple of Saturdays we were all going to have practices until our first games.

Our school had two gymnasiums for practice. Of course, the boys' team got the larger of the two while we girls were stuck in the much smaller one for practice. However, all games for both genders were played in the larger one.

The four of us sat in silence while Jenna drove us to school. I sat in the backseat with Jackson and rested my head on his shoulder, nodding off along the way. It was too early to be up on a Saturday morning. This was the one thing I truly hated about playing sports.

Practice was long and strenuous, as I knew it would be. We ran through all the same ol' drills that we've been doing since junior high all the while being reminded by Coach Smith that 'fundamentals are the backbone' of winning.

Hilary and Caitlyn dragged themselves into the locker room at the end of practice along with Jenna and I and the rest of the team. We changed back into our sweats and washed our faces off with cool water, trying to make ourselves presentable again before rejoining the guys.

It was almost noon and we'd been in practice since eight. Each of us was suffering from exhaustion as we slowly hauled ourselves through the chilly parking lot. Cody had his arm draped around Hilary's waist and Caitlyn and Zak held hands beside Jackson and me. Jenna and Ethan walked together since the rest of us were paired off.

"What's everyone doing tonight?" Jenna asked, switching sides with Ethan.

"I don't know. Any good movies come out this week?" Hilary asked.

"No. Nothing, I want to see. Besides I'm broke," Caitlyn added.

"Me too," Zak laughed. "I'd love to get a part-time job or something, but of course that will have to wait until the end of basketball season."

"I know what you mean. You can't do both, so you must choose, play sports and be broke, or get a job and miss out. It sucks," Cody whined.

"What are you talking about? Your parents give you money anytime you ask for it," Hilary teased.

"I know," Cody laughed. "Any ideas?" he asked the group as the eight of us stood huddled freezing together between Jenna's and Cody's cars.

"We can watch a movie at our house," Ethan offered.

"I hate always hanging out at our place. Let's go somewhere else," I complained, snuggled up against Jackson's warm body.

"Where? There's really nowhere for us all to just hang out," Jenna stated, jumping up and down attempting to stay warm.

"Fine," I rolled my eyes at her. "Our place."

"What time?" Zak asked.

"Whenever. We'll be home all day," Ethan said, happy to have everyone clustered at our place so that he'd be sure to be included.

"Great. We'll see you guys in a few."

Caitlyn seemed satisfied with the solution and climbed into the backseat of Cody's car with Zak.

"See you all later then," Jackson replied, opening Jenna's door for me.

After a long hot shower, I stood in front of my full-length mirror imagining what it would be like to be a bride. I tried to picture it and struggled with exactly what type of bride I wanted to be. *Do I want a long full dress with ruffles? No. What about a slim silk dress or a strapless stylish number? Maybe.*

I turned sideways and stood on my toes wondering what type of shoes would be appropriate. That would depend on the dress. And my hair—down or up? Curls or straight? Veil or not?

I was going to need a lot of help with this. Emily was probably going to be a huge asset in this department. Mom, not so much. Her wedding was very simple yet elegant. I only hoped to be surrounded by all my family and friends.

I sighed heavily and confronted the mirror. *How am I ever going to explain this to everyone?* I knew they would all immediately jump to the same conclusion. She's pregnant! I could hear them all now. Even if I eventually convinced them that I wasn't I knew they would all decide that I was insane for getting married the summer before heading off to college.

College. Good God! I was going to have to apply to Boston University within the next week or sooner. Hell, I hadn't even decided on a major yet.

My mother really wanted me to follow in her footsteps, but I wasn't sure if I wanted to be a physician or not. I hated the long hours she worked and the fact that she was always on call, exhausted, and cranky. I really didn't want a career that made me spend so much time away from my family. I wanted more of a nine to five type or something with a more flexible schedule.

My reflection stared back at me with wonder, confusion, and utter disbelief. I wanted so badly to talk with Jenna and share my excitement and terror with her. I knew I could trust her with the secret of my upcoming wedding, but I wasn't sure how she herself would take the news. As much as she dearly loved Kyle, I doubted if the two of them had ever even discussed marriage or even attending the same university.

It was almost two o'clock, certainly Jenna would have showered and had lunch by now. I grabbed my cell on my nightstand and pushed her button. She finally answered on the fourth ring just as I was about to give up.

"Hello?"

"Whatcha' doing?" I tried to act as casual as possible, but inside I was ready to explode.

"Physics. I really hate this shit," she complained.

"Can you come over for a few? I need to talk to you about something."

"All right, but only for a few. I really need to study. There are four hundred different formulas and I'm completely lost."

AP physics was her worst class and she'd been struggling with it all semester long.

"Wish I could help, but I don't take that class until next semester."

"I know. Anyway, I'll be over in a minute," She hung up the phone.

I ran downstairs and waited anxiously for her to arrive. I sat down on the bottom step and tried to figure out how I was going to tell her.

"What in the world is so important?" Jenna waltzed in the front door wearing old sweats and her hair pulled up in a ponytail.

"Upstairs." I turned and ran up the grand staircase with her on my heels.

We reached my room, and I shuffled her in and closed the door behind her. She walked over and sat down on my bed.

"Okay, I'm here now. What's so important?" She looked peeved.

"I have some great news, but it's a huge secret." I sat down next to her on the bed.

"Okay." Her face was full of apprehension.

"I mean it. You can't tell anyone," I warned her sternly.

"You know better than that." She gave me a strange look. "I won't say a word."

"Promise?"

"Promise. This had better be good."

"It is. Jackson asked me to marry him!"

"What!" Jenna screamed and jumped off my bed. "What in the hell are you talking about?" Her voice was so loud I was positive the entire house heard her.

I grabbed her arm and pulled her back down on the bed. "Would you keep your voice down? Damn, Jenna!"

"Sorry. How am I supposed to react to some crazy ass crap like that? Please tell me you laughed when he asked, before you said no."

"No. Not exactly."

"Are you insane? You've been going out with him for less than a month."

"Can't you just be supportive?"

"I am supportive of everything you do. But this is insane! How can you even be considering marriage? You're a senior in high school and you want to go to college. Remember?" She got up and paced back and forth across the length of my room.

"Will you please calm down? I am still going to college," I explained.

"There is no way in hell that your parents are ever going to allow this. You realize that don't you? Even if you decide to do this anyway, there's no way they're going to pay for your education if you get married." Her arms were wailing about for emphasis and dramatization.

"We haven't worked out all the details yet, but I believe we are going to Boston University."

"Boston? Are you serious? Did you even apply there?" she confronted me.

"No. But I am this week. Jackson's already been accepted," I tried to explain rationally.

Jenna returned to pacing again with a discontented expression across her face. "Good for him." She stood facing me with her hands on her hips. "Please. Tell me you aren't seriously considering this?"

Her face went void of expression. "Oh God, why? You're eighteen! You have your entire life ahead of you! Why would you even consider marriage to a guy you barely know? Think of all the people you're going to meet in college? And what about grad school?" She sat back down beside me. "Why would you want to throw everything away for a guy you've known a few weeks? It makes no sense, Jocelyn."

"Haven't you and Kyle ever talked about getting married?"

"Yeah. After we graduate from college, not before. We both want to enjoy school, grow up a little." She narrowed her eyes at me. "You know. Mature a little. We're both eighteen and at least we realize that there's a good chance our relationship may not survive four years apart at different universities."

I wanted so badly to tell her that Jackson was almost twenty-two and already completed his undergrad degree. But that was something else I couldn't explain since he was currently impersonating a high school senior to get close to me here in 2015. This was all getting too complicated.

"Jenna, please. Can't you just be happy for me?" I sank back on my bed. I knew she was going to be shocked, but I hadn't expected her to react like this.

"I'm sorry, but I think this is a really big mistake, Jocelyn. Don't get me wrong, I really like Jackson. He's a great guy, but you're both too young and haven't known each other long enough to even be thinking about marriage." She shook her head in disbelief.

I was sorry I'd told her. Perhaps it would be best if Jackson and I eloped and didn't tell anyone about it but his family. At least they were not only supportive, but excited about the idea of us getting married.

I got up and walked over to the closet for my jacket. "All right. If that's how you feel, then I'm sorry. But I have to live my own life and Jackson makes me very happy. I love him, Jenna."

"I'm glad he makes you happy. We can all see that he does, but you haven't known him long enough to say you love him." She lowered her voice and stood up. "Don't do this, Jocelyn. You'll regret it for the rest of your life if you do. Maybe not right away, but what if you get pregnant and have to drop out of school? All your dreams will be gone. Everything you ever wanted to do with your life will disappear and you will hate yourself and resent him for killing your dreams."

I felt tears burning up behind my eyes and I wanted to get as far away from her as possible. I couldn't believe she had to say such horrible things even though I had thought of them myself. *Marriage wasn't something I was considering lightly. How could she believe it was?*

"I have to go, and you need to study." I walked over to my door and opened it. "I'll see you later." I headed down the stairs with Jenna running behind me.

"Jocelyn! Wait!" she hollered after me, but I took off out the front door and ran across the yard towards Jackson's.

By the time I reached his front door and knocked loudly on it, Jenna was standing in the street between the houses still hollering my name. I ignored her and opened his door myself and walked in. Emily came around the corner to answer the door only to discover me standing in their foyer in tears.

She hurried over and put her arms around me at once. "Jocelyn, honey. What is wrong?" I wrapped my arms around her sobbing.

"I cannot believe she reacted so badly. All I wanted was for her to be happy and excited for me," I choked out.

Robert and Jackson walked around the corner to investigate all the commotion. They both looked concerned to see me in such a state but lingered back a little letting Emily try and calm me down. I went on to recount the conversation between Jenna and I while the three of them listened attentively.

The four of us retreated to the front room and gathered around the roaring fire. I sat down on the couch beside Jackson, who immediately placed his arm protectively around me. I felt so much better just being in their presence. It was so natural, like coming home. This, I knew, was where I truly belonged. This family, who were going to be with me wherever I traveled.

"I am so sorry Jenna reacted the way she did, Jocelyn." Robert smiled at me sympathetically from across the room on the loveseat beside his wife.

My sadness over her reaction was slowly turning to anger. "I'm more upset about how she could think that marriage is something I would consider entering so lightly. I mean, it's not like I can tell her the whole truth but still, I wanted her to be happy for me. I knew she'd never understand the way I feel about you." I looked over at Jackson who gently tightened his grip around me. "I know she's never felt this way before, even for Kyle."

"You knew most people were going to react poorly when you two made the official announcement." Emily's face looked forlorn.

"But she's my best friend. I honestly thought she'd be excited about this. Instead, she was furious. Like I was throwing my life away over a schoolgirl crush or something."

"So, is it safe to say that you two have agreed to get married over the summer?" Robert inquired with obvious apprehension.

I smiled over at Jackson who looked at me lovingly. "Yes. I believe so." I replied with confidence.

"Of course, I haven't officially proposed yet. But that will be soon," he smirked. "I believe that we should probably wait until spring break to make the announcement though."

"Spring break? That does not give us any time to plan a proper wedding," Emily complained.

"I am not saying I do not want you and Jocelyn to go ahead and start making plans, just don't mention them to anyone until spring break." A coy grin spread across his shapely lips.

"Fair enough." Emily seemed satisfied with that condition. "We will have to get started soon, Jocelyn. We can sit down with some magazines and planners and decide what you two would like."

I shifted uncomfortably in my seat.

"I know it's customary for the bride's family to pay for the wedding. I do have a college fund set up by my parents, but I'm honestly not sure if they're going to let me use it if I get married. I'm not sure what my parents are going to say, but I can guarantee they will *not* take this well. My dad found the engraving on the watch and freaked over that. He already thinks we're getting too serious."

Robert let out a small chuckle. "Jocelyn, Emily, and I honestly expected this type of reaction when we were still in Boston. At that time, we decided to put away some money for the wedding and your college education."

I started to object, but Robert put up his hand to silence me. "I know it is not customary, but the groom is our son and we want you both to have everything you want to make the day extraordinary. And as far as your education, we have watched you thrive *here* academically, and we know how important continuing your education is to you and that is something we would never deny you. Especially after watching you sneak around for years *there* to read and learn things that Patrick has forbidden you."

I was shocked and speechless. This was entirely unexpected. "I sincerely appreciate the gesture, but I cannot ask so much of you. College is entirely too expensive to put that type of burden on your family."

"It is no burden, Jocelyn. Honestly, my husband is a very successful attorney and I have been blessed in my success as a novelist. We are very comfortable and if we cannot use our success to care for our loved ones, then what good is it?"

Emily gave me a look that made me feel as if I truly was family in her eyes. It was such an incredible feeling. I fought back the overwhelming tears of joy as my brain searched for the appropriate response to such unselfish generosity. "Thank you both so much."

Jackson leaned over and kissed me tenderly on my forehead. "See, everything is going to be fine."

I nodded my head stupidly afraid to open my mouth knowing it would open the floodgate behind my eyes.

"We will leave you two alone now to talk. I will pick up some magazines and we will start planning things tomorrow afternoon. Is that all right with you, Jocelyn?" Emily asked as she and Robert got up. They both gave me a hug.

"That sounds wonderful, Emily. Thank you both so much for everything."

I hated that those few words caused the reaction I had feared, and tears began falling down my cheeks. Jackson grinned softly and wiped them away.

"We are going to run to the market for a few things for dinner. We shall return shortly." Robert strolled by and placed his hand on my shoulder, giving me a gentle squeeze before they left.

I snuggled in close to Jackson feeling wonderful about the turn of events. A heavy burden had been lifted concerning our marriage and my education. I closed my eyes and imagined how wonderful it would be to spend my life in the arms of the man I love. In both time periods, I was truly blessed to have him and his amazing family. Jenna's words no longer stung as they had earlier cause now, I knew that no matter what, I was going to have Jackson and that was all that truly mattered.

"Feeling better?" he whispered in my ear.

"Yes. Much." I leaned up and kissed him passionately.

A loud knock on the front door interrupted our exchange. Jackson climbed off the couch with an inquisitive look on his face. "Must be Ethan looking for you," he said as he left the room to answer the door.

I sat there absorbing the heat from the fire and waiting to hear my brother's voice from the foyer. Instead, it was Kyle's voice that rang out. "Hey, Jackson. Is Jocelyn still here?"

"Yes." Jackson's voice sounded strange.

"Can I speak with her?" Jenna asked rudely.

"Let me ask. Please, come in."

I heard their footsteps on the ceramic tile in the foyer. "Wait right here, please." The front door closed, and I heard his steps returning to me.

I got up and walked over to the fire staring blindly at it. I really didn't want to talk with Jenna right now. I was feeling too good and confident about the new course my life was taking and her negativity only spoiled my happiness.

Jackson walked up behind me and slid his arms around my waist. I closed my eyes and leaned back against him. "Jenna and Kyle are here."

I nodded silently not wanting to lose this moment in time.

"She wants to speak with you. What would you like me to tell her?"

I turned around in his arms to face him. His bright green eyes sparkled in the firelight as he gazed upon my face so lovingly that it literally took my breath away. "I don't want her to spoil this for me," I whispered, leaning my head against his chest.

"Then don't let her." He put his index finger under my chin lifting my face to look at his. "This is about you and me, Jocelyn. Not them, not your family. You and me. I love you. Always. Do not ever doubt that." I nodded, locked in the trance his eyes held me tightly in. "Shall I invite them in?"

"All right," I reluctantly nodded.

Jackson let go of me and retreated to the foyer. Seconds later the three of them returned. Jenna looked extremely uncomfortable. I wasn't sure if it was because she was in Jackson's house or because of our argument.

They sat down on the loveseat and Jackson joined me on the couch. There was an uneasy silence coated with tension that hung in the space between us.

"Jocelyn, I'm sorry," Jenna began. "You just caught me off guard with your news. I wasn't expecting it and didn't react very well." Her voice was less than sincere. Almost forced. It gave me the feeling that the only reason she was here was that she had gone running to Kyle when we parted and told him about our interlude. He must have made her come over and apologize.

I had no words for her less than sincere apology. Rather I glanced between Kyle and Jackson to get a sense of their reaction. Both looked bored and uncomfortable.

"See? I told you this was pointless," Jenna huffed over at Kyle.

"No. This is silly! You both are." Kyle looked over at me then back at Jenna. "You two are the best of friends who fight like two grumpy old men. Frankly, I'm getting a little tired of it."

"I'm not the one who wanted to come over here. Remember?" Jenna nearly shouted at him. "If she's stupid enough to ruin her life, then let her! It's not my responsibility to save her."

"Now wait a damn minute." Jackson was suddenly very irritated. "What gives you the right to come into my house and make such accusations? This decision is between us, not you or anyone else."

"That's where you're wrong, Jackson! You have known her for what? Five minutes? Well, I have known her for eighteen years. I think I know her better than you ever will. I know how much she has always wanted to go to college and grad school and have a career of her own. Not be some little wife and play house somewhere with you and a house full of snot-nosed little brats! You're ruining her life, and you don't even care about it. If you truly love her, like she claims, then you would wait until you both at least finished your bachelor's degrees before you decide to get married!" Jenna screamed back at him. Her face was crimson with anger and her hands were shaking uncontrollably.

Kyle placed his hands over hers attempting to calm her down. I looked over at Jackson who was fuming with fury and struggling to remain composed.

"This is my decision. Not yours, Jenna. I love Jackson more than you can ever comprehend and if you can't be happy for me then I don't think we have anything more to say to one another."

I considered telling her about my conversation with Robert and Emily earlier and their offer to help, but immediately decided against it. After all, it was none of her business anyway.

"If that's how you feel, then fine." Jenna stood up, but Kyle pulled her back down with her arm. Jenna flashed a hateful look at him and jerked her arm away. "Don't!" She glared.

"Calm down. Now this is stupid. Why can't you just be happy for them? If this is what they want, then it's their decision to make. Be supportive and stop acting like such a bitch," Kyle scolded her like a child.

Jenna crossed her arms and narrowed her eyes at Jackson and me. I took a deep breath and sighed heavily.

"I can't. I know this is wrong. He's going to ruin her life." She narrowed her eyes.

"Jenna, there are some things I can't explain to you between Jackson and me. You must trust me. This is the best decision I've ever made," I reluctantly stated.

"Bull shit! We have never kept secrets from one another. You know you can tell me anything," she complained.

"Not this." I shook my head in despair.

"What? Now, because you have *him* in your life you can no longer trust me?" I swear, if looks could truly kill, then Jackson would have been dead from the look she shot him.

"It's not about him. It's about me crying out loud! Something happened to me in the last several weeks that I cannot explain to you, because I don't really understand it myself." My voice raised an octave.

"But it involves *him*. Right?" Her voice was accusing.

"No! Actually, it doesn't!" I lied.

"See, I told you." She looked over at Kyle. "This is completely pointless. If she won't be honest then this conversation is over."

"Then I guess you can leave now and stop ruining my afternoon." I glared over at her.

"Fine." Jenna got up leaving Kyle baffled on the loveseat.

"This has gone on long enough," Kyle raised his voice, an unusual rarity. "Jenna, sit your ass down. Now!"

She exhaled deeply and leaned against the bookcase glaring at him.

"I cannot believe you two. This whole thing is beyond ridiculous. Jenna, you are going to have to accept the fact that Jocelyn is with Jackson, and they are getting married. You also must accept the fact that the two of you are different people and there are some things in her life she can't share with you. That doesn't mean she doesn't trust you or love you. It means that some things that she may feel she cannot share."

Jenna remained silent, but her face softened a bit. "And Jocelyn, you must accept the fact that Jenna loves you like a sister and only has your best interest at heart. She's terrified of you making a mistake when you two have only known each other for such a short time. It seems so fast and that makes the possibility of it being a mistake even greater. Can you at least understand where she is coming from?"

"I do, but she must trust me when I say I'm not making a mistake. This decision is the one thing I am the most certain about in my life."

I reached over and took Jackson's hand in mine and looked over at Jenna. "I just want you to be happy for me. For us."

Jenna came over and sat back down beside Kyle. "What about college? You know if you get married your parents aren't going to pay for it. And what if you get pregnant?" She slowly shook her head. "Birth control isn't a hundred percent," she pointed out as if I wasn't aware of that.

"I promise you. She will go to college and graduate. I will take care of that. And as far as having children, that is between us. However, I can tell you that her education is every bit as important to me as it is to her." Jackson leaned over and lovingly kissed me on the cheek.

"I seriously doubt that." Jenna mumbled, and Kyle elbowed her in the ribs.

"I am sorry that you doubt my sincerity. I love Jocelyn more than I can explain." Jackson laughed a little and looked over at me. "You know, I thought I would be having this conversation with your parents. Not your friends."

"Aren't you lucky? You get to have it twice!" I smirked.

"Yeah. Lucky me," he grimaced.

"Kyle, Jenna was not supposed to tell you about this. We want to keep it quiet for now because we figure everyone else is going to react much the same. Therefore, we want to wait until spring break before announcing our engagement."

I knew Kyle wouldn't breathe a word, but now that Jenna was so against us, I only hoped she could keep her mouth shut for once in her life.

"Fine, but aren't you going to at least tell Caitlyn and Hilary?" Kyle looked surprised.

"Not yet. We don't want the entire school to know because once Ethan gets wind of this, my parents are going to attack," I laughed.

"Point taken." Jenna finally laughed.

Robert and Emily returned shortly before seven o'clock with armloads of groceries. Robert hollered at Jackson that there was more in the car and both guys went out to retrieve them. Jenna and I joined his parents in the kitchen to help unpack everything.

"Is there a party at your house this evening?" Emily inquired, putting her perishables in the refrigerator.

I looked over at Jenna who busted out laughing. We had both forgotten that everyone was congregating at my house for the evening.

"I can't believe this. Kind of, I guess. A few of our friends were coming over to hang out." I shook my head in disbelief.

"I had forgotten all about that," Jackson remarked as he entered the kitchen and placed more bags down on the counter.

"Forgot about what?" Kyle asked, coming in behind him.

"Everyone was meeting over at my house to hang out tonight," I answered.

Kyle started laughing. "So that's why there's so many cars. Who'd all you invite?"

"Caitlyn, Zak, Cody, and Hilary, plus us four. Why? How many people are over there?" *Dear God, what has Ethan done now?*

"About six, I think," Jackson answered.

"Wonderful, guess we'd better head over."

"Excuse me, Jocelyn," Emily spoke up. "I got those things we discussed earlier if you want to come by tomorrow evening for dinner and we can start sorting through them."

"Wonderful," I gave her a big hug. "Thank you, for everything. I really appreciate it."

The four of us headed over to my house to discover that my idiot brother had invited several of his friends as well. My parents were held up in the living room watching television and didn't look all too thrilled about hosting a house full of teenagers.

My mother hollered at me as soon as we walked in the door. The other three headed downstairs while I approached my parents. Neither appeared to be in a very good mood.

"Did you invite all these people over and then take off to Jackson's?" she asked.

"Not exactly."

"What's that supposed to mean?" My dad was clearly annoyed.

"After practice, this morning it was suggested that since all of us are broke, that we hang out here this evening and watch movies. But I only invited my usual group. I am not responsible for the rest of the people down there. That's all Ethan."

"Jocelyn, you know we don't mind if your friends hang out here. That's why we finished the basement for you kids. But we would appreciate it if you would at least be considerate enough to clear it with us first." She used her scolding voice to make me feel like a four-year-old.

"I'm sorry. It won't happen again," I apologized to them.

"All right. Now go join your friends. And clean up the mess when they leave." My father returned to his paper obviously still not happy about the impromptu party.

I was stunned by the time I reached the basement. Now I understood why my parents were so upset. There must have been at least twenty people milling about. Some playing pool, others dancing like morons by the jukebox, and others lounging on the sofas talking over the noise of the television and music.

My eyes quickly scanned the room for Ethan. I finally located him over in the corner talking with a blond girl whom I recognized from school but didn't know.

I stormed over to him angrily and grabbed his arm. "What in the world were you thinking?" I demanded.

"What? You invited your friends over, so I invited some of mine," he shrugged.

"And I just got yelled at because you didn't get permission for this mess. And my friends know how to behave themselves. Look at this place! I'm not cleaning this up, Ethan!"

I left him with his jaw hanging open to locate my group of friends amid the crowd of blurred faces. The seven of them were huddled in the corner talking amongst themselves.

"Why didn't you tell us there was a party here tonight?" Caitlyn asked teasing.

"I didn't know myself." I rolled my eyes in disgust.

"What'll you guys want to do?" Hilary asked.

"Leave," I answered.

"And go where?" Cody asked.

"Anywhere. I don't care. Just not here," I responded.

"We could go over to my house and watch a movie," Jackson offered.

"What about your parents? Won't they mind?" Hilary asked.

"Let me check." Jackson took out his cell and began texting.

He turned back around to face us with a big grin. "All set. My parents would be happy to have us all."

"Fabulous. Let's go." Caitlyn clapped her hands together and headed for the stairs with the rest of our group following right behind her.

Jackson and I curled up once again on the sofa in his living room. The rest of our friends were all coupled off and relaxing. Emily set out drinks, chips, and dips for us before she and Robert disappeared into the study.

Zak riffled through the Chandler's DVD collection in the family room bookcase hollering out different suggestions hoping that something of a consensus could be met amongst the eight of us. Anything remotely feminine was universally booed by all four of the men while all the action and fantasy were given thumbs down by us females.

"Oh. Fabulous! I love this movie!" Zak jumped back up and ran over to the Blu-ray player.

"What did you put in?" Cody tossed a throw pillow in Zak's direction.

"*Back to the Future.*"

"Sounds good." Cody leaned back against Hilary.

"Can you imagine how cool it would be to travel through time?" Caitlyn asked about the room.

"I wouldn't go back to when my parents were teens," Zak replied.

"Me neither," Hilary concurred.

"I agree," I stated.

Jackson tightened his grip around my shoulder and smiled slightly. He looked utterly at ease in this world of mine.

The movie started, and the room went silent. The only sound was the occasional crunch of a chip or a sip of soda.

"I don't know it might be fun," Jenna piped up. "I think it is funny the way the mom tells her children she never drank, called a boy, or sat in a parked car with a boy. Then Marty finds out she wasn't exactly as innocent as she wanted her children to believe she was." Jenna wrinkled her nose.

Jackson and I both stifled a laugh as Caitlyn responded, "Yeah, my mom wants me to think she was so innocent when she was a teen."

"Can you imagine seeing the 80s firsthand? That would be so cool. They had great clothes, and the music was so cool," Hilary added.

"Who cares? Gee whiz. Hush up. We're trying to watch the movie." Cody glared up at her.

"Oh, shut up. You've seen it before." Hilary playfully shoved him off her lap.

"Hey!" Cody hollered when he hit the floor.

"Will you both shut up?" Zak threw a blanket at them on the floor.

"Hey. Thanks." Cody picked it up and snuggled back into Hilary who giggled, wrapping her arms back around him.

"Seriously. Where would you go if you could travel through time and go anywhere you wanted?" Jenna asked the room.

"Oh, I don't know. That's a hard one. Would we still know everything we know now?" Zak looked over at Jenna.

"Ummmm...yes. I suppose so. Why?"

"Because that makes all the difference in the world." Zak shifted his position, and his face took on a serious look. "See, if you knew everything you've learned in our history classes about the wars, famine, and misery suffered by our ancestors it would be hard to pick a time in history you'd want to see."

"That's true. Knowing what we do about the Revolutionary War, the Civil War, the World Wars, Korea, and the Vietnam War," Kyle's voice trailed off as he got lost in his own thoughts.

"I love the beautiful gowns the women wore in the mid nineteenth century, like the ones from *Gone with the Wind*." Hilary added.

"Can you imagine how hot those gowns must have been during the summer? Especially in the South with no AC or electricity? It would have been miserable." Caitlyn turned toward Hilary.

"Yeah, I'm not so sure I would want to live or even visit that time period," Zak added. "The Civil War literally tore the country in half, even families in half.

I wouldn't want to live through that."

"Yeah, me neither. The Revolutionary Era couldn't have been any better," Cody remarked.

"At least the World Wars weren't fought on American soil," Caitlyn stated.

"Maybe not the battles, but we had internment camps here for Japanese citizens and immigrants. There were a lot of things going on here because of the war. Granted, not as much as what the country went through protesting Vietnam, but still our country was turned upside down," Jackson informed the rest of us.

"I suppose so." Hilary turned toward Jackson. "I guess there really isn't a time in history that is without its own conflicts."

She was quiet for a moment while she and the rest of us tried to think of a period that wasn't wrought with misery.

"What about right after the Civil War? That was a peaceful period. Oh. What did Mrs. Ulbright call it? The Industrial Era," Hilary said.

"You're forgetting about Reconstruction. The South was a complete disaster after the war," Jackson explained.

"Okay fine, then I would stay in the North," Hilary laughed. "But it would have to be in the fall or spring. The summer would be miserable and so would the winter."

"You're not picky, are you? What if you couldn't pick the time and just ended up some place in history? What would you do then?" I inquired.

"Do everything I could to get back home," Zak immediately responded.

"That depends on where I ended up and what my social status was." Jenna tilted her head with a slight grin.

"You are such a snob," laughed Kyle.

"I am not," Jenna declared. "I just wouldn't want to be a maid or shopkeeper or farmer's wife."

"Like he said. Snob!" Caitlyn giggled and we all laughed.

The eight of us settled back down and became engrossed in the film. It was the perfect escape from all the worries and headaches that were waiting for me just around the bend. I wanted to enjoy these precious moments of tranquility with my friends because something in my gut was screaming at me that these days were about to abruptly end.

CHAPTER 8

Sunday, November 10, 1878

I SLOWLY OPENED MY EYES determined to forget the images that were now burned upon my retinas. I wanted desperately to physically scrub them off my brain and erase everything I had seen since that first night. I climbed out of bed and threw on my robe. I splashed some cold water from the basin on my face trying to shock my brain into focusing on something else. Anything else.

I sat down at my vanity and toweled off before picking up my brush and running it through my hair. My crowning glory was dull and lifeless and in dire need of being washed. But I didn't care. I numbly went through the motions. The image staring back at me in the mirror resembled nothing of the face I once knew. It had been replaced by a thinner, paler version with heavy eyes surrounded by blackish purple puffy rings. Tears silently dripped down my cheeks, yet I felt completely void of all emotion.

I picked up the blanket off the window seat and sat back down in the same spot I had spent the previous day. However, today, the cool air creeping between the panes felt amazing on my hot skin and was a welcome friend on my exhausted soul.

Mimi came in a little while later and exchanged pleasantries. She began changing the sheets quietly and cleaning up my room. The whole time she was busy I kept my eyes shut and rested my head against the cold window. My entire body ached, my head hurt, and I never wanted to move from this spot. I was so thankful that she worked as silently as she did.

Mimi placed her hand gently on my shoulder when she finished her work. "How ya feelin', chil?"

I opened my eyes and looked up at her. "Not very well."

She put her hand over my forehead. "M'goodness chil, you's burnin' up! Let's git ya bac ta bed."

She wrapped her arm around me and helped me over to my bed. "Ya stay's rite ere, Ah's be right bac." She tucked in the covers around me before she hurried out of my room.

Seconds later I heard her voice and that of both my parents on the stairs and then they all got louder before the three of them came bustling into my room.

"Ah's kno she's gotta bad feva, Dr. Timmons." Mimi started ringing out a rag in the basin.

My parents sat down on my bed on either side of me. My mother started brushing my hair out of my face with her hand and smiled down at me. "Sweetheart, what is wrong?"

"Does it hurt anywhere?" my father asked before I could answer my mother.

"My head is killing me and my stomach hurts."

Mimi handed the rag to my mother who placed it across my forehead. I winced a little from the cold. Suddenly, I was freezing to death. My teeth started chattering uncontrollably and I wanted to push the rag off my head, but I knew my mother would just put it back.

"Patrick, she is burning up. What is wrong with her?" I could see the fear in my mother's eyes.

"Probably influenza." My father glanced over at my mother whose hand immediately went up over her mouth.

"Mimi, go on downstairs and tell everyone that Jocelyn's room is restricted. I do not want Olivia or anyone else near her room until I know for sure what she has," Father ordered in a firm voice.

Mimi stepped out the door and closed it softly behind her. My eyes drifted from my father's face over to my mother, who looked like she was ready to cry.

"There is no need for that now, Annabelle. I am being overly cautious for Olivia's sake. Whether she has an ordinary cold or influenza, we need to keep everyone from being exposed." He placed his hand on my mother's arm to reassure her.

My father instructed Mother to retrieve his medical bag and some fresh water for the basin. She nodded and left the room silently. He turned his attention back to me with a grim smile. "You know something, Jocelyn. I believe you have worked yourself up into feeling so poorly."

I scrunched my eyes up at him. "What do you mean?"

"I think you have gotten yourself so upset about these night terrors that you have made yourself sick from worry. I know you will not talk about them with anyone, but you really should. They are obviously having more of an impact on you than you are letting on."

"They scare me," I replied softly, feeling silly and childish.

"What is it about them that frightens you so much?"

"Many things. It is too difficult to explain."

"Can you try?"

"I would rather not."

There was no way I could confide in my father about such things. He would certainly think I was crazy if I spoke about moving picture boxes, horseless carriages, the strange clothes, the people, and my strange emotional attachment to them.

"Jocelyn, you know that dreams, even night terrors, are our mind's way of dealing with problems that we do not want to face. Perhaps your dreams are trying to tell you something. Maybe there is something that you do not want to accept or deal with that your mind is telling you it is time to take that extra step."

"It is not like that, Father. I cannot explain to you what it is, but I can see what you are saying."

"I know you have been avoiding Mr. Jackson lately. Do they have something to do with him or your marriage?"

"Sort of. I guess. In a way, but not directly."

"Have you tried talking with him about them?"

"No. He has repeatedly asked because William has a big mouth, but I have told him nothing. He would not understand."

"You do not know that unless you have tried. Besides, it is not like you to give up on something without even trying," he pointed out.

"I know." I looked towards the door at the sound of approaching footsteps.

"Then I suggest you should and soon. Otherwise, you are going to go on feeling very poorly," he whispered quickly before my mother reentered my room.

My parents took turns with Mimi keeping watch over me for the rest of the day. They hadn't been this vigilant since I had influenza when I was nine. I knew that both Mimi and my mother were keeping watch over me out of genuine concern for my wellbeing, but I had the strongest feeling that my father was only there because he hoped I would eventually break down and talk with him about my night terrors. He spent countless hours sitting in the rocking chair by the fire reading the newspaper or some other book, rarely speaking but always keeping one eye keen on everything I was doing.

I finished my homework early and began reading Jane Austen's *Sense and Sensibility*. It was a great escape, which enabled me to ignore the constant glances from my father. I got lost in the story and dreamed of what Europe looked like and how it would be to live there instead of Chicago. I wondered if things there were easier but as I became engrossed in the story it became clear they weren't.

By midafternoon my mother came in to relieve my father so that he could eat some lunch. I had just set my book on my nightstand to give my eyes a break. After hours of reading the words were becoming blurry and starting to run together.

My mother picked up the book and flipped it open to my bookmark. "You know, I read this story years ago. It is my second favorite story by Jane Austen. *Pride and Prejudice* was always first. I love Elizabeth Bennet and Mr. Darcy. Mrs. Bennet was so socially ungraceful and an obvious embarrassment to the entire family except for the younger two daughters who behaved just like her."

"*Pride and Prejudice* is my favorite also."

"Would you like me to read to you aloud?"

"That would be nice. Thank you."

I closed my eyes and listened to the words flow smoothly from her. My mother's voice was soft and soothing. She spoke with confidence and strength. I looked over at her for a moment and wished I could be more like her. Her thick blond hair was woven up in a stylish bun at the base of her neck and her vibrant blue eyes shone brightly as they read the words across the pages. She was graceful, kind and everyone in the city regarded her as a lady of the highest morals and character.

My mother read until I drifted off to sleep. For the first time in a long time no dreams or visions invaded my mind. I am not sure how long my mother continued reading after she realized I was asleep, but the sound of her voice stayed with me throughout the night, and I slept straight on until the next morning.

CHAPTER 9

I REMAINED STILL, too afraid to open my eyes, utterly unsure of the images dancing around behind my eyelids. It was getting harder to differentiate between ones that were dreams and those that were remembrances from my *other* life. I hated that the only way to be positive was by calling Jackson and telling him about it, but not enough to stop me from picking up the phone. He answered on the third ring.

"Hello," a sleepy voice responded.

"Did I wake you?" I hadn't even checked to see what time it was before I called.

"What time is it?"

I had a horrible suspicion that it was extremely early, and I suddenly regretted phoning. I glanced over at my alarm clock on the nightstand: 7:34. Ouch!

"Early. I'm sorry. I didn't mean to wake you."

"No. It is all right."

"Go back to sleep, baby. I'm sorry." I started to hang up, but I heard him reply.

"Wait! Are you okay?" His voice was soft and sweet.

"Just another memory. Or dream. I'm not sure."

"What was it about?" he inquired, clearly interested.

"Who is Maryanne and Elizabeth?"

"Friends of yours. Well, Elizabeth is. Not so much Maryanne. I guess she was at some point, but not any longer. Why?"

I went on to recall all that I had seen. I gave him explicit details of my encounters with these young women apparently after some altercation I had with Olivia about our wedding and my brother William. I wasn't sure how I knew that, but I did. It was so incredibly strange. I was seeing things so much clearer now and the pieces were starting to fall into place.

I couldn't help but wonder how my *other* self was reacting to these episodes or glimpses of *my* world or if I was having them *there* at all. I had no way of putting it together or reaching out—tearing down or breaking through that barrier to connect with my *other* self. I wished there was some way of touching the perception between each conscious where the two halves of my psyche collided. I thought of asking Jackson, but I truly feared his reply.

"Jocelyn?" Jackson broke my interlude.

"I'm sorry. What were you saying?"

"Did you hear anything I said?" he chuckled.

"Of course." *Most of it anyway.*

"Would you like some breakfast?" he offered, still laughing at me.

"What do you have in mind?"

"My house. Twenty minutes?"

"What? No! I'm still lying in bed in my pajamas."

"So?"

"I'm not even dressed," my voice trailed off.

"So, come over in your PJ's. We'll have a pajama party."

"No thanks. I'm not quite ready for you to see me like that. You'd turn tail and run."

"How can you say that? I saw you in the hospital. Remember?" *Guess he has seen me at my worst.*

"Fine, give me thirty minutes." I couldn't help but laugh at his logic.

"See you then."

I took the fastest shower, for me at least, in recorded history. After throwing on some jeans and a light hooded sweater, not being sure yet how cold it was out, I quietly snuck down the stairs. No one else was awake so I scribbled down a quick note and left it on the island before heading out.

Jackson answered his front door wearing jeans and a light grey button-down shirt over a dark grey thermal. He was too breathtaking for this early in the morning. His hair was still damp from his own shower and the normally gentle waves were much more prominent. His face was unshaven and held that sexy stubble of growth.

He smiled warmly and invited me inside. I could smell his cologne as I paused in the doorway for an eagerly anticipated morning kiss. I melted into him as he drew me closer. Everything about him was intoxicating.

"I missed you," he whispered in my ear, closing the door behind him. I smiled and followed him into the kitchen.

The most amazing aroma of bacon and blueberry pancakes filled the air. I was surprised to see both his parents up, dressed, and looking perfect standing over the island stove.

"Good morning, Jocelyn. How are you?" Emily greeted me.

"Wonderful. Thank you." I leaned against the bar stool. "I wasn't expecting you both up so early."

I was suddenly embarrassed for intruding on their morning.

"We always get up early," Robert stated nonchalantly. "Old habit."

"I see. Not me. I could sleep until noon or later if allowed," I smiled sheepishly.

Robert flipped over another pancake absentmindedly. "Do you have any plans for today?"

"Not really." I looked over at Jackson wondering what was up.

"We were planning on driving into the city to wander around and do some early Christmas shopping. Would you care to join us?" Emily offered. She was slicing up some bananas and placing them in little fruit bowls with strawberries and green grapes.

I watched her for a moment utterly amazed at how carefully she prepared every detail of their meals with such precision. I was beginning to doubt if this house even had a box of cereal in it.

"I'd love to. What time are you planning on leaving?" I helped her carry the bowls over to the table that was already perfectly set as if expecting a dinner party instead of a typical Sunday breakfast.

"Right after we eat. I wanted to get an early start. There is so much I want to buy this year for my grandbabies." Her voice was so sweet and caring.

I thought how wonderful it must be for those lucky babies to have such grandparents. Then it dawned on me. They were going to be my children's grandparents as well. The mere thought of it filled me with warmth and happiness.

"My mom isn't on call this weekend. So, my parents will probably sleep until noon and trust me, I know better than to wake them up," I laughed, following her back into the kitchen.

"Oh, do not worry about that. I spoke with your mother last evening and asked her if we could take you with us. She said that it was fine." *This woman never ceases to amaze me.*

Robert carried in the mountain of blueberry pancakes and Jackson brought in the platter of bacon into the dining room. There was a pitcher of orange juice on the table beside an elegant antique sterling silver kettle filled with freshly brewed coffee. I stiffened back a giggle to myself at the drastic comparison of their family dynamics as opposed to my own. I couldn't recall ever in my life sitting down and having a family breakfast together unless we were on vacation somewhere and eating at a restaurant.

Jackson pulled out my chair for me as Robert did the same for Emily. There was certainly something to be said about them being gentlemen and their mannerisms were definitely from another time period.

"Jackson mentioned that you are starting to remember flashes." Robert passed the platter of pancakes to his son.

"Yes. Almost every morning I wake up with clear images of different things. Unfortunately, I'm only seeing glimpses of events. Most of them don't make much sense so I must ask him to explain the context of them. I'm sure I'm driving him insane with my constant questioning." I smiled across the table at Jackson who was taking a bite of his fruit, but still a grin slid across his stunning face.

"Not at all. I am thrilled things are coming together so nicely and that you are no longer passing out around me. It is quite disheartening to make your fiancée physically ill every time you are near." His eyes shone as his smile deepened.

"I admit that was a bit of a downer," I laughed. "At least that part is behind us."

The four of us drove into downtown Chicago and parked in a large parking garage off the busy city streets. We headed off on foot to explore the various shops. The air was cool, but not too bad for early November. It seemed so far, at least this year, we had been lucky as far as the weather was concerned. The rain hadn't been nearly as bad as it typically was for this time and year, and so far, it hadn't snowed.

Jackson and I followed behind his parents, holding hands, and enjoying ourselves. His parents were holding hands and occasionally laughing at something the other said. I was still taken aback by the amount of affection the two of them displayed towards one another. Just the simple things, like holding hands, a tender glance, or an arm draped around a waist. My parents never displayed such behavior around the house let alone out in public. I almost felt sorry for the relationship they shared as I glanced over at Jackson's face shining under the late morning sun. I wanted desperately to believe it would be impossible for us to fall so far out of love with one another.

After several hours of browsing through an enormous number of shops, Emily had purchased a small toy store of gifts for her three grandchildren. She was practically floating with anticipation for her family to arrive for Thanksgiving break. It saddened her they were away from them so much.

We headed to some quaint little upscale old-fashioned restaurant around one o'clock for lunch. The place was charming, with an old-world atmosphere that fit in perfect conjunction with the company I was keeping.

Once we placed our orders, Robert turned to me with a very serious look on his face. "Have you considered yet how you are going to approach your parents about the wedding?"

"We were discussing the possibility of breaking the news around spring break."

"Do you believe your engagement can remain a secret that long?" He gave me an inquisitive look.

"I hope so. Only the four of us and Jenna and Kyle know about it."

"And you do not believe they will accidently let it slip?" Emily asked.

"I don't believe so. I would hate for my family to hear about it from someone other than me. It's going to be difficult enough to explain without that kind of added pressure." I took a deep breath.

"I am sure that Jenna and Kyle are trustworthy. Jocelyn should be fine until spring break," Jackson assured his parents.

"Fair enough." Robert dropped the subject even though I got the impression he was far from satisfied with the situation.

"Are there a lot of people who have this *EVE* gift?" I asked to change the expression on Robert's face and the concern plaguing Emily's. Robert cleared his throat and glanced for a second over at his wife.

"I wish I could give you exact figures, but there really is no way of knowing for sure. Since it is inherited, it typically stays within families. However, occasionally it does skip generations, like in your case. Typically, family members recognize the signs when it begins in late adolescence or early adulthood and are there to help and guide the individual through the transition. But there are always some who have lost their families, or their families have broken apart, who do not have help and unfortunately those individuals usually do not fare as well."

"How do people deal with this without help? I mean I thought I was losing my mind or something."

I was so engrossed in his words that I barely noticed the waiter dropping off our food.

"There are a few theories about that," Emily offered.

"Theories. No proven facts mind you. It gets extremely complicated fast and will make you crazy if you concentrate on it too hard trying to figure it out," Jackson laughed, breaking off a piece of his dinner roll and popping it in his mouth.

"True. There are some who have *EVE* who strongly believe that those who have no assistance or experience this alone are those who are normally diagnosed with schizophrenia." Robert's expression made me think that this look was how he must appear in a courtroom, serious yet compassionate.

"Schizophrenia?"

"Are you very familiar with the disorder?" Robert asked me.

"Some. We covered it in AP Psych. I remember Mr. Rand talking about the positive and negative symptoms." I locked eyes with Jackson who nodded with a slight grin.

"Some people with *EVE* believe that the positive symptoms of experiencing hallucinations, delusions, and oddities of perception are the individual seeing and hearing episodes as the barrier begins to break down between the two consciousnesses. The absence of emotions, jumbled words, and lack of ability to adjust and relate to their ever-changing perception of reality is believed to be the result of a deep depression brought about by their inability to cope. It is believed, by some, that their fall from grace and the bizarre reports of their symptoms lead physicians to diagnose schizophrenia," Robert explained.

"All of that makes sense if they had inherited *EVE*. I experienced all those things," I interjected.

"But if no one was there to explain it to you, guide you through the transition, there is a good chance you would be lost also," Emily added.

"Yes, I can see that." The mere thought gave me chills. I honestly couldn't imagine going through this alone. "But what if a physician, who also had *EVE*, was there to guide them?"

"Most individuals who have *EVE*, that we know of anyway, tend to shy away from the medical profession. It tends to become incredibly frustrating, leaving the person feeling more helpless than anything else." Robert gestured helplessly, but I looked at him with confusion.

"Why? That doesn't make any sense."

"Everyone's time varies. Some are a great deal more extensive than ours. For us, it varies over a hundred and thirty years, give or take, but there are some that vary as much as five hundred or more. The most I have ever heard of was seven hundred years. In the medical profession, imagine that you had learned and been trained within the current era, and you have almost completed your education when the barriers begin to crumble. Let's say your family is there for you and you make a smooth transition into both your realities. Let's also say you now conceive that you live in the time of the American Revolution and are also a physician *there*. However, everything that you know you can perform to help save the lives of patients in 2015 is not available, neither the instruments nor the medications. You have virtually no ability to do what you have been trained to do. You would feel completely frustrated by the extreme limitations of the circumstances, which in turn, leaves you feeling utterly helpless," Robert painted a grim picture.

"The majority of those with *EVE*, somehow unconsciously, have the same professions in both their existences," Jackson added with a chuckle. "Of course, there are some exceptions."

The four of us sat in silence numbly eating our lunch, lost in our own thoughts. I guess I never really considered that the time difference between eras could be so great. I was so consumed with the abnormalities within my own eras that the numerous others and their dilemmas hadn't really crossed over into my consciousness. That brought about an entire new realm of questions.

"You said the time difference between some eras can sometimes be quite substantial, right?" I interrupted the silence.

"Yes, it can be. Obviously, none of them would be close enough to overlap. I have never heard of one being less than ninety years," Emily replied.

"If that is true, doesn't that leave quite a lot of speculation about prophets and their so-called predictions about future events?" This was much more complicated than I could have ever imagined.

Robert looked between his son and wife before he suddenly broke into a low chuckle with a wide grin. "You are quick. I believe that I severely underestimated your wit because I am more familiar with your *other* self. Jackson was correct in saying that your education *here* has had a direct impact on the differences in your two personalities."

"I don't understand." *Could my other self be that different?*

"It normally takes others much longer to come to that realization. Most are more focused on their own eras and concentrating on how to adjust to the vast differences between them." Emily grinned and placed her hand over mine.

"I told you she was different," Jackson laughed, looking directly at his father.

"Yes, much," he concluded.

The thought that the three of them had apparently been discussing the differences between my *two* selves left me feeling incredibly uncomfortable. I desperately wished I knew more about my *other* self, but the glimpses I had told me very little about my actual personality, and from what I could feel there was not a whole lot of differences. Yet, the look on their faces told me that I was wrong in that assumption. Now I wanted to know just how wrong I was.

"Please, explain." I looked at the three of them trying not to get upset.

"Nothing bad, Jocelyn. It is only that you speak much more freely here. It also appears that some of your personality traits *here* are unconsciously coming through to your *other* self because recently you have become more aggressive in speaking your mind *there* than you ever were before," Jackson attempted to assure me. "Lately, you have been more forward with your thinking, but also very evasive in your behavior. I have the feeling that you have been having episodes *there* since your birthday, perhaps triggered by the identical pocket watches that I gave you, but you are extremely stubborn and refuse to talk about it."

I snorted unintentionally, my face reddened. "I can't imagine why? Have you even bothered to attempt to explain anything to me?" I asked Jackson directly.

"No," he answered quietly.

"And why not?" I could only imagine what I must possibly be thinking.

I had to be terrified out of my mind.

"It is not as if I can approach the subject with you. The same conditions apply *there* as *here* you know. I have tried to drop various hints in attempts to get you to talk to me, but you have closed yourself off completely as of late." He looked almost ashamed.

"Of course." I knew he was right, but I was still concerned about the mental standing of my *other* self.

The mood had somehow shifted and become sullen. The four of us never said another word while we finished our lunches. I knew it was going to take me some time before the entire concept, with its many variables, fully registered upon my consciousness. They were right, it was simply too enormous to comprehend.

The atmosphere hadn't improved much on our ride home. Robert and Emily made small talk about their grandkids and how much they were looking forward to the holidays with them while Jackson and I sat silently in the backseat. I stared out the window watching the world go by and wondered how many of us were out there with this inherited gift. The scope seemed so unrealistic to me, as did all of it. I wondered if I would ever get used to *this* the way his family had and if someday it would all be second nature to me like it was to them.

We arrived back in our neighborhood shortly before four. I quickly explained that I needed to run home to check in with my parents and see what was going on over there. I thanked them for lunch and taking me with them, assuring them that I had a great time and took off before any of them, including Jackson, could say anything to stop me.

I quickly closed my front door behind me and leaned back against it. I could hear the television and loud obnoxious ranting coming from the family room and I could tell my dad and Ethan were already engrossed in their Sunday NFL games. It was a relief knowing I wouldn't be drilled by either of them. I wondered briefly where my mom was wandering around but dismissed it as I ran silently up the stairs to hide in my room.

I sat down at my desk and wiggled the mouse to bring my computer back to life. I waited impatiently as the screen saver, a stupid photo of me with Jenna, Hilary, and Caitlyn last summer at the pool, came into view.

I stared stupidly at it wondering what had happened to those four girls as they all smiled back at me. So much had changed in such a short period of time that they all looked like strangers to me now. My heart ached for those days when life was much less complicated, and my biggest worry was making sure that my college applications were sent out before the deadlines. There was no concern about dual consciousness, Jackson, wedding plans, and keeping secrets from my closest confidants.

I felt like such a phony every time I was around my friends now. I hated all this sneaking around about the wedding and my true relationship with Jackson. Mostly I hated that I couldn't confide in any of them about *EVE* and all its dimensions. I longed for the days when my life consisted of school, friends, and sports.

I clicked on the Internet icon and typed EVE in the search engine curious to see what would come up. All I got was a hip-hop queen named Eve along with a bunch of biblical links. I knew what I was searching for wouldn't be there, but I still couldn't stop myself from looking. I even typed out the full name and got nothing. I exited out and went back over to my bed throwing myself across it, feeling emotionally drained. I closed my eyes wishing all of this would disappear and I had never inherited this *thing*, whatever it truly was.

A knock on my door brought me out of my daydream and back to the frightful reality that consumed me. I rolled over and quickly wiped tears, I hadn't even noticed before, off my cheeks.

"Come in," I hollered as I sat up.

My mother opened my door and came over, sitting down beside me. "I thought I heard you come in."

"I got here a little while ago." I tried to muster up the best smile I could for her.

"Did you have fun shopping with the Chandlers?"

I noticed her scanning my messy room and wondered if she was going to remind me again that I needed to pick it up.

"It was fun. Emily bought a lot of Christmas gifts for her grandchildren, and we went out to lunch."

"That sounds nice. I'm glad you had a good time." She sighed and absentmindedly stacked the papers on my bed and placed them on my nightstand. "I can't even fathom having grandchildren yet," she giggled. "I don't feel old enough to have any of those, so give me another ten years or so, all right?"

"Don't worry, Mom. I'm in no hurry to have kids," I reassured her.

Children are the last thing I need right now.

"Good. Just keep that in mind when you are with Jackson. I know he's a nice boy and all and I know how good-looking he is but think about your future and your dreams before things get too serious between you two." She gave me a warning look that she had perfected over the years both as a physician and a mother.

I playfully rolled my eyes at her. "I know, Mom. I am still going to college. So, don't worry about it."

"But I am worried. You two seem too close and spend too much time together. I just don't want him to talk you into doing anything that you are not ready for."

Oh God, could this get any worse?

"We are not having sex, Mom. I promise."

"Just don't be in any hurry. Don't let him pressure you." She put her hand over mine.

"Trust me, he's not."

"Good. Good. I'm glad to hear that. I know when you're young, you feel invincible and all those bad things that happen always happen to someone else, not you. But let me assure you that you are not exempt from pregnancy, AIDS, drunk driving accidents or a million and one other things that can happen. Just be smart and make wise choices," she lectured, even though she had told me all this a million times before.

"I know, Mom."

I stood up and walked over to my desk. I turned around to face her, leaning back on my desk chair. "I am still a virgin. Jackson doesn't have AIDS or any other STDs for that matter. He's not pressuring me into sex. I'm still planning on going to college. I'm not stupid, Mom."

I knew she was only saying these things because she cared and was concerned about me, but I was not in the mood for a lecture about my relationship with Jackson. I knew the battle I was facing when she and my dad found out I was already engaged.

"I'm not lecturing you, Jocelyn. I just want you to be smart about the choices you make right now. I can assure you that they will affect your future and the kind of woman you will become."

"I'm sorry, Mom. I've had a lot on my mind lately."

"Like what?"

"Just stuff I can't discuss."

"You can tell me anything, you know that honey. I'm always here for you." Her eyes were pleading with me. I hated it when she tried to make me feel guilty.

"I know, but this is something I need to figure out on my own." I went over and sat back down beside her. "It's difficult to explain. But don't worry, I'll figure it out."

"But it does have to do with Jackson, right?" Her eyes were imploring.

"Mostly. Yes. But not in the way that you think."

"What I believe is that you are in love with this boy," she stated. "And I also believe that he is in love with you as well."

I could only stare at her numbly and nod my head. She nodded back solemnly.

"I thought so. Are you worried about going away to school next year and you two being separated at different universities?"

"No. Not really. We have been talking about going to the same school."

"Emily said that he was already accepted at the University of Boston. You haven't even applied there." She gave me an inquisitive look.

I dropped my eyes down to the floor not wanting to admit what she already knew.

"I see. You plan to attend there as well?"

"Yes." My voice was meek, barely audible to my own ears.

"I don't think that it's such a good idea, Jocelyn. There are tons of young men out there, sweetheart, and a whole world of opportunities. College is the time when you can truly discover yourself. You need to enjoy it and meet new people, explore life a little before you commit yourself to one man."

"Mom," I tried to interrupt.

She placed her hands back over mine and squeezed them tightly looking at me. "Jocelyn, you're young, beautiful, smart, and talented. I don't want to see you revolve your entire world and future around one boy. You're far too young to even consider doing something so stupid. It's idiotic."

I stood up and began pacing the floor in front of my bed. "You *really* don't understand at all, Mom. I love him. More than I can explain. And he *is* the one for me. He *is* the one I am destined to be with. I am more positive of that than I am anything else in this world." My hands were gesturing wildly as I struggled to keep my voice calm.

She calmly approached me and put her hands on my shoulders causing me to stop pacing. She took a deep breath shaking her head slightly. "You've already decided this after knowing him only a few weeks?" she inquired full of skepticism.

I nodded my head looking down at the floor instead of meeting her eye.

"You're so young, honey. And I know you think that everything is going to work out between you two. But you must realize that you can't possibly *know* something like that. I understand what you're feeling. I honestly do. I was young once. I've been there, but I cannot let you throw your life away on a high school crush."

She dropped her arms and headed towards my door before she turned around again and looked at me. "I'm not trying to hurt you, Jocelyn. I love you and I only want what's best for you. You're not going to Boston University and that's final. If you want to date him until next fall, that's fine. He's a nice young man so I won't say anything, but it's only going to hurt that much more when he leaves you."

Something inside me snapped. I was furious. My hands began to shake as my entire body started shivering. I was so sick of people telling me about my future and how I was going to live it. Jackson was the only thing holding me together and I was not about to let anything stand in my way of being with him.

"You're wrong!" I nearly shouted at her. My mother was almost out the door when my words halted her in her tracks. She turned around stunned at the tone of voice I used.

"Excuse me," she was strangely calm. "What did you say?"

"You're wrong. I'm going to be with Jackson next fall at BU! It's a great school so why do you care?" I couldn't keep my voice steady, and the tears were soaking my face.

"I care because you're my daughter and I'm not going to let you throw your life away on some boy. Not as long as I'm paying for your education." Her eyes narrowed at my defiance.

"He's not just some boy," I blubbered.

"Yes. He is. And there are millions of them out there." She walked slowly back over to me. "If it's meant to be for you two then it can happen after you graduate from college and finish grad school. But until then, you need to focus on your goals, your education and go to a school that is best suited for you, not him."

"BU is a great school. They have wonderful programs and I'm not a hundred percent positive about my major right now anyway," I tried to reason with her, but I knew I was losing this battle.

"I'm sure it is. But you have talked about joining Sidney at Northwestern or going to Indiana University. You loved the campus when we went down there this past summer. You said it was exactly like you pictured college. Remember how excited you were about it? And I thought that Hilary was planning to go there also. You two could room together."

She looked genuinely upset and I felt horrible. "IU has an outstanding pre-med program and a first-class Medical School in Indianapolis. It would be perfect for you."

"Mom, I told you I'm not positive what I'm going to major in."

She is never going to allow me to be anything other than a doctor.

"I know. I know. I just want you to have the option." She smoothed my hair away from my face and wiped the tears on my cheeks.

"And I'm positive that once your classes get underway, you will meet someone new and forget all about Jackson."

Her words burned through me like a hot fire poker. I stepped back from her and glared. "You really don't get it, do you?" I shook my head in frustrated disbelief. "There *is* no one else. Not now, not *ever*!"

Damn. She's not listening to me at all.

"Jocelyn, I'm not going to spend the evening arguing with you."

She turned to walk away again, but I was too pissed to drop it now. "I'm going to marry him! I'm eighteen and there's nothing you can do about it!"

As soon as the words fell out of my mouth, I immediately regretted it.

"Well, if you want to throw your life away then that is certainly your choice. But if you do, don't look at us to pay for your education."

She slammed my bedroom door and seconds later, I heard her slam her own as well.

I flopped back down across my bed and screamed into my pillow. I knew it was childish, but it helped. I couldn't stop the tears and I didn't care. I should have kept my mouth shut; I knew that. I should have just let her lecture and agreed with whatever she said to keep the peace. Instead, I was sure I had rattled a hornet's nest, and it was going to take quite a bit to calm it down again.

The hours passed, and I never bothered to go downstairs for dinner. Even though my dad was engrossed in his Sunday football games, I had a feeling my mom had already given him an earful. Plus, after he had already voiced his concerns about my relationship, I knew he was not likely to take my threat lying down. But the more time passed the more at ease I was feeling. If my dad thought there was any merit to my tantrum threat, he would have been up here already with threats of his own.

My cell phone rang shortly after seven o'clock, waking me up in a startle. I must have fallen asleep. My room was dark, and I fumbled around on my nightstand blindly searching for the annoying sound only to make it stop.

"Yeah?" I finally answered.

"Jocelyn?" Jackson's voice sounded like a lullaby to my ears.

"Hi, sweetheart."

"Are you alright?"

"Fine. Just dosed off is all." I wasn't about to tell him about my argument with my mother. Not after Jenna's reaction yesterday. "I'm sorry I ran off so quickly this afternoon. I just had a lot on my mind."

He let out a small laugh. "Don't give it a second thought. We understand that when something big occurs or changes, you hibernate until you have time to process it in your own fashion and once you have, you are fine."

"I do not."

"Yes, you do." he laughed again. "But it's okay. Everyone deals with things in their own manner."

"Whatever," I muttered.

"Anyway, I was calling to see if you were still going to come over and look over some wedding material."

I had completely forgotten about agreeing to that tonight.

"When does she want me to come over?"

"As soon as you can." His Boston accent curled my toes. "You should see what she is doing. There are papers, patterns, and magazines scattered all over her office."

I took a deep breath and exhaled slowly. I was hardly in the mood now to discuss wedding plans, but I had already told Emily I would start things with her tonight.

"Okay. I'll be over in just a minute."

"Great. I will see you soon. I love you."

"I love you too."

I shoved my cell phone into my pocket and wondered how I was going to get out of the house. If my mom had spoken with my dad, I knew he wasn't going to let me leave if he believed there was a hint of validity to my threat.

I quietly opened my door and peeked down the darkened hallway. There was a soft glow coming from under my parents' bedroom door assuring me that my mom was still hiding inside. As I stepped out on the landing, I could hear the obnoxious sounds from both guys in the house glued to the game as with every Sunday throughout the NFL season.

I entered the family room and found Ethan and my dad knee deep in chips and salsa. My dad had numerous empty beer bottles on the end table next to him while Ethan's was covered with Dr. Pepper cans. An empty pizza box rested on the coffee table in front of the two of them as they repeatedly shouted and gestured wildly at the television screen.

"Dad?" No acknowledgment.

"Dad," I hollered a little louder.

He glanced at me for half a second then turned back to the game.

"I'm going over to Jackson's for a while. Okay?"

He waved acknowledgment, so I took full advantage of his preoccupation and split before a commercial kicked in.

CHAPTER 10

Thursday, November 14, 1878

I MANAGED TO MAKE IT TO ALL MY CLASSES thus far all week except for Monday. I pulled myself together as best as I could and focused all my energy on maintaining the status quo. Jackson and William had come home for the weekend, and both returned to campus without either of them setting eyes on me. My absence over the past weekend left little doubt that I was faking about not feeling well. I watched from my window as Jackson walked to and from my home each day, yet I made no effort to see or speak with him. I was not looking forward to their return home tomorrow evening.

While the visions continued daily without a stimulus, the screaming had been reduced to a single episode on Tuesday morning this week. I was still waking in uncontrollable sobs with vivid pictures still seen clearly in my mind's eye and there was nothing I could do to stop them or even reduce their effects on me. However, it felt good to be functioning again, even on such a disconnected level. My head felt like I was under a constant fog, but at least I was out of my room and moving my aching muscles. The cool air moving in and out of my lungs burned life back into my disenchanted soul.

"Are you looking forward to Jackson coming home tomorrow?" Elizabeth asked lightly as we sat surrounded by Christina and Laurie eating lunch.

"I know you must have hated not seeing him last weekend being sick and all."

"Yes. I imagine he will be waiting at my home by the end of classes tomorrow," I responded casually before taking a bite of my apple.

"You have to be excited about him almost being done with classes," Laurie said cheerfully, brushing her blond hair away from her face.

Luckily, my mouth was still full, and I could only nod in response.

"Have any of you spoken with Maryanne since the festival?" Christina asked, and the three of us shook our heads in unison and glanced over to the corner of the small lunchroom where Maryanne was sitting alone in the corner eating lunch and reading a book.

"I heard that Dimitri has refused to speak with her since their break-up."

Laurie nodded in agreement. "Yes. He told me the same thing last Sunday after services. I know she brought it on herself, but I still feel bad for her with the holidays upon us and her being all alone. She not only lost the man she planned on marrying, but all her friends in one day."

"It is sad," Elizabeth agreed.

"How can either of you say that after what she did to Olivia? It was horrible. Even if she and William made a mistake, they did the right thing to correct it." Christina glared over in the direction of Maryanne. "I do not feel bad for her at all. She is a cruel woman, just like her mother, and she got exactly what she deserved."

"And on that happy note, I believe it is time for us to be heading off to class. Mr. Grahame is going to lecture me again if I am late." I gathered my belongings and quickly headed towards our classroom. This was one conversation I did not want to be involved in.

"Would you like me to come by Sunday after services, so we can figure out my dress for the wedding?" Elizabeth asked on our way home.

"That would be wonderful. Please invite Lee also and you can both join my family for Sunday dinner," I offered, still feeling guilty about last Saturday.

"Wonderful. We would love to. I will speak with him this evening," she smiled brightly.

"I am sorry about last weekend. I was not feeling well."

"Will you stop apologizing," she replied. "People get sick. I am just happy that you are feeling better. You did not look so great earlier this week, but you seem to be getting some color back in your cheeks."

We parted in front of my house with the promise of seeing one another again in the morning to walk to school together. I continued up the walkway to our front porch feeling better than I had all week.

Olivia was playing the piano when I arrived home. Mother was rocking beside the hearth knitting contently with a slight smile upon her lips. The house was peaceful and calm. I placed my books down on the table in the foyer and handed my caplet and scarf to Eddie before I joined the ladies by the fire.

Mother excused herself to check on dinner while I finished the last of my assignments. Olivia stood up and moved over to the side window. I tucked my papers inside my books and stacked them neatly on the corner of the desk. I knew Olivia must have noticed the activity taking place over at her old home.

I got up and walked over beside her. "Are you alright?"

"Someone bought our home," she said in a low voice without looking at me.

"Yes. I believe so."

"There have been people moving things in and out all day. I am not sure who the new owners are. I have not seen anyone whom I recognize."

"Me neither. I have not even heard who bought the place."

I saw several strong young men carrying a beautiful cherry oak hutch up the walkway.

"William said my father sold it before my family left, but this is the first time I have seen anyone over there. I wonder why it took them so long to move in?" she turned slightly towards me.

"I am not sure," I answered, barely loud enough for her to hear me.

"They have been emptying the house all day long. It appears that my parents left a great many things behind when they left. I have no idea what the new owners are going to do with them. They have been loading up wagons all day long."

"Perhaps they have different taste in decorating than your parents."

"Perhaps," her voice trailed off weakly.

We stood in silence for what felt like an eternity. I was so uncomfortable and the words to comfort her failed me. The sun was fading quickly as the evening hours took hold on the day. Very few leaves remained on the trees, but those that held on tightly in the autumn winds had lost their vibrant luster and faded into a dull grayish brown.

"I wonder where they are now." Olivia's pleading eyes ripped at my heart.

I placed my hand on her shoulder and grinned meekly. "I wish I knew."

"Not I, but I do wish that I could see my little brothers again. I do miss them dearly." She turned back toward the window. "I hate to think of what my parents must have told them about me. The last thing I want is for them to hate me."

"Olivia, there is no way either of them could ever hate you. They adore you."

I did not want to tell her the truth, which was that her parents probably did everything they could to erase her from their lives.

"I hope that someday they will come looking for me and I can explain to them the truth rather than them spending their lives only knowing my parents' version of the truth."

"I am sure they will once they grow up."

My father came home a short while later and was in an unusually good mood. The four of us enjoyed a delicious dinner Sarah prepared and wonderful light-hearted conversation. I informed Mother that I had invited Elizabeth and her beau to join us for Sunday dinner and that she was joining us after services to finalize her dress for the wedding. It seemed my renewed interest in the wedding preparations excited everyone that I was back to myself, as my mother had politely put it.

My father settled in next to the hearth completing his patient charts from the day while my mother knitted silently beside him. Olivia was fielding her way through the works of Emerson and absentmindedly twirled a lock of her dark brown hair between two fingers. I finished an essay that was due in the morning, enjoying the break from reality it provided.

Mimi met me in my room at half past nine to help me prepare for bed. I watched her reflection carefully in the mirror as she unlaced my corsets, freeing me from my daily binding, and I realized that the lines on her face had deepened over the past few weeks. Her fingers, though still graceful, moved slower than before. It saddened me to think she was growing older, and I would only be living with her for a short while longer.

"How's school today?" Her voice rang with her strong spirit.

"Good. Maryanne's little tirade at the Autumn Festival seems to have replaced Olivia's fall from grace as the topic of lunchroom discussion."

"Ah's figuas much. Ah hears 'em talkin' bout it wen Ah's at ta sto dis wek."

"I know it may sound horrible for me to say, but I cannot bring myself to feel sorry for her. Besides, I believe Dimitri to be better off without her. I know it must be hard on him right now because he loves her. Still, I know that he will someday meet someone who will treat him much better than Maryanne ever did."

"Ah's tink so's too."

She brushed out my hair until it was shiny and soft before she helped me into bed. Eddie came in quietly and put a couple more logs on the fire. He nodded in our direction and exited without a sound. Mimi leaned over and kissed me softly on the forehead.

"Wat me to tun down da lamp?" She crossed over to the mantel.

"No. Thank you, Mimi. I feel like reading for a while."

She nodded and smiled. "Don't stay up too late. Ya've skool 'n da mornin'."

"I promise. Sweet dreams, Mimi."

"Sweet dreams, chil."

She closed my door softly. I listened briefly to her footsteps fade down the stairs. I picked up my copy of *Sense and Sensibility* off my night table and flipped it open to where I left off. I quickly lost myself in words and thought nothing more of what might happen when I finally drifted off to sleep. It seemed for a moment, the storm had passed and the clouds, while they hadn't quite lifted yet, were starting to make way for bluer, brighter skies on the horizon.

CHAPTER 11

I WAS TRYING MY BEST TO KEEP UP on all my schoolwork. Yet, between basketball practice every afternoon and Saturday mornings, and Emily consuming my evenings with wedding plans, I was quickly falling behind. I stayed up later than normal trying to get it all done.

The flashes that I remembered from my dreams were almost comforting as each day passed. They almost seemed like little movie trailers tailored to a specific place and time. Most of the time they were not in any sequential order so deciphering them was becoming more challenging. I would try my best to put the pieces together and when frustration inevitably took over, I would turn to Jackson for clarification.

My mom kept up her cold façade, refusing to even look at me let alone speak to me. Both Ethan and my dad, I suppose, figured they'd stay out of it for a few days and let us work it out. However, with the stubborn streak ingrained in both of us, the likelihood of that happening was slim to none.

The noise level in the cafeteria maintained an unhealthy level as Jackson and I joined the others around our usual table. Everyone was anxious for the weekend and still gossiping about who did what at the Halloween party. Several of my classmates had made utter fools of themselves. Better still was the rumor that Taylor had drank just a tad bit too much and passed out while getting sick in the downstairs bathroom.

Someone apparently had photographed her intoxicated elegance with their phone. From what I understood, Taylor in her little Playboy bunny outfit had been caught seated in front of the toilet with her legs wrapped around the bottom, head down in the toilet and the lid on top of her head. Apparently, it was such a great photo that it was plastered all over Facebook under a pseudo name.

"I think it's funny," Hilary giggled.

"Couldn't have happened to a nicer person," Caitlyn added. "I'm only sorry I didn't get to see it for myself."

"Me too," Zak added while Jackson only smiled.

"I'm just glad that she made it to the bathroom before she got sick. My parents were mad enough because of all the antics," Cody stated flatly.

"Really? Your parents? They never get mad." Hilary gave him an odd look.

"They were after the party. Some of my so-called friends took a few liberties that my parents didn't appreciate very much."

Later, the four of us gathered around our lockers after practice gasping for air and covered in perspiration. Coach Smith was determined to kill each of us in a slow and agonizing fashion before we ever played our first game this season.

"I need a nap," Jenna complained, leaning against her locker.

"You and me both," Hilary added, kicking off her shoes.

"Shower first. Then nap." Caitlyn started peeling off her sweaty garments.

"I can't. I have so much freakin' homework to catch up on it isn't funny," I whined.

"Ditto," Jenna half-laughed to keep from crying. "I can't wait for Christmas break."

After a long hot shower and a quick-frozen pizza, I ran across the yards to the Chandler estate. The air was cold, and the brisk wind tore at my clothes. It wasn't even seven o'clock, but the sky was as dark as midnight. The moon drifted slightly from behind the thick cover of clouds offering little illumination. The smell of the Chandler's fireplace hung heavy on the breeze as the leaves crunched under my feet in their front yard.

Jackson answered the door looking amazing in his school sweatpants and hoodie. His hair was still slightly wet from his shower, and I could smell the Axe body wash radiating off his skin. I immediately wrapped my arms around his neck and kissed him eagerly.

"I brought my homework with me."

"Good. I was getting ready to start mine." He flashed my favorite lop-sided grin and took my backpack from me.

"I can only imagine how simple this homework must seem to you after already completing your bachelor's," I remarked as we made our way to the family room.

"Not as easy as you may believe," he slightly smirked. "The little trivial things seem harder to remember than the larger more complex ones."

"Kyle and Jenna will be here before eight to watch *Vampire Diaries* and *Grey's Anatomy*."

I sat down on the couch and opened my bag. I pulled out my books and set them on the coffee table in front of me.

"All right. Let me get my study materials from my room. I will be right back." Jackson walked quietly out of the room.

I opened my calculus book and placed my notebook beside it on the table. I read the instructions again for tonight's assignment and took a deep breath. *I don't know what in the world I was thinking about taking AP Calculus this semester.*

"Good evening, Jocelyn. I thought I heard your voice." Emily walked into the room carrying a silver tray with a couple of mugs on it.

"I brought you both some hot chocolate. It is really getting cold out this evening."

"How sweet of you. Thank you very much." I stood up and reached for one of the mugs. It was just hot enough with several fluffy marshmallows floating on top. I sipped it briefly before I sat back down.

"It's delicious."

"Thank you. It is my mother's recipe." She smiled sweetly and sat down on the loveseat across from me.

"She must be an amazing cook."

"She was. She passed away several years ago."

"I'm sorry."

Emily looked down for a moment and picked up her mug and took a sip. "She loved to cook. We used to spend hours cooking and baking." Her voice was soft, and she looked like she was almost in tears.

I was sorry that I mentioned anything. "Well, you are an amazing cook."

"Thank you. I enjoy it."

"Can I ask you a question, Emily?"

"Of course."

"When Jackson and I leave for Boston next fall, are you and Robert going to move back as well?"

"Yes. You were the reason we came back here. I am looking forward to going home. Chicago is home in our *other* lives, but Boston is home in *this* one."

"I was hoping you would say that. As strange as it may seem, both you and Robert really feel like family to me. I would be thrilled to have you both nearby."

"Thank you, Jocelyn. You are like a second daughter to me, and perhaps you do not recall me saying to you *there*, but I will tell you again *here*, I could not be happier with my son's choice in wife."

I got up and sat down beside her on the loveseat, wrapping my arms around her neck. "Thank you so much, Emily. That means a great deal to me."

"You are a wonderful, young lady, Jocelyn. I know you make my son very happy." She hugged me back tightly.

"Am I interrupting?" Jackson paused in the doorway with a couple books in his hand.

"No. Come on in. I will let you two get your studies done. Holler if you need anything." Emily smiled sweetly and left the room as silently as she'd entered.

"Your mother is so incredible," I said to Jackson as we reconvened on the sofa.

"I think so, but I may be a little biased, so thank you."

We dove into our homework hoping to get it all completed before the others arrived. Jackson had his physics done in less than fifteen minutes while I was still struggling with my calculus. I finally relented and let him walk me through it step by step.

"That's it?" I looked at him with disbelief. "Mr. Clark never explained it like that." I laughed at my own stupidity. "Damn, that's easy. I wish I'd asked you sooner."

"I told you I would help you. All you had to do was ask."

"Don't rub it in." I playfully shoved him away from me.

"You are so amazingly stubborn, silly woman."

Those simple few instructions allowed me to complete all my assignments a full ten minutes before eight. Just in time for Jenna and Kyle to arrive for *Vampire Diaries*. It was our favorite show and somehow the guys had joined in. She and I were addicted to books and devoured each one of them only to have heated discussions over who should be with whom and our opinion over every little detail.

I climbed into bed and opened my psych textbook. I wanted to try and get through the chapter we were covering this week in class on social psychology. However, my mind simply would not focus. It would wander off somewhere into my *other* life and I soon found myself wondering about my *other* family, friends, my relationship with Jackson and his family. All the things that I could not afford to be thinking about at this moment and the very reason I was behind in the first place.

I finally tossed my text on the floor in frustration. This was completely pointless. I shouldn't worry about where I was going to college in the fall because if I couldn't get it together right now, I wasn't going to graduate high school.

There had to be a way for me to compartmentalize my life and priorities. And I had to figure it out fast because this way was not working.

Chapter 12

Saturday, November 16, 1878

THE ROOM WAS STRANGELY FAMILIAR, very familiar in fact, but the furnishings were different. I was half lying on the couch leaning against someone who had their arms wrapped around me holding me lovingly. The light was low, and a roaring fire was ablaze in the hearth. I was surrounded by three other couples that were curled up in various postures looking comfortable and happy. We were all facing a weird-looking rectangular box that hung above the fireplace and watching the moving picture. The sounds the images produced seemed to be coming from every direction.

The three females I recognized from other visions and knew they were good friends of mine, but the boys they were with I had never seen before. I was becoming so accustomed to the bizarre attire that we all wore that I no longer paid any mind. There were platters of bizarre looking appetizers resting on the coffee table in the middle of the room that appeared to be well picked over.

A voice from behind tensed every muscle in my body and completely stopped my breathing. I didn't dare turn around.

"Do you kids need anything else?"

The familiarity was uncanny, and I knew at once without even looking who the voice belonged to. Emily. I sat numbly as a chorus from my peers rang out about me, declining any further assistance. Fear was the only thing that rooted me in the spot it was sitting.

"Well, then. Have fun kids. We will be in the study if you need anything else," Robert's distinctive voice added.

I closed my eyes tightly and forced myself to take a breath. I suddenly realized whose arms I was wrapped in, Jackson's. It had to be. But how? I couldn't bring myself to turn my head ever so slightly to confirm my theory.

As that detail truly sank into my thick skull, it became obvious whose house

I was in and why the structure was so familiar to me. This was the Chandler Estate; the same one I had been to a million times and served as a second home to me in recent years. *But how? How could I be here with these friends, at this time, in this house, with Jackson and his parents?* I fought the urge to run screaming from the room or collapse into a fit of hysterics.

The arms around me tightened noticeably. "Are you alright? You seem tense." I felt lips brush slightly against my cheek.

I inhaled deeply and looked over to confirm my hypothesis. Jackson's brilliant green eyes glowed back into mine. A broad smile stretched across his shapely lips and his familiar fingers lightly traced lovingly across my face. It was him. Holding me in his arms in this strange period that was rapidly becoming commonplace to me. It brought about a mixture of excitement and terror that coalesced into nothing short of a pure panic attack. I felt a scream in the back of my throat that I consciously struggled not to let escape. I was scared to respond, not trusting what my shaky vocal cords would produce. I opted simply to kiss him lightly in return to remain silent.

Luckily, he paid no notice and only tightened his grip around me, becoming engrossed again in the moving picture box.

I rested my head back against him once more but was still unable to control my whirling thoughts. Thousands of questions I wanted to demand answers for screamed loudly in my head. Everything I had believed to be true and false about this time of period was shattered. All that I loved about the prospects that were laid before me *here* were the same opportunities I felt denied in my actual reality and all hinged on the fact that I feared a life in this period.

This world. This period. Where I was given the opportunity to explore my education, become anyone whom I desired, have my own career, be something other than a wife and mother, can speak freely on any topic, and have equal footing with any male, granted with equal rights and freedoms, was truly where I belonged. But now I knew it was nothing more than simply a dream I could never have.

The already dim light began to fade before my eyes. My heart and mind screamed violently not to return to my *other* reality. I reached out my hands towards Jackson trying to grasp hold to him, but as always, my efforts were fruitless, and the world disappeared before me.

I bolted upright in my bed, screaming with intense insanity. Arms quickly locked onto my shoulders, and I vaguely heard my named called repeatedly. But I refused to open my eyes. Tears streamed down my face as the world I longed for became nothing but an incredible memory of the life I was denied. I pulled violently away from the grip of my captor, determined not to be forced back into this reality. My voice soon became raw and harsh, but the screams would not subside.

"Jocelyn! Look at me!" rang repeatedly in my tainted ears.

"No! No! Let me go!" I shouted blindly at whoever was holding me. "I want to go back! I don't belong here! Please! Let go!"

But to no avail. My captor only tightened his grip, forcing me back against my pillows with a strength I could not compete with. "Open your eyes, Jocelyn! It's me, Jackson!"

His name broke through my hysterics and the comfort of his familiar voice opened my eyes to see the frightened face before me.

"Jocelyn?" He lowered his tone, but his breathing was still panicked. "Are you with me?"

I nodded numbly unable to form any words. He swiftly wrapped me up in his arms and pulled me close to his body. I could feel his body heaving in sobs that he fought against and felt his tears falling upon my face.

"I am so sorry, so sorry darling. I should have realized the depths sooner. Please forgive me. I would have never let it go this far. I am so sorry my love." He repeatedly kissed the top of my head and held me tightly.

He gently and almost numbly rocked us back and forth as he continued to sob uncontrollably, babbling words that made no sense to me whatsoever. The only thing that was clear in all his mutterings was that he was indeed responsible for the visions I was witnessing. But I couldn't understand how.

He slowly let me go as I edged myself back away from him, sitting up staring at the face I loved in pure bewilderment. "You did this to me?" My voice was raw, and my throat screamed painfully. "But why? Why would you do this to me?" I wiped the steady stream of tears off my cheeks with rapid haste. My body was quivering unsteadily. My mind and heart were being ripped in two.

"I am so sorry. I had no idea you were seeing so much. I looked for clues, questioned my parents, your parents, Mimi, Olivia, your brother, about your nightmares, trying to figure out what you were seeing, but no one knew. You wouldn't tell anyone." His eyes pleaded with me to understand that I couldn't give him.

"Why would you do this to me?"

He reached out for my hand, gently taking it in his and looked longingly into my eyes. "For us to be together. Always." His shaky words only confused me more.

"We are together. Always," I sobbed. "I love you. We are getting married and…and…" But words failed me.

We sat in silence for a long time, calming down, each lost in our own thoughts. After all that had transpired in the last several weeks, I began to doubt whether I even knew the man sitting before me. Then I realized for the first time my room was still dark and the only light was coming from the embers of the fire. *Why would he be in my room in the middle of the night? What would my parents say? His parents?*

I straightened myself up and took a deep breath trying to calm myself. I desperately needed to clear my head and attempt to make some sense out of what he was trying to explain to me.

"Jackson, what are you doing here? How did you get in my room? My father will kill you if he finds you in here."

My throat was still screaming raw at me, and every word escaped painfully.

Jackson took several noticeable deep breaths, and finally, a small smile etched across his defined lips. "God, I love you." A full-hearted laugh burst forth from him followed by a deep sigh of relief. "It is so like you, in the throes of hysterics, you notice something so incredibly trivial."

"Trivial?" *He certainly wouldn't think it was trivial if someone caught him in here.*

"Do you honestly believe that I would be in here without permission?" He continued to smile at my naivety. "Your parents know I am in here, as do mine. Everyone is greatly concerned about these night terrors."

I nodded numbly, absorbing every word that flowed from his lips. "After you went to bed last evening, I spoke with your parents about them, and they told me that Mimi has been staying close to you most nights. Given her age and the toll that this is having on her, I asked your parents if I could sleep in the rocking chair next to your bed in case you had another episode. Since they trust me and are genuinely concerned, they agreed with the stipulation that I not enter your room until you were in a sound sleep so that you would not be aware of my presence."

Unbelievable!

Jackson got up and crossed over to the pitcher next to the basin and poured me a glass of water. He sat back down on the corner of my bed and handed the glass to me. I reluctantly took a sip knowing it was going to enflame my throat going down. It did.

"Thank you," I squeaked between sips.

"Confused?"

"Very," I answered flatly. "I do not know what to say or think. None of this makes any sense."

"I imagine not. I felt the same way when it happened to me." Jackson slid a little closer to me on the bed and took both my hands in his. "I need you to be completely honest with me. None of these, 'it is nothing' or 'I can handle it' responses, you *must* tell me what you are seeing!"

His face was plainly serious. A knot in my stomach clenched tightly and I felt like I was going to get sick.

I cannot possibly tell him the truth. He will think I am insane. Maybe I am?

I stared at him blankly, unable to give him the answers he desperately needed.

"Please, darling. You must tell me. I know how you are feeling. I have been there also. It terrified me, and I was sure I was losing my mind."

I loved him for being empathic, but there was no way he could possibly understand what I was feeling. Again, I shook my head numbly unable to find any words for him.

Jackson cleared his throat and exhaled loudly. "Let me see, you have seen objects like horseless carriages, talking and moving picture boxes, people talking or pushing buttons on small objects, um…things like wires plugged into people's ears."

How could he possibly know all this?

"I am sure you are confused by the unusual styles and clothing, weird furniture, and accessories. Things like that."

I nodded stupidly, filled with an indescribable amount of fear and confusion as the tears poured down my cheeks.

"I am sure that you have seen Jenna, Caitlyn, Hilary, their boyfriends, your younger brother, Ethan, and your *other* parents too."

My jaw literally hit the floor. *There was no way he could possibly know their names! Can he read my mind? See my visions too?*

"And by the expression on your face I am going to take a guess and say that you have seen either me or my parents or all of us there as well." He patted my hands reassuringly.

How can he be so casual and calm?

My entire body had gone numb. Thousands of words were screaming in my head, and I couldn't put them in any sensible order to convey any type of message.

"Jocelyn? Please, say something."

He paused and looked deeply into my eyes searching for some sort of recognition. But I had nothing. I couldn't form words to express the overwhelming number of emotions that were coursing through me.

"Sweetheart, please." He gently brushed my hair away from my face. "You are starting to scare me."

"This is too much," I stuttered softly.

"I know, darling."

"How? Why? I do not understand. You say you know what I am experiencing, but that is not possible."

"Please. Get dressed and come with me over to my house. I believe that my parents may explain everything to you better than I can."

He climbed back off my bed waiting for me to get up also, but I didn't. I couldn't.

"Are you serious? It is still dark outside. Look." I pointed over towards the windows. "Everyone is asleep. What time is it anyway?"

Jackson lifted the pocket watch off the night table and flipped it open leaning towards the light of the fireplace.

"Four-thirty," he answered casually.

"Four-thirty in the morning? How can you expect me to go over there and wake up your parents? Absolutely not!" My arms gestured wildly expressing my disbelief with his suggestion.

"Trust me. They will not mind. They will be thrilled to finally get the truth out in the open."

My eyes scrunched up in confusion. *The truth? The truth about what?*

"Come on, throw something on, and I will leave your parents a note downstairs telling them where you are."

But I still didn't move.

"Jackson, I am not going anywhere at four-thirty in the morning."

"Will you please trust me on this?" he pleaded impatiently by the door.

"No. I will not. And if it is that important, then you can come back over here and explain it to me yourself."

Jackson reluctantly let his hand drop from the doorknob and walked back over to my bed. My out-spoken behavior not only surprised him, but I surprisingly shocked myself as well.

"All right." He took a deep breath and sat back down on my bed facing me. "I still do not believe that I can explain this to you properly, but I will give it my best. Then later, we will go over and speak with my parents." He readjusted himself. "This is very difficult to explain. First answer this. Was I correct in the statements that I said before about what you were seeing?"

I nodded.

"Do you have any idea as to what time period you were seeing?"

"No. But it was so amazingly different from anything I had ever seen before in my life." I was doing my best to push the memories out of my mind and remain focused on Jackson's words.

"I believe you were seeing your life in the twenty-first century."

"What? How? My life? But..." I hated myself for sounding like an idiot, but I couldn't form the right words to put together.

"The 2000s to be more precise. Many, many years from now. And yes, you have a full complete life in that period also. Much the same as you do in this one. Of course, there are numerous differences. Many of which I am sure you have noticed. Women in the twenty-first century have many liberties and freedoms that you do not share here."

I numbly sat and stared at Jackson, intensely absorbing every word that rolled off his lips.

Everything that I had seen—could it really be real?

"You see, Jocelyn. You have been blessed with a special gift that you inherited from your Uncle Monte. It is called *Essence Voyager Era* or rather, *EVE*. As I understand it, our consciousness shifts between two planes, often in sleep, one in the twenty-first century and one in the nineteenth. Of course, it is not you that physically travels, just your soul."

"How could you know such a thing?" I babbled in disbelief.

"Because I have the same gift, my whole family does." Jackson squeezed my hands tenderly, full of love and understanding.

"So, you see, yes, I do understand what you are experiencing. I went through it also several years ago and I know how terrifying it is."

I remained rooted in my spot, unable to fully comprehend what he was saying. It made no sense.

How could something like this even be possible? "I…I do not understand."

"I know it is a lot to take in, but it is okay. I promise. Everything is going to be fine."

I knew his words were sincere, but I found no comfort in them. "How can you say that? Everything is *not* fine!" I could feel the blood rushing to my face and found it hard to even breathe. "If what you are saying is remotely true, then you are telling me that I am some kind of freak of nature. Cursed!" I scrambled out of bed as quickly as I could. I had to get away from him.

He did this to me. This was all his fault! The visions, the terror, the sleepless nights, fearing I was losing my mind. It was all his fault!

My mind was screaming a thousand different things all at once. None of which made any rational sense whatsoever. I paced back and forth across my room, mumbling to myself.

Jackson sat quietly on my bed watching me rant and rave a path across my bedroom floor.

"Why? Why did you do this to me?" I stopped a few feet from him and demanded.

"Jocelyn, I did not do this to you. You inherited it. It is genetic," he calmly stated.

"What? What do you mean genetic?" I shouted.

"It is a trait that is passed down through families, like eye and hair color. Things like that."

"Then why am I the only one in my family who has this?" I fired back.

"Your Uncle Monte has it as well. You inherited it from him. He *is* your father's brother," Jackson shook his head at me.

"Why would you put me through something like this?" I shouted.

"Will you please keep your voice down before you wake up the entire house?" he calmly asked.

"I don't care if they wake up." I fell back atop my bed in sobs.

Jackson moved over beside me and softly brushed my hair back. "I am so sorry, darling. I know how hard all of this is. I wish there was something I could do to make this easier."

I looked up at his blurry face through my tears. "Do have any idea how absurd this all sounds?"

Jackson smiled slightly and nodded.

"How am I supposed to believe something like this?"

"You must trust me. Trust your faith in us. You will know that I am being honest with you." His eyes were imploring me, but I simply couldn't wrap my brain around this concept.

I inhaled deeply and ran my fingers through my hair in exasperation.

Jackson pulled me closer to him and wrapped his arms securely around me. I rested my head against his shoulder and waited anxiously to hear everything he had to say.

For the next two hours I listened intently while he explained the whole sordid truth about having a dual conscious, the barrier between them disintegrating, my life there, our relationship, his life in Boston, my Uncle Monte approaching him after our engagement announcement and him returning to High School in Chicago to get closer to me. His story sounded like something closer to some fairytale that Mimi had told me as a child rather than something that was happening to me.

I gently pulled back away from him to better see his face. "So, are you telling me that since both of my consciousnesses are aware of one another that this barrier between them is now broken down completely?"

"That will take some time. Right now, you are seeing glimpses of your *other* life in each period but not in any chronological order. Some memories are more current while others are from your childhoods. It could still be some time before the wall is completely down between the two. Maybe a month or so, perhaps longer, maybe shorter. I really do not know. Everyone is different."

I laughed inwardly to myself thinking that he should write all this down because no one would ever believe that something like this was possible.

I stared at him numbly shaking my head. "This is unbelievable. You realize that, right?" I halfheartedly laughed. "I cannot believe that you went searching for me and actually returned to school to get closer to me. And to think that everything I have seen was real. The family, the school, the people." The images of all the bizarre objects and things clouded my memory.

"Very real. I know that it all seems impossible. Strange. Unimaginable. But I can assure you that it is all very real. And you know, you have a very good life *there*. You are very happy. You have a wonderful family, friends, you are an outstanding athlete and student. It was rather a shock to see you in such a setting. It is like you are the person you wished you had the opportunity to be *here*."

His words brought back all those feelings of jealousy that I had felt for that girl's life, and it was beyond weird to think it was truly me. Not someone else.

"So, I'm happy *there*?" Somehow, I already knew the answer before the words even fell off my lips.

"Yes. Very."

"And we are together?"

"Yes. And planning on getting married after graduation before we go off to the university in Boston next fall. I am going to continue studying for my law degree," he smiled. "I am afraid it is a little more in-depth *there* than *here* and takes somewhat longer. And you are going to start your undergraduate studies."

"Really?" It was amazing to think that I was preparing to go off to college like my brothers.

"What am I planning on studying?"

Curiosity was overwhelming me. These were all my dreams come true. Jackson in my life and the opportunity to attend college.

"You haven't decided on a major yet, but I know it is…"

"Something in the sciences," I interrupted. "I remember Indiana University and telling my parents that I was considering my options within the sciences. The woman," I snorted unexpectedly, blushing red. "I mean my mother *there;* she wants me to be a physician like her. It is so strange to think that I have a mother who is so educated and has a career of her own. To think that she has her own life and that it does not revolve around her house, the servants, and a house full of children."

Jackson looked at me with stunned disbelief. "I believe I truly underestimated your desire to further your education." Then he let out something that sounded like a cough. "I believe you have more of your mother, Amy, in you than I had previously estimated."

"I have always wanted to further my education. You know that."

"Yes, only I did not realize how strong of a drive you had for it." He reached out and pulled me closer, engulfing me in his strong arms.

Long after the sun had finally risen, Jackson and I sat huddled on my bed discussing all the strange and wonderful aspects of the twenty-first century.

The glimpses that I had seen apparently did not do justice to all the amazing things that had changed in the world over the vast distance of time between my two eras.

He explained to me the horrific tragedies and wars that in my mind were still yet to come. He talked about flying machines, horseless carriages, computers, and cell phones. My imagination had never conceived of such possibilities. Jackson spoke of televisions, movies, stereos, iPods, and various oddities. If his expression hadn't been so serious, I would have been positive he was making this stuff up. The wondrous progress that had been made completely baffled me. He even told me that a man named Neil Armstrong took a spacecraft to the moon, landed on it, and even walked on it in the summer of 1969! *How absurd!*

I sat there totally dumbfounded as I listened intently to something that was in some aspects part of my history, but in another, a future that was slowly beginning to unfold before me.

By nine o'clock, he had retreated downstairs to have breakfast with my family while I quickly got myself dressed to go over to his house. My fingers trembled with nervousness as I fumbled with Mimi trying to get my corset tied and dress fastened. I could hardly sit still long enough for her to fix my hair. I had a million questions stirring within me and I was ready to explode with anticipation.

His parents were sitting quietly by the hearth when we arrived. Robert was consumed by piles of papers from his legal practice while Emily was writing next to the fire. They appeared the same as always as we sat down across from them, exactly like they always did on any other typical Saturday morning.

All I could think was, *what had they been doing in 2015 when I was upstairs struggling to find a good night's rest? Did they see me, talk to me, my family? Did they drive around in one of those horseless carriages that Jackson described to me or were they playing games on some rectangular box that appeared on the moving picture screen? Had they eaten food prepared in a microwave or picked it up, what Jackson had referred to as fast food?*

I couldn't stop my mind from feeling muffled and obscured. I wish I could remember fully the life that I had *there*. It seemed so unreal to me, just out of my grasp. I wanted desperately to reach out and hold onto it, but it kept slipping through my fingers like running water.

"Good morning, you two." Emily was the first to welcome us. "Are you feeling better this morning, Miss Jocelyn?"

"Yes, thank you." I replied with a shaky harsh voice.

"Mother, Father, we have some news to share with you both," Jackson started. Both his parents stopped what they were working on and turned towards us. "Last night, Jocelyn woke up screaming again. After I finally got her calmed down, I explained everything to her about *EVE*."

Robert's eyes widened. "Really?"

I nodded.

"And how do you feel?" Emily asked sweetly in a motherly tone.

"I am not sure to be honest."

"I would imagine so. It is a lot to take in and very hard to imagine, let alone believe." Robert got up and crossed the room to refresh his cup of coffee. "I remember how hard it was when Jackson found out. He came unhinged."

"Don't exaggerate," Jackson blushed and shifted uncomfortably.

"I wish I was." Robert couldn't stifle his laugh as he sat back down next to his pile of papers.

"Anyway," Emily said calmly. "Jocelyn is the focus here, not Jackson. There is plenty of time later for retelling horror stories."

Their casualness and laughter regarding such a bizarre topic immediately put me at ease. I felt like an intruder overhearing an intimate conversation between two lovers. Yet somehow, I knew I was a part of the insider group, a part of something so much bigger than myself. This amazing gift that I apparently received from my Uncle Monte seemed so commonplace and familiar to them, like nothing out of the ordinary to these people.

"All right," Robert composed himself. "A story for another time then. I am sure that all of this is quite confusing, and you must have a million questions."

"Yes, about that many," I laughed. "I do not even know where to start."

Robert started off by explaining the more current effects of our industrial revolution and expanding up to the turn of the century. I had no idea how complicated it all was. I wanted to write it all down for myself just to attempt to keep things straight, but all three of them strongly advised me never to do such a thing.

Apparently, Nostradamus, a name I was vaguely familiar with, had made the mistake of keeping journals of the history between his two lives. Robert explained that even though he tried to write in code, numerous scholars have spent centuries trying to decipher the meanings behind his writings. Emily added that most people with *EVE* figured that he wrote most of his journals while the wall between his two consciousnesses was coming down and he was attempting to keep it all straight by creating some sort of timeline.

"The extreme distance between his two worlds was astounding, by any standards. The amount of history that took place had to be a hundred times more difficult to explain and comprehend than I could even begin to imagine.

However, the fact that he left all his writings behind has caused so much speculation about the future that it scares people," Robert explained.

"I believe I have heard the name somewhere before," I stated more to myself than anyone else, but for the life of me I couldn't remember the context in which I had.

"Nostradamus was known as a great prophet that predicted future events, supposedly by astronomy. His journals, called *The Centuries*, have been interpreted as foreseeing upcoming events such as the coming of three Anti-Christ's as well as other major events. Many scholars believe that the first was Napoleon, the second, a horrible German Nazi dictator named Adolf Hitler that was single-handedly responsible for the second World War at the end of the 1930s, and the third one has yet to be revealed, at least to our current knowledge in 2015." Robert paused for a moment before continuing.

"There has been some controversy over whether a man named Saddam Hussein was the third, but I personally doubt it. The other two were much worse, it is hard to imagine that he is the one Nostradamus was referring to, but I could be wrong. Some even say that Osama Bin Laden is the third because of some images of a burning tower found among Nostradamus' journals. Still, others speculate the picture predicts the terrorist attacks on the Twin Towers on September 11, 2001, but I do not believe that either." Robert shrugged his shoulders.

"Who really knows? I personally do not believe it was either of them because they did not have the army, navy or in Hitler's case, Air Force size that the other two had during their reign. Plus, the part of the world where they reside is such an unstable region and is more of a religious war than the gaining of land and power like the other two."

I crinkled my eyebrows at him with complete confusion. I had no clue who Hitler was, or the other two men he was referring to. Let alone the words like Air Force, Twin Towers, or German Nazi dictator. I had certainly heard of Germany or rather Germania. I knew it was a country on the other side of the world, but that was all I knew of it.

"I know who Napoleon was but who were Hitler and the other two men?"

Robert glanced over as Emily nodded slightly.

"They were horrible men who did terrible things. Saddam ruled in the Middle East and is already dead in 2015, but Bin Laden is still evading capture. I am not sure how, but he is."

Robert chuckled uncharacteristically, and his action was bizarre to me. "And Hitler, well Adolf Hitler was an evil dictator who started World War II and killed over six million Jews, gypsies, homosexuals, and disabled individuals in Europe in the 1930s and 40s, men, women, and children alike."

"There are so many events that happen within the hundred-plus years or so between your current states that it would be best if we explain it to you step by step, so you can better understand it all," Emily explained softly.

I spent the rest of the day over at the Chandler's home getting the ins and outs of this *EVE* thing and a more in-depth look at the world as it slowly unfolded into my *other* existence in the twenty-first century. There were so many amazing differences between my two lives that the vast structures and core of my existence were not even parallel. I was warned about the struggles I would encounter once I had full awareness of both worlds, informed that it could get complicated and they reinforced to me the foreign world in which I was like myself yet, in many ways, drastically different. All of which was overwhelming.

Chapter 13

Saturday, November 14, 2015

I RODE HOME FROM PRACTICE with Jenna, Ethan, and Jackson. I leaned against Jackson in the backseat listening to the other three rambling on about practice and our upcoming opening games. I was barely listening to their conversation as the short drive brought me closer to our dreaded home. I had avoided being alone with my parents for almost a week, ever since my tantrum. Luckily, my mother had not addressed the subject of Jackson or BU with me again and thankfully, my dad hadn't mentioned anything either.

But I knew that my mother was not on-call this weekend, so she would be hanging around the house. I was positive my dad had heard everything by now and I was certain that I was headed for an ambush.

We pulled into Jenna's driveway where Kyle was waiting for her. He opened the door even before she had the chance to put her car in park.

"Hello, beautiful. How was practice?" he greeted her.

"Long. As always." He pulled her up into his arms and kissed her lightly on the lips. "Kyle, stop." She pulled away from him. "I'm all hot and sweaty and dying to take a shower."

"Cool. I'll join you," he teased.

"Yeah, right. No problem. Of course, my parents won't mind that." Jenna couldn't stop smiling. She turned back to the three of us. "I'll catch up with you all later. Give me a call this afternoon." She turned with Kyle and headed up her drive.

"Sure." I waved as the rest of us headed over towards my house.

Jackson and I paused on the walkway. He pulled me close in his arms while I struggled to free myself. "Jackson, don't. I'm all nasty!"

"I do not care," he smiled and kissed me passionately.

I relented, pulling his body closer to mine. I could taste the sweet salty sweat from his practice on his luscious lips and it only made me want him more. I twisted my fingers through the back of his hair crushing his mouth onto mine. I could never get enough of him. I wanted him so badly my body physically ached for him.

"Come over after you shower. I have a big surprise for you," he gave me a devilish grin.

"What are you up to?"

"You will see. Just hurry."

"You realize I hate it when you do this."

"I know," he leaned over and quickly kissed me on the cheek. "See you soon." And before I could reply, he sprinted across the street and disappeared into his house.

"Great," I muttered to myself, walking up to the porch where Ethan stood waiting for me.

"So, what's going on with you two?" he asked opening the front door.

"I don't know. He's up to something," I shrugged, following him into the house. "He said he has a surprise for me."

"Good luck with that," he laughed. Ethan knew how much I hated surprises. "I'm going to get something to eat before I shower so if you're going take one, make it quick and don't use up all the hot water."

"Sure. No problem," I hollered, already heading up the stairs.

I was sitting at my vanity table blow-drying my hair when someone knocked on my door.

"Jocelyn? You decent?" my dad hollered.

A chill of panic rushed down my spine. I placed the brush back on the table and turned towards the door. "Sure. Come in."

My door slowly opened. He hardly ever visited my room unless he really had to, which meant that Mom had sent him. He crossed over and took a seat on the edge of my bed. He looked even more uncomfortable than I felt.

"I understand that you had an intense conversation with your mother last weekend." He fidgeted with his hands, glancing slightly over at me. I only nodded, hoping it was a safe response since I didn't trust my voice.

"She also told me you applied to BU next fall."

Again, I only nodded.

"Do you really think that is such a good idea?"

"Yes," I squeaked.

"I know you really like Jackson. I understand that. It's just that …. Well Jocelyn, you're so young," he mumbled.

"I'm eighteen, Daddy. I know you both think I'm too young to know what love is, but I'm not. I honestly love him, and BU is a great school. I don't understand why it would be so terrible for me to go there with him next fall."

"You're right, BU is a great school, and you would get an excellent education there. That's not what concerns us." He was still looking more at the floor than me.

"I'm not stupid, Daddy. I'm not going to get pregnant and drop out of school. I promise. That is not why I want to be with him," I tried to explain.

"Most pregnancies are not planned, honey. You know that." He shook his head. "I don't want to see something like that happen to you."

I got up and walked over to my bed and sat down beside him. "Daddy, whether we go to the same school, we're still going to be together. But I can tell you that I would be much happier if we were together." I took a deep breath trying to believe that I was saying this to my dad of all people. "Daddy," I placed my hands over his. "Jackson is not pressuring me to have sex. He respects me too much to do that. He loves me and doesn't believe in sex before marriage. I promise, Daddy. I'm still a virgin." I could feel the blood rushing to my face.

I glanced up at my dad, whose face had blushed every bit as red as my own. "I'm—I'm glad to hear that. But the more time you spend with him and the longer you two are together, the less likely you are to retain that status."

Wow, his bluntness caught me off guard. "I agree. But that is also my decision, and it has nothing to do with where I attend college. I believe we both know that."

"Yes."

"Then Daddy, you must trust me. My decision to be with Jackson is not going to change. Neither are my feelings for him." I looked at him, pleading for understanding.

"Did he ask you to marry him?"

I looked into his mournful eyes that were so like my own and I couldn't lie. I only nodded slowly.

"And you said yes."

I nodded once more, afraid to speak.

He looked down at his hands briefly and exhaled deeply. "And when were you planning on telling us about this?"

"Spring Break," I answered in a low voice feeling horrible about my betrayal.

"And the wedding?" He looked up at me with tears in his own eyes. "Before next fall I'd imagine."

"Yes."

My dad wrapped his arms around me and held me tightly. "Well then, I guess I'd better go have a long talk with this young man."

He let go of me and stood up.

"What? Daddy! No!"

But he was already outside the door and down the stairs.

I rushed over to the window and saw my dad crossing the street towards Jackson's house. There wasn't even time for me to call and forewarn him. I pulled the curtain back and sat down pressing my forehead against the cool window. I hated to think of what he was going to say to Jackson, let alone his parents.

Ethan strolled into my room silently and snuck up behind me. "Hey what's going on? I heard the front door slam. Where's Dad going in such a rush?"

"Damn, Ethan." I nearly jumped out of my skin, "Dad's going over to Jackson's."

He took a seat at the other end of my bay window and glanced outside. "So? What's the big deal about that? He's probably just going to talk to Robert about something."

I looked over at him unable to hide my own tears. "No. He's going over there to talk with Jackson."

Ethan gave me a confused look. Then his eyes grew bigger and bigger. "Oh my God! You're pregnant! Damn, Dad's gonna kill him!"

I reached over and slapped his arm. "No, stupid. I'm not pregnant."

"Then what?"

"I told him that I plan to go to BU next fall with Jackson."

"So?" he shrugged slightly.

"And" I hesitated, not wanting him to also explode on me. "I told him that Jackson proposed to me, and I said yes."

"No shit! Wow. I wasn't expecting that."

He took a deep breath and looked back out the window across the street. The Chandler household remained silent with my father tucked neatly inside saying God only knows what to Jackson and his parents.

"I wonder what's going on over there," I muttered in a soft voice.

"I'm sure you'll find out soon enough," he chuckled.

"Yeah, I know." I couldn't tear my eyes off the house across the way.

Ethan looked over at me crinkling his eyebrows. "Are you sure about this?"

I gave him a scornful look in return.

"I'm being serious. Aren't you a little too young to even be thinking about marriage? What about college and grad school?"

"I'm still going to college and grad school. And yes, I am positive about this." I knew he wasn't going to take this well either.

"But you've only known him," Ethan reasoned.

I immediately cut him off, getting irritated with always hearing the same excuses. "A few weeks. Yes, I am aware of how long I have known Jackson Chandler." I took a deep breath and leaned my head back against the window. "I can't explain it, but I know he's the one I'm destined to be with."

Ethan stared at me for several moments trying to decide what to say. I could tell from the look on his face that he was struggling to find the right words. "Trust me on this E. Jackson is everything, and I promise you, I love him with all that I am."

"When are you planning on getting married?" his voice dropped an octave.

"July."

"That soon? What did Mom say?" He had his all-knowing smirk across his face.

"That if I decide to do this then I'm on my own to pay for my education." I rolled my eyes and couldn't help but laugh.

Ethan laughed too. "Sounds like her."

"I know, doesn't it? And I believe her too."

"No, I don't think Dad would jeopardize your education as a punishment. So, she's probably going to kick and scream about this for a while and then accept it. You know how she is."

"Yeah, I hope you're right." I wished I was as optimistic as he was.

We both fell into an uncomfortable silence with our eyes locked on the house across the street. There was no movement from within and I wasn't sure if that was a good sign or not. Occasionally, Ethan would lean over and touch my hand in reassurance, but he never uttered another word.

Two hours passed before my father emerged from the gray shadows. He appeared years older as he slowly crossed back towards our home. A part of me wanted to call Jackson, but the other wanted to interrogate my dad first. Either way, I was terrified of what one had to say about the other. I was frozen in my place unable to react. Ethan's eyes were locked on me curious to see what I was going to do next. So was I.

I couldn't breathe when I heard the front door open and shut and then footsteps on the stairs. Within moments, there he stood, in my doorway looking worn out from the encounter.

"Ethan. Out." Dad's voice was soft which scared me even more. It was always better when he screamed. At least then I knew that he was getting it off his chest. When he was calm, that was when I truly needed to be scared.

My brother scrambled to his feet and left quickly without saying a word. He didn't even bother to glance back at me before he rushed out, closing my door behind him.

My dad took a seat on the corner of my bed facing me. I shifted towards him but couldn't find a way to break the silence between us. Several minutes of awkward silence passed before he finally opened his mouth.

"Well, I had a long talk with Jackson and his parents."

I said nothing but stared at the floor, only looking at him uncomfortably when he spoke.

"And I can tell you that you have a very mature young man with a good head on his shoulders who seems to be very much in love with you."

I only nodded.

"And it seems that there is no way of changing his mind about getting married to you next summer, either" he shifted with tense emotion. "Jackson has also reassured me that he respects you enough not to pressure you about your intimate relationship before you are married. He promised me that you would finish college and grad school and I can tell you I'm going to hold him to that." His voice got a little harsher but remained low.

My dad took a deep breath and exhaled slowly before continuing, "So I guess we are planning a wedding then." He looked over at me and smiled weakly.

I jumped up and rushed into his arms as a flood of relief fell over me. "Oh, thank you, Daddy. Thank you!" I kissed him repeatedly on the cheek.

"All right. All right. Calm down. We still have to deal with your mother and that's not going to be easy," he laughed lightly.

I straightened up and tried to compose myself. "Your support means the world to me Daddy, you know, that right?"

"Yes, I do. And I want you to know that I'd rather be supportive of you in this and gain a great son, and he really is great, Jocelyn, than risk alienating you and ruining our relationship. I love you, sweetheart. And don't worry about your school money. You will still be able to use the trust we set up for you," he smiled lovingly with tears in his eyes. "It's just going to be very difficult for me to let you go."

"Don't worry about that, Daddy. You'll never have to do that." I leaned over and gave him a reassuring hug. "Thank you so much, Daddy. Oh God, I need to go see Jackson."

I jumped back off the bed. "I'll be home later."

"What about your mother? We still need to talk to her," he hollered as I headed for my door.

I paused, turning around to face him with a smirk. "You talk to her. You can calm her down before I get back."

"Great," I heard him mutter as I smiled and ran out the door.

Jackson was waiting for me when I arrived hours behind our earlier intended schedule. He opened the door before I even reached his porch.

"It is about time," he greeted me. "What happened? Your father caught me completely off guard."

I leaned on the doorframe feeling completely foolish. "I'm sorry. My mom and I had an argument last weekend about our relationship and us going to the same university. She kept pushing all the right buttons and I blew it. I acted like a two-year-old and told her fine, I'm an adult and I could marry you if I wanted to and there was nothing, she could do about it."

Jackson busted out laughing, "Wow. I am glad I missed that one."

"Yeah, me too. I didn't come across very well. I'm sorry about my dad. I'm surprised he waited this long to confront me about my tantrum. He was probably trying to figure out how to handle it before he blew up also."

I wrapped my arms around his waist and pulled him to me kissing him lightly on his full lips.

"Oh, sorry." Emily paused midway down the stairs. "I thought maybe Amy was coming over to yell at me next."

"Sorry about my dad."

"Do not worry. He was very polite and gracious. Just being a concerned father. I would be the same way if Phoebe was in your place." Robert walked into the foyer. Emily walked down and joined her husband, putting her arm around him. "No, darling. Shane handled things calmly and rationally. You would not have been nearly as gracious in this situation. And if I recall, even though Phoebe was quite older, you still did not take the news well," she patted him lovingly on his chest.

"No man likes giving up his little girl. It is hard," he pouted, and I couldn't keep from giggling.

I was so happy that my dad had not come over here and made a complete ass of his self.

"Come on in. I have some incredible news to share with you." Jackson pulled me into the living room.

I joined him on the couch while Emily brought us in some hot chocolate before she and Robert disappeared into another part of the house. Jackson was beside himself with excitement.

"Guess what happened last night, or rather 1878!"

"What?"

"You finally found out about *EVE*."

"Are you serious?" I couldn't believe it. Was all this barrier crap over with, finally?

"Very much so."

"And? How did it go?" I wondered if I'd handled it any better *there* than I did *here*.

"Not great. Worse than *here*, but you are dealing," he grimaced.

We snuggled up on the sofa and he gave me a detailed account of all the excitement. I was embarrassed by my behavior and reactions even though I had no control over any of it. The more he described the events, the worse I sounded and felt. I was thrilled that at least I was aware of everything now in both my lives, but for some strange reason I didn't feel any different.

"So why has nothing changed? I mean, if I am now aware of both worlds, in both worlds, shouldn't I be completely conscious of both lives now?" I rested my head on his shoulder with my arm across his chest.

"It will probably still take a little time for everything to set in for you to become fully aware of both existences," he shrugged casually.

"I wish it would speed up. I'm so sick and tired of asking you every day what happened in my *other* life and all the strange memories. They're almost annoying because they tell me so little," I complained. "And here I thought this day couldn't get any worse."

"This is great news, Jocelyn. Now it is only a matter of time before the barrier is completely gone. You should be happy." He kissed me lightly on the forehead.

"I know. I'm sorry. I just figured that knowing would somehow magically change everything and that suddenly the barrier in my consciousness would disappear."

"It will. You need to give it a little more time. Soon it will seem normal to you to exist on two separate planes, and we will be laughing at the comparisons between the two worlds." Jackson gave me a gentle squeeze of reassurance.

"It's so hard to imagine," I said more to myself than him, staring off into space. "I mean, the two worlds are so drastically different. Everything about them couldn't be further apart and the more research I do on the period, the harder it is for me to imagine living *there*."

"I know, but you will get used to it."

"It's so strange to think of myself living in a time when there's no electricity, no cars, no refrigerators, microwaves, computers, cell phones. All the stuff that I take for granted every day and think nothing of."

"It definitely gives you a new perspective on life," he laughed. "I remember once when I slipped up and made a remark to my brother about antibiotics in front of your father Patrick when Olivia's little brother was fighting pneumonia, and he almost clobbered me. Penicillin was not discovered by Alexander Fleming until 1928, and even then, it took years of studying to figure out how it worked and wasn't available in quantity until 1944, just in time to treat the Allied soldiers wounded on D-Day. My brother ripped me a new one when we got home and so did my father. Luckily, your father never said anything further about it, but it could have caused a lot of problems. We must always be very careful of what we say when others are around."

"It's not going to be easy. Is it?" I stared into his deep green eyes.

"Not at first, but you will get used to it. Hopefully, the barrier will not be completely gone by the time we get married. That way, you will be protected around your family, and it will give you some time to adjust without risking exposure," he grinned slightly.

"I keep trying to wrap my brain around all this. It's so hard to make sense of it. Having two totally different lives, it sounds exhausting."

"It can be. You should try going to college in both existences at the same time. It is hell! All I ever did was study," he shook his head with his adorable lop-sided grin across his face. "It makes high school seem like a breeze now."

"How am I supposed to switch from being who I am *here* and what I am accustomed to currently, to a place where women are subservient and have no rights at all? I'm not sure I can do that. I am too outspoken to sit by and not be able to offer an opinion on anything that happens. That's going to be impossible for me." I knew my big mouth was going to get me into a world of trouble *there*. It was only a matter of time.

"Trust me. It will not be as bad as you believe. You have to remember that once the barrier is gone, not only will your personality *here* shine through *there*, but who you are *there* will merge into your personality *here*. You will become an even mixture of both with full memories and the cultures of each world. It will not be nearly as difficult as you imagine."

I sighed deeply, resting my body against his. A silence fell between us as we both became lost to our own thoughts. I closed my eyes and listened to his heartbeat, feeling the warmth of his body flowing into mine. My mind recalled all the various episodes of my life in *there* that I witnessed trying to put them all into chronological order and perspective.

From all that I had seen, I did have a good life and was very happy. My family really loved me and I them. Still, it felt more like a movie than a world I lived in.

The doorbell rang, breaking my thoughts and bringing me back to reality. My mind immediately jumped to my mom and her occasional irrational behavior. I hoped that she hadn't decided to come over here after talking with

Dad about my plans for next summer and screamed her displeasure at Jackson and his parents. While it wouldn't surprise me at all, I could only hope that my dad had managed to calm her down a bit before she embarrassed me to no end.

I heard Emily greet someone at the door and felt a rush of relief when Jenna's voice responded. Jenna came storming into the living room followed closely by Ethan and Kyle. With her hands on her hips and a smirk across her lips she demanded, "Okay, explain!"

"Excuse me?" I was baffled.

"The wedding? Your parents know! We just stopped by your house," she gestured towards Kyle, "because you hadn't bothered to call like you said you would, and Ethan tells me that you're over here and then asks me if I know you're getting married next summer. When I didn't answer him, he told me that your parents know about it and that your dad came over here this afternoon and had a talk with Jackson! What in the world is going on?" She couldn't keep herself from laughing.

"It's nothing. I had a fight with my mom over Jackson and going to BU next fall and it all sort of slipped out." I rolled my eyes.

Jenna flopped down on the loveseat giggling like an idiot. "Man, I wish I could have seen that. She must be coming unglued."

Kyle sat down beside her, and Ethan sat down in the chair next to the hearth.

"I'm not sure. I'm hiding over here while my dad calms her down."

Ethan smirked at me. "Coward. Mom's going ballistic. I could hear her screaming downstairs from their room while Dad was trying to talk with her. You might want to consider staying over at Jenna's until…um, graduation." He raised his eyebrows and tilted his head to the side.

"Really? That bad, huh?"

"Yep, pretty bad! She's going to read you the riot act when you get home. Dad told her she's not allowed to come over here and make a scene. She was going to, but he stopped her." Ethan shook his head at me. "I'm glad I'm not in your shoes right now."

"She will come around," Jackson piped in.

But Ethan interjected, "You don't know our mom. This is exactly what she didn't want for any of us, especially Jocelyn and Sidney. She has pushed college down our throats even before we started kindergarten."

It was the first time I ever saw my brother look at Jackson with such scorn. He had always liked him and been supportive of our relationship, but I suppose it was different when Jackson was only my boyfriend and not someone planning to marry his sister before college.

The room fell into an uncomfortable silence for several minutes until

Jenna, who never handled silence well, finally spoke up. "Well, now that everything is out in the open, we can really start with the wedding preparations." She bounced excitedly in her seat. "I texted Caitlyn and Hilary on my way over here and told them to get here ASAP, that you had a surprise for them."

"You didn't."

But somehow, I wasn't surprised at all. Honestly, I was truly grateful that she was now comfortable, even excited about my upcoming nuptials. I was going to really need her support since my mother, and probably Sidney also, were going to give me so much grief about it.

"Of course, you're not going to stick us in some hideous bridesmaid dresses that we're never going to wear again."

"Like I would do that," I grinned and rolled my eyes playfully at her.

"Oh, yes you would, just to see us suffer and laugh at us," she laughed and so did Kyle and Jackson, but Ethan sat there glaring over at Jackson who pretended not to notice.

"I would not," I defended myself. "I'm not going to ruin my wedding pictures just to make you three look goofy." I had to laugh because it certainly seemed like something Jenna would do just for the fun of it. "Plus, Emily's already bought every wedding magazine on the market. She's even got a wedding planner started."

"Great. Have you found anything you like? What about colors? Have you decided on what colors you want?" Jenna settled back a little and snuggled up to Kyle who grinned and rolled his eyes across to Jackson.

"Not yet. There's so many to choose from. It's a bit overwhelming. I'm really going to need you three and Emily to help me decide."

Shortly thereafter, Caitlyn and Hilary showed up dragging Cody and Zak along with them. After the shock of the news settled in and the barrage of questions were finally answered, the four of us, along with Emily, disappeared into the dining room to begin to sort through what Emily and I had already started on the wedding plans.

The guys all remained in the front room watching a movie. Zak and Cody seemed as if they couldn't care less one way or another about the wedding, but my little brother remained quiet. I wanted to go in there and talk to him, but I decided it would be best if I waited until we got home. I hated the thought of Ethan being upset or disappointed with me. He and I were so close and his support in all of this was going to make a world of difference to me. It really hadn't occurred to me before now that he would be bothered by any of this. I guess I took his unconditional affection for me and his friendship with Jackson for granted, thinking that he would certainly be supportive of a marriage between us. I was wrong.

Ethan and I returned home by midnight. Luckily my parents had already retired for the evening, and I wouldn't have to deal with my mom until at least tomorrow. For that I was grateful.

I crawled into bed and snuggled down under my comforter. My thoughts had turned completely to what was going on in my *other* world and how I had behaved on Sunday, the day after finding out about *EVE*. I turned off the light on my nightstand when I heard someone enter.

"Ethan?" I whispered.

"Yeah. It's me." He came over and sat down on the edge of my bed next to me.

"Are you okay? You didn't say a word all evening." I rolled over towards him.

"I guess it bothers me more than I thought it would. I mean, when you and I were in here earlier and Dad was over at Jackson's, it never occurred to me that he would give you his blessing to do something so stupid. I figured that he would put a stop to all this, and you'd pout, but life would go on like it is now," his voice sounded sad.

"I thought you liked Jackson."

"I did. I do. I just sat here for over an hour after you left and listened to our parents screaming about this wedding and to be honest, Mom had some really good points, Jocelyn."

Now it all made sense. "Like what?"

"That the possibly of you getting pregnant before you even finished your undergraduate work is very likely, making the likelihood of you graduating very slim, let alone completing grad school. All your hard work up until now will have been for nothing."

"I'm not going to get pregnant, E. There are ways to prevent it."

"Nothing is full proof. You know that."

"True, but we're going to be very careful. My education is every bit as important to Jackson as it is to me," I tried to explain, but I could tell my efforts were falling on deaf ears.

"What about the fact that you have only known him for a few weeks? If one of your friends, Caitlyn, or Hilary, or even Jenna was planning to marry some new guy that just moved to town a few weeks ago you'd be going ballistic, ranting, and raving about how insane they were to be even considering something so stupid," he took a deep breath and sighed. "You and I both know you would."

I sat there for a moment and considered carefully what he was saying and as much as I hated to agree with him, I knew he was right. "True. I would be, but this isn't one of my friends, it's me and I need your support, Ethan. I really do. I need to know that you are with me whether you agree with my decision or not," I pleaded with him for understanding.

"Jocelyn, you know the odds of this marriage lasting are so low it's ridiculous. You both are so young. I mean, I'm barely younger than you and I can't imagine making a commitment to someone like that. I can't imagine even wanting to. I want to play football in college and then maybe grad school. I would never let some girl derail me from my dreams. Why would you let Jackson do that to you? Do you really want to be divorced before you even finish your Bachelor's?"

"No, of course not. Look, I understand why you feel the way you do, but you have to realize that he is not trying to rob me of my dreams. He supports them. In fact, his parents even offered to pay for my tuition if our parents withheld my trust from me." I propped myself up on my elbow to see him more clearly and read his facial expressions. He looked so sad.

"Either way, you have known him for such a short amount of time. What do you really know about this guy…I mean seriously? Why not just go to school with him, share an apartment if that's what you really want, but don't marry him until after you at least complete your undergrad."

"Because I want to marry him Ethan, more than anything. I don't know how to explain it to you. We belong together."

"Great! Wonderful! I'm not saying that you shouldn't be with him, just wait to get married." He placed his hand on my side as if pleading with me. It only made me feel more horrible.

"Please E, I need you with me in all this. I want you to stand up there with Jackson when we get married. It would mean a lot to me." I felt like I was begging, and I guess in a way I was.

"I don't know, Jocelyn," he shook his head looking down at the floor. "I just don't know." He slowly rose and walked over to my door.

"Ethan don't go. Let's talk about this," I hollered after him.

"Not right now. I've had enough for one day." He paused with his hand on the door but did not turn around towards me. "Good night, Jocelyn, sweet dreams. I love you." He closed the door behind him.

I rolled back over with a sharp pain in my stomach. I knew Ethan must really be hurting if he told me he loves me. He never speaks to me like that. I knew he loved me; I've always known that. However, he and I never say it. It's always just a given between us.

His words stung deep into my soul, and I couldn't shake it. I knew I could never get through all this without him. I hated the thought of hurting him. It killed me to know that I was the source of all the pain sweeping over my family and even worse, I felt incredibly selfish because I knew I was doing it for my own happiness despite their well-founded and good intentioned objections.

CHAPTER 14

Sunday, November 17, 1878

TIME, I BELIEVE, STOPPED. Reverend Jacobs was never going to conclude his services and it was taking every ounce of my willpower to remain seated. Now I regretted my decision to attend this morning. I wished I had followed my first instinct and stayed home with Olivia and William. Mother had even said it was all right if I did since I was still looking pale and hadn't gotten a good night's sleep for some time now. The fact that I had invited Elizabeth and Lee over afterwards was the only reason I was stuck sitting here. I couldn't cancel on her again. I knew she was excited about being a part of my wedding party and I didn't want her to feel as if I was postponing her inclusion.

It was a quarter after one before Reverend Jacobs finally shut up. A full forty-five minutes longer than his typical sermon.

Figures, today of all days he had to be so darn long-winded.

Elizabeth and Lee came home with us directly after services. It gave me no time to spend alone with Jackson and grill him a little further. I was doing my best to remain as pleasant as possible even though I felt as if it was physically killing me. The last thing on my mind was picking out another bridesmaid dress.

After our Sunday supper, I spent another full four hours going over patterns with all the ladies in my father's study trying to pick out the perfect dress, fabric, lace, ribbons…you name it. I honestly wanted to throw up my hands in the air and tell them to decide for themselves, that I truly did not care what they chose. However, I knew any behavior of that nature would only end up causing everyone to be more concerned about me. My family was still treating me like I was some fragile China that might break at any moment.

Strangely, all day Jackson had been giving me the quirkiest grins, like he either knew something or was up to something. I was not sure which it was. I wanted to get him alone, but Sunday family gatherings never really allowed it.

Our oversized families were practically hanging from the rafters and there was no place to escape since the weather had turned so cold.

Having decided upon a dark emerald satin fabric for the gowns and similar patterns for both Elizabeth and Olivia, we retired to the front parlor to relax around the hearth. Mother and Emily along with my brothers' wives were going over the final details of the gowns while Olivia and Elizabeth joined me closer to the fire.

Olivia was starting to look more like her old self. She looked healthy and was glowing with her new pregnancy although she was not showing yet. She was, however, beginning to thicken a little bit around her midsection and there was a little more fullness to her now constantly rosy cheeks. She was the perfect image of an expecting mother and she and my brother seemed to be very happy with one another. I felt so relieved and thrilled for the two of them that despite all the obstacles they have had to hurdle and the more they had before them, they seemed determined to tackle them all together.

"Are you getting excited about the Thanksgiving holiday and meeting Lee's family?" Olivia turned her attention to Elizabeth.

"Nervous more than excited." Elizabeth let out a weak laugh. Her shyness was going to make this introduction very painful for her.

"You have nothing to worry about. His family is going to love you as much as he does," I reassured her.

"Well, of course they are, and Lee seems to be a lovely young man," Olivia added.

Elizabeth's face flushed with embarrassment. "I truly hope so," she took a deep breath and sighed audibly. "It is amazing to me how much things have changed since summer. I mean, you married William and are starting a family," she gestured over at Olivia. "You, Jocelyn, are almost done with your studies and making the final preparations for your own wedding; Maryanne and Dimitri separated; and both Christine and Laura are engaged and finishing up classes, also."

"Time certainly has gone quickly," Olivia smiled.

"It feels like such a short time ago when we were all starting school and playing with dolls," I laughed. "I remember chasing my brothers around in the backyard and them teasing me relentlessly to leave them alone because I was too small and a girl. I hated the fact that I was always excluded from everything they did like playing baseball and fishing. Now it all seems so trivial."

"Yes, but it sure was fun," Olivia said. "I had the biggest crush on William for as long as I can remember. I certainly never imagined marrying him."

"I know what you mean. I remember following Jackson around like a lost puppy and he never gave me a second look. He was always busy with my brothers and oh…that girl he dated when he was in prep. What was her name?" I paused trying to recall.

"Sue Ellen," Elizabeth remembered.

Olivia smirked. "I remember her always trying to be so perfect. Little Miss 'I cannot get dirty', 'I cannot run or play or do anything that would mess my dress or hair'," she laughed out loud, and Elizabeth and I joined in at her mocking impression of the girl.

"What ever happened to her?" Elizabeth looked between the two of us.

"I believe she married one of the Conley boys and moved somewhere out West."

"Why did she and Jackson ever split up?"

"Oh, their relationship was a childhood crush," I smirked. "They were fourteen or fifteen when they separated so it was not like it was a serious relationship. Although I do remember being so jealous of her."

"Yes, I remember that too," Olivia grinned at me. I was sure she recalled all those long hours I complained about how much I hated that girl.

"But you ended up with Jackson," Elizabeth beamed.

"Yes, I did," I could not help but giggle. "And who did you have a crush on growing up?"

"Probably, no one," Olivia laughed with Elizabeth who was turning red again. "You were always so serious, studying all the time."

"Yes, I read a lot growing up. Still do actually," she shrugged. "But I did have a crush on someone." She gave us a slight smirk that intrigued both Olivia and me.

"Really? On whom?" I could never recall Elizabeth paying special attention to anyone while we were growing up.

"You will laugh." She looked down at the floor embarrassed.

"No, we won't," Olivia reassured her.

"It's silly really. He never even noticed that I was alive, honestly."

"Who?" I urged.

"Dimitri," she said quietly.

Our eyes grew much larger with the shocking news. I would never have guessed such a thing. Funny enough, they really would have made a cute couple, much more so than Dimitri and Maryanne. Plus, Elizabeth would have made him very happy with her sweet gentle ways that truly complimented his.

Olivia shook her head. "I had no idea."

"Me neither. How come you never said anything?" I inquired.

Elizabeth shrugged. "Why would I? He has been with Maryanne for the last two years and before that, well, I was always buried in a book, and he never noticed me."

"Imagine how things could have been different if he had known," Olivia said absentmindedly.

"Well, I believe that it all worked out for the best. I am with Lee now and he makes me very happy. Therefore, I know that it was not ever meant to be for Dimitri and me," Elizabeth glowed.

"I think it is wonderful about the two of you. You deserve someone who makes you this happy," I added.

We fell in a short silence. I rocked gently, absorbing the heat from the fire, and thinking about my conversation with Emily last evening. She had spoken to me at great length about why her family had gone looking for me in 2015 and about pregnancy. We discussed my goals and dreams in my *other* life and how getting pregnant *here* would destroy my world *there*.

I spent all evening and morning thinking about how much I envied my *other* self and the opportunities that lay before me in that world. Going to a large university and even obtaining a graduate degree was something I knew I could not risk jeopardizing. I was excited about the barrier disintegrating completely so that my conscious self would be living the dream I had always longed for. I knew it was a matter of time and that I would not be starting college until next fall, but I was so anxious to witness firsthand a world in which I never otherwise could have possibly imagined.

It was after seven o'clock before everyone departed. It had been a grueling day that had been mentally and emotionally draining to me.

Jackson strolled into the parlor and joined me on the lounge. Finally, we were alone. I leaned over and kissed his soft full lips then hugged him tightly. It felt wonderful, safe to be in his arms again. The world was in balance once more.

"How are you holding up?" His voice was soft and sincere as he leaned up and his lips gently brushed across my forehead.

"Better now that I am with you."

"I am sorry that it took so long for us to be alone today. I could not escape from everyone long enough to get two words with you in private."

"I know. There is so much going on with finalizing all the wedding preparations. Your mother has been truly wonderful in volunteering to create the gowns for Olivia and Elizabeth. I know she will do such a beautiful job."

"Your mother mentioned that you were hiding your new wedding dress from everyone and that only my mother knows what you are up to." His lopsided grin slid across his face mischievously.

"I want it to be a surprise." I raised my eyebrows and wrinkled my nose at him.

A short laugh escaped from his chest. "Somehow, I am not surprised by that. I hope you do realize that even though the barrier is not completely down, some of your personality traits from your *other* world are starting to shine through into this one."

"Really? How so?"

"You are becoming much more independent and forthright in your opinions and actions."

"Is that a good thing?" I asked, curious as to whether it was disappointing to him to see me behave in such a manner, even though I felt like it was natural of me to act this way even though I was fully aware that a year ago I never would have taken such an initiative.

"It is a wonderful thing. I like you like this," he laughed at my hesitation.

"Good, I am glad." Relief flooded over me.

"I have some good news for you," his mischievous grin returned.

"And what is that? Cause you know, I am not sure how many more surprises I can take in such a short amount of time," I teased, but honestly it was true.

"Shane, your *other* father, has agreed to let us get married next summer," he leaned in close and whispered in my ear.

"Okay." I looked at him with my eyebrows crinkled unsure as to why my *other* father would ever disapprove of our union.

"Jocelyn, this is wonderful news! We have been hiding the fact that we are getting married from your family because well, typically people do not get married this young *there* and we knew that your parents were going to be very unhappy about it."

"Really? Why is that?"

"Because of college and grad school."

"Yes, but I am still going to college and grad school. Right?"

"Of course, but you see, your mother is very strong minded in that you complete your education before you ever get seriously involved with someone, let alone get married, and she is terrified that getting married so young will ruin your life."

"But that is silly. How could marriage ruin my life?"

"People do not typically get married at eighteen in the twenty-first century. Especially people who plan to continue their education. The divorce rate is around sixty percent and is even higher for those who get married at a young age," he tried to explain.

"Sixty percent! How is that possible? Do people not believe in the commitment and sanctity of marriage anymore?"

"Divorce, I am afraid, is quite common. A large percentage of the population has had multiple marriages and divorces. Many families and children are torn apart because of them."

"That is unbelievable. Do these people get divorced even when there are children involved? That is horrible!"

"Yes. However, there are many factors *there* that make the world a much different place than it is *here*. Children divide their time between their parents' households and adjust to an unconventional family life. What is unusual is for a child to make it through school with their original parents still happily married."

"I hope you realize that once we get married, divorce will never be an option for us." I shook my head in disbelief.

"I never considered it to be," he grinned and kissed me softly. "Until death do us part."

"I love you." I snuggled up into his arms and rested my head on his chest.

"I love you, too," he whispered back.

I looked up at him with an overwhelming sense that something else was heavily weighing on my heart. "Ethan is not happy about us getting married." It was more of a statement than a question since somehow, I knew it was true and that fact deeply troubled me.

"He's struggling with it only because he is concerned. You two are close, much like you and William. Yet, in a way, even closer. You two share so much in your athletics and common personality traits that despite the eleven months between you, you two seem more like twins," he laughed a little.

"It is strange. I have not *seen* anything that told me he was unhappy about us getting married, but when you mentioned it …. I felt it!" I gave Jackson a strange look. I couldn't explain it any better but somehow, I was having some of my *other* self's feelings.

"Really? That's amazing." Jackson looked away for a moment and muttered more to his self than to me, "Perhaps the barrier is coming down faster than I thought."

"I hope so," I whispered.

"Well, that could be a good thing or not. I am not sure. If it happens too quickly, you will not have the necessary time to adjust and learn everything you need to. That is what concerns me. Slip-ups can cause major problems and we have to be very careful about what is said and in front of whom." His eyes widened, and he seemed more lost in his own thoughts than here with me.

"But would I not know everything from both worlds and already know how to behave in each?"

"Yes. However, sometimes, especially in the beginning, any small silly almost trivial thing can be difficult to not comment on and that is when accidents happen."

I looked at him completely confused.

"Okay, for instance, in 2015 people use a lot of slang words and contractions. Here, we do not. It is very easy to accidentally say something inappropriate at the wrong time just out of sheer habit. Granted, you do not use curse words very often, but occasionally you have muttered *shit* when you have stubbed your toe, or something frustrates you."

I looked at him completely appalled. I could not imagine ever saying such a thing. My parents would kill me if such a word slid across my lips.

Jackson laughed noticing my expression. "Trust me. It is not a big deal to say that word in 2015. Anyway, you can imagine what would happen if that word slipped from your lips here in front of your family. There would be quite the fallout," he laughed again. "Plus, like I said, people use slang and contractions mostly when they speak. Formal grammar is rarely used *there,* and people do notice it when you have it. Even you noticed that I speak differently than all your other peers."

"How odd."

"Not really. It truly is a very different world *there*. But once you become adjusted, it really is an amazing experience to live in both. The everyday things that we hardly notice *here* are now studied in history books and seem so refined and old-fashioned *there*. It is hard to imagine how we survive *here* without so many of the conveniences that we have in the twenty-first century."

"Is life really easier *there*?" That world fascinated me so much and I wanted to learn everything about it.

"It is in some ways, yet in others…not at all. It's almost sad in many of the ways the world has changed. Yes, we have washing machines and clothes dryers, and our laundry is done now with the push of a button. We can get to any destination either across the country or around the world by driving a car or flying in an airplane. We have microwaves that can cook an entire dinner in five minutes, cell phones that fit in our pockets that give us the ability to talk to anyone in the world at the push of a button, but none of that seems to replace all that was lost. Things like family values, spending time with your family on Sundays after church, living close to them and being involved in their lives. Working out marital problems rather than just giving up and filing for a divorce. Morals and values seem not to exist nearly as much *there*. People have sexual relationships with individuals they have only known for a few hours and never see again. Kids bring guns to school and shoot their peers. Most mothers work outside the home and have flourishing careers of their own because things are so expensive that it takes two incomes to survive." Jackson shrugged his shoulders casually.

"Therefore, children grow up in daycare centers and only see their parents in the evenings for a few hours and weekends. And typically, during that time, the children are involved in some sort of extracurricular activity so the family grabs dinner from a fast-food restaurant and hardly ever eat a meal at the table with one another. There simply are not enough hours in the day to allow for it. People are rushed, tired, irritable, and never happy with what they have."

"That sounds horrific!" My mind could not fathom living such a life.

"Of course, there are always exceptions. Not every family is like that."

"What about mine?"

"What do you mean?"

"Is my family close? Do we spend time together at all?"

Jackson's eyes dropped to the floor, and I knew his answer even before he gave me one. "Well, you know that your mother, Amy, is a physician and your father, Shane, works at the hospital as well. They both have very demanding careers that take up a great deal of their time. Amy usually does not cook and trust me," he laughed, "that is not exactly a bad thing. The woman is a horrible cook. But from what I have seen, you all sort of fix your own dinners whenever you get hungry. You found it very strange that my parents cook dinner together and we eat at the table as a family."

"That's sad," I muttered in a low voice.

"Well, you and Ethan both play sports, so you are not home until after dinner time. And you spend most of your time on the weekends with your friends…and me," he grinned.

"What about Sundays? Do we not attend church together as a family and then have a big family dinner afterwards?"

"No, your family does not go to church that I know of and your extended family, well I honestly do not know. You have never mentioned your grandparents, so I do not believe you see them very often or that they even live anywhere close to you. However, you and Ethan are extremely close, and I believe you two always will be." He tried to give me a comforting smile.

"What about my sister, Sidney?"

"I'm not sure. I only met her once at your birthday party. You two made some small talk but did not really spend any time together. I know she looks a lot like Amy, and I believe them to have a similar personality from what I have heard of her. You and Ethan are more like Shane. You look more like Shane while Ethan has features evenly split between your parents. But I do not believe that you and Sidney are very close. You have hardly spoken to her in the time that I met you *there*, nor has she come home from school to visit your family, and she is only at Northwestern like me. I do know she is very feminine and you, well, you are more athletic. I believe you two are very different people with really nothing much in common," he shrugged slightly.

"You know, growing up with four older brothers I always dreamed of having an older sister to confide in, do things with, and such. Now, it seems so strange knowing that I have one, but have no real relationship with her." This new world was starting to not seem so wonderful after all.

"Trust me, your relationship with Sidney is not all that unusual. Family dynamics changed a great deal in the 1960s to early 1970s. Everyone became more independent. At least they did in the United States. A lot of things happened in a short period of time that altered the country forever."

"Like what?"

"Well, let me see…." Jackson paused a moment to think. "There was the Korean War in the 1950s, the president of the country was assassinated in the fall of 1963, followed shortly by the Vietnam Conflict. Rock-n-roll evolved, and there were protests over the war and with it came a lot of drugs, flower children, hippies, the Civil Rights movement, the women's movement, Watergate, and the sexual revolution. The entire country went into chaos for a long time, and everything changed again when the economy crashed in the early 1980s."

"I don't understand."

"You will. It's very difficult to explain. There was so much going on during that time, and then you throw in the explosion of technology on top of it all and things just could never return to the way they were once structured. People became very independent, and women came out of the kitchen, so to speak, and started having careers of their own. Of course, there are still some cultures that have strong family ties, but not so much among most Americans, I am sorry to say."

"That sounds depressing. It is hard to imagine not having my family so involved in my life."

"Most people in the latter half of the twentieth century and the first part of the twenty-first have become more focused on themselves and their careers and immediate families rather than extended family. However, there are many expectations for that, and I am generalizing. But because of the way the world is structured and the fast rate at which everything moves, most people only get the opportunity to see their extended family on major holidays such as Thanksgiving or Christmas, and sometimes Easter. Like I said before, there simply are not enough hours in the day to do all the things that you would like to do."

His words disheartened me, and I wished I hadn't inquired about the status of my family. It was too depressing to think about. The rest of the evening left me feeling cold and empty.

I crawled under the covers as Mimi straightened up my clothes for school in the morning. I watched her stroll casually around my room, placing things here and there. Her constant presence in my life gave me a great deal of comfort. Eddie came in briefly and put some more wood on my fire and stoked it before he disappeared. Mimi came over and adjusted my covers tightly around my neck before she kissed my forehead and turned down my oil lamp and was gone.

Jackson's gift was still lying in the little blue box on my night table. It glowed in the moonlight that danced around my room. The trivial little pocket watch that was responsible for opening this wide new fascinating world to me no longer held the intense intrigue it once had. Instead, it now had turned into another frivolous trinket that resembled everything else that rested throughout my room.

I rolled over and closed my eyes tightly. Jackson's words flooded my brain to the evolving world that I had not yet witnessed, nor now, had any desire to. The foreign concepts he had offered as explanations for it made no sense to my naive brain. As much as I truly desired and loved the idea of continuing my education and having the freedom to do so, I wasn't sure if everything that was lost along the way for me to win that battle was truly worth the cost. I dearly loved my family.

I could not imagine living without my brothers and their wives and children so close by. The idea of us all being spread out, perhaps across the country from one another, and only seeing each other a couple times a year, broke my heart. I considered my little nieces and nephews and how much I would miss them if they were not living so close by.

I tried to imagine how my *other* self felt about not having a close relationship with Sidney or any of my extended family. I wondered if I was bothered by it or if it was just something I considered normal. It was weird to imagine fixing my own dinner every evening whenever I chose rather than sitting down every night with my family and discussing our days.

How do people there ever really get to know each other with such informal ways of communication? Do the parents there know anything about their children and how they feel and what is going on in their lives?

I seriously doubted it. It seemed to me though that everyone was too consumed with their own lives to take the time to get involved with their family. In my heart of hearts, I sincerely hoped that Jackson was exaggerating when he stated that this new structure was the norm and not the exception. I wanted so badly to believe that he had it reversed.

Chapter 15

Sunday, November 15, 2015

THE SUN WAS STRUGGLING TO FIGHT ITS WAY through a thick blanket of clouds when I finally opened my eyes. I snuggled the covers up around my chin, trying to keep the cold that lingered in the air away from my warm body. The images in my mind played over repeatedly like a movie on a screen. I saw myself looking horrified and confused as Jackson described the dynamics of life in 2015. I sat there on an oversized loveseat next to the fire wearing a dark blue dress that felt incredibly heavy on my torso and fell all the way to my ankles. My hair hung curled around my shoulders, and I held a white handkerchief in my hand. I looked truly elegant, but the corset was extremely constricting. I wondered if it would ever feel commonplace to me.

Jackson looked so incredibly handsome in his navy suit with a vest, tie, and pocket watch with the chain hanging down across him. He was trying to be patient with me as he attempted to explain a world I couldn't comprehend. It was the oddest feeling because I could feel what I felt as he spoke of such foreign concepts. Yet, I knew in my mind's eye the other side of it as well. It was so bizarre.

I also recalled sitting by the fire with Olivia and Elizabeth while Annabelle, Emily, and a couple of other women who I knew were married to my brothers, sat across the room with sewing items scattered about. I felt comfortable in their presence, yet strangely anxious to be with Jackson. However, the scene before my eyes looked like something out of *Gone with the Wind*. The clothes, furniture, atmosphere—all of it was surreal to my evolved eyes.

It was all so simple. Children running around with old fashioned toys, clothes, things that I had never personally seen before yet saw in history books and museums, flooded my vision. Apparently, my family was extremely large and almost always present. A young black girl who worked for my family would come in periodically with a fresh pot of hot coffee, and an older black man maintained the fire keeping the room warm and toasty. This bizarre world unfolded before me like a dream I could no longer awaken from.

I reluctantly climbed out of bed and headed for the bathroom. The hot water rained down on me and my tense muscles began to finally relax. I took a deep breath and wondered if this experience was ever going to get any easier.

I am barely juggling all the drama in one life, how am I going to manage two?

I finished blow-drying my hair and attempted to do something with it when someone knocked on my door. Instantly, all the muscles in my body tensed up again. "Yeah?"

My door slowly opened, and my mom poked her head in. "Can I come in?"

"Sure."

I tried to keep my voice as light as possible. She looked drained, not angry. I noticed she had dark circles under both her eyes like she hadn't slept at all last night, and I instantly felt guilty.

She hesitated just inside my doorway as if she was unsure of what to do.

"Have a seat," I offered, gesturing towards my bed.

"Thanks." Her voice was melancholy.

She sat down on the corner of my bed looking as if she was about to burst into tears at any moment. I could handle almost anything except my mother's tears. The guilt was unbearable. "I had a long talk with your dad last night."

"Ethan told me." My own voice dropped several octaves.

"I guess your mind is made up and there's nothing I can do or say that is going to change it," she stared down at the floor not bothering to look up at me when she spoke.

"Mom, please don't look at it that way."

"I did not come in here to start another argument with you, Jocelyn," she said coldly. "I just wanted to tell you that if this is what you truly want, then I will keep my mouth shut. However, I refuse to watch my daughter throw her life away on some silly crush for a boy she's only known a few weeks and sit idly by while college and graduate school disappear. Therefore, you cannot expect me to participate in the events leading up to your downfall."

My heart jumped in my throat, and I could not speak. My entire body went numb. I couldn't believe she was saying these words to me.

"Therefore, I have decided that I will not help you with planning anything for this disaster nor will I be attending it." She got up and walked back to my door.

"Mom? Mom, stop. Please. You can't mean that," I pleaded, jumping to my feet. Tears poured down my face as I rushed over to her side. "Please. Don't do this to me."

"I am not the one who is doing this. You are. I will not watch you throw your life away," she continued to avoid making eye contact with me.

"Mom...Please!" I begged through my tears.

"I'm sorry, Jocelyn. I always thought you were going to be something when you grew up, make a difference in this world, accomplish something incredible. Not waste your life on a man who is going to turn you into a homemaker and mother. I honestly believed you were better than that, that I had raised you better than that. I guess I was wrong. I am sorry I failed you." She took a deep breath and exhaled slowly and walked out of my room.

I stood rooted in place. Her words ripped through my very soul. Endless tears poured down my cheeks, but I made no effort to brush them away. Something inside me died. I knew she was going to have a difficult time accepting my decision, but I never dreamed she would feel this extreme.

I blindly took a step forward, then another. I stumbled down the front stairs and sprinted out the door gathering momentum as my legs carried me blindly where my heart wanted to go. My mind was empty, screaming, numb. My breathing was rapid yet there was not enough oxygen to fill my aching lungs. My legs forced my body forward over my front lawn, across the street to Jackson's front porch. I didn't even hesitate as I threw open their front door unexpectedly.

Jackson and his parents were seated at the dining room table enjoying their peaceful breakfast when I came bursting through their front door. I could only imagine the sight I must have been to cause the three of them to leap from their seats and rush to my side. I collapsed into Jackson's arms in hysterical sobs as he lifted me up into his arms and carried me over to their couch with Robert and Emily directly behind him.

Jackson sat down cradling me and trying to calm me down. My brain would not function properly for me to form words. He wiped the tears from my cheeks with a tissue his mother handed him and soothed my hair away from my face. But my body would not stop trembling uncontrollably. Words would not come. The tears would not relent. Nothing was ever going to be right again. Somewhere in the back of my mind I heard a door close, and the sound of distant footsteps drew closer in on me.

"Is she alright?" My dad's voice broke through my foggy consciousness. I scrambled off Jackson's lap and rushed into the strong arms of my father. With my face buried in his chest like a small child, I cried endlessly.

He stroked my hair and rubbed my back as he did when I was much younger. "Jocelyn, baby, you have to calm down."

His voice was soft and soothing. My breathing began to level out into a low rhythm. "That's it, that's my girl."

He spoke to me like I was still four years old and for some reason, at this moment, it gave me great comfort and security. "Daddy, she said,"

I couldn't get the words to come out. It was as if I knew if I said them aloud, it would make them real, and I knew I couldn't handle the pain and rejection.

"I know, littlen'. I know. She didn't mean it. I promise. She's only hurting and lashing out." My father continued to comfort me while Jackson and his parents looked on at us baffled as to what could have happened or been said to warrant such a reaction.

I shook my head slightly with my face still buried in his chest. "No, no, not this time. She meant it, every word of it. She's so disappointed in me. I let her down and she's never going to forgive me." I cried.

"Jocelyn don't be such a drama queen. You know how your mother can be. She'll come around. She always does," he whispered, still stroking my hair.

My dad looked over at the three faces staring back at him with confusion and wonder. "I apologize for the intrusion. I am afraid that Amy is not taking the news of the wedding very well. She is deeply upset and has refused to participate or attend any aspect of it."

"My goodness, no wonder she's so upset," I heard Emily whisper from behind.

"Ethan is also pretty upset about it," Jackson said in a low voice.

"I know my wife can be challenging at times. But I do believe that once she realizes this is what Jocelyn wants and that it is not going to affect her education, she will come around." Dad's voice sounded more wishful than reassuring.

"Hopefully, before the ceremony begins," Jackson muttered.

"I hope so, too." My dad patted my back again as if he had just remembered I was there.

"Dad," I lifted my face up to his. "I know how important it is for her to see me graduate college, but can't she at least realize that perhaps I can have both?"

"Give her some time littlen', show her you can. She'll come around."

"Shane, would you like some coffee? I just brewed a pot," Emily offered.

"No thank you, Emily. I really must get back home. I'm trying to sort through some of the old things in the basement storage closet," he left out a half chuckle. "Lord only knows what I'm going to find in there. I cannot even remember the last time I attempted to clean out that room and it's probably going to take me all day."

Emily nodded silently.

My father shifted his focus back to me. "Are you alright?"

I nodded numbly and wiped my cheeks off again as the tears subsided. "I think I'm going to stay over here for a while if that's okay."

"Sure," he squeezed me tightly. "And don't worry, I'll talk to her," he whispered softly in my ear before he released me. "I'll see you in a little while." He smiled towards my new family and headed back home.

Robert disappeared into the kitchen, and I took a seat beside Jackson back on the couch with Emily on the other side of me.

"I am so sorry about your mother's reaction," Emily said in a soft voice, placing her hands over mine. "I had no idea she would take it so hard."

"I did. That's why I wanted to wait until the last possible minute to tell her. Like the night before the wedding." I tried to smile, but don't believe I pulled it off so well.

"Well, that's not going to happen," Jackson chuckled, and Emily gave him a look of disapproval.

"I'm sorry, this is my fault. I never should have let her push my buttons like that and throw a childish tantrum like I did."

"It happens," Robert spoke up as he walked back into the room carrying a tray with teacups and a pot.

"Coffee?"

"Thank you," I answered.

Jackson placed his arm around my waist while his father poured each of us a cup of coffee. I couldn't imagine joining a more loving supportive and closely-knit group of people. I would be so proud to call them my family.

I spent the day with Jackson and his family. The four of us watched movies together relaxing in the living room by a roaring fire. Emily made us some popcorn and it turned into a lazy afternoon.

Shortly before five, his parents excused themselves to start dinner. I offered my help, but they both politely declined. I wasn't sure whether it was because cooking together was something they both enjoyed or their lack of faith in my cooking abilities, which wasn't completely unfounded.

The meal they created was as incredible as the conversation. We sat around the table and discussed more plans for the wedding along with various courses at the university and the beginning of our basketball season. The atmosphere was so relaxed and calm that I felt perfectly at ease. I was in no hurry to get back home. I hated the idea of getting into another altercation with my mother or worse, her silent treatment.

I arrived back at my house before eight. I could hear sounds of Sunday night football blaring from the family room and my father and Ethan shouting at the television. I smiled to myself and headed upstairs to hibernate in my room and catch up on some neglected homework that was due the next day.

I finished my last calculus problem and shoved the book aside. I looked over at my psych book lying dormant on the corner of my nightstand and knew I should probably do some reading to prepare for my next exam, but I really wasn't in the mood. We were now covering research methods and I found it incredibly boring. I knew it would put me to sleep in a matter of minutes. Instead, I decided to work on some other research of my own.

I sat at my computer and began searching for more information on anything I could find from the 1870s, trying to learn as much as I could about the culture, traditions, and lifestyle. I read several old newspaper articles from the *Chicago Sun*. Everything that I came across only offered a small glimpse of the life that I wanted so desperately to understand. The sites I found on customary clothing seemed so incredibly strange to me. Looking at them on a computer screen was so entirely different than how I viewed them in the first person. The styles were similar, yet on a computer they looked very out of place.

My dad knocked on my open doorframe interrupting my train of thought. "Working on schoolwork?" he asked, glancing over at my monitor.

"Um…Something like that, yeah." I turned around noticing something behind his back. "Whatcha got there?"

"You'll never believe what I found in the basement today," he waltzed in and took a seat on my bed.

"What's that?"

He held out a stack of old looking journals on his lap.

"I'm not sure if you remember my brother Monte, who passed away when you were really young." Instantly I felt every muscle in my body tense up. "Well, I was going through some boxes of his things and came across these," he patted the stack of journals. "At first, I had no clue what they were, but then, when I started reading them, I couldn't put them down. They're really fascinating. I had no idea my brother was such a talented imaginative writer. In fact, if I didn't know any better, I would swear he lived every word written."

I slowly got up and joined my father on my bed. "What do they say?" I could hardly breathe as fear ripped through my body.

Could he have possibly written about EVE? Did my father now believe his brother to be insane, schizophrenic?

"They're like the personal journals of a Union soldier that chronicles his life shortly before the Civil War erupts and then continues with his experiences during the war. Then they abruptly just stop about a year after the war ends. There really is no conclusion or anything, which is strange. It was like the man just dies, but it doesn't say how or anything," he shrugged.

"Really? Can I read them?"

"Well, I figured you'd be interested. I noticed lately you've been doing a lot of research on that period for history class," he nodded towards my computer. "So, I thought I'd let you read them. Just please be careful with them." He put the stack over on my lap. "Are you feeling any better?"

I looked down at the journals, dying to tear into them. "Yeah, I'm fine. Just feeling really tired."

"Well, get a good night's sleep," he stood back up. "I'll see you in the morning."

He started to leave. "Hey, Dad?" I spoke up before he could escape. "Thanks for everything."

He smiled back. "Love ya, littlen'. Sweet dreams."

"Love you too, Daddy."

I sprawled out across my bed next to the stack of journals. Anticipation was nearly killing me. I could only imagine what my father must have thought reading something so personal of his brother's. However, for my own selfish gain, I truly desired some personal insight into a period that still felt so foreign to me.

Perhaps my uncle's journals would provide me with a foundation to their way of thinking that would help me in understanding my *other* world. Yet for some reason, I thought about the warnings that Robert had given me about writing things down—both past and future events that could be misinterpreted by others if they happened to fall into the wrong hands.

I cracked open the first journal. The pages were crinkled with age and were adorned with perfect letters scribed in black ink. In the top left-hand corner was the name *Montgomery Floyd Timmons* with the date *December 25, 1860.* I held my breath almost scared to continue.

I spent the day over at my brother Patrick's house with him and his family. It was a delight to witness all four of my nephews opening their Christmas gifts. They were so excited and gleeful. His wife, Annabelle, has done an amazing job decorating their newly built house and shaping it into a home. She certainly has her hands full with the boys and the recent birth of their daughter, Jocelyn Alyssa, two months ago. Their sons are quite spirited and require near constant attention. Their little girl has a complete head of brownish hair that maintains a red tint in the light and her eyes are so prominent and such a dark brown they appear black. She will most certainly grow into the most stunning young lady. However, Jocelyn is very calm and easily contented. I do believe that this little girl is going to be quite smothered with love and protection from everyone in our family not only because of her being the only female, but because of her amazing appearance and features.

Yet despite the joyous occasion, the elaborate meal, decorations and the comforts of family, the threat that we are all currently living with hung heavy in the air. The war! It is all everyone speaks of in these times. I know that Patrick and Annabelle are deeply afraid of what will happen if the war comes. My brother will most certainly be utilized for his talents as a gifted physician. While the threat of performing on the battlefield will not fall upon him, he will still be close to the front lines and traveling with the military troops, which will most certainly place him in the path of danger. I know that they are also deeply concerned about our younger brother Nicholas as well as my prospects. Since we made the decision not to follow in our father's footsteps in the medical community, we will most certainly be drawn into the front lines.

However, I am not afraid. I will do as my country asks of me if that is the journey that I must take. My only regret is that I waited to wed Miss Vivian. I should have done it sooner. Now I am afraid that if the war does come and if I should die on the field of battle, that she would be left without a husband to care for her. I should have married her last year. I wish that I had a family like Patrick's to keep me strong and give me faith.

I closed the notebook and flopped back on my pillows. I couldn't read anymore. I felt like an intruder on his personal thoughts, the sincerest form of invasion. A part of me wanted to continue, wanted to learn as much as I could. However, I wasn't sure if this was the way to go about it.

I stacked the notebooks on my nightstand and crawled under the covers, flipping off my light. I considered telling Jackson and his parents about the journals but didn't know if it was the right thing to do before I'd had the chance to look through them. Surely, my uncle didn't mention anything regarding *EVE*, but then again maybe he did. My father did say that his writing was imaginative. Just how imaginative, I didn't know.

CHAPTER 16

Tuesday, November 19, 1878

IT WAS ALWAYS HARD WHEN JACKSON LEFT for school, but now it was particularly difficult. There were so many things I wanted to discuss with him and couldn't. Instead, I spent all last evening with Emily and Robert asking them thousands of questions about this strange new world and the customs it was so enriched in. I had told my parents that I was helping Emily with the dresses for the wedding and neither of them questioned my time away from home.

The short abstracts I was seeing were only strengthening my fears of this era. I could see myself spending time with my friends, attending classes or sporting events, and my parents would rarely make an appearance. However, my brother did seem to have a constant presence in my life. It saddened me to think that my marriage to Jackson was causing a strain on my relationship with him, especially since familial relationships at that time seemed so strained anyway.

Elizabeth, Laurie, and I stood in the archway after our last class of the day and watched the rain pouring from the sky. The wind was unusually cold and cut straight through clothing to reach far inside chilling actual bone. I leaned my head against the frame wishing I had asked Eddie to pick us up after school while Elizabeth explained in elaborate detail her new gown for my wedding.

"Excuse me, Miss Jocelyn. May I speak with you for a minute?" Her voice both startled and surprised me. Maryanne was the last person I expected to approach me.

"Of course."

Both Elizabeth and Laurie gave me an inquisitive look, but I shrugged and followed Maryanne a short distance back into the school building for some privacy.

"What can I help you with?" I couldn't imagine anything she would have to say to me after her little stunt.

"I wanted to apologize for my behavior. I am sorry that I acted so rudely towards you and your family." Maryanne looked down at the ground and fumbled with her books.

"I appreciate that. However, I believe that you owe my brother and his wife an apology rather than I."

"I know. But they have not been at Sunday services in a long time, and I have not seen them in town lately. I promise that I will apologize to them the first chance I see them."

"Maryanne, you know where I live. All you have to do is come by." I knew that going over to my house was something she would find impossible to do.

"Yes, I know. I only was not sure how I would be received." Her voice dropped down an octave almost sounding as if she was honestly sincere.

"No one in my house would be rude to you. I believe they would appreciate an apology."

Maryanne nodded, still looking down.

"Why did you say those things, Maryanne? I know you have never been the best of friends with Olivia, but you were friends and for you to treat her that way in front of everyone was just so …. well, it was cruel."

A part of me wanted to tell her exactly how cruel I believed her actions had been over the years and that I completely agreed with Dimitri in his assessment of her and her mother, but I did not want to stoop to her level of insults.

"I was just so angry with Miss Olivia," she muttered.

"Why? She did nothing to you."

"I saw her speaking with Dimitri on several different occasions and once I saw her hug him when she was crying." Maryanne looked up at me with pure hate in her eyes. "It seemed to me she was trying to take him away from me."

"Dimitri was Sean's best friend. The two of them were like brothers. Olivia went through a horrible time when she lost Sean and I know that she leaned on Dimitri a lot after his death because she knew he was going through the same thing she was. But they are only friends, nothing more. She would never do something to directly hurt anyone she cares about. And she cared about you. She was grieving and so was Dimitri. Sean's death brought them closer together, but not in the way that you are accusing," I attempted to explain.

"Perhaps, but it was inappropriate for her to hug him and cry on his shoulder." Her eyes narrowed, and I knew that her apology was anything but sincere. She had not changed at all.

"I am sorry to disagree, and I hope that you never have to experience the kind of loss the two of them have." I started to walk away having nothing more to say to her.

"Jocelyn?" she hollered. I paused a moment and turned back to face her. "Do you not understand, I have. I lost Dimitri."

"No. You have not. Mr. Dimitri is still very much alive and well."

How could she possibly make such a comparison between a break-up and the death of a loved one?

"Well, I am not with him now, am I?" she fired back.

"Maryanne, you are not with him because of the way you treat people. Not because he died!"

"But I lost him just the same!" She walked up to me with her hand on her hip and nearly shouted. People nearby turned to look at us with curiosity.

"I am not going to argue with you. If you would like to apologize to my brother and his wife, you know where we live." I started to walk away again.

"You are so incredibly selfish, Jocelyn," she hollered at my back.

I could hear whispers behind me as I walked back over to Laurie and Elizabeth. The audacity of Maryanne never ceased to amaze me. *Some apology.*

I stopped at my house to drop off my schoolbooks before I headed back over to Jackson's house to speak with Emily. I found Olivia working on her cross-stitch by the fire in the front room. She was listening to the phonograph and humming softly to herself. I hesitated a moment in the doorway, not wanting to interrupt her contentment. I considered telling her about my altercation with Maryanne but immediately changed my mind.

Perhaps she was better off not hearing of all the little trivial events that happened at school with our friends. As much as I knew she still wanted to be included in everything with our group of friends, maybe it was for the best that she wasn't.

"Are you having fun?" I smiled over at her, and her face lit up as I approached.

"A little bit. I keep trying to find ways to occupy my time while you are at class. I get so bored." She sighed deeply, placing her needlework aside.

"I am sorry. I know it must be driving you crazy being around here all day." I sat down in the rocking chair across from her.

She smiled politely and began to work once more on her cross-stitch, although the expression on her face told me that her thoughts were elsewhere. She looked almost as if she were about to cry at any second.

After dinner, I excused myself to visit the Chandlers. I told my mother we were doing something special for Jackson for Christmas and I wanted it to be a surprise. That way I knew she would not want to follow me over.

The rain had picked up and was coming down sideways in sheets. It was as dark as midnight despite only being early evening. The trees stood bare and were shivering in the cold breeze. I pulled my shawl over my head and tighter around my shoulders. Then I pulled up the hem of my skirt a bit and ran as fast as I could over to the Chandler household.

"Miss Jocelyn, good evening, I was expecting you earlier," Emily greeted me with a cheery smile.

"I am sorry. I was held up at my house," I apologized.

"That is all right. I made some peach cobbler this afternoon. Please join me, I will have Susan bring some in." I followed Emily back into the front room where Robert was sitting by the hearth looking over some legal briefs.

"Good evening, Miss Jocelyn. It is good to see you. How are you?" Robert stood as we entered the room.

"Good evening, Mr. Chandler. I am doing very well, thank you. How are you this evening?" I took a seat on the lounge by the fire and Robert sat back in his chair. The blazing heat from the fire felt incredible after being in the cold rain. I rubbed my hands together trying to warm them as Emily sat down beside me.

"Did you have a nice day at school?" she inquired.

"Yes, thank you."

Susan came in carrying a tray with three saucers of peach cobbler and silverware, napkins, and hot tea. She placed them on the coffee table and excused herself before exiting.

Emily poured the tea with lemon and handed out the cobbler. She settled back in her seat looking like a picture of loveliness.

"I am sure you are here with a thousand more questions," Robert laughed.

I blushed, thinking of how much I had grilled them last evening. I had listened for hours to them talking about Prohibition, the Titanic, automobiles, and all the amazing inventions that were still to come into my life *here*.

"I am sorry. This *EVE* thing is very difficult to comprehend and just thinking of this new world with all the differences is a little bit overwhelming."

"I know it is darling. Have you had any other visions?" Emily politely asked.

"Yes, I wake up with them every morning and even have them when I sit quietly unfocused. I know it sounds strange, but I am feeling things from my *other* life, emotions that I cannot explain, but have a strong intuition about." It was difficult to explain in words all the unique events that were now unfolding.

"Such as?" Robert was clearly intrigued.

"Well…like I know Jackson told me that my family *there* is now aware of us getting married this summer, but I told him that I knew Ethan was not happy about it." They nodded but said nothing. "And well…I get the feeling that my mother is extremely upset about it also. I have this horrible feeling that she is being very hurtful to me, but I cannot explain it."

Robert and Emily exchanged a strange look that I didn't understand. "Yes, she is struggling with you getting married so young," Emily said in a low voice. "But I do believe that in time, she will come around. Your father is being very supportive," she tried to brighten her voice.

"Sunday, Jackson tried to explain a few things that did not make sense to me. I know that once I have full awareness everything will be clear. However, at this point it is all very frustrating." I took a bite of the cobbler. It was so sweet and delicious.

"What in particular?" Robert asked.

"Everything," I laughed. "Mainly things like the Civil Rights movement, the Women's Movement, the two World Wars, Vietnam, the Korean War… rock-n-roll?" I shook my head. Such strange concepts. Robert and Emily laughed, making me feel even more embarrassed.

"The 1960s and '70s were an interesting time in American history. I can see why Jackson wanted to let you understand it for yourself once the barrier is down. Those things that you mentioned changed the lives of everyone in America in more ways than we could possibly explain to you." Robert shuffled his papers and put them back in his satchel.

"That is what Jackson said," I added.

"It probably is better for you to wait until the barrier disappears. These things would take a long time to explain. Plus, the foreground you would need to understand everything would take us longer to explain than the time it would take for you to come to realize them for yourself," Emily said much to my despair.

"But I want to understand."

"I know this is incredibly aggravating for you, but you have to understand that some things are better left for you to understand on your own. I realize that it makes the images you are seeing rather confusing, but I do promise that once you have full awareness, you will understand our hesitation in telling you too much too soon." Robert acted like it was no big deal, which only heightened my frustration at being left in the dark.

"I appreciate the fact that you both have my best interest at heart. However, I am at a place where I feel that I am unsure as to what is real and what is purely my imagination. Is there not something either of you can tell me?"

Emily placed her hands over mine. "I am sorry, Jocelyn. Time is the only thing that can make a difference now."

I wanted so badly to cry. The aggravation was building within me, and I felt as if I was ready to explode. Yet sitting here next to my future in-laws, the two people with whom I held the upmost respect for, I knew I had to maintain my composure and behave like a lady.

"Well, then I guess I should say that this is absolutely the best peach cobbler I have ever had." I tried to laugh it off just to keep the tears from breaking through.

"Do not worry so much about it, Jocelyn. I do promise you it will get easier," Robert said with a comforting smile.

CHAPTER 17

Tuesday, November 17, 2015

I CRAWLED OUT OF BED feeling like I'd been hit by a Mac truck and dragged for several miles. I had fallen asleep on top of my uncle's notebooks. I'd become so engrossed in them and had read my way up to the second year of the Civil War. I could not get over the amount of detail and emotional anguish that screamed through the words on each page. It was like nothing I had ever experienced before, and his words made me feel as if I was living the experience with him. The vivid descriptions of his fellow soldiers, their personality characteristics, his commanding officers, and the horrid battles that surrounded him left little to the imagination of how it really was to fight every day to stay alive.

I had studied American history since the third grade and each year we covered the Civil War. Last year I took a history class that concentrated on the causes leading up to the war, the battles, and the aftermath. The course was interesting and gave more detail than any general American History course before it yet, but everything that I'd studied had never given me the emotional side of what it was like to live everyday fighting for the cause.

My uncle's words touched my soul. He wrote of his true love who I knew he eventually married and left his life in the 1990s for, to exist only on one plane with her since she had not inherited *EVE*. He spoke of coming across my *other* father at the makeshift military hospital where Patrick was covered in blood, scrambling about and hectically trying to save as many men as possible. His choice of words allowed me to almost see my father standing over a table by the light of poorly luminous oil lamps. I could almost see him digging ball shots and shrapnel out of men as young as sixteen years old while they hollered out in pain and an assistant continuously poured whiskey down the patient's throat while others held them down.

Uncle Monte had only been home once for Christmas in those last two years. It was so difficult to hear him describe my brothers and I, and how much he had missed watching us grow and change. It was obvious from his words that he loved us all. His deep love and affection for Vivian jumped off the page and enraptured my heart. He left me in tears describing his last moments with her, holding her tight on our front porch never wanting to let her go.

My father had managed to join him that holiday and he and Annabelle had sobbed in one another's arms while my brothers and I had cried around them, holding tightly to our father's pant legs. The image he painted ripped the heart from my chest leaving me gasping for air. It was as if I was standing there again holding onto my daddy for dear life begging and pleading with him not to leave me. However, I knew it was impossible for me to recall such a memory even if the barrier was completely down. I was barely two years old when this event took place and in 2015, I had no memories of that age.

What I found so difficult to read was Monte's deep worry for their younger brother Nicholas. They had spent the first nine months of the war fighting side by side but then Nicholas had gone missing when he and several other men in their battalion went out on a search party for food. None of them had returned.

After their visit home for Christmas, the despair grew deeper after Monte learned that no letters had arrived home from Nicholas since they had separated. He continually asked every group of soldiers he encountered but no one knew anything about him. Monte feared he had been captured by the Confederates and was being held in a Southern prison. He had heard numerous horror stories about one in Andersonville where the men were dying by the dozens every day from starvation and disease. All he could do was hope and pray that someday he would see his younger brother again, but with each passing day his faith diminished a little more.

I climbed into the shower wondering again if I had made the right decision in not sharing the discovery of the journals with Jackson and his parents. I hated to think what they would say about them or maybe I was afraid they would warn me against reading them. I considered how they were impacting my view of this foreign world that I was rapidly becoming more aware of and how witnessing it through my uncle's eyes made me yearn for simpler times in days long forgotten. I thought about how his words could impact not only me, but the rest of the world if his journals were ever published. It had changed my perception completely of all that I thought I knew about the Civil War, and I knew it would do the same for anyone who read them.

All day long his journals haunted me. I couldn't wait to get back home and engross myself in them. I repeatedly tried to concentrate on my schoolwork, but it was pointless.

Caitlyn and Zak were arguing loudly once again outside his locker right after the lunch bell rang. She had overheard him joking with some of the guys on the basketball team and stupidly referred to her as a *trophy*. She went ballistic. Her face was bright red, and her words grew louder and louder with each second. Poor Zak looked like he was ready to crawl into his locker from the embarrassment. Like all immature boys, Ethan and Cody stood behind him snickering as Caitlyn ripped Zak a new one.

As soon as Hilary realized what Cody was doing, she approached him with a stern look, smacked him on the arm and pulled him towards the lunchroom. I immediately followed her example and pulled my idiot brother away as well. They already had enough people watching the spectacle and didn't need us witnessing it too.

Ten minutes later, Zak cowered into the cafeteria looking like a beaten puppy. He slumped down in the chair beside Cody and stared down at his tray of untouched food. Hilary, Jenna, and I all exchanged looks, wondering if Caitlyn was going to follow him in or if we should go looking for her.

"I can't believe she got so pissed. It was a compliment for crying out loud," Zak muttered under his breath.

Cody let out a giggle and Hilary quickly smacked him again on the shoulder. "It's not a compliment," she scowled.

"I'm going to go find Caitlyn." I leaned over and gave Jackson a quick peck on the cheek before I climbed out of my seat. He smiled and nodded.

Hilary and Jenna got up as well and the three of us headed back towards the bathrooms by Zak's locker. I figured that was where she was hiding.

Sure enough, Caitlyn was crouched down in the corner with her knees drawn up in her arms, crying when we walked in. The three of us knelt around her.

"Sweetie don't worry about him. You know how Zak is. In his mind, I'm sure he did believe it was a compliment." Jenna rested her hand on Caitlyn's shoulder.

"I'm so sick of this crap with him. I'm not a trophy and if that's how he really thinks of me, then I don't want to be with him," Caitlyn sobbed.

"I know, but honey, he's just an immature little boy. You know he has the maturity level of a twelve-year-old, just like Cody," Hilary added, trying to reassure her.

"Kyle and Jackson don't act like that," Caitlyn nearly shouted through her sobs. "They would never make a remark like that about either of you."

Jenna and I exchanged a knowing look. Her statement was true. It was not in either of their make-up to utter something so immature and thoughtless.

"Why can't he act more like them? I don't see them hanging out with a bunch of idiots trying to be cool. They act more like men than little high school boys," Caitlyn complained.

"They are just different, I guess," I said in a low voice feeling horrible. I could never imagine Kyle behaving with such disrespect, it just wasn't him. Jackson, on the other hand, was almost twenty-two, and I knew he had behaved like Zak and Cody when he was younger. He had told me so himself. However, I seriously doubted if he had ever been so crude to a woman before. That really wasn't part of his personality.

"Well, Cody and Zak could certainly learn a lot from them both." Hilary sat back against the wall beside Caitlyn. "But you have to make up with him. We're all going to see the midnight showing of *Mockingjay* on Thursday night. We already have the tickets. Do you realize how hard it was for me to convince my mom to let me go on a school night?" She tried to laugh, but we all knew she was serious. She had battled her mom for over a month to be able to go to the midnight showing, and I knew she wasn't going to let anyone, or anything ruin it for her.

"Oh, we're still going. Don't worry about that. But Zak can choke on his ticket as far as I'm concerned. I wouldn't sit by him now anyway. Besides, he really didn't want to go. He was only doing it to pacify me." Caitlyn brushed the tears off her cheeks smearing her make-up across her face.

I stood up and got some paper towels and wetted them down a bit. I went back over to Caitlyn and tried my best to fix the smeared mascara around her eyes. She gave me a weak smile. "Are you sure you're ready to get married? I mean, Jackson's great, don't get me wrong, but I just can't imagine being married to Zak and having to put up with his crap forever."

"Jackson is nothing like Zak." I sat down in front of her. "He's more mature and I love him." I knew none of them were ever going to understand my decision. They couldn't see why I didn't want to wait, and I could never explain to them the entire truth. I laughed to myself imagining their facial expressions if I ever spoke of *EVE* and the truth about why Jackson and I needed to get married.

Besides, we are getting married next month anyways….in 1878! Wow, they would surely understand that one!

They all noticed my giggle and gave me an odd look. "What?"

"What's so funny?" Jenna asked.

"Just thinking of something Jackson had said about the assumptions people were going to make about us getting married," I quickly lied to my three best friends.

"Yeah, I've had people already ask me if you're pregnant," Hilary spoke up.

"Really?" I rolled my eyes at their stupidity.

"Yeah, me too," Jenna added, and Caitlyn nodded in agreement.

"Well, I'm not. I can promise you that," I laughed, trying to lighten the mood.

"Haven't you guys done it yet?" Hilary piped up.

"No," I shouldn't have been surprised by her bluntness, but it caught me off guard.

"Why not?" Caitlyn asked. "I mean, if you're getting married in seven months, why wait? It seems silly."

I shrugged my shoulders again. I couldn't have agreed with them more. I wasn't the one who wanted to wait, Jackson was. But that information wasn't something I wanted to share with them. I wasn't sure how they would judge him for it.

"Well, it's not that we're actually going to wait until we're married," I lied again. Jackson and I had already decided to only wait until our wedding night in 1878.

"We're more or less waiting for the time to be right." I looked between the three of them to see if they were buying it. "You know how it is, parents or brothers always around. We never get much opportunity to be alone." It seemed plausible enough of an excuse.

"Yeah, I do know. My parents are always home and watching us like hawks," Hilary laughed.

"It's hard to be romantic when Ethan keeps walking in on us every five minutes," I complained.

"I can sympathize. My parents always seem to find some excuse never to leave Kyle and me alone," Jenna added.

"Zak's folks aren't that bad. They trust us," Caitlyn laughed. "Either that or they don't care." She shrugged slightly. "But those days are over." Her head dropped, and the tears started back up again.

Jenna and Hilary patted each of her shoulders softly while I placed my hand on her knee trying to comfort her.

"It's not over. You will forgive him, as always. We all know this," Jenna spoke in a low voice. We all knew she was right. Caitlyn always forgave Zak for his stupid antics in the end.

"Not this time," she shook her head. "I've had enough. He went too far and has no respect for me at all."

"Yes, he does," Hilary assured her, giving Jenna and me a contradictive look. "He loves you. He was just showing off to his cronies. You know how he and Cody can be…. completely thoughtless and immature. But they really mean nothing by it."

"Of course, they don't," I added, trying to calm her down.

"Guys act stupid around other guys, Caitlyn. You know that. It's in their DNA. They can't help it. They're prewired for stupidity," Jenna giggled, attempting to make Caitlyn laugh.

It worked. Caitlyn giggled, and I wiped the tears from her cheeks once more.

"Better?" I asked.

Caitlyn grinned and nodded. "Thanks."

"Good. Can we go eat now? I'm starving." Hilary climbed back off the floor.

The guys were all still seated around the table when we walked back into the cafeteria. There was only ten minutes left for lunch, and I too was starving.

I took my seat back beside Jackson. He leaned over and whispered, "Is everything okay?"

I watched Caitlyn sit down in the chair beside Zak and smile softly.

"I think so," I whispered back.

After a quick bite and a shower after basketball practice, I flipped on an 80s music video marathon on *YouTube* and flopped myself back down across my bed with my uncle's journals. I quickly lost myself in his world as the words took hold of my soul and ran away with it.

My cell rang at eight-thirty, bringing me out of the battle of Gettysburg. I absentmindedly wiped the tears from my face, not even realizing I had been crying before I reached for the phone.

"Hello."

"Hi, darling. How are you?" Jackson's sweet accent flooded my ears.

"Fine." I cleared my throat trying not to sound like I had been crying.

"I was wondering if you are avoiding me."

"Why would you think something like that?" I teased.

"Normally, you practically live at my place, but for the last couple days you have been going home after practice and disappearing for the entire evening." He sounded like a hurt child, and I knew he was playing with me.

"Well, if I keep that up then I'm never going to graduate, let alone get into college. I do have to study sometime, you know." Which was very true, and I reminded myself again of how far behind I was falling in my current classes. I was seriously going to have to bury myself in my books sometime soon or my grades were going to slip.

"I know," a little laugh escaped from his chest. "I just love giving you a hard time. What are you studying?"

"History."

"I didn't think you were taking history this semester." I could hear the intrigue in his voice. He knew I wasn't studying schoolwork. I should have told him psychology, but since he was in my class and I hadn't read the current material, I didn't want him quizzing me.

"Well, it's more personal research than anything else." I hoped he wouldn't read anything more into it.

"Let me guess. You're playing on Ancestry.com. Right?" he laughed. "Tracing down your family tree?"

His words hit me like a bolt of lightning. *Yes! That was the answer I couldn't think of that was staring me straight in the face. It was perfect.*

I jumped off my bed and leapt over to the computer. I quickly wiggled the mouse to bring it back to life and paced impatiently around my room waiting for it to come alive.

"I'm sorry, Jackson. I have to take care of something really quick. Let me call you back in a little while. I love you." I clicked the button on my cell before he had the chance to respond.

My mind was rushing in a thousand different directions at once. My monitor finally sprang to life, and I sat down and typed the website into the search engine. I typed in our last name and played around with the dates until I saw the name that I wanted to pop up on my screen: Montgomery Floyd Timmons 1839-1904. I quickly did the math in my head. My uncle was only twenty-two years old when the Civil War had begun.

With the proof glaring at me across the monitor, I plotted preciously what I was going to say to my dad to convince him there was another explanation for the journals. I ran down the stairs to my father's office where he was buried under a pile of paperwork looking exhausted from an apparently long day.

"Dad?" I leaned against the doorframe trying not to appear too anxious.

"Yeah?" He didn't bother looking up.

"Can I show you something really quick?"

"Not right now, Jocelyn. I'm really busy." He kept his eyes on his papers.

"Seriously, it will only take a second. It's important," I pleaded.

"Maybe later." He finally looked up and gave me a haphazard smile.

"It's after nine already. I promise it will only take a second of your time." I was not against begging at this point.

"I don't have time for any wedding things, Jocelyn." He went back to his papers.

"It has nothing to do with the wedding," I explained. "It's about the journals. I found something. Trust me you really want to see this."

His eyes darted back up with intrigue. "All right." He got up from his desk chair and followed me to the stairs.

"I did some digging after reading half of the journals because they seemed too authentic to me, and you're not going to believe what I found." I could no longer hide my excitement as we ascended the stairs two at a time. I practically danced over to my monitor and pointed to the name and dates behind it.

"Can you believe that? Uncle Monte must be named after him. According to the dates on our family tree, he was twenty-two years old when the Civil War broke out." I moved my finger over to point at my *other* parents' names followed by my brothers and even my name. "And look, they are mentioned in the journals as well. His brother Patrick, his wife Annabelle, their children, Patrick II, James, Jonathon, William, and check this out, she and I have the same name, Jocelyn Alyssa! Can you believe that?" I tried to act astonished by the discovery.

My dad stared at the monitor in silence for several minutes. "Well, I'll be damned," he said more to himself than to me, rubbing his chin slightly. Then he looked over at me and smiled.

"Uncle Monte must have somehow come across his namesake's journals in your parents' things, and they had to have been falling apart by then. He must have just recopied them in their original form. There's no other explanation for it. They are too authentic, way too real not to be written firsthand. I can't believe how real they are. It is just like living the war through his eyes and being there with him experiencing all of it." The words rushed out of me as I tried to get my dad onboard with my train of thought, hoping he would buy the story.

Yet he just stared at me with a coy smile across his face. Several minutes passed before he went over and sat down on the edge of my bed. "Have a seat, baby."

He nodded towards my desk chair. "I suppose your mother and I should have told you all this a long time ago. I'm not sure why we never did to be honest. It's not like it was some big secret we were trying to keep from you or something." He paused, looking at his hands fidgeting in his lap. "This house was built by my family in the summer of 1860, less than a year before the Civil War started. It stayed in my family, I believe, until sometime after the turn of the century when it fell into disarray and was sold because it would have cost too much to update it and make all the necessary repairs. Anyway, I grew up listening to stories of this place and it always intrigued me.

So, when it went up for sale when your mother was pregnant with you, we bought it. At that time, we had done a lot of research on my family history and the history of the house. Your mother thought it was more than a coincidence that we got the house back into our family when she was carrying you and it was built when Annabelle was carrying her only daughter, Jocelyn Alyssa. Therefore, she wanted to name you after her as a kind of tradition. So, you truly have a family name," he laughed. "I wanted to name you Zoe Nichole, but I was overruled."

I wrinkled my nose. "Zoe Nichole? I don't look like a Zoe."

"No. You don't. You look like a Jocelyn Alyssa. Your mother was right about that," he agreed with a loving smile and patted my knee. "Come with me, I want to show you something else you'll find interesting." He stood up and walked to my door. I quickly followed him eager to see what else he had to show me.

I followed my father down to the basement to the back corner of the room where there was a large storage closet containing all the holiday decorations. He opened the door and flipped on the light. Various boxes and tubs were stacked against the walls and labeled with various topics.

"Wait just a sec. It's kind of crowded in here." He squeezed his way to the back of the little room and began tugging on something large, trying to maneuver it through the little maze of stuff packed in there.

"Here we go." He reappeared with a very old, extremely large, ancient-looking trunk. "This was given to me when Monte passed away. I had never gone through it until the other day. I never could bring myself to sort through his things, but this is where I found the journals. There are some fascinating things here. A lot of family history stuff that I never knew existed must have been passed down through the family. He must have gotten it from your grandparents when they passed away. But I can't figure out why I'd never seen any of this stuff before. Neither Monte nor my parents ever mentioned to me that there were so many artifacts left from our family."

He rambled on absentmindedly as he unlocked the trunk and started to pull out various papers and items that were obviously old and fragile. I waited impatiently yet, scared to my very core of what I was about to discover. I could almost hear Jackson, Emily and Robert's voices ordering me to return to my room, not to look at any of it—the dangers of knowing too much about a world that I was only starting to discover. I pushed their voices aside and plopped down beside my dad. The curiosity was too great and there was no way I could stop myself. I wanted to know everything. I had to know.

"You know, I think you might be right about the journals. My brother must have seen how fragile they were, if they were anything like this other stuff, and recopied them. It certainly seems like something he would do. Family history was always something that intrigued him a great deal, so it didn't surprise me much to discover the contents of this trunk and that it was left in his possession," he shrugged casually and handed me a faded white binder.

I held it in my hand shaking slightly. The butterflies were dancing around in my stomach, and I struggled to calm my breathing. I didn't want him to notice anything peculiar.

"Look, littlen', I wish I could sit down here with you and sort through all this stuff, but I really must get this presentation done for a meeting I have first thing tomorrow morning." My dad rose back to his feet. "Don't worry about putting the trunk back in the closet tonight. When you're done looking through this stuff, just close the trunk and leave it here. I'll put it away tomorrow," he patted me on the head. "Have fun and don't stay up too late."

"All right, thanks, Daddy," I managed to squeak out before he disappeared.

I sat with my legs crossed in front of me and the album across my lap, surrounded with the answers I ever wanted to know about my life *there*. Before and after. I closed my eyes trying to steady my accelerating heart rate and the uncontrollable shaking in my hands. A part of me knew I shouldn't be doing this, but I truly couldn't help myself. This was for me. It was far beyond time that I knew the truth—the whole truth.

I slowly turned the cover of the album. It crackled with age and the black pages felt like they were about to crumble under my light touch. There on the front page was a faded black and white photograph of my Uncle Monte in his Union uniform. There was no smile across his face, just an intensity and fear of what was to come. I closely studied his features. They were so like my father Shane's. Yet, I could also see a trace of Patrick in his eyes and around his lips. It was so weird to comprehend how they were so intertwined with one another.

I turned the page slowly. On the backside of the front page was a photograph of my uncle again in his military uniform but beside him was Vivian in a wedding gown. She held a slight smile across her lips, as did he. Even though I already knew that he survived the war, it was so incredible to see him with his true love. The way he spoke of her in his journals, his decision to leave this plane of existence behind and live solely with her no longer surprised me in the slightest. His love for her was intense and true.

My eyes drifted over to the page opposite and my breath caught in my chest. There I was, standing beside the happy couple on their wedding day. I was wearing a very frilly, old-fashioned dress with little white gloves and my hair adorned in curls around my face. Even though I looked different than any other photo of me at this age, there was no mistaking it was me. The smile across my lips was slightly wider than the bride and groom's. I looked very happy, delicate, and so beautiful. I couldn't tear my eyes off the image of myself. Somehow, even with all the episodes, glimpses, and visions, this was the first time *EVE* had felt so amazingly real to me.

I reluctantly turned the page again with great care. There were several pictures of a baby boy fastened to the page. None of which I recognized. I carefully turned the page again. There, I found photos of a toddler boy sitting on a rocking chair and another of him playing with a toy wagon on the floor. I assumed that this had to be one of my uncle's sons, but I had no idea which. The next few pages were photos of my uncle, his wife, and his boys.

I began to casually flip the pages, only glancing at the faces that stared up at me until I turned the page and felt like someone punched me in the stomach. There was my entire family, well, my family *there*. My parents, all four brothers, and me, somewhere in my early teens I think, looking up at me with a knowing look upon their faces. I could barely breathe. I had seen all these faces before in my mind's eye, so they were familiar to me, but this was real.

They were real!

I couldn't believe what I was seeing in front of me, holding in my hands—proof! They had lived during that period. All that Jackson and his parents had told me was true!

My hands began to shake uncontrollably, and I felt like my heart was going to leap out of my chest. My breathing quickened as if there was no longer any oxygen in the room to fill my lungs.

The strange, yet beautiful, gowns that my mother and I wore were breathtaking. The men were all dressed in suits and hats. I only wished the photo was in color, so I could see the brilliant hues of the fabrics and the background. The picture was taken on the front porch of the house—this house—my house! These faces were the ones that had been haunting me for weeks. To see them so clearly in this photo stirred so many mixed emotions, I wasn't sure what I was feeling or if I could even put a label on it.

Slowly my eyes slid over to the adjoining page. There stood Robert, Emily, and a much younger Jackson, Alexander, and Phoebe. The five of them looked like a model of the perfect upper scale Victorian era family. The three familiar faces instantly made me feel incredibly guilty for looking at these pictures of the world I longed to be a part of. I shifted my eyes back to my family one more time before I turned the page over.

The rest of the album was filled with various photos of our family, mostly of Uncle Monte's boys and Vivian. I closed that album and set it aside nervously picking up the next one. I looked up at the ceiling wondering what the rest of my family was doing. I was sure my dad was still in his office and my mother had been successful in her silent avoidance of me.

Ethan had stopped coming by my room to talk and was only being polite now to Jackson when they rode back and forth to school together. Although Jackson hadn't mentioned anything to me, I knew Ethan's behavior was bothering him also.

The next several albums I flipped through had pictures of relatives from the early 1920s and up. One clearly had belonged to my brother James and was filled with pictures of his family. Finally, I came across an album that belonged to William and Olivia.

A smile stretched wide across my face as I recognized the wedding photo of them on the first page. Standing on either side of them was Jackson and me. I stared at the picture for a long time. It looked as though it could have been taken yesterday, apart from the styles. Olivia's wedding gown was so beautiful I couldn't take my eyes off it.

The following page contained a picture of William and Olivia, who were holding a little baby boy in her arms. I stared at her face for a long moment. It was exactly as I recalled it in my mind's eye. She was a pretty, young woman who looked much younger than she really was. The baby was adorable and looked exactly like his father. The chubby little baby with dark blond hair smiled happily up at the person taking the photograph. He looked to be maybe four or five months old.

I knew Olivia was due in March, so I figured this picture had to be taken this upcoming summer. It all seemed so weird to think that I was looking at photos that were one part my family history and yet in other events that haven't occurred yet. I was still unable to wrap my brain around it fully and if I concentrated too hard on it, the concept drove me nuts.

The next several pages were covered with photos of the little boy at various ages. He was such a beautiful child, and with each passing stage, he resembled William more. The following page showed the same little guy on William's lap sitting next to his mother who was now holding another baby boy in her arms. Both parents appeared very happy as did the chubby little boy who looked about three on his daddy's lap. I watched their children change through various stages of their childhood with each passing page. A third brother again joined them several years after the second and eventually a fourth before I reached the end of the album.

I closed the book in my lap and let out a deep sigh. I rolled over in my mind the idea that the Olivia I was currently aware of was only a few months pregnant, yet I was looking at aged photographs of individuals who had surely passed away now in this current reality. The concept of it was giving me a headache.

I picked up the next album without giving it much thought. Careful as always, I opened the front cover and a gasp of air escaped from deep inside me. Staring up at me was mine and Jackson's wedding photo. The picture captured us from our midsections on up and our faces were clearly shown. Jackson had his arm around my waist, and I held a bouquet of violets and lilies in my hands.

There were no words to describe the rush of emotions that poured out of me. Jackson was a breathtaking sight, and I could not have looked more perfect if I had been professionally done up in today's standards. We were standing in front of the hearth in the room upstairs. I absorbed every detail I could take in. I lightly traced my fingers longingly over the photograph. Then my brain flashed light a bolt.

Did my dad see this picture as well? How could he not have recognized the two people staring back off the pages? It is so obvious that it is Jackson and me. We look the same, especially Jackson. Everything about him except for the clothes is identical. There is simply no denying it is us in this picture. How in the world did my dad rationalize this in his own mind? The resemblance between his Jocelyn and the Jocelyn in this picture and the man standing beside her and my current fiancé is uncanny and must have boggled his mind for sure. Is that why he wanted me to look through these alone? Is he curious as to my reaction once I notice it for myself? Is he testing me?

I had no clue what could possibly be running through his head at this moment. My only hope was that he hadn't taken the time to look through all the albums since this was next to the bottom of the pile. I was almost afraid to turn the next page and see where my life was taking me next. Jackson's voice screamed out in the back of my mind warning me against knowing too much about my future in the past. I hesitated, my fingers toying lightly with the edge of the page.

Do I really need to know what is in store for us? Should I be so curious or just let the events unfold over the natural course of time?

I let out a small laugh.

Natural course of time. There is nothing natural about my course of time. There never has been apparently. What difference could this possibly make now? It's not like I have the power to change anything about the past anyway.

I held my breath and flipped the page over. There was Jackson and I standing beside William, Olivia, Elizabeth, and Alex on our wedding day.

See, nothing to be afraid of. I'm just being silly.

The next several pages were various photos of different family members on our wedding day.

Completely harmless.

The next page showed a picture of Jackson and me standing on the front porch with our arms around each other's waists looking happy. But the porch was not the one on this house, or the Chandler's home. It had to be our new home. I sucked in a large amount of air and almost choked. It was Jenna's, or Olivia's parents' home!

Why are we standing on the porch of their house?

It didn't make any sense. I rattled it around in my brain, but the images I had previously seen of that time told me nothing. It made no sense at all.

Perhaps we just happened to be over there visiting the new owners and someone took a picture of us on the porch.

It was the only explanation I could reason.

I slowly turned the page again. There were various photos of us together or us alone in numerous settings. I could tell with each passing page, the subtle differences in our faces, maturity setting in on each of us. It showed me the passing years as Jackson, and I was obviously still childless.

In my heart I knew it was because during this time, Jackson was keeping true to his word to my father that I would finish graduate school without having a child. The thought of it pleased me to no end, knowing that this man truly loved me a great deal and put my dreams and the goals that I held for myself before his own of having a family.

However, the following page showed me standing sideways with a clearly extended belly and Jackson's arms wrapped happily around it. A smile stretched across my face from ear to ear.

So, we do have a family, eventually.

It was so strange looking at a picture of me pregnant. I felt a mixture of pure joy and horrifying terror. My fingers played with the edge of the page.

Do I really want to know what we have? Would it ruin it for me when the time finally comes?

All that I had dreamed of had already come true.

Is it selfish to ask for more? Desire to know more?

I decided quickly that I didn't care. I was going to be selfish, I had to know. Besides, I probably wouldn't remember any of this anyhow since the barrier was still pretty much intact.

The next page showed me holding an angelic baby boy with dark eyes and dark wavy hair like Jackson's. I stared down at his tiny little face as tears covered my cheeks. He was perfect in every way. I wanted to reach out and hold him, cradle him in my arms, never let him go.

Now I realized why this was such a bad idea—the knowing. My heart physically ached for this child, my child. I could almost feel him in my arms and now they felt so empty. I ran my fingertip lightly over his face. It was as if I could feel the softness of his skin against mine, smell his scent, the fine texture of his hair against my cheek. I didn't want to wait another eight or ten years to have this child. I wanted him now.

I never should have turned the page. My heart broke as I carefully closed the album and set it apart from all the rest. I covered my face with my hands and sobbed uncontrollably for the child that was still years away from my reality.

I placed all the stuff back into the trunk. I hadn't put a dent in all that was in there. I would ask my dad in the morning to leave it out a little longer, so I could spend more time with it. I was sure he wouldn't mind. I straightened myself back up and picked up the album of Jackson and me and headed to my bedroom. The house was silent as I moved around. I had lost all track of time while I was in the basement, and I was guessing it was later than I had thought.

The alarm clock on my nightstand informed me that it was two in the morning when I arrived back in my room. I picked up my cell phone off my pillow feeling horrible that I had forgotten to call Jackson back after getting off the phone so abruptly with him earlier. My phone told me that I had five missed calls, four from him and one from Jenna.

I stacked my uncle's journals on my nightstand next to my cell. My body felt emotionally drained as I climbed into bed with the album on my lap. I flipped open the cover for one last look at the first wedding picture of us when my cell phone went off again. I reached for it quickly before it had the chance to make any more noise and possibly wake my parents.

"Hello," I whispered.

"Jocelyn are you alright?" Jackson's voice sounded alarmed.

"What? I'm fine. Do you know what time it is?" I couldn't believe he was calling my house in the middle of the night.

"Yes. I am sorry, but I was worried. You never called me back and your bedroom light was still on. I just noticed you moving around so I wanted to catch you before you went to bed to make sure everything is all right," he explained in a hurt voice.

"I'm sorry. I got busy with my dad and lost track of time. Were you watching my room?"

"Not really," he sounded embarrassed. "I was only keeping an eye out since I had called you several times and you never answered. I wasn't sure if you were fighting with Amy or Ethan or what was going on."

"No, nothing like that. I was in the basement with my dad. He was showing me some old stuff he'd come across cleaning out the storage room. No big deal." I wanted to sound as casual as possible considering I was staring at a wedding photo of the two of us from about one hundred-thirty years ago. I shook my head in disbelief at the entire situation and struggled to keep myself from busting out laughing at the absurdity of it all.

"It must have been pretty interesting if it held your attention for five hours." The tone of his voice shifted slightly.

"It was," I mumbled. I flipped over to the next page as my *other* family and friends smiled up at me. A part of me couldn't wait to get to sleep to be with them again.

"What did he show you?"

"Nothing." I was no longer paying much attention to him as I became enraptured in the photos of our *other* life again.

"If it was nothing, then why are you being so secretive about it?"

"Just some old family things. Nothing really."

"Which side of the family?" His voice sounded distant and faded, only a slight murmur in my ears. I wasn't paying much attention and had stupidly flipped the forbidden page. There he was again, my son!

"Jocelyn? Which side of the family?"

Silence.

"Jocelyn? Hello? Are you there?"

I could no longer hear his muffled words. The little boy had captured my full attention — nothing else in the world existed.

"Jocelyn? Will you please answer me? Jocelyn?"

Silent tears returned and ran freely down my face. My heart was physically torn from my chest and the pain was unbearable.

I numbly turned the page over, and my little angel had grown even more. He appeared to be happy and healthy as he crawled across the floor. The next shot showed him taking his first steps with Jackson kneeling beside him ready to catch him if he should happen to fall. My child had such a proud expression on his face as if he knew this was an important moment in his young life and he had made a great achievement. The next page showed me sitting next to my son who was somewhere between two and three years old, and from the looks of it I was pregnant again.

The tears continued to flow freely, and I had all but forgotten my future husband on the phone and instead was lost to a world that lay before me. I couldn't hear Jackson calling out to me with panic in his voice. I didn't even notice when the phone had gone dead or that I had let it slip from my shoulder and fall beside me on the bed. The entire outside world had disappeared around me.

With the flip of a page, again I saw Jackson and me in front of the hearth where we had gotten married. He was holding our oldest son while I cradled our new son in my arms!

Two boys! I have two boys!

The reality of it floored me. I turned the page once more and my youngest angel had grown a little more. He was perhaps six months old, barely sitting upright beside his brother. Our oldest son looked like an exact copy of Jackson with the same black wavy hair and dimples, yet he appeared to have my brown eyes instead of Jackson's emerald, green.

But it was hard to tell from the black and white pictures. On the other hand, our youngest seemed to favor me more than his father. He had a small trace of freckles around his nose exactly like mine and what appeared to be my hair color.

I brushed away the tears again and numbly turned the page once more. My boys were growing up right before my eyes. Their chubby little bodies seemed to slim down as they got older and they looked to be very happy children, always with big smiles covering their little faces.

The following page caused a startled squeak to escape my lips when I saw we were also blessed with a daughter. There before my eyes was a photo of our happy little family at the white gazebo where Jackson had proposed. Our little boys stood on the bench on either side of us and I held a little girl in my arms. She was adorned in a long flowing gown and was sucking on her thumb. It appeared to be a beautiful spring day and all the lilies around us were in full bloom.

My sons were wearing little knickers with suspenders and buttoned up shirts and little ties. They each held their hats in their hands and smiled up at me. Jackson looked as handsome as ever and even had a trace of gray starting to show in his black hair. I was also happy to see that I appeared to still be thin and maintaining my figure. Then again, I probably couldn't breathe being stuffed into a corset. I smiled through my tears, but I couldn't take my eyes away from my family.

Nothing else in the world mattered to me now. I was positive that I had made the right decision for the course of my life. I was going to be able to go to college and graduate school, graduate and have my family and a successful career. I was sure of it.

It was all going to work out. I had the proof before my eyes. Jackson and I were going to be together always. This marriage was successful, going to last. Nothing was going to come between us. We were going to have two beautiful sons and a gorgeous little girl, and they all appeared to be happy and healthy. I wiped the tears away again but still could not turn away. I no longer cared that I had to get up in a couple of hours and go to class. It really didn't matter if the roof caved in, and the house fell all around me. I couldn't tear my eyes off my beautiful family.

"Jocelyn?" A low voice came out of nowhere causing me to jump out of my skin. My eyes immediately landed on my door where Jackson stood leaning against the frame.

"Jackson," I whispered. "What in the world do you think you're doing? My dad will kill you if he finds you in here." I quickly shoved the album under my comforter and brushed the tears off my cheeks.

Jackson quietly closed the door behind him before walking over to my bed and taking a seat beside me. "What is going on with you? You would not answer me, and I could hear you crying on the phone."

I brushed my cheeks off again. I couldn't seem to get the tears to stop flowing. "Nothing. I'm sorry. I didn't mean to worry you." I gave my best attempt at a smile. "How did you get in here?"

"The basement window," he blushed. "I am afraid your brother William and I know every nook and cranny in this house and how to sneak in and out of it undetected."

"Why am I not surprised?" I muttered shaking my head.

"Jocelyn," he placed his hands over mine and stared intently at me. "Tell me what is going on."

I hated it when he did this, it made it impossible for me to deceive him. "Nothing is going on. You really should leave. We can talk tomorrow. I need to get some sleep and so do you." I tried to change the subject to give me some time to figure out something to tell him, anything but the truth.

"I am not going anywhere until I find out what you are hiding. Something has clearly upset you. Something you obviously do not want me to know about." He raised his eyebrows at me, and I felt like a little kid.

In one swift motion, Jackson reached under my comforter and grabbed the album before I could do anything to stop him.

"Hey, give me that!" I nearly shouted as the hysterics built inside me. "It's very old. You're going to damage it." But I was too late. He had already turned his back to me and opened the front cover.

"Oh my God," he gasped in a low voice that trailed off into nothing. He was stiff and silent for several minutes before he turned to face me with pure horror in his beautiful green eyes. "Where did you get this?"

I exhaled deeply and explained to him how my dad had found my uncle's journals.

Jackson sat silently and listened. He never turned the page of the album to see what came after our wedding picture. He just sat frozen and pale and stared at me in disbelief. Even after I stopped talking, he was silent for some time.

"Say something, Jackson. Please," I begged, but his eyes were unfocused. I wasn't even sure if he could hear me. "Jackson, this wasn't my fault. I didn't know what was in the trunk. I had no idea there were photos of us and our family in there. How could I have known that?" The tears returned stronger than before, but he remained silent.

Ten minutes of agony passed before Jackson seemed to return to the present. He gently closed the album and slid it off his lap onto my bed. His eyes never looked up to meet mine. They seemed to be somewhere far off in the distance.

"I have to go," he whispered in a soft voice as he slowly stood up. It was almost as if the world was moving in slow motion, and nothing was real.

"Jackson? No! Wait! Talk to me!" I nearly said in a normal tone reaching out for his arm. But he had managed to pull it away before I had the chance. He silently shook his head and slowly walked to my door.

I jumped out of bed and leapt between him and my door. I knew he wouldn't make a scene in the middle of the night with my parents asleep down the hall. I guess he knew I wouldn't either.

"Jackson, please talk to me. What's wrong? Why are you upset with me about this?" I blocked his departure and placed both my hands on each of his arms. His eyes finally focused back on me and locked on mine.

"Not now, Jocelyn." His voice was low but firm. I had never heard him take such a tone with me before. "Later. I need to calm down. You will have to drive yourself to school in the morning."

His expression told me he was serious, and I needed to back off. I let go of his arms and stepped aside, giving him space to leave my room. He didn't frighten me, but I knew I had crossed the line, and it was one I really didn't want to dance along.

Jackson left my room without uttering another word. I stood there quietly and watched him leave, not having a clue as to what to say to bring him back. I had never seen him behave that way and I didn't know what to make of it. I slowly walked back over to the bed and crawled under the covers. I picked the album back up and stared at our picture.

A part of me half expected it to have changed, like in the *Back to the Future* movie when future actions had changed the past and the picture Michael J. Fox was carrying of him, and his siblings had started to disappear. I laughed at myself, yet I caught myself closely examining the photo making sure a part of it hadn't begun to fade or change in some way. I felt silly and closed the album and slid it under my bed for safekeeping.

I flipped off the lights and wandered over to the bay window, pulling the drapes back slightly. I wondered what Jackson was doing at this moment. Was he across the street explaining to his parents what had happened? I couldn't help but worry what they would think of the photos and the implications of them. I knew they were going to be extremely upset with me. Even though it wasn't technically my fault, I knew I shouldn't have looked through that trunk because I had found exactly what I was hoping I would find, and that fact alone made me feel much worse.

CHAPTER 18

I SHOT UP STRAIGHT IN MY BED with intense feelings of pure panic. Something was wrong. Terribly wrong. I struggled to calm my breathing as my eyes quickly scanned my room. Everything appeared the same as always. I closed my eyes, drawing my legs up to me and wrapping my arms around them resting my head on my knees. I focused on what I had seen the night before. Something had gone horribly awry I was positive about it.

My chest began to ache, and I rocked back and forth, not even sure why a sudden rush of tears was now falling from my eyes. Jackson, it was Jackson.

Something had happened to Jackson... No. That wasn't it. Something had happened between Jackson and I. Something that I was responsible for. Something I had done that he did not approve of. But what?

I continued rocking back and forth searching my brain for what I had done. Nothing came.

I jumped out of bed as Mimi came in to wake me. She helped me dress quickly. I knew I had to speak to Emily as soon as possible. Certainly, she or Robert would know what had happened. I didn't even consider the fact that I had classes this morning. I didn't care. I had no idea what I'd done, but I knew it was something bad.

It was bitter cold, and the frosted grass crunched under my feet as I quickly ran across the lawns. A low light beamed from the front window, and I was sure that at least someone was awake. I tapped nervously on the front door waiting for someone to let me in. I shifted my weight from one foot to the next shivering in the cold before Barnaby finally came to the door.

"Gud mornin', Miss Jocelyn," he greeted me with a startled look.

I quickly stepped into the foyer still shivering. "Has Mrs. Chandler arisen?" I asked through my still chattering teeth.

"No ma'am, but Mr. Chandler's in da dining room havin' his mornin' coffee," he nodded towards the opposite direction.

I rushed into the dining room not even considering how inappropriate my actions were. "I am sorry to intrude, Mr. Chandler," I said as I entered the room.

Robert was sipping on his coffee buried behind the morning newspaper when I approached. He looked up at the sound of my voice, obviously startled by my behavior. "Miss Jocelyn, what's wrong?"

He knew something was off. I had never behaved so informally before in my life. "I am not sure, but something is. I am not sure what happened, but I think I did something to really upset Jackson."

He gently guided me over to a chair and pulled it out for me. I sat down, and he kneeled beside me offering me his handkerchief. Susan came in with a confused look on her face and quietly poured me a cup of coffee before exiting quickly without a sound.

"Jackson is at school. You could not have done anything to upset him." The confusion on his face was plain to read. I shook my head at him.

"No, *there*. I did something *there* last night, but I have no idea what it was. I can't remember." Tears welled up in my eyes. "I know he is really upset with me. I woke up with this pain in my chest and for some reason I feel like he is close to calling off our wedding."

I could hardly get the words out. I was close to hysterics. I could not imagine living in a world where Jackson was not by my side.

"Oh, I see." He sat down in the chair next to mine and leaned his elbow on the table, rubbing his chin like he was lost in his own thoughts. I stared at him as he contemplated his next words.

What had I done? What horrible thing could I have possibly done to cause such a reaction in the man I loved, and why was his father struggling to tell me about it? It had to be absolutely wretched.

"Jocelyn, I am sorry." Robert stopped rubbing his chin and placed his hand over mine. "I am afraid I cannot tell you what happened because it can greatly affect your life *here*."

"What is that supposed to mean?" I demanded in a tone I immediately regretted using.

Robert looked stunned by my bluntness then slowly laughed. "Yes, your traits from *there* are starting to come through as well, I see."

"I apologize, Mr. Chandler. I sincerely do. I feel like I have so little control over my actions and behaviors. Some of the things I am doing are so out of character for me," I cried, but he only smiled gently.

"I know, Jocelyn. It is to be expected."

"Please. You must tell me what I did. I must know. I have to correct it."

The tears fell steadily down my face, but I made no effort to wipe them away. "I have to speak with him," I pleaded.

"I am truly sorry, my dear. I wish there was some way I could help you." Robert got up and walked over to the window and stared out at the veranda.

"Please," I begged. "Can't you call him?"

I knew they had a telephone installed in their home the same time we did. Although I could never recall them ever calling upon Jackson while he was away at school. I also knew they had a phone in his residence building since Olivia had called William there before they were married. Jackson had told me so himself.

"I do not believe that would be a good idea. My son is fully aware of what transpired between you two *there* and if he felt it necessary, I am sure he will contact you. I think it may be best for you to give him some time and space right now." He continued to stare out the window, so he wouldn't have to face me.

"But what did I do that was so horrible?" I begged.

"I am sorry, but it is not my place to discuss what transpired between the two of you." He walked back over and sat beside me again. "I know this is difficult for you and I do wish I could do or say something to make this all easier." He inhaled deeply and sighed, placing his hands over mine. "All I can say is that what you discovered can greatly affect your life *here* and therefore, I cannot say anything about it. I am truly sorry, Jocelyn."

I nodded slowly with no words or fight left in me. I sat numbly for several minutes, holding his hand, searching my brain for any sort of glimpse into what I had done to cause such a state. But my mind was blank, and I found no answers, only more questions.

I smiled softly at the man whom I was no longer sure would be my father-in-law and walked hesitantly to the front door. "Please, forgive my intrusion," I whispered softly before turning to leave.

Robert surprised me by wrapping his arms around me in a fatherly manner and kissing the top of my head. "Try not to worry, my dear. I am sure you two will work this out. All couples have disagreements from time to time. It does not mean that he has stopped loving you. I am positive he has not. Give him some time and things will work out fine."

I undressed numbly with my head in a fog. Nothing felt real. I crawled back into my bed and informed Mimi that I did not feel well and would not be attending my classes that day. She brushed my sweat-matted hair away from my face, gave me a slight nod and departed, closing the door softly behind her.

I watched the flames dance across the wall in various shapes and forms. I tried to imagine what was going on in this bizarre new world that was finally becoming clear. My eyes became more unfocused as my mind drifted away to the unusual things in my *other* world. I pictured the clothes, moving photo boxes, and my friends, those three amazing young women who always seemed to be by my side. Their faces had become ingrained in my mind, their smiles and the sound of their laughter gave me great comfort.

I pictured my room *there*. The unique differences between the two of them were astounding. My picturesque ivory, violet, and sage pristine room was all class and elegance. My *other* room was stuffed with vibrant colors and photos of things I had only read about in fairytales. It had brilliant lights and fabrics that felt elaborate to the touch. Everything about it was all that I wanted yet failed to have the strength to be *here*.

I got up and walked over to my vanity and sat down in front of the chair. The reflection that stared back at me appeared tired and weak, lost and alone. I envied the strength that dwelled deep within my *other* self. This *other* version of me was strong, independent, and willful. Those small little personality traits from *there* were bleeding over into my life *here* felt amazing. I loved the fire that burned within me when I acted spontaneously and spoke my true feelings.

I picked up my brush and ran long strokes through my hair and wondered if I should call Jackson directly myself. Olivia had called William numerous times at their dorm, and I knew the number was written on the chalkboard downstairs by the phone. *Would Jackson be terribly upset with me if I called?* He had never told me *not* to call him at school. I placed the brush back on the table and went over to my nightstand. I picked up my copy of *Sense & Sensibility* and sat down in the rocking chair next to the hearth.

Unfortunately, I was on the part of the story where Marianne discovers that her Mr. Willoughby is going to marry another woman. I read about half a page of her heartache and grief then tossed the book over on my bed. It was only making me feel worse plus it confirmed that happily ever after never happens for anyone no matter where or what period they reside.

I walked over to my bookcase and glanced over the titles of every book I owned. Nothing remotely appealed to me. It seemed every one of them was a love story of some sort or another and each with its own version of happily ever after. I wished I had something different to read, something to distract my mind off this heartache. My sewing basket sat beside the rocker but also held no appeal to me. I had nothing to do to occupy the countless hours ahead of me. I crawled back into bed and pulled the covers up over my head.

CHAPTER 19

Wednesday, November 18, 2015

I EXPLAINED JACKSON'S ABSENCE by saying he was sick to justify why I was driving Ethan and myself to school. I hated the thought of admitting to anyone, especially my brother, that we'd had an argument and were not speaking. I knew he would fully enjoy it and hope that I would call off the wedding and things would return to the way they were before Jackson ever entered our lives.

I continued about my day, moving from one classroom to the next, trying not to think at all about the damage I had done. I sat numbly and listened to one lecture after the next without hearing anything my teachers said. It was like running on autopilot, functioning without consciously being aware or feeling anything.

After basketball practice, I considered going over to his house and demanding to know what his problem was or calling him up and begging for forgiveness. However, the stubbornness deep inside me wouldn't allow me to give in, either. I kept telling myself repeatedly that if he wanted to speak with me, he knew where to find me. But even that didn't stop me from keeping my cell phone beside me all evening in hopes that he would give in and call. And of course, he didn't.

CHAPTER 20

Thursday, November 21, 1878

I COULDN'T MOVE. My chest ached with pain and my head throbbed from the nonstop crying for the last two days. Tears no longer fell from my eyes; I had none left. But the dry sobs still returned every time Jackson entered my thoughts.

The morning sun glared through my windows making my head throb. It was painful to even open my eyes. My vision was blurred, and I swear my eyeballs hurt. I made no effort to get out of bed. There was no life in me.

Mimi was the only one I would allow to enter my room. I didn't want to see anyone else. She never questioned my haggard state but spoke comforting words when she tried throughout the day to get me to eat something. Food was the furthest thing from my mind. I had no appetite or desire for anything but Jackson.

The hours passed slowly as I sat lifelessly in my bay window. The coolness of the window felt comforting on my aching head while I stared off into nothingness. The sun shifted gently in the sky as I witnessed it glide gracefully with the passing hours until it finally set on my torment and darkness took over once more.

CHAPTER 21

Thursday, November 19, 2015

FOR THE SECOND DAY IN A ROW, I drove Ethan and I to school. I was hoping that Jackson would make an appearance, but by the time the first bell rang I realized that he wasn't coming. I slammed my locker shut in frustration and stomped off to class. I was so angry with him for behaving so childishly. Yet, in the back of my mind, the photo of my future family kept reappearing and my heart would break all over again, making the anger disappear.

By the time lunch rolled around and we were all gathered in the cafeteria, I felt like the smallest little thing was going to cause me to burst into tears.

"Where's Jackson?" Hilary asked innocently. "I hope he's not sick. What about the movie tonight?"

"He's not sick," I answered flatly. "We just had a fight, and he's acting like a baby and avoiding me!" Every eyebrow in the vicinity rose with curiosity.

"Must have been some fight." Zak tried his best to hide his smirk from me. I thought briefly about kicking him under the table but decided he wasn't worth the effort. Luckily, Caitlyn elbowed him in the stomach for me with a smile in my direction.

"Does that mean the wedding is off?" Ethan asked with hopefulness in his voice.

I flashed him the evilest look I could muster, and the smile quickly faded from his lips.

"Sorry," he responded in a weak voice.

"Well, you'd better make up with him after practice. I'm not about to let some silly argument between you two ruin this movie for me. I have been waiting months for this night," Jenna ordered. "I'm going straight home after practice, showering, grabbing a bite to eat and taking a long nap."

"We're all meeting at your house around ten o'clock, right?" Caitlyn asked.

"Right, so I'll get up at nine forty-five," Jenna laughed.

"Do you really think it's going to be that crowded?" Hilary looked between them.

"Six theaters are sold out already. It's going to be stupid," Caitlyn answered.

"And cold. I guess we should be thankful that it stopped raining for once," Jenna added.

"Wonderful," Hilary muttered and turned her attention back to Cody.

I sat there and listened to everyone chat around me, but I didn't join in on any of the conversation.

I pulled out of the school parking lot thinking of nothing else but making up with Jackson. Ethan sat in the passenger seat looking out the side window. He really hadn't said more than two words to me in days and I was at the point that he was the least of my problems.

"You really love him, don't you?" The sound of his voice caused me to glance over at him, but he was still staring out the window.

"Very much."

"Then why the rush?"

"I don't feel like I am."

"You do realize that everyone thinks you're pregnant. It's all over school. People are openly talking about you behind your back. Do you even care about that? I do. It's embarrassing." His voice was thick.

"Nope. I honestly don't. I'm not an idiot. I know what people are saying. But I'm not pregnant. Besides, it's no one's business but mine and Jackson's anyway."

He could tell he was upsetting me, and I knew he didn't care. When Ethan was upset, he generally liked to spread it around, so everyone felt a little bit of his misery.

"Whatever," he muttered still looking out the window.

I ran up to the bathroom as soon as we walked in the door and turned the hot water on high. I stripped down as quickly as possible and jumped under the hot water. I didn't care if it took an hour for the hot water to run out, I was determined to stay in there until I had used up every drop of hot water in the tank just so Ethan would have to take a cold shower. I knew it was mean and my actions were purely out of childish spite, but his words stung, and I knew one of his biggest pet peeves was having to take a cold shower.

After all, all's fair in love and war.

I toweled off feeling immensely satisfied with myself no matter how childish my actions were. It served him right for being so judgmental, I thought as I climbed into my sweats.

I quickly blew my hair dry and put on some light makeup before I went over to confront Jackson. I had finally reached my limit with his childish avoidance of me.

As I stopped in the kitchen to fix myself a sandwich first, I heard the shower turn on. It was quickly followed by a barrage of swearing mixed with my name. I giggled to myself as I sat down on one of the bar stools to enjoy my quick dinner.

The knot in my stomach had grown to the size of a bowling ball before I managed to cross the street. My palms were sweaty and shaky, and I had to remind myself numerous times that my futures in both worlds were not in fact, at stake.

I waited impatiently after I rang the bell for someone to answer the door. Finally, the door opened slowly, and Jackson emerged from behind it.

"Hello." His greeting was as hollow as his voice.

"May I speak with you?" I desperately tried to keep my voice calm and steady.

"Of course."

He opened the door a little wider, so I could pass through. He offered no kiss, no hug, none of the normal enthusiasm that he always showed with each encounter. My heart immediately sank to my toes while I followed him silently into the living room.

He took a seat on the couch and stared back at me. I wasn't sure if I should join him or take a seat across the room on the loveseat. I swallowed hard and decided that I was going to take my future into my own hands. I was not going to give up my family so easily. So, I sat down on the edge of the sofa beside him but kept a little distance between us.

We sat in an awkward silence for a few minutes. I kept waiting for Robert or Emily to pop in with their normal cheerfulness, but neither of them made an appearance. I wondered where they were since the house was deadly quiet. He offered no explanation for their absence, so I didn't inquire.

"Are you going to speak to me?" The silence was worse than the anger.

"What would you like me to say?" he asked without looking at me.

"Well, you can start with explaining why you're so upset with me."

"You really have no clue?" He finally looked at me and I could see the anger in his eyes.

"You didn't even give me a chance to explain everything. It's not as if I went searching for proof. I had no idea that stuff was down there." I hated the way he kept looking at me.

Jackson sat silently for several minutes fidgeting with his hands. I considered getting up and leaving when he took a deep breath and sighed heavily.

"To be honest, I truly thought you were a better person than I. Not to say anything about the fact that I have been dying for the last eight months for our wedding day and the fact that you have been keeping your wedding gown some big secret from everyone….and well," His voice trailed off and I immediately felt ashamed.

"You have no one to blame for that, but yourself," I pointed out. "I did not hand you the album. In fact, if memory serves me correctly, you yanked it out from beneath my comforter without my permission because of your own selfish agenda."

"Yes, I did, and I do apologize for that. However, in my defense, you would not tell me what was upsetting you so much and forced me into finding out for myself."

"You can't be serious." I shifted towards him in full confrontation mode. "You're unbelievable. Just because I don't want to share every single detail of my life with you, you must take it upon yourself to investigate. Are you always so selfish and childish?" I demanded.

"Do you know the background of the gown you are wearing in that picture?" he said hotly.

"No, I don't. How could I?" I could feel the blood rushing to my face and my hands began to tremble with fury.

"Well, just so you know. It is *my mother's* wedding gown you are wearing. Not even my sister got married in her dress."

"That's only because she couldn't fit into it!" I shot back, having no idea how I knew that information but positive it was true.

Jackson stared at me with his face covered in astonishment. His mouth fell open, looking at me as if I had just slapped him. "How do you know that?" he said weakly.

"I don't know, I just do." I shrugged, still trying to control the trembling in my hands.

"My mother just told me that yesterday when I told my parents about the pictures. You could not have known that. She said she has never spoken with you about your wedding gown *there*." His expression held, but his eyes widened further. "What else are you not telling me?"

"Nothing." I couldn't figure out what he was getting at.

"You know about our kids, don't you?"

"Yes. And I know you do too." My eyes narrowed in on him.

Jackson fell back against the couch and let out a loud laugh, shaking his head in disbelief. I sat there dumbfounded like an idiot staring at him.

"When I said I thought you were a better person than I, well," He covered his face with both his hands for a moment almost as if he was ashamed of his own actions. "How far did you scroll down on the ancestry website once you pulled up your uncle's name?"

"I didn't."

"Don't you get it?"

I stared at him and shook my head stupidly.

"Last spring when your uncle told us about you inheriting *EVE* .... Well, I got curious and did some digging myself on the same website. So yes, I know about our children. I even know their names!"

He turned his body towards mine. "I am sorry, but it is not like it was something I could just tell you. I honestly figured you would discover the information for yourself. And well, you never did."

Now I was mad. All that guilt, their voices repeatedly warning me not to look, and here he knew everything I had discovered and never told me.

"I can't believe you," I nearly shouted as I leapt to my feet. "You warned me. Your parents warned me. Don't go digging around. Don't Google yourself. How could you not tell me the truth? How could you sit there and warn me after you did it yourself? And I can't believe you had the nerve to act angry with me for looking into our past when you'd already done the same thing! At least mine was an accident. You did it on purpose!"

But Jackson just laughed even harder at my outburst. "Calm down. I am sorry." Yet, his laughter was only increasing my anger.

"Oh, forget it." I stormed out of the room, but he chased after me.

"Jocelyn, stop! Seriously, do not leave. I am sorry. Honest I am. Please, come back in and have a seat." He gently touched my arm and guided me back over to the couch.

I sat down a little further away from him and Jackson laughed, and noticing the distance I put between us, he scooted closer to me. He gently pulled me into his arms and kissed my cheek. As much as I really didn't want to, I could feel myself relenting in his arms. I made a vague attempt to pull away from him, but it was obvious to us both that my heart wasn't in it.

"No. I'm still mad at you."

He flashed my favorite lop-sided grin knowing it would render me powerless. "You cannot be mad at me forever. After all, we are getting married in a month."

"If I'll still have you!"

"Oh, you love me," he pulled me closer and pressed his lips against mine.

The passion soared between us, and I could no longer resist him. Yes, I loved him. With every fiber of my being, I loved him. There would never be anyone ever who could invade my heart and soul the way he had. He truly was my life.

I pulled myself away reluctantly, breathing hard. "Yes, I do." I leaned my forehead against his.

"Are you curious?" he smirked as if he was hiding a glorious secret.

"About?" I had no clue what else there could be.

"Our children?" his smile widened.

"What about them?" I narrowed my eyes again with suspicion.

"I know their names," he chimed smugly.

"Well, I have the album of our family," I one-upped him.

His eyes widened and sparkled. "Can I see it again?"

"Not until you tell me their names," I teased, enjoying having the upper hand again.

"You are malicious."

"Always."

"Fine then, be that way," he laughed at my coyness. "Well, our eldest son is Gavin Harold."

"Gavin Harold? Are you kidding?" His words took me by surprise. That was certainly not a name I had ever expected to come from his lips.

He looked hurt. "No. Why? What is wrong with that?"

I slumped back against the couch and whispered the name again to myself trying to figure out where in the world I had ever come up with such a name for my son. "Gavin...I like that," I whispered softly to myself, sitting a moment longer considering it. "Gavin Harold...yeah, I can see it." A smile slid across my face and Jackson looked at me with curiosity. "Don't you get it? Gavin Harold...it's a strong masculine name that is perfect for both time periods." He still looked confused. "Gavin...well, Gavin is just a great name. And Harold...can you guess where I got that from?" I couldn't stop myself from laughing at the irony of my logical thinking, but Jackson only shrugged his shoulders. "The children's book, *Harold and the Purple Crayon*."

I looked at his blank stare as if he was a complete idiot and still, he shook his head again. "It was my favorite book as a kid. Oh. Come on. Don't you get it? Harold has this magic purple crayon that allows him to draw his own world the way he wants it to be. Therefore, Harold's world is as he sees it, not conforming to the way everyone else sees it." I laughed again even harder "It's the perfect name for a child born with *EVE*, because he will view the world entirely different from all his peers."

Jackson burst out laughing. "You are right. It is perfect." He shook his head in disbelief at me. "You never cease to amaze me," he muttered softly and quickly kissed my cheek again.

"And our second son? What's his name?" I held my breath, scared to imagine what other twisted logic I could possibly have come up with.

"Ethan Alexander, after our brothers," he announced with pride.

"I love that!" And I truly did. It was perfect for the darling little man from the photo. Plus, I was thrilled that this meant my relationship with my brother would someday mend.

"And our daughter?"

"Alyssa Nichole."

"That's so beautiful and it fits her perfectly." I sighed, remembering the little princess in the long flowing dress on my lap. "Actually, all their names fit each of them," I grinned over at him. "We did really well."

"I think so," he agreed before standing up. "Now, can I see the album?"

"Of course, but let me bring it over here. My house isn't exactly friendly these days."

"Yes, I have noticed that." He walked me to the door. "Do you think they will ever forgive me?"

"In time," I assured him. I leaned up and kissed him passionately before running back across the street.

Ethan pounced on me as soon as I opened the front door. He raced up the stairs hot on my heels.

"You think you're real cute. Don't you?" he shouted, following me into my bedroom. "Using up all the hot water so I had to take a cold shower. You know how much I hate a cold shower and you did it purely out of spite."

"So, what if I did? Maybe next time you have a comment you'll learn to keep it to yourself, or you will find yourself riding the bus to school and walking home from practice," I threatened.

"You're not the only one who drives, you know." He glared and took a step closer to me. But despite his physical advantage, I did not step back. I knew he wouldn't lay a hand on me. Our dad would skin him alive if he did and he'd be grounded until his graduation.

"True, but I'm the one with a car and don't even think about asking any of my friends for a ride," I replied smugly. I had reached my limit with his opinions.

Ethan glared at me, narrowing his eyes a little further and took another step toward me. "We'll see about that." His voice was surprisingly low and cold.

"Yes, we will little brother." He turned to leave, but I added, "Oh, and don't even think that you're riding with me or any of my friends to the movie tonight, because I can assure you, you're not!"

He stopped in his tracks and turned slowly around. "You can't stop me."

I let out a small laugh. "Wanna bet?"

"If I don't go, you don't go!" A satisfied look flashed on his face.

"Really? Well, let's see. One of us is eighteen and one of us is not," my voice rang triumphantly. "Now, let's think about this. Who can our parents forbid to go out on a school night? Not me!" I sang out, laughing.

"I hate you," he said calmly. "And I'm going whether you like it or not."

"I don't care if you go or not. But you're not going with me or my friends. You have your own, stop being a leech on mine," I said clearly, only because I knew my words stung.

"I have my own friends. Besides, Zak, Kyle, and Cody are my friends. More so than they are yours!"

"Yeah, probably, but their girlfriends are my best friends, and they are going to the movie tonight with their girlfriends," I reminded him. "Besides, this is more of a couple's thing. Do you really want to be an extra wheel? It's sort of sad, don't you think?" I added just for a cheap shot.

He stared at me fuming, trying to come up with a good retort. His breathing was uneven, and his ears were bright pink, as they always were when he worked himself up into a tizzy. Finally, all he said was, "I really do hate you; I hope you know that. And I really hope you do get pregnant by your precious husband and have to drop out of college."

"Wow. That one hurt!" I shouted back at him as he stormed out of my room.

I sat down on the corner of my bed and rested my head in my hands. I hated fighting with him. He was such an important part of my world, and unfortunately, when you're that close with someone, you know exactly what to say to hurt them the most. As good as it may feel in the heat of the argument, immense remorse and guilt always followed.

I reached under my bed and pulled out the ancient looking brittle album. I carefully wrapped it in a fleece blanket to protect it from the elements and headed back downstairs. I paused at the bottom of the staircase. I could hear the television coming from the family room and I knew Ethan was probably sulking and munching on anything he'd found in the kitchen.

He didn't bother to look over at me when I sat down in the recliner next to him. "Hey E, I'm sorry. I didn't mean what I said."

"Whatever," he muttered.

"Come on, Ethan. Talk to me."

"I have nothing else to say to you except leave me alone." He turned and glared at me again.

"Damn it, Ethan, I'm tired of this! You're acting like a spoiled brat! Why should you care if I get married or not? It's none of your business, so just butt out and keep your snide remarks to yourself because I don't want to hear it anymore!"

"Fine. Now will you leave?" he growled.

"You're such an ass! No wonder you can't keep a girlfriend," I muttered loud enough for him to hear before I stormed out of the room.

Jackson and I snuggled back down on the couch together with the album resting across both our legs.

"Aren't your parents going to be upset that we're looking at these?" I inquired.

"My parents left for Boston yesterday. My sister has the flu and they decided to take a long weekend to help her." A sly grin slid across his face.

"You're telling me that we have an empty house for the next several days?" My heart leapt out of my chest with excitement.

"Yes. And we're going to remember that we're waiting." He played like he was trying to escape from me, and I burst out laughing.

"Yes. Yes. Right. Waiting." I pulled him closer to me laughing at the shocked expression he pretended.

"Miss Jocelyn, I never…" he covered his face before I could kiss him.

"Oh bull," I shook my head. "You seem to forget. You have. I have not!"

"Oh, right. Sorry," he dropped his head to his chest trying to act ashamed of himself. "Can we just look at the album? Please?" His eyes met back up with mine.

We settled back down beside one another. I placed my hand calmly over the album and thought about all that this held for the two of us, the story of our lives yet to come. My eyes drifted back up to Jackson's face and our eyes held each other for a moment in time.

"Are you ready for this?" I whispered.

"Yes, very." A slight grin crossed his shapely full lips.

I slowly opened the cover revealing the first wedding photo. We both stared at it with disbelief.

"You certainly are a beautiful bride."

"And you are a stunningly handsome groom."

He smiled softly and turned the page. We sat in silence as we watched our future unfold on the pages across our lap. The years of college danced before our eyes in the various snapshots taken of us as the family's disappointment. The childless couple. I wondered for a brief second how we must have been perceived by everyone except Jackson's family, of course, as a couple who were married for almost ten years without ever producing one child. It must have been so hard on my parents since they were so family oriented. But it was also a comfort to know that in the end, I didn't let them down. I gave my parents three very beautiful grandchildren to be proud of.

Jackson turned to the page where he had his arms wrapped around my enormous belly. His smile brightened and he traced his finger lightly over the photo of my protruding stomach. "Wow. Look at that. Amazing," his eyes met mine. "I love you," he whispered.

"I love you, too."

Jackson stared back down at the pregnant picture for several more minutes without saying a word. My eyes shifted from the image on the page to the expression of adoration across his face.

With hesitation and a slight tremble in his fingers, he gently flipped the page over.

"Gavin," he whispered in a small voice broken up with a smile and tears gleaming in his eyes. I choked back my own tears and couldn't manage to utter a sound.

More than two hours after we opened the album, we found the strength to close it again. We sat together, both unsure what to say. I had managed not to look any further, so the final two thirds of the album were just as new to me as they were to him. From all that we had witnessed, we felt truly blessed, and had every reason to believe that we lived a very full and happy life together. The final page in the album finished with the photos of our eldest son's wedding ceremony. It was perfect, almost too perfect.

I rested my head back on his chest, fully content with the world. The grandfather clocked chimed in the foyer breaking the silence. Without thinking, I absentmindedly counted the gongs and for the first time I realized how late it really was.

"It's nine o'clock already?"

Jackson turned towards me. "Yeah. So?"

"We have that *Mockingjay* showing at midnight. I was supposed to be taking a nap this evening," I complained with a grin.

"And how is that working out for you?"

"Not so well. It's going to be a long day at school tomorrow."

"You don't have to go to school tomorrow, you know. You could just spend the day here with me." He pulled me back down to his chest.

"Hold on just a sec."

I pulled my cell from my sweatshirt pocket. I quickly dialed my dad's number and waited for him to answer. He finally answered on the third ring. I told him I was across the street then reminded him that I was going to the midnight show and promised to be home directly afterwards. He told me to be careful and that was it. I was surprised he didn't ask me if Ethan was going.

"Is everything all right?" Jackson asked.

"Sure. Just one more thing."

I quickly texted Jenna a message asking her to call my phone at ten o'clock in case I dozed off and didn't hear my phone alarm. I knew she was sound asleep but would check her phone as soon as her eyes popped open.

"Okay. I'm good." I rolled back over and snuggled into his chest.

"This is how I want to spend the rest of my life. Holding you in my arms," he leaned down and kissed the top of my head.

CHAPTER 22

Friday, November 22, 1878

MY EYES OPENED WITH RENEWED SPIRIT. The morning light barely broke through the curtains as the grey skies threatened rain at any moment. The ground was once again covered with frost and the cold air was so thick it could be seen through thin glass.

However, none of that mattered. Things between Jackson and I were wonderful once more. Whatever issue or disagreement we experienced had been resolved *there*. I was positive about it. We were back on solid ground together and closer than before. I could feel it in my very soul. Even though I could not explain the rush of relief that flooded my entire body, I was elated to experience it.

I arose quickly and gathered my robe off my vanity chair. I washed my face with the cool water in the basin and struggled with trying to brush the knots out of my matted hair. It wasn't long before I realized that my efforts were fruitless, and Mimi was going to have to take care of it for me.

Taking a closer look at myself in the mirror, I laughed aloud in the hollow room thinking that there was no possible way I could show up at the breakfast table looking like I did. My family's opinion of my fragile state was already concerning them, and this would most certainly cause them nothing but alarm.

After a long, hot bubble bath, Mimi helped me dress before she skillfully curled my hair and pinned it up properly. She carefully applied a subtle amount of make-up to my ashen skin in a vague attempt to cover the effects of the last several weeks and the obvious toll they had taken physically on me. By the time she had completed her craft, I looked almost back to my former self.

I arrived downstairs shortly before nine. The house was quiet with only the usual sounds of the crackling fire and the staff going about their daily chores. Mother and Olivia were reading by the fire.

"Good morning. You are looking much better. How are you feeling?" My mother greeted me.

They both looked up and smiled when I entered the room.

"Wonderful, absolutely wonderful," I declared, taking a seat on the lounge.

They both gave me an inquisitive look with a hint of confusion. I casually ignored their unspoken questions and happily accepted the cup of coffee Missy brought in for me. Neither mentioned my behavior as of late or the fact that I had missed several days of school. Instead, we turned our attention to discussing various novels that we had previously read. It was a safe enough topic that filled the time without allowing them the opportunity to ask the questions they truly wanted the answers to.

William came home a short while before Sarah put dinner on the table. I heard him greet Eddie when he entered the foyer and I rushed in front of Olivia and my mother to see him, hoping desperately that Jackson was with him.

I stopped short in my steps when I saw him standing alone handing his coat and hat to Eddie.

"Good afternoon, Jocelyn. You seem to be feeling better," he happily greeted me.

"Hello William," I leaned against the doorframe disappointed. "Where is Jackson?"

"He went home."

I ran to the door and yanked it open, but my brother grabbed my arm.

"Jocelyn, wait. He said he will be here after dinner."

But I couldn't wait. I had waited long enough. I jerked my arm away from his grasp and took off out the front door. William hollered after me, but my legs were already carrying me towards the man I desperately needed to see. The chilly air whipped around my face and through my hair as I ran as fast as I could in the heavy gown.

I came to an abrupt halt on the Chandler's front porch. I hunched over breathing heavily, trying to catch my breath before I knocked on the door. Anxiety rippled through my body making it more difficult to calm my breathing.

I stood there for several minutes inwardly talking myself down, continually reminding myself that everything between Jackson and I was fine. The storm had passed and had made us stronger. However, that shred of doubt and the unknown about what the details of the disagreement contained still frightened me. I wished I had some idea of what I had done to cause such a fight that threatened the continuation of our very relationship. I had nearly driven myself insane for two days trying to uncover the answer to that very question.

I took one last deep breath and exhaled slowly as I rapped lightly on their door. Dreadful moments passed before I finally heard footsteps drawing closer.

"Miss Jocelyn, how nice to see you. Please, come in," Robert unexpectedly greeted me and stepped aside.

"Good evening, Mr. Chandler," I said, my voice slightly cracked. "Is Mr. Jackson available?"

"Of course." We walked into their front room. "Please, have a seat. Jackson is upstairs putting his things away. I will let him know you are here."

Robert placed his hand on my shoulder and gave it a gentle squeeze before exiting the room.

I stood in front of the fire and fidgeted nervously hearing the distant sounds of their staff bustling about the house. Minutes later, I turned around at the sound of footsteps descending the stairs. Jackson entered the room looking stunningly handsome in his deep gray suit. He had removed his jacket and tie but still had his vest on with his pocket watch chain dangling across his midsection.

"Hello, darling," he waltzed to me and embraced me tightly. "I have missed you this week." He leaned down and kissed the top of my head.

"Oh, I missed you too." My eyes welled up as I gazed into his emerald eyes. "I am so sorry for whatever I did to upset you," I gushed, making a smile widen across his full lips.

"I got an interesting call from my father on Wednesday about that," he chuckled. "He said you were in quite a state about it. He felt badly that he could not explain it to you."

"I see nothing funny about my torment." I dropped my arms from around his neck and walked over to the window. It had started raining lightly and the sky was starting to grow darker with evening settling in. Jackson came up behind me and wrapped his arms back around my waist.

"I am sorry, darling. I know you must have been very concerned." He rested his cheek against the top of my head, and I let myself lean back into him, giving up all unsettling feelings I had.

"I was. I woke up knowing. I mean feeling something horrible had happened between us, but I had no inkling as to what it was. It made no logical sense," I complained. "However, nothing in my life makes any sense anymore."

"I understand. I wish there was something I could do to make all this easier for you," he tightened his hold on me.

"Will you please explain to me what we had a disagreement over?" I turned to face him and pleaded for answers.

His face dropped a little further and I knew his answer before he could speak the words.

"But why not?" I almost shouted, catching even myself by surprise with my tone.

"Jocelyn."

I pulled away from him once more and paced around the room.

"Please, try and understand," he gestured with open arms.

I spun around to confront him from across the room with my hands placed firmly upon my hips. "Understand? What is there to understand? My world is falling apart around me. I am experiencing a rush of emotions that I cannot reason, and you refuse to tell me why!"

"Trust me. Everything is fine now. We worked it out Thursday after school. There is nothing for you to worry about."

He took a step closer to me.

I took a step back, and he stopped in his steps. "No. Not this time. I cannot continue to live like this. You either decide to be completely honest from this moment forward or our relationship is over!"

"You must be fair about this. There are some things I cannot discuss because it could jeopardize our future."

"Fair? Nothing about this has been fair. I am serious, Jackson. You tell me everything right now or our relationship is through."

"You cannot mean that," Jackson spoke in a low voice.

"I most certainly do."

"Jocelyn, there are some things you must understand that I cannot tell you because it will affect your life *here*," he pleaded.

Silent tears rolled down my face despite my anger with him. He was ripping my heart right out of my chest. "If that is your decision then I guess we have nothing further to discuss."

I stared at him for one last moment, begging with my eyes for him to say the right words to stop me. He didn't.

I burst into tears and fled from the room. Jackson said nothing to bring me back. He remained rooted where he stood while I ran through the rain back towards my own home.

I slammed our front door, drawing everyone's attention towards the foyer. William rushed out to investigate the racket as I ran up the stairs.

"Jocelyn!" he hollered, but I did not respond. He took the steps two at a time and caught me quickly about halfway up. "What happened? Why are you crying?"

I grabbed a hold of my dearest brother and sobbed against his chest. "It's over. The wedding is off."

"What?" He turned towards the door like he was expecting to see Jackson standing there. "What do you mean the wedding is off? What happened?"

I pulled myself away from him. "I don't want to talk about it!"

I lifted the hem of my gown and fled the rest of the way up the stairs. I didn't stop until I was safe alone in my room. I closed the door behind me and locked it. I didn't want to see or talk with anyone. I threw myself across my bed and let the tears flow freely.

I could hear the muffled sounds of voices in the foyer below. Shortly thereafter, the front door slammed. I climbed over to the bay window and saw William walking quickly towards the Chandler estate. I knew his trip was going to be fruitless. There was nothing that Jackson could tell him about why we separated.

I peeled the wet garments from my chilled skin and slipped into a warm dry nightgown. I washed my face off once again and towel dried my hair. My head was clouded while my body moved about automatically. I slid down into my vanity chair and picked up my brush. I could feel nothing. I watched the reflection staring back at me in the mirror brushing my hair in long strokes. My head jerked towards the door at the sound of someone trying to turn the handle. Realizing it was locked, the person stopped jiggling it. No voice rang out. No one knocked or called my name. Everything was silent.

The room was dark with only the light from the fire to illuminate the empty space. I watched the shadows from the flames dance along the wall as I sat alone in my window seat curled up in a blanket. No tears fell. No sharp pain was felt in my chest. That was all experienced days earlier. I slid into a place inside myself that was compiled of nothingness, devoid of all feelings and emotions.

CHAPTER 23

Friday, November 20, 2015

THE EIGHT OF US TOOK OUR SEATS in the already crowded theater. Jenna sat on one side of me while Jackson, of course, was on the other. I briefly wondered if Ethan had hooked up with some of his friends and was wandering around somewhere.

The lights dimmed, and the previews filled the screen. I leaned back against Jackson and rested my head on his shoulder. Ten minutes later the actual movie started, and I was struggling to stay awake. I glanced over at Jenna who was wide-awake and quickly becoming lost in the film.

Twenty minutes later, I was so engrossed that sleep never invaded my thoughts any further. Jackson put his arm tightly around me and whispered quietly in my ear, "See. We are not the only ones who have challenges in their relationship."

I could feel the chuckle struggling to remain silent in his chest and had to fight to stiffen my own.

"I seriously don't think it's quite the same thing," I whispered back, a nagging feeling in the back of my mind making me pause for a moment before I shook it off.

"Challenges are challenges regardless of the nature of it," he spoke softly in my ear.

"At least you're not attacking and trying to kill me," I giggled back.

"No, just two lives on parallel planes," he grinned back. "The best of both existences."

I accidentally snorted loudly at his response, which immediately caused Jenna to lean over. "If you two don't knock it off I'm going to smack you both," she glared.

Jackson and I grinned at each other, trying to restrain ourselves, which only made it worse. But Jenna just glared all the harder before turning her attention back to the screen.

As the credits rolled, we filed out of the theatre and into the parking lot. It was almost three in the morning and all of us were expected to be in class by seven-thirty. It was certainly going to be a rough day at school today. Jackson opened the passenger door for me, and I slid into the car. The same unsettling feeling I'd felt earlier washed over me, but unable to place its origin, I brushed it off.

I almost ripped my alarm clock out of the wall when it started screaming at me. I hit the snooze three times before I finally rolled out of bed and stumbled into the shower. The steam and hot water barely roused me out of my sleep-deprived stupor. My head felt groggy and congested. I knew there was no way I was going to make it through the day.

By the time I strolled into the hallway, Ethan was coming out of his room looking worse than I felt. He passed by me without uttering a word and I was too out of it to bother with him. All I could think about was going back to bed and pulling the covers over my head for the rest of the day.

Thankfully, my mom had already left for the office before I managed to make my way downstairs, but my dad was still hovering over his coffee and the morning paper. I poured myself a tall mug and joined him at the table.

"You look awful," he glanced up from the paper. "What time did you guys get in?"

"I don't know what time Ethan rolled in, but I got home around three," I muttered.

"Are you two still not speaking?"

"Not so much. He's ignoring me at this point," I shrugged. "And Mom's been leaving before I get up. She won't even talk with me in the evenings," I half complained, resting my head down on the table. "I can't believe they have such little faith in me," I whined, closing my eyes.

"It's not that. They're both just concerned," he placed his hand over mine. "So am I, but I know I'm not willing to sacrifice our relationship to prove a point. Don't worry, they aren't either. They are hurt but will come around. They always do," he tried to assure me, but in my current state, nothing mattered, but sleep.

"I know."

"You sure you really want to go to school today?"

"Mom said I had to if I went to the premiere." I barely looked up at him.

"You've been through a lot lately. I think it would be okay if you took the day off. Go back to bed and get some sleep. Don't worry, I'll call the school and drop Ethan off on my way in. I was going to take you both since Jackson called while you were in the shower and said he wasn't going to make it in," he chuckled. "I'll bet half your school doesn't show up because of all the hype surrounding the midnight showing."

"Probably not. Thanks, Daddy." I half grinned and slumped out of my chair leaving my coffee mug on the table.

Ethan stumbled into the kitchen with his sweatshirt and pants stuck to his wet body. He didn't even look like he'd attempted to towel dry his hair. He paused, looked at Dad and I, then started to walk back out.

"Ethan?" Our dad's voice halted him in his tracks.

"Yeah?" He half turned back.

"If I let you stay home today since I'm letting Jocelyn stay home also, can you two promise me not to kill each other while I'm gone?" Dad looked between us. I was pretty sure he knew neither of us had the energy to fight.

"I don't care what she does. I just want to sleep," he grumbled back.

"Jocelyn?" His eyes rested in my direction.

"Ditto," I muttered in return.

"Good. Then you both can go back to bed, but I don't want to see the house destroyed today if you both wake up with renewed energy. No fighting or you'll both be grounded," he warned before picking up his briefcase. "Sweet dreams." He kissed my cheek lightly and headed out the door.

Ethan glared over at me while I waited for him to move out of the doorway. He was blocking my exit, and I knew he was standing there just to annoy me.

"Told you I'd see the movie anyway," he grumbled.

"Good for you," I snapped back, getting aggravated enough that I pushed past him and headed up the stairs.

I flopped down across my bed and dug my cell out of my backpack. As glad as I was that my dad was letting me miss a day of school, I really didn't want to spend that time alone with Ethan. I knew we were going to start again as soon as we woke up. I dialed Jackson's number hoping he hadn't fallen back asleep yet.

"Hello?" a barely audible voice inquired.

"Jackson?"

"Yes?"

"It's me."

"Didn't your dad tell you I called?" He sounded sleepy again.

"Yes. He did. That's not why I'm calling."

"Oh. What's going on then?"

"My dad's letting me stay home today."

"That's good. Well, call me when you wake up."

"Ethan's here too."

"Oh, I see."

"Is it all right if I sleep over there?" I gushed before I could stop myself. "I just don't want to be here alone with him."

"Of course. I'll leave the front door unlocked. Come on in and make yourself at home. I'll be upstairs in my room."

"Thanks, darling. I'll be there in a minute."

I tossed my phone back into my bag and headed back downstairs. I could hear the television blaring in the family room, and I was sure Ethan had probably fallen asleep in the recliner. I opened the door as quietly as possible just to escape the argument and accusations that were sure to come.

The cold morning air hit me straight away nearly knocking the breath out of me. I wished I'd brought a heavier jacket, but there was no way I was going back inside to retrieve one. Instead, I took off in a half jog that was the best my sleepy legs could muster.

Even though I'd been in Jackson's house more times than I could count in the last month or so, as I opened their front door, it hit me that I'd never seen his room. The only time I had even been on the second floor was with Emily. I was always curious about what his room looked like. A person's bedroom is such a personal space it offers great insight into who they truly are and reflects so much of their personality. Anyone who didn't know me could simply stand in the middle of my room, look around and know everything from where I attend school, what sports I play, music I love, to the styles I'm into. I couldn't help but wonder what adorned the walls of Jackson's room.

The house was dark and lifeless. It felt so strange without Emily and Robert. I hesitated a moment as I quietly closed the front door behind me and scanned over the darkened vastness surrounding me. I stood at the foot of the stairs with my hand resting on the rail staring nervously upwards.

I slowly ascended the tiger oak stairway filled with anxiety, butterflies, and terror all jumbled together. Jackson's bedroom was at the opposite end of the hall from his parents' room. I stood in the doorway of the nearly darkened room, and I could see him lying peacefully under the covers. I walked in as quietly as I could and set my bag on top of his desk. He stirred a little and lifted his head.

"Hello, sweetheart. What took you so long?"

"It hasn't been five minutes yet." I smiled and walked to him.

He pulled the comforter back with a sleepy grin. "Come to bed. I am exhausted."

I set my jacket on the desk chair and kicked off my sneakers. He turned over on his back and I crawled in bed beside him. He was wearing pajama bottoms but was absent a shirt. He had just a small amount of hair on his chest, not even enough to run my fingers through. His pecs and abs were stunningly well defined. It was the first time I had seen him so scarcely dressed and all it did was enhance my desire for him.

I curled up beside him and rested my head on his chest. Jackson wrapped his arms around me kissing the top of my head. "Do you always sleep in so many clothes?" he inquired.

I was wearing sweat shorts, a T-shirt, and socks. It was typical sleeping apparel for me.

"Usually." I could feel his bare legs rubbing up against mine as I draped mine over his.

"Well, after we are married, we must get you something a little more appealing to sleep in," he whispered.

"Are you saying you don't like my pajamas?"

"I bet this is what you had planned on wearing to school today."

I tried not to laugh because we both knew he was right.

"Hush." I started to lean up towards his face, but he stopped me.

"Please. Don't. I am struggling enough lying here in bed holding you and if you kiss me, I am afraid I would not have the strength to stop."

"Do you want me to go home or downstairs to the couch?"

"No. Do not be silly, I'm fine. I want to hold you and never let you go." I felt his lips press softly against my hair.

"If you want me to behave, then you'd better stop that." I placed my arms over his while he held me tightly. I could feel him breathing and hear the strong steady rhythm of his heart.

"Sorry. Sweet dreams."

"Sweet dreams, my love."

The alarm on his nightstand told me it was almost three o'clock when I opened my eyes. For a minute I wasn't sure where Jackson was but then I heard him moving around in the kitchen below. I sat up and looked around. The sunlight was trying to break through the cracks in the blinds but was largely unsuccessful.

Jackson's room was painted in a grayish blue color and had posters of Walter Payton, Peyton Manning, and other football heroes scattered on the walls, alongside various awards. His desk was neat and organized, unlike my own. He had various sport trophies on top of his dresser with several pictures of family and friends tucked around the mirror. Except for being extremely clean and organized, it closely resembled my brother's room.

I felt uneasy alone in his room. I scanned over everything, taking it all in. Something was different, something had changed. I reluctantly climbed out of the warm covers and wandered aimlessly about the spacious room. I searched my brain for some clue, some trigger, something that would give me the slightest hint as to what had transpired while our bodies rested in peaceful slumber. The nagging feeling I'd felt at the movie theater rushed back even stronger than before.

Jackson walked into the room carrying a tray covered in delicious looking foods. "Good afternoon, sleepy head." His voice was cheerful and bright.

I froze to the spot I stood in. The moment my eyes reached his, I knew. It hit me so fast that it literally knocked the air right out of my lungs. Jackson stopped in the doorway and stared at me with a frightened look on his face. A wave of ice soared through my body causing me to drop to my knees. I felt close to hysterics as the realization and magnitude of it fully rested deep within my heart.

Deep sobs escaped from somewhere inside my soul. I wrapped my arms around my stomach in some futile attempt to hold myself together. Jackson dropped the tray without hesitation and rushed to my side. He pulled me into his arms as I went into full blown hysterical sobs clinging to him for my very life.

"Why? Why didn't you just tell me the truth? You let me leave!" I looked at his tear-streaked face and realized for the first time that he was crying also.

"I don't know. I couldn't," he squeaked out in a weak voice, shaking his head slowly.

I pushed him away and scrambled to my feet. Jackson gazed at me helplessly, pleading for understanding as he rose slowly. He reached out his arms for me, taking a step forward, which only made me take a step back away from him. I was too shocked and stunned with disbelief that this had happened.

"You don't know? You don't know?" I shouted through my tears. My body rippled with pain and rage.

How could he do this to me? To us?

"What the hell do you mean, you don't know? What kind of answer is that?"

"Jocelyn. Please! Let me explain," he begged.

"Oh, now you want to explain? Too little too late, don't you think?"

"We can fix this. It is all intertwined, don't you see? If we fix it *here* it will directly affect the outcome *there*. Please! Jocelyn!" He took another step towards me, but I backed away again.

My head was screaming, and my entire body was numb. Everything that I had been through, my parents, my brother. It had all been in vain. I shook my head wildly. "No! No! Not now. I can't do this now." I backed myself around the room towards the door. "I've got to go."

I blindly ducked out the doorway and took off at a sprint.

I slammed the front door and ran up the stairs. I barely made it to the bathroom before I vomited. Between the sobbing and the never-ending dry heaves, my body was spent. I splashed some cold water on my face and reached for my toothbrush.

"Are you sure you aren't pregnant?" The sound of Ethan's voice made me jump.

"Not now, Ethan! Please! Save your insults for later." I looked up at him and could see he was shocked by my appearance.

"Are you alright? What happened?" he asked in a gentle voice.

"As if you care."

"I do."

"Right," I scoffed at him, "Well, you can celebrate now. I'm not pregnant and I'm not getting married."

I started brushing my teeth leaving him standing with his mouth hanging open. I finished and rinsed my mouth before tossing my toothbrush on the counter. I turned to leave but Ethan stood blocking the doorway.

"What?" I asked in a loud tone.

"What happened?" he asked again.

"You won. That's what happened. Now get out of my way!"

I shoved him as hard as I could to get past him. He relented and watched me storm into my room and slam the door behind me.

I paced around my room trying to focus on one topic. My mind jumped back and forth between scenes from both places. I could see myself standing in Jackson's bedroom arguing with him, then I was *there* having an almost identical argument with him downstairs in his living room where we were both dressed in dated attire. I could feel the agony that ripped my heart in two for days on end. The never-ending abyss of not knowing. The dark uncertain future that loomed before me as I contemplated living without the man, I loved more than life. The pain was unreal.

I spun around my room searching for my bag when I realized I had left it on Jackson's desk. I had left my coat, bag, and cell phone in his room. I screamed out in frustration and grabbed Jackson's birthday gift, the beautiful delicate pocket-watch, off my nightstand and threw it as hard as I could against the wall. It broke into several pieces and the inside parts scattered across my floor near the broken remains.

I rushed over to the shattered metal and collapsed on the floor, gathering it up in my hands. The tears and sobs returned full force and I gave myself over to them. It was too much.

I would never again let someone into my heart.

Chapter 24

Saturday, November 23, 1878

THE RAIN PATTERED AGAINST MY WINDOW, bringing me out of a restless slumber. Tears immediately brimmed in my eyes as images of the scene in Jackson's modern bedroom replayed over again. On both planes, I witnessed the man I love refuse to be completely honest with me and fight to save our love.

I could not fathom what had transpired, that I was unaware of causing him to have such a change of heart. Then it rushed over me so quickly, like a veil had lifted over my darkened eyes. I rolled over with my eyes tightly shut. I could see the photos plainly as if I was the one holding the brittle antique album in my hands. My three babies, that were so amazingly beautiful, I would now never hold in my arms. I would never have a picturesque family that smiled lovingly from the white gazebo. My sons Gavin, Ethan, and my sweet, beautiful Alyssa would never be born into this painful existence.

It felt so silly to miss something that I'd never had in the first place, yet in some strange way, I did. I saw them, held them, loved them. We were a happy family and it had all been documented in black and white, plain as day. Why was Jackson so willing to let them go? I realized he had no way of knowing that the holes in my consciousnesses were enlarging by the day and that events were becoming vividly clear in my mind shortly after they occurred.

Should I tell him that I know about the album, the journals, his mother's wedding dress…our children? Should I inform him that he can no longer hide things from me because events are invading this world making his frivolous attempts to keep them from me pointless? No, I will not tell him.

For the life of me I couldn't understand why he was willing to believe me to be so naïve and trusting that I would never see the truth.

He knows the barrier between my two worlds is falling apart, how could he think I wouldn't discover the photos of our life together—that would now never exist?

A soft tapping on my door brought me back into this current reality and the misery it held.

"Yes," I responded in a low voice.

William hesitantly entered my room and took a seat on the corner of my bed. He looked tired like he did in the time before his own wedding, when his world was falling apart.

"How are you feeling?" he gently placed his hand on my side.

"Not well."

"What happened between you two?" His voice was gentle and full of concern, but it was impossible for me to tell him the truth. All I could do was slowly shake my head.

"I spoke with Jackson last evening." He started, but I did not want to hear it.

"William, please," I quickly interrupted him.

"Jocelyn, you two must work this out. I do not know what happened, but I am sure it is nothing that is worth losing the love of your life for."

"What did he tell you?"

"Not much really. He aggravated me more than anything," he glanced towards the window. "He told me that you called off the engagement because of something he did, but he would not go into detail. He kept saying that it was between you two and if you wanted to tell me, that was your decision, but he would not."

"The reason no longer matters. The outcome remains the same. The wedding is canceled. Our relationship is over." I brushed the tears away angrily. I wished they would just stop, but broken hearts don't tend to mend so quickly.

"Jocelyn, Jackson is destroyed. I have never seen him so distraught. Is there no possible way to work this out?"

I shook my head slightly.

"There must be a way. I have never seen two people more in love and perfectly suited for one another. You cannot throw it all away."

"I did not throw anything away. He did." The words sounded childish to my own ears. I could only imagine how they sounded to him.

William cracked a smile. "You are so incredibly stubborn."

"I wonder where I get that from, big brother?" I couldn't help but smile through my tears.

"Perhaps, but I do know that stubbornness and pride are not worth throwing away a lifetime of happiness with the one you love." He admitted.

"I did not do anything wrong. Jackson did this to us, not I."

"Now is not the time to place blame. It is a time for forgiveness," he patted my arm. "He is truly destroyed, Jocelyn. He loves you more than life and the very thought of living without you is killing him. Please, just talk with him. I know you two can work this out."

"Not this time. It is too late for that. It is over." My declaration ripped the fragile strings that were barely holding my heart intact. I leaned forward and wrapped my arms around William's neck as the hysterical sobbing took hold of me once more.

I cried for everything I had lost, everything that I was losing, everything that I would never have now that Jackson was no longer in my life. I cried until the pain overtook me and I drifted back off in a restless slumber.

It was early evening when I opened my eyes again. Only the warm glow of the embers added to the darkness. I crawled out of bed and wandered over to the bay window. I pulled the curtain aside and found my eyes resting on the house that once felt like a second home. I slid down the wall and slumped into the seat. My dry eyes could not turn away. Even the dim lights from behind their curtains no longer looked inviting.

"You should really talk with him, my dear." Mother's voice startled me out of my stupor.

"I was just checking to see if it had finally stopped raining," I lied, and we both knew it.

She came over and joined me in the window seat. "Jocelyn, I believe this entire thing has been blown way out of proportion. So, you and Mr. Jackson had a disagreement. It will happen from time to time. That is no reason to throw away a three-year relationship and call off the wedding."

"It is more involved than that, Mother."

"I am sure it is my dear, and I know that what happened is between the two of you." Instantly I felt a rush of relief. "Your father and I have been married over thirty years and during that time, we have had some heated disagreements. The ability to compromise and forgive is crucial in any successful relationship. I know you can be stubborn but allowing your pride to stand in the way of love is going to only make you unhappy."

I turned back towards the window and wondered what Jackson was doing at that moment.

Is he as miserable as I? I doubt it. How could he be? After all, this was his choice, not mine! Obviously, this is what he wanted, or he would have stopped me yesterday evening.

"Darling," I turned back to meet her eye. "Mr. Jackson is downstairs and would very much like to speak with you."

I got up and walked back over to my bed. "I have nothing to say to Jackson. Please, send him home," I stated as calmly as possible, hoping my voice wouldn't crack.

"I believe you have plenty to say to him and I think you should be honest with him."

"I was honest with him. That is what started the beginning of the end. It was he who could not be honest with me. A marriage cannot be built on dishonesty. I must know that he is not covering up something because he believes it is in my best interest to do so. Honesty and trust are the foundation of every successful marriage, and I cannot spend my life with a man whom I cannot trust to be honest with me!"

Mother came over and joined me on the bed, "I know, but love is not easy and working things out can be hard, forgiving is even harder."

"Mother," I sighed deeply. "Please, just send him home. There is nothing to work out or forgive."

"If that is what you want, my darling, I will take care of it." She hugged me tightly. "But only on one condition, you get yourself out of this nightgown, clean up and come downstairs and have dinner with your family."

"I will, but I would prefer not to join the family for dinner if that is all right with you. I really do not feel like seeing anyone just yet."

"You will have to face the family eventually, Jocelyn. No one is going to say anything, and you might as well start small. Remember, Thanksgiving is only a few days away and everyone will be here."

"Fine," I huffed. "I will be down within the hour."

"Thank you. I will send Mimi up to help you after I speak with Mr. Jackson." She smiled lovingly before she exited the room.

I returned to the window and rested my head against the cold pane hoping and praying I was making the right decision. My head believed everything I had said to my mother, but my heart was screaming at me to run downstairs and beg Jackson to forgive me for my irrational behavior. I wanted nothing more than to put things right between us, but I knew I had to stand firmly on my beliefs. I was so lost in my own thoughts that I didn't hear Mimi come up the stairs.

"He's still talkin' wif Mrs. Timmons," Mimi said on her way into my room.

"I wanted to make sure he was gone before I went downstairs," I answered flatly.

"Ah's sor ya ma'll tak car of dat, honey," she smiled warmly.

After soaking in a long, hot bubble bath and washing the tears and sweat out of my matted hair, Mimi picked out the most beautiful gown for me. I noticed while she was searching for my gowns in the armoire that the beautiful gown that Emily had designed for my birthday was suddenly missing. I said nothing about its absence since I knew I'd never wear it again anyway.

Mimi applied a little subtle make-up before she worked her magic on my hair. She hummed softly as she worked just as she always had for as long as I can remember.

"How ya holdin' up, chil?" she asked, twisting my hair.

"Not well. How are you feeling?" I gave her a weak smile and tried to change the subject.

"My back's still achin', but Ah's alri'." She lightly patted my shoulder and continued, "Ah's real sorra 'bout…" she let her voice trail off.

"Thank you, Mimi. So am I." I gently laid my hand over hers for a moment and locked my eyes with hers for a second in my reflection in the mirror.

"Ya sur?"

"Yes, I wish I was not, but I am." A single teardrop fell upon my cheek.

I joined my parents, William, and Olivia in the dining room for dinner. The men stood as I entered, and I hated feeling their eyes upon me knowing full well what each of them was thinking.

"Good evening sweetheart, you look lovely." My father came over and pulled my chair out.

"Thank you, Father."

Sarah and Cora brought the food in and the rest of them fell into mindless conversation. Although I was seated next to them their words fell on deaf ears. I aimlessly fiddled around with the food on my plate without ever tasting it. In the back of my mind, I was aware that the four of them were still paying close attention to everything I was doing, but I didn't care. I had no desire to eat. Jackson was the only nourishment my body and soul required and without him, nothing could fill that void.

I finally excused myself and fled to my room about halfway through the meal. I could no longer stand the sympathetic stares from each of them. I heard another chair scoot across the floor as I reached the stairs only to be followed by the voice of my mother telling William to let me go and give me time. For that I was very grateful.

A low rapping on the door forced me back into the dreariness that surrounded me. An image of Jackson standing on the other side of my door was the first thought that entered my mind, but the small voice in my head reminded me that he would never do such a thing and my heart sank instantly to my feet.

"Jocelyn?" Phoebe's voice whispered softly.

"Yes?"

Why would she of all people be at my door?

"May I please speak with you?"

"Of course." I walked over to the door and slowly opened it. "I apologize, I was not expecting you."

"I know. I am sorry to just drop by, but my parents told me this afternoon what happened. I wanted to see how you are doing." She walked in with hesitation and took a seat in my vanity chair.

"I see." I sat down on the edge of my bed. "How are Wallace and Mr. Silas?"

"Very well, thank you. But we both know I did not come here to discuss my family."

"Phoebe," I began, but she quickly cut me off.

"Jocelyn, you and I both know that this whole mess is completely silly and juvenile."

"Is that your way of calling me a child?" I could feel the heat rising to my cheeks.

"No....no, not at all." She got up and took a seat beside me on my bed. "What I am trying to say is that this whole *EVE* thing is very new to you and in that sense, the stage you are in with that, well you essentially are a child, an infant really." She placed her hands gently over mine.

"Jackson was not honest with me."

"I know, he told me."

"I cannot spend my life with someone whom I cannot trust to be honest with me."

"I am not saying you are wrong. What I am trying to say is that you must put a little blind faith in him and trust that what he was doing was with your best interest at heart and only for your protection."

"He did not even try to explain the truth. Does he not realize the barrier is disintegrating a little more every day and he cannot protect me from my own mind?" I pleaded.

"I do not believe he was aware of how much you were witnessing. If he was, he would have been more open to discussing things with you." Phoebe tilted her head to the side in the same fashion as her brother.

"Why did he not bother to ask me? He assumed that I was completely ignorant."

"Yes, and he was wrong and now he is paying a very high price for it, do you not agree?"

"It does not matter now, our engagement is over, the wedding — canceled." A single tear slid down my cheek and I hated myself for it.

"Jackson is miserable. I have never seen a man so destroyed." A slight snort escaped from inside me. "Jocelyn, I am serious. He is a complete mess. He cried."

"Well, he is not the only one."

"Is there no way you will reconsider speaking with him? He is so sorry for the way he has behaved and wants so badly to correct things between you."

"No. I do not believe that is possible."

"Anything is possible," Phoebe chuckled. "If you have learned anything recently with this whole *EVE* gift, it is that."

A slight smile slid across my lips. "Very true, but that does not apply to the area of love or relationships."

"I believe it does," she stated flatly.

"Then we will have to agree to disagree," I retorted.

"I know there is so much about all of this you cannot see right now. But I know my brother loves you dearly and you love him also. I know you do."

"Yes, very much so. But this has nothing to do with lack of love. It is about trust and honesty and his lack of putting his in me."

"He does have trust in you. However, it seems to me that you lack a great deal of faith in him. He was only trying to protect you, not be deceiving in any way," she said angrily as she stood up and walked over to the door. "You know something Jocelyn, if this is how much faith you have in my brother then perhaps, he is better off without you."

"Perhaps he is Phoebe. Perhaps you should go tell him that. I did not want this — this *EVE* curse. This awakening. This new world that has been thrust upon me. I hate it. I hate that I have little control over every aspect of my life now. I cannot tell what is real, what is a memory or what is simply part of my overactive imagination. This is not the life I wanted. I wish I could change everything back to the way it was before this entire nightmare began."

"Don't you realize that we all went through this?" she walked back towards me. "We understand everything you are going through because we each experienced it as well. Therefore, you must trust us when we tell you some things are better left unknown."

She tried to put her hand on my shoulder, but I backed away from her. "You had your family there for you. I do not. My parents, and obviously none of my brothers, inherited this curse. Only me. I am the one who must face this alone," I said softly.

"You are not alone Jocelyn. We are all here for you, especially Jackson. Plus, you have your Uncle Monte."

"My Uncle Monte? He has never bothered to discuss any of this with me. Not once," I scoffed back.

"Maybe he does not know how much you need him. He probably believes that since you have my family you are doing well with the transition. Maybe you should go talk with him," she suggested.

"No, I cannot do that. He obviously wanted to put the whole *EVE* thing behind him. Otherwise, he would have tried to talk to me since he found out

I have it also," I said in a low voice. "He is happy now. I cannot dredge up a past that he worked so hard to put behind him."

"I am sure he would be more than happy to talk with you."

"Phoebe, I do appreciate your concern for me about *EVE* and especially my relationship with your brother or the lack thereof. But I really would like to be alone right now if you do not mind."

"You know you cannot hide from everyone forever." She picked up a throw pillow off my bed and absentmindedly fluffed it.

"I am not hiding from anyone."

"All right, but would you please hear Jackson out? He loves you so very much. He needs you. You two are so perfect for each other and I hate to see you both in so much pain." She tossed the pillow back onto my bed.

"I will think about it. I promise." I was about to promise her anything if it meant she would go away.

She walked over and hugged me tightly. "Thank you, I know you will make the right decision." She kissed my cheek and left without another word.

I paced around my room recalling my conversation with Phoebe. I wished it were so easy to do as she suggested, but I knew it wasn't. I could never have the voice *here* to say or do as I please. There were so many things passing through my mind that I could never let slip pass my lips…not *here*, not in this time. In this time, I was not allowed to have a voice of my own, it was simply not proper for a lady to speak her mind. I truly hated that.

CHAPTER 25

Saturday, November 21, 2015

I LAY WITH MY EYES CLOSED, not wanting to face the long, lonely hours that were to come. The soothing sounds of the rain on the roof brought some comfort, but not much. I pulled the covers up over my head and dreaded the fourteen million questions that I knew were coming. I was sure the news of what had happened yesterday afternoon had already circulated amongst our group and probably others by now. I could only imagine the rumors, the speculation, the accusations—but those were the least of my problems. The love of my life was gone.

The very thought of living without Jackson pulled the breath from my lungs and sucked the life right out of me. I reached under my bed and pulled out the antique photo album. Resting it in on my lap, I sat staring at the cover wondering if the photographs had somehow changed, altered in some strange way now that events had so dramatically veered off the course of the past and somehow taken my future with it.

I took a deep breath and reluctantly opened the cover. Staring up at me was the exact same photograph that I'd previously seen, Jackson and I smiling happily on our wedding day. The appearance of it triggered tears and shot a sharp stabbing pain through the middle of my chest. It felt like a hot dagger had plunged deep into my heart. Hyperventilation took over as I closely studied the face of the man who meant everything to me. My very existence was wrapped totally around his, my happiness, my sorrow, my very soul, every breath I would ever take was intrinsically linked with him.

I flipped through the pages for the next several hours, memorizing the smallest details of every one of them. I couldn't stop myself—the power of what was lost was hypnotizing. My aching head could not grasp the realization that these gorgeous children, our children, my children, would never exist. I wrapped my arms tightly around myself and gently rocked back and forth numbly trying to accept what was lost.

But I couldn't. I pushed the album off my lap and climbed out of bed. My mind was racing, there had to be a way, some way I could stop this pain. My hands twisted nervously while I scrambled for a solution that would save us both from a lifetime of misery. I knew I would never love again. But I also knew that I could not stand the thought of seeing Jackson. Having him near me, on either plane, was killing me. I couldn't stand the thought of him moving on with his life, finding someone else, falling in love, marrying her, and having the children that were destined to be mine.

My eyes landed on my Uncle Monte's journals resting safely on my nightstand. The very answer I needed was sitting right there before me. I wondered if it was at all possible for me to do what my uncle had done.

Could I leave that place forever and only have a life in 2015? Could I never see my family or my friends again?

If I did, if that is what I decided to do, I knew I would have to give Jackson up *here* as well.

Besides, with us no longer getting married there, we would have no reason to get married here. In fact, he and his family could then move back to Boston, and we could all go on with our lives before all this insanity ever began.

The heaviness in my chest grew deeper and settled into a mind-numbing pain. Thanksgiving was less than a week away. That would give me time to absorb all I could and a chance to say good-bye. On Thanksgiving night, I would speak with my Uncle Monte alone about how he left one plane to live happily in the other. I knew the only way I could survive a life without Jackson was to not survive.

I showered quickly, fully determined to do what I had to do. It was the only way to ease the pain. I threw on some old jeans and a hooded sweatshirt. My wet hair was brushed back away from my face, but I had no desire to fix it or put on any make-up. Appearances didn't matter anymore.

The house was quiet with only the sound of the television coming from the family room. I numbly opened the front door without a word to anyone. I closed the door behind me, and the cold air slapped me across the face, but I continued forward.

I walked past Jenna's house and thought of the photograph of Jackson and me standing on her front porch. I shook my head blindly trying to force the image from my brain. The rain was coming down in sheets soaking through my clothes. My jacket, I assumed, was still draped over Jackson's desk chair.

I continued down the sidewalk, my mind flashing back and forth between the concrete beneath my feet and the cobblestoned one that was here yesteryear. The barrier was crumbling and in its place was the realization that the world around me was no longer as it once seemed. My feet wandered where my heart wanted to go without any conscious effort by my brain.

Blocks away from my house stood a park that I had played in throughout my childhood. The various playground equipment, basketball courts, the baseball diamonds on one corner and soccer fields on the other had replaced what I now knew was once a scenic reign of beauty. The lavish rows of flowers, the cobblestone walkways, the multiple rows of blossoming trees had all been replaced by the modern world, just like everything else. Progress.

My feet carried me to the spot where the gazebo had once stood. A place where my happy family had once gathered for a picture, where Jackson had asked me to be his wife, a place where he had told me the truth about William and Olivia, where we'd had the most intimate talks. It had been torn down. Just as our love had been.

I sat down on the saturated ground letting the rain pour down on me. It was bitter cold. The wind whipped around me blowing the rain in every direction. Yet I felt nothing. No rain, no wind, nothing but emptiness.

"You are going to catch pneumonia sitting out here like this." His voice came up behind me. I didn't even bother to turn and look. I knew Jackson was standing only a few feet away from me.

"Jocelyn, please," he hesitated, expecting a reply, but I had none.

I wondered how long he would stand there waiting for me to say something. I closed my eyes and waited for him to disappear. He didn't.

"Will you please speak to me? I know we can work this out."

He sat down beside me and tried to put his arm around me, but I shrugged him off.

"Will you please leave me alone?" I continued to look at the ground.

"No, I love you. I want to marry you — *there* and *here*. I want to spend my life with you. I know you still love me. You would not be sitting here, in this place, if you did not," he pointed out.

"Of course, I still love you. That's not the point, Jackson, and you know it." I still wouldn't look at him.

"That *is* the point, Jocelyn. If two people love each other, there is nothing so great that they cannot work out," he said softly.

"Jackson, please go away. I really want to be alone," I begged. His being here with me made everything all the worse.

"Not until we talk first." His persistence was beyond irritating. I could feel the frustration building within me. I knew I needed to talk with him, tell him everything that I was thinking. I just didn't know how to start. I knew he was not going to make it easy. In fact, I expected him to make it as difficult as possible.

"Fine, you want to talk? Let's talk," I finally relented and faced him.

"Jocelyn why are you acting this way?" His eyes were clouded, and raindrops were dripping from his nose and eyelashes.

"Acting what way?"

"Cold."

"It's freezing out here."

"That is not what I meant."

"I know what you meant. I was being literal." I wished he wouldn't look at me. Those green eyes that I loved so much, I hated looking at them.

"Jocelyn," he lowered his eyes and fidgeted with his hands. "I hate fighting with you."

"I hate fighting with you too." I took a deep breath trying to gather up my courage. "That is why I believe it would be best for both of us if you went back to BU. You can start the spring semester and move on with your life. You can leave this mess behind you and never look back."

"What?" He looked stunned by my words. "What do you mean? You want me to leave?"

I nodded slowly while my heart screamed out in agony. "If we aren't getting married *there*, then there's no reason for us to be together *here*. Our marriage was the only reason you came in the first place anyway," I reasoned.

"My leaving is not going to change anything, Jocelyn," he stated flatly.

"Yes, it will. I won't have to look at you every day. We can both try to start putting our lives back together. I can't do that with you here. It's too hard." I hated myself for the tears that started up again.

"I will still be *there*," he claimed softly before the realization of what I meant fully set in. "No!" he exclaimed. Jackson's face twisted up in pain.

"It's the only way either of us can move on," I claimed.

"Please, Jocelyn. Do not do this! Think of what it will do." His breathing increased. "This will kill your family! Think of Annabelle, Patrick…" he stood up and began pacing back and forth in front of me. "How can you do this to them? How selfish can you be?" Jackson raised his voice over the sound of the rain.

I climbed to my feet to confront him. "I'm not being selfish. I'm trying to put my life back together after you demolished it!" I shouted back. "And I barely even know them. They aren't even real to me at this point. They're more of a weird dream than anything else!" I screamed knowing full well we both knew I was lying. "Besides, you're the one who came here, lied about your age, integrated yourself within my group of friends, turned my world upside down, and now my family is torn apart! My mother and my brother aren't even speaking to me because of you. Don't you think you've done enough damage?"

We faced one another with a silent tension filling the space between us. Jackson fumed in frustration. His face was turning pink despite the cold air, and he placed his hands in his pockets to keep them from shaking. I wasn't exactly sure what he was going to do to try and sabotage my plan, but I was positive he was going to do something.

"Is that what you really think?" he questioned.

"Yes!" I struggled to remain strong.

"Why would you even consider something so devious? You have an amazing family that loves you more than you realize. They would be devastated if they lost you." His eyes softened a bit.

"I am trying to be logical. I know this world. I'm comfortable here. I have a life here."

"You have a life *there! We* have a life *there!*"

"Jackson, please." I shifted my weight and started to feel the cold dampness in my bones for the first time. "Try to understand," I pleaded. "*That* life is still not entirely real to me yet, but this one is. I want to end this before the holes in my consciousness get any larger and it becomes impossible to do so. I haven't reached that point yet. Now, while it still feels mostly surreal and if I keep telling myself it is, I can put it all behind me."

"You honestly believe that hurting them just to hurt me is going to make this all better?"

"I am not deliberately hurting them," I rebuked. "I don't even know them."

"Yes, you do. Look into your heart and you know that is true," he stated hotly.

I could not meet his eye, I knew what he was saying was true, but I couldn't admit that, especially to myself. If I kept reminding myself that they weren't, I'd be able to do this. The pain would be too much if I admitted it.

"Jackson, please just go back to Boston. Go to school and move on with your life. I want you to be happy."

He took a step forward, reaching out for me. I was frozen in my stance. "I will never be happy without you in my life." His hands rested on my arms. His powerful green eyes implored me. "You are my life, Jocelyn. I will never stop loving you. Please. Do not ask me to walk away."

"I have no other choice. Don't you understand that?"

"You do have a choice. We can work this out. I know we can."

"Why didn't you tell me the truth *there?*" I had to know.

Jackson's face went blank. "How much are you seeing?" he questioned in a low voice.

"How do you expect us to work this out if I cannot trust that you will always be honest with me?"

"You have not answered me, Jocelyn. How much are you aware of on both planes?"

I immediately jerked myself away from his grasp and took a couple steps back. "Does it matter? You're going to lie to me anyway, for my own good. I can't believe anything that you say to me!" I sobbed through the tears and the rain. Jackson's face looked pain stricken.

"Jocelyn," he stepped towards me.

In great haste, I fled across the field. My lungs screamed for air as I ran as fast as my legs would carry me. I heard him call out to me a couple more times, but I never stopped. I didn't trust myself. I knew he would wear me down and I would give in. I loved him more than life. It was killing me to let him go. My heart splintered into pieces with every step that carried me away from all I had ever wanted.

Jenna came by before dinner. I had Ethan tell her I was sick and would call her later. He gave me a pitiful look but did as I asked. I wasn't sure if he'd told her about our break-up. It really didn't matter either way, she'd find out soon enough. Everyone would.

My dad knocked on my door right before ten o'clock, waking me out of an exhausted sleep brought about by endless tears and a throbbing headache.

"Jocelyn?" he whispered, poking his head in my room.

"Yeah?" I forced my eyes open.

He entered and took a seat on my bed. I could tell he was carrying something but couldn't make out what he held in his hands.

"How ya feelin'?" he lightly patted my leg.

"Guess Ethan told you."

"Yeah."

"Great," I muttered under my voice.

"Jackson dropped this off earlier for you." He put my bag and jacket on my desk chair. "He also wanted me to give you this and to tell you that loves you and he's sorry for all his shortcomings."

I half sat up in my bed and turned on the lamp on my nightstand. My dad handed me a sealed ivory envelope with my name on it in Jackson's familiar handwriting.

"I'm not sure what happened between you two and I know it's none of my business, but I do know you, and you have never once acted impulsively. For you to make such a declaration of love in such a short amount of time leads me to believe that it had to be the real thing," he smiled lovingly at me.

"I do love him, Daddy, more than anything. I can't imagine spending my life with anyone else," I confirmed softly.

"Then if you truly love him, baby, there's nothing you can't work out. The boy's a mess, I've never seen a young man so heartbroken," he laughed lightly. "And to be perfectly honest, Pumpkin, you don't look so great either."

"Gee thanks, Daddy, you really know how to make someone feel better." I couldn't help but crack a smile.

"Relationships are difficult at best, and men are jerks. To put it nicely," he laughed. "We are stupid, prideful creatures who hate to admit when we're wrong."

"I won't argue with you on that."

"But *your* young man knows what he did was wrong, and I believe him when he says he's sorry. I've never seen someone look so pitiful. You really should consider hearing him out." He gave me a mournful, pleading look.

"I'll think about it," I said just to appease him.

"Good. Well, you get some sleep. I'll see you in the morning." He leaned over and kissed my forehead. "Sweet dreams."

"You too, Daddy."

I waited until my door was safely closed before ripping open the envelope. I was terrified to see what Jackson had to say. My hands shook steadily as I attempted to remove the pages. His elegant handwriting gleamed up at me from the parchment.

My Dearest Jocelyn,

I have given the greatest consideration to everything we have discussed and all that you said to me in the last two days. I apologize for being so thoughtless. I was only trying to protect you. I am afraid I was unaware of how much you were witnessing and the extent of the disintegration of your consciousness between your two worlds. My only excuse for my behavior is that I was attempting to protect you there from the realization of your accidental discovery here. My concern was in your knowing too much about what your future held and the impact it could have on you.

I assure you that I only had the sincerest of intentions in my decision. I would never do anything to disappoint you or cause you to doubt your ability to trust and have faith in my love for you. I implore you to reconsider your decision. I understand your reasoning and to prevent such drastic actions, I have decided to relocate upon the completion of my courses. I promise you that I will in no way interfere with your life.

As far as your life here is concerned, I apologize for all the discord I have caused.

I never intended to upset you or your family. Therefore, I have come to the decision to return to Boston this evening. I will be residing with my sister and her family and will make the necessary arrangements to resume my classes at the university in the spring. My parents shall be returning after the holiday to arrange for the sale of our home here. I will not be returning. I sincerely apologize for any inconvenience I have put upon you, your family, and your friends.

I do want you to know that I am always here for you. I will always love you with all my heart and soul. Nothing or no one will ever take your place in my heart. If you ever feel alone or ever need a friend, I will be here for you until the very end.

Love Always & Forever,

Jackson Chandler

His words stabbed right through my heart. I dropped the letter and dashed over to the bay window throwing the curtains aside. Jackson's house sat lonely and dark in the night. His CRV was missing from its usual location. I grabbed my cell phone out of my bag and dialed his number as fast as my fingers would move. It went straight to voicemail. I threw the phone on my bed in despair. He was gone! Even though he had done exactly what I had requested of him, the realization that I would never set eyes on his beautifully sculpted face again was unbearable.

I collapsed into a ball on the window seat, crying out in agony. The future that was so certain such a short time ago had slipped through my fingers. My husband to be, my children, the happy life that had been carefully documented was all but gone. My life, the very essence of my being, the reason for my existence had disappeared in a matter of moments. All I could do was weep.

Chapter 26

Sunday, November 24, 1878

WILLIAM KNOCKED LIGHTLY ON MY DOOR before entering my room. I was still seated in the window looking longingly across the street. I just wanted to catch a glimpse of him when he left for church. I had to see him. The last vision I had of him could not be of the two of us standing in the rain arguing and me fleeing.

Why had I been so stubborn? Why didn't I tell him how much I love him, that I was sorry? Why didn't I beg him to forgive my foolishness? Why didn't I put an end to all this stupidity when he came over to speak with me?

"He is not there," William's voice broke the silence of my hollow room.

"What do you mean? Where is he?"

I couldn't take my eyes off his house. I saw Emily and Robert walk out the front door and Robert helped her into their carriage. They had closed the door behind them with no Jackson anywhere to be seen.

"He left late last night for his aunt's place in Boston." He came over and sat down on the other end of the window seat. His face was sad and concerned. "He said he would be back for finals on campus but plans on returning to Boston for a couple weeks to study for the bar. He told me last night that instead of joining his father's practice, he has decided that he is going to join his uncles in Boston."

A silent tear ran down my cheek as the complete magnitude of my decision fully set in.

"Jackson said that without you, he could not bring himself to stay here." He reached out and pulled me into his arms. "I am so sorry, Jocelyn."

I curled up in the security of my brother's arms and wept uncontrollably. It was truly over. He was gone forever.

CHAPTER 27

Sunday, November 22, 2015

I WOKE UP CRAMPED IN A BALL on the window seat. My legs and back ached from the uncomfortable position my body had been in for hours. The faded light couldn't break through the cloud-covered skies. The rain had stopped, but the moisture still held heavy over the air. I stretched my muscles and my head screamed out in pain. The long hours of sobbing had taken its toll both mentally and physically.

I made my way over to my bed and flopped across it. I never wanted to move. I closed my eyes just wishing the world around me would disappear and take me with it. I shifted my legs and heard paper crumbling beneath me. I pulled Jackson's note back into view. It was smudged with tears. I held it tightly in my hands rereading each carefully chosen word he'd written to say farewell and knew they would haunt me for the rest of my life.

Jenna arrived in the early afternoon after several unsuccessful tries to reach me on my cell. She never bothered to knock, just walked in, and sat down on the corner of my bed. I barely opened my eyes when I felt her weight disrupt the loneliness of my hell.

"Jocelyn?"

"What?" I muttered, closing my eyes once again. Even the small amount of light in my dreary room hurt my aching head.

"Can I get you anything?"

"No."

"Ethan told me what happened. I'm sorry." She reached over and brushed my hair away from my face.

"Doesn't matter," I whispered, feeling the tears sting my eyes again.

Silence filled the four walls. She had no words to ease my pain and we both knew nothing she could say would. She continued to stroke my hair doing the only thing she could think of, and it was more than I deserved. If I hadn't been so hard-headed, so prideful, so incredibly stubborn, and stupid, I would have Jackson in my arms at this moment. I had no one to blame for the hell I was consumed in but myself. Jackson tried relentlessly to speak with me, explain his behavior, and I would not listen. I had shoved him away, asked him to leave my life and never return.

How can I blame him for doing precisely what I asked?

I knew I could not.

Jenna stayed beside me for the remainder of the day. Though we rarely spoke, and she never inquired as to the details of our break-up, her very presence was a great comfort.

CHAPTER 28

Wednesday, November 27, 1878

I NUMBLY LISTENED TO ELIZABETH CHATTER about her and her mother's endless preparations for the arrival of Lee's family that evening and the enormous amount of food necessary for hosting such a large holiday feast. The moist, chilly wind blew around us as we made our way the several blocks to school. She was being kind in trying to fill the silence with mindless chatter and to distract me from the thought my mind possessed.

The news of our separation had already made its rounds, and everyone was giving me pitiful looks and offering their condolences. I hated the way everyone was staring at me and even worse, the hushed whispers behind my back when they naively believed me to be out of earshot. The countless speculations on the whereabouts of Jackson and his sudden disappearance placed all the blame of his departure on my shoulders.

Maryanne and another classmate of ours, Greta, were huddled together at the bottom of the steps of the main entrance, whispering and giggling in our direction as Elizabeth, Laurie, Christina, and I approached.

"Perhaps I will call upon Mr. Jackson to make sure he is doing all right. I would hate to think of him spending Thanksgiving all alone," Maryanne giggled. "You realize Greta, Miss Jocelyn certainly is not as bright as her new sister-in-law. If she would have gotten herself in a family way too, perhaps Mr. Jackson never would have left her."

"It is most likely the only way she would be able to keep a man like that. But then again, he would have to touch her first and that is most unlikely," Greta responded laughing.

I stopped in my tracks causing the other three girls to stop also. Elizabeth placed her hand gently on my arm. "Pay them no mind, Miss Jocelyn," she said calmly.

"Not this time," I said hotly and stalked over to where the other two were waiting, knowing full well they'd aroused my attention.

"Hello, Miss Jocelyn. I am sorry to hear you have had a difficult week," Maryanne smirked.

"Well, I must say, you seem very satisfied with yourself," I stated coyly.

"What is that supposed to mean?" Greta asked, looking ignorant.

I rolled my eyes at her and focused my attention back on Maryanne. "You know it is such a shame that Mr. Jackson is visiting family in Boston. However, Mr. Dimitri happens to still be in Chicago," I couldn't help myself. "I would hate to think of *him* spending the holidays alone. I was uncertain as to whether I was going to call upon him this afternoon and invite him over tomorrow evening for some dessert, now I believe I will."

"Mr. Dimitri would never give you the time of day," she stated coldly.

"We shall see about that," I sneered.

"We will work our problems out. You stay away from him," she demanded.

"It seems to me Mr. Dimitri does not believe it is going to snow in hell any time soon," I snickered.

Maryanne was flabbergasted, much to my own selfish enjoyment. "I do hate you, Jocelyn Timmons! You deserve all the pain and heartache from losing Mr. Jackson that I suffered losing Mr. Dimitri. I truly hope you are miserable!" she shouted, her face turning beat red.

"Thank you, Maryanne. I appreciate that. It is such a comfort to know that there are people like you in this world who take such pleasure in other people's misfortunes. I am sure that someday you will get everything you deserve," I said evenly before walking away.

Laura, Christina and even Elizabeth were snickering when I rejoined them. "Sorry," I apologized to them. "I could not help myself."

"Understandable," Laura giggled.

"I could not have said it better myself," Christina added. "Are you really going to invite Mr. Dimitri over for dessert?"

"Of course not," I whispered back. "I just wanted to get a rise out of her. As much as I think of Mr. Dimitri, I am not interested in being counterproductive in working things out with Jackson."

"I believe you are right," Elizabeth concluded, and the other two nodded in agreement.

William was waiting for me in the front room when I returned home. The house seemed unusually quiet for midafternoon, and I wondered where everyone had gone.

"How were your classes today?" he greeted.

"Fine." I sat down beside him by the hearth trying to warm myself up.

"Are you feeling any better?" he inquired.

"No," I smiled glumly. "But I am afraid it is my own fault. I am the one who told him to go away."

William gave me a confused look. "Why in the world would you do that?"

"Is it not obvious?" I stared off into the flames. "I am stupid." I hated the tears that welled back up in my eyes.

"You are not stupid," he half-laughed. "Selfish perhaps, but not stupid." He placed his hands over mine attempting to comfort me.

"Well, I suppose I am that also," I sighed heavily. "I only wish I could speak with him and apologize."

"I believe you should," he smiled brightly. "Then perhaps we can put all of this foolishness behind us."

"I wish it were so easy."

"It is," he acted thrilled by the prospect.

"No, it is not I am afraid. I believe that this time I went too far and nothing I could say to him could make him reconsider his decision." I brushed the tears aside.

"I do not believe that for one-minute, little sister. I know Jackson very well and his love for you, his faith in you, will never wane," he squeezed my hand firmly.

I shook my head somberly wishing I too could be so naïve in spirit and belief. "William please, I do not enjoy entertaining such topics. Let us not speak of it again."

I patted the top of his hand and rose out of the rocking chair to leave.

As I exited the room William responded, "Only you can set this right, Jocelyn."

"That is exactly what I intend to do — tomorrow night," I whispered back under my breath, so he could not hear me.

I sat in my window seat, staring out into the evening sky, wishing that I had more time. More time to absorb every fiber, every smell, every single detail of my life *here* before I let it go forever. With the gaps increasing daily it was becoming almost exhausting trying to keep it all straight. Thank goodness for the drastic differences in the fashion and all the other variances. It was the only thing that was allowing me to maintain some semblance of sanity.

I knew without the guidance of Jackson and his parents, the possibility of me preserving anything remotely close to sanity as the barrier in my consciousness crumbled between my two lives was minuscule. Just in the last five days since their departure, I had been feeling as if I was constantly walking on quicksand, falling through time from one plane to the other without any true rest or solace in between.

The darkness covered the outside world like a warm blanket. Everything around me was peaceful and calm. The aroma of Sarah's amazing cooking drifted beneath my door letting me know that dinner would be on the table shortly. I knew the comforting sense of home that her cooking brought me would never be found *there* and I felt a dreaded sense of loss. Amy was barely capable of boiling water and the mere thought made me smile.

The absurdity of the reality that I was living in was nothing short of unimaginable. The many hours that I spent fixating on the concept, attempting to somehow wrap my fragile brain around this ever-increasing insanity, had only reinforced my decision to end it now. I wanted the fog to lift and disappear forever. I wanted to be normal again, whatever that may be. The impossible paradox that I existed within flooded every sense of reality that I waded through. Nothing seemed real anymore. I no longer had any inkling as to who I was supposed to be.

Perhaps it was all simply a dream.

I was ready to awaken.

CHAPTER 29

DESPITE THE FACT THAT JACKSON HAD LEFT for Boston and had not been at school all week, my dear sweet brother was kind enough to let everyone know that my relationship with Jackson had ended. It seemed I was getting looks and whispers behind my back constantly from people in the school. By the time I sat down at our table in the cafeteria, my nerves were shot.

I angrily set my lunch down on the table and kicked what would normally have been Jackson's seat out of my way. "Could this day get any worse?"

"Just ignore them. It's no one's business what happened," Jenna tried to comfort me.

"I hate high school," I muttered, picking at the disgusting pizza in front of me.

"I'm sure by the time we come back from Thanksgiving break there will be something new to occupy their time," Caitlyn offered.

"Is Jackson coming back?" Zak leaned around Caitlyn and asked. Caitlyn shot him a dirty look and elbowed him in the ribs. "What? I'm just asking because Coach was pissed that he took off without saying anything and missed practices all week."

"I don't know, Zak," I stated flatly.

I couldn't bring myself to answer him honestly. In the back of my heart, I didn't want to admit the truth even to myself. I wanted to cling to the hope that Jackson would come rushing back and take me into his arms and all would be forgiven.

"Nice, Zak." Hilary glared at him from across the table.

"No, really," I sighed and pushed my lunch tray away from me. "I'm sorry, Zak. I really don't know anything. I haven't spoken to him since he left."

Zak nodded and thankfully dropped the subject.

I was almost feeling better when Taylor and Dakota came up behind me purposely, casually carrying their lunches. The two of them paused long enough to flaunt their delight in my pain.

"You knew it was only a matter of time before he dumped her. He was way too good for her," Dakota smirked.

"Yeah, he probably dumped her when he found out she wasn't pregnant. Guess she had to lie to try and keep him. It's not like he would be with her for any other reason," Taylor laughed.

Something inside my head snapped and I saw red for the first time ever in my life. Before any of my friends could even think of responding to the two of them, I shoved myself back from the table, ramming my chair into Dakota. Without any thought whatsoever, I tackled Taylor down to the cafeteria floor between the tables.

I blindly started swinging at her smug hateful face. I was vaguely aware of the muffled voices screaming around me as I screamed out everything I had ever thought of this girl since grade school while continually pounding my fists against her face. All the anger, all the hurt, all the frustration that had been building up in me for weeks came pouring out in a blind rage like nothing I had ever experienced before in my life.

Mrs. Neal-Beliveau grabbed me under my arms and pulled me off Taylor. I was still screaming and throwing punches, trying my damnest to free myself so I could continue pounding on Taylor as my biology teacher literally dragged me out of the cafeteria.

"Jocelyn Timmons!" she shouted in my ear, "Calm down!" She held me tightly against her in the hall until I finally returned to my senses.

"Are you okay?" she asked, and I nodded still fuming, but calmer. "Can I let you go, and you won't do anything stupid?"

"Yes."

She released me, and I leaned back against the wall and slid down completely spent.

"What in the world has gotten into you, Jocelyn?" she kneeled beside me.

"I'm so sick and tired of her thinking she owns this place. She prances around here like some queen with her smart remarks making people feel like crap." I looked up into her understanding eyes. "She and Dakota made a couple snide comments about Jackson and I breaking up and I snapped," I explained.

"I'm sorry. I understand what you're going through." She looked at me and laughed. "Believe it or not, I was in high school once too. I know how those girls are. The same ones went to my school. You realize that even though time has passed, the crowds are still the same. It has always been that way and it always will be. Only the styles change. But there will always be jocks, cheerleaders, nerds, geeks. Every high school in the country is the same."

"Yeah, you're right. It's just she's been a wench since grade school, her, and Dakota both."

Normally I would never talk to a teacher like this, but Mrs. Neal-Beliveau was different. She treated us like we were people, not just something she had to deal with between summer breaks.

"Taylor has been relentless in her pursuit of Jackson since he moved here and today, she danced all over my last nerve and I snapped."

"You know that's no excuse for your behavior."

"I know."

The cafeteria door swung open and Mr. Dunn, our chemistry teacher, came out aiding a sobbing Taylor who was holding a wad of napkins against her bloody nose. The rest of her face was already swollen and bright red.

"I'll meet you both down in Mrs. Cosgrove's office," Mr. Dunn said.

I wasn't sure, but I could've sworn I saw him smile slightly over at us.

"We'll be down in a moment. Is she all right?" Mrs. Neal-Beliveau inquired with a half grin despite herself.

"She'll be fine. We are going to stop at the nurse's office for some ice," he replied.

Taylor was still sobbing like a baby as they walked off.

"You did a nice job on her."

I glanced over at my teacher who seemed to be doing her best to restrain herself from smiling.

"Thanks." I couldn't help it; I busted out laughing and she joined in.

"Oh, we're terrible," she wiped her eyes. "The high school kid in me always wanted to do that." She leaned back and shook her head. "You do know we never had this conversation, right?"

"Nope, never. You've been out here chastising me for my childish behavior," I smirked.

"You do know you might end up with an extra-long vacation for this."

"Yeah, and my parents will be so thrilled."

"Probably, but look at the bright side,"

I looked over at her confused.

What could be the bright side in all this except that I finally got to do what every girl in school has been dying to do?

"At least you've already sent in your college applications."

"True." I laughed again, and she joined me. I was glad that it was her that was with me.

"Come on. Might as well get this over with." She stood back up and offered me her hand.

Principal Julia Cosgrove was seated behind her desk looking upset when the four of us entered. Her long, curly brown hair was in disarray and behind her glasses her big brown eyes looked overwhelmed. Her desk was cluttered with papers and post-it notes. She crossed her arms and sat back in her chair looking like this was the last thing she wanted to deal with today. It immediately made me feel guilty, not for attacking Taylor, but for making Mrs. Cosgrove deal with it.

I got a three-day in-school suspension thanks to both Mr. Dunn and Mrs. Neal-Beliveau who told Principal Cosgrove that Taylor started it. As I sat in her office with both teachers, Taylor, and the principal, I realized neither of them said I threw the first punch, was the one who tackled Taylor in the cafeteria, only that Taylor was responsible for starting the altercation.

Taylor whined when she received a five-day out of school suspension along with a three-game cheerleading suspension. I had to fight not to smile at her battered and bruised face when she was informed that her suspension meant all her homework and exams that week would go into the books as zeroes, and she couldn't make up the work.

I was silently thrilled that although I had to spend three days sitting in the office, at least I could still turn in my work and get credit. At least there was some justice in this screwed up reality.

I walked out of the school with my dad, fully anticipating him to start in on me for being so stupid and childish.

I climbed into his car waiting for the bomb to drop. I couldn't imagine how long I was going to be grounded for this one. He turned the key before he finally looked my way. "I only have one question for you," he started.

"Yes?" My voice was almost a squeak.

"I saw Taylor. Where are your injuries?" he smiled, raising his eyebrows.

"Not a scratch." I couldn't stiffen my smile and his grin widened.

"That's my girl!" he laughed.

I fidgeted around my room, putting my things away after destroying my room last weekend. I flipped on the radio and began singing along trying to distract myself when Buckcherry's *Sorry* began to play. I didn't want to hear it, but I couldn't turn it off either. It's such a beautiful honest song. My voice began to crack, and the tears started all over again. I found myself absentmindedly drawn to my bay window where I stood softly singing along in my cracking voice, staring at Jackson's silent house.

I slowly sat down in the window seat and leaned my forehead against the cold pane. His house looked as empty and hollow as I felt. The tears ran silently down as the song finally ended. I hastily stomped over and switched my player off and brushed the tears aside. My alarm told me that I had another hour or so before everyone else got out of school. I truly hated idle time these days. My heart always overtook my mind and strayed back to the longing pain for Jackson.

I picked up my uncle's journal and returned to my window seat with a fleece blanket. I snuggled into it and opened the journal across my lap, yet my eyes diverted back across the street again. I knew what I had to do after Thanksgiving dinner *there*. I would have to get my uncle alone and somehow get him to tell me how he left this life to remain solely *there*. I wasn't sure how receptive he was going to be, but I knew I had to convince him to tell me how he did it.

With the holes in my consciousness becoming larger by the day, the more difficult it was going to be to leave my *other* family and friends behind. I didn't want to hurt them, and I knew this was going to be very difficult on them all. I felt so selfish for deliberately putting them through this because I couldn't cope with witnessing Jackson's life move forward and knowing mine never would.

I had such an amazing, close-knit family and friends *there*. I hated the idea of never seeing any of them again and letting them fade into a distant memory that hopefully, along with Jackson and his parents, would someday disappear from my mind all together.

I read a couple pages of the journal trying to concentrate on anything but what I was faced with having to do. Yet my uncle repeatedly wrote about missing Vivian and how being away from her was like trying to live without air. His tender emotional expressions of love only managed to make me feel even worse. Closing the journal, I set it aside and blindly stared out the window once more.

Because of the holiday weekend, all our practices were cancelled. Jenna, Caitlyn, and Hilary came over right after school bringing with them their men and my little brother. The silent house sprang to life, and I happily ran down the stairs to greet them.

"Hey guys!" I called out, descending the stairs as they entered the foyer.

A round of applause broke out. I stopped a few steps shy of the floor and playfully took a bow.

"I can't believe you. I'm so jealous!" Jenna began.

"Me too. I have been dying to do that for years!" Caitlyn added.

"Well, I guess we all learned not to piss off Jocelyn," Cody laughed. "I never knew you had it in you."

"Neither did I," I said.

All of us retreated to the basement. Ethan put in a movie, and everyone got comfortable, chattering endlessly about how fast the news spread through the school. It seemed I had become quite the celebrity for my stupid stunt.

"Dakota says she's going to pay you back for this," Hilary rolled her eyes with a smirk. "I told her to go ahead. You'd have no problem making her look like Taylor."

"That's true. I really wouldn't mind," I giggled. "The only thing that makes me mad is that she got a five-day suspension out of it."

"Jocelyn, that's good news." Jenna looked at me like I was stupid. "It's five days we don't have to deal with her."

"Nah, I think it'd be more fun to see her back at school on Monday so that everyone can appreciate my artwork."

"You're real sweet, sis." Ethan playfully hit me with a throw pillow before he sat down beside me on the couch. It was wonderful to goof around with him again, but I couldn't help but think of the price I'd paid for it.

"I know. I try." I grabbed the pillow from him and wrapped my arms around it holding it to my chest.

By six o'clock the eight of us were starving and the popcorn and chips had long since disappeared. I decided I'd go upstairs and see if my dad cared if we ordered a pizza. Between all of us, we had managed to scrape up enough to order a couple of larges.

I put the paper plates and a stack of napkins on the island. I opened the pantry door looking for the plastic cups and for the two-liter when my mom entered the kitchen nearly scaring the life out of me.

"A three day in-school suspension! What in the world were you thinking getting into a fight at school?"

I spun around to find her standing in the doorway with her hands on her hips. Apparently, she was still not ready to forgive me for my almost marriage, but at least she decided to finally speak to me.

"I don't know, it just sorta happened." That was the truth.

"I don't even know who you are anymore," she huffed.

I almost fired back with that makes two of us, but from the look on her face I decided against it.

"You had better get your head on straight young lady or you're never going to amount to anything!"

My mouth dropped open, but no words came out. I stood there in stunned silence.

"And what are your friends doing here? Do you think you get to have some sort of party to celebrate your stupidity? You'd better think again because you are grounded, for a very long time." She raised her voice, and I cringed knowing everyone downstairs could hear her.

"She's not grounded for defending herself," my dad spoke up, entering the kitchen from the other side. "The principal even told me she didn't start it when I picked her up."

My mother fumed, glaring between my father and I. Minutes passed and none of us said a word. Finally, she spun around on her heels and stormed back upstairs. Seconds later, we heard their bedroom door slam.

"I'm sorry, Daddy." I truly was. I felt horrible for putting him in this position.

"You did nothing to be sorry for. Don't worry about it, enjoy your friends. I'll talk with her after she calms down a bit," he smiled half-heartedly.

I pulled the covers up around my chin and considered how great it would be if I could utilize the fireplace in my room to take the chill out of the air. My parents would have a nervous breakdown if I even suggested it, claiming that I would most certainly burn the house down. It amazed me, the degree to which *here,* at the age of eighteen, I was legally an adult yet still viewed by most of society as a kid still too immature to make rational decisions regarding my own life. Yet, *there,* at the age of eighteen, most of men and women were already married, some with one child, others more, and they were already running their own careers and households. I couldn't figure out where along the line the shift happened. Best I could figure was somewhere in the sixties and seventies when a large portion of America's youth decided growing up and having responsibilities wasn't much fun and did everything possible to avoid it.

I rolled over trying to find a comfortable position. My out of character behavior at lunch seemed rather trivial in comparison to the magnitude of what was waiting for me once sleep found me. Part of my brain was eager to have it over with, the other, was still somewhat on the fence. My heart physically ached in my chest. The thought of never seeing Jackson again was almost more than I could handle. Sending him to Boston was the right thing to do, my brain kept reminding me. I wanted him to find happiness and I knew that someday he would move on with his life. With him living in Boston and me in Chicago, it would be much easier for him to move forward. Yet, having to live across the street *there* from him and his wonderful family that I dearly loved was more than my heart could conceive.

I knew my decision was the right one for both of us. I was sure of it, but even that knowledge did not make it any easier for me to contemplate a life without the man I loved. I knew that no man ever to enter my life in the future would fill the void that Jackson left. My heart would never heal. Never love again.

CHAPTER 30

Thursday, November 28, 1878

THE SKIES WERE DARK AND GRAY and the rain pattered heavily on the roof. Dread filled my heart. I knew what had to be done. It wasn't going to be easy I was sure of it. Saying good-bye to those I loved dearly a life I loved dearly, a world that would forever disappear and become only a faded memory.

Yet I had to believe that this was as it should be. I was positive that I could not reside between the two worlds. I knew I could never find that happy medium that the Chandlers found.

One life is difficult enough without contemplating the idea of entertaining two. I know I am not strong enough for that. Not alone anyway, and that is exactly where I am in this bizarre scenario that has consumed me.

None of this is real. None of this is real. None of this is real, I repeated over and over in my mind in some vague attempt to convince myself. Yet as I stumbled out of bed, I stubbed my little toe on the corner of my bed. Intense pain shot through my body assuring me that this was indeed real, as I grabbed my foot and hopped around my room trying to verbally censor my pain.

I hobbled over to the window and sat down rubbing my aching foot until it finally subsided. I leaned back and laughed to myself again for being foolish enough to try and convince myself of anything other than this never-ending nightmare which I was finally hoping to awaken from. I pulled the curtains back and looked out at the soggy dreary day that engulfed everything within my view. In the foggy haze across the way sat the vacant building that had once been my second home. It had always been a warm and welcoming atmosphere that I always felt comfortable and at ease within. Now it loomed cold and heartbroken, a place I desperately wished I could erase from both planes.

A low rapping on my door broke my train of thought.

"Yes?"

"Good mornin', Miss. Jocelyn." Mimi appeared in an overly festive mood.

"Good morning, Mimi. How are you this morning?" I tried to match her enthusiasm.

"Ah's doin' well, ben up since five gettin' everadang reada. Ya'r ma's in rare form."

"I would imagine so," I smiled, envisioning the havoc that my mother was most likely inflicting upon the staff.

"What time is everyone arriving?"

"Suppa time."

She walked over to the armoire and started sorting through my gowns. She pulled out an Amherst shaded gown and laid it gently across my bed. It was the exact color of the gown that Emily had created for the Halloween party even though the style was somewhat different.

I remained silent and sat down at the vanity table. Mimi came over and began brushing my hair in long strokes. I closed my eyes trying not to think that this may well be the last time she and I performed this ritual that we had danced every day for as long as I could remember. I closely watched her skillful fingers work their perfected craft and absorbed every movement. She moved her graceful fingers with such precision and delicacy that it amazed me.

I held onto the bedpost while Mimi pulled and tugged on the corset strings until I felt like I couldn't inhale before she finally tied the knot. *This is one thing I certainly will not miss at all. Yet, I must admit that I do love the degree to which it enhances my figure.*

I climbed into the heavy gown and instantly felt the weight of the material against my frame as Mimi fastened it together. After the tactile recall of the almost weightless attire, I wore daily *there,* the multiple layers of articles adorned *here* felt oddly more comforting over the other. In a sense I felt as if I was stepping into a role, the role of the proper young lady in the year 1878. It was absurd to imagine styling the fashions of the twenty-first century in such a setting. I smiled at myself in the full-length mirror thinking of the reaction it would cause if I were to attempt such a thing.

"Ya luk vera lovely, Miss Jocelyn." Mimi smiled, stepping back, and admiring her work.

"Thank you, Mimi. You did a beautiful job." I hugged her tightly.

Mimi excused herself to return downstairs to assist the others. I assured her that I would follow shortly. It was half past ten and I still had some time before the remainder of my family arrived. I paced restlessly around my room, tracing my fingers over the silliest and most trivial of objects just to encode them into my memory forever. I wanted nothing to go left unexplored. The smells of the fresh linens on my bed, the embers in the hearth, the dried violets and lilies of a spring long forgotten left at my request. Even though I resided within the same four walls on both planes, each was so drastically different they appeared in my mind as separate entities.

My mind drifted from one source of intrigue to another while spontaneously entertaining minute-by-minute shifts in my emotions. It was impossible to focus on one topic or contemplate anything for longer than it took me to take two steps. I wanted to absorb everything all at once, remember every single detail of the last eighteen years. All the holidays, birthdays, special occasions that transpired under this roof.

The most aggravating of all was the fact that while the holes were enlarging, they mainly consisted of recent events across planes with only rare flashes of the past that were hard to differentiate. It seemed while on each individual plane, everything was normal, and memories of years past were as clear as day, full memories had not been totally exposed across time. I picked up the silver pocket watch from Jackson and held it tightly against my chest. I suppose it's a good thing because having those memories would only make it harder to let go of my life *here*.

I had spent the last several years of my life thinking of how wonderful it would be to finally be Jackson's wife, the mother of his children, have our own home, and be able to spend every evening by his side. Now it was gone. I sat down on the corner of the bed and leaned my head against the post, closing my eyes. I could see the photographs of our family that my *other* self had discovered. My three beautiful babies and the proof that our little family had prospered and persevered were painful reminders.

I sighed heavily and wiped a single tear off my cheek. I knew I had to pull myself together if I was going to get through this day. I couldn't give anyone anything to be suspicious about. I would play my role to perfection until I could seize the opportunity to get my Uncle Monte alone and beg him for his help.

Sarah, Cora, and Mimi were working endlessly making sure that the huge Thanksgiving dinner was prepared perfectly. The smell of turkey and pumpkin pie hung heavy throughout the house. The enticing aroma brought back a flood of memories from yesteryears when all of us were much younger, and the world was somehow a much friendlier place. It was strange to think of how that wasn't long ago yet, so much has occurred since those times that the carefree innocence was now lost forever and had been replaced with something much colder and harder than I could ever have imagined.

Mother was almost frantic, making sure all the last-minute details were attended to before the first of our family arrived. Father was doing his best to keep her under control but even he looked as if he had almost hit his breaking point. I never could figure out why these occasions were referred to as a holiday when they always seemed to wreak more havoc than all the other days combined.

"Everything looks beautiful, Mother," I complimented upon entering the dining room.

"Do you really think so?" she looked apprehensive.

"Yes." I placed my arm around her. "And you look lovely, too."

"So, do you, darling. It is good to see you looking more like yourself again."

"I feel better," I catered. "And this is going to be a great day."

My parents looked at me as if they weren't buying my fake façade.

"Yes, it is," William spoke up as he and Olivia entered the room.

Two of my brothers showed up with their wives and in Jonathon's case, children. As soon as I saw Patrick II and his wife Kathrine, I flashed back to the memory that I'd had of their wedding in my life *there*. It was the first time I had ever seen Jackson and his parents in one of my visions. Even then, strong emotions were coming across my thinning consciousness. I knew how much I did not like my brother's choice of wife.

Kathrine was a very cold woman whom I truly believed only married my brother for his choice in profession and the financial gain he received from it. Even though they had been married for several years, they had yet to produce a child. Mainly, I believed, because she would hate to share the spotlight with someone else. Kathrine was a very vain individual that always thought of herself first. She couldn't care less about the long hours my brother put in at the hospital to afford the type of lifestyle she felt entitled to. If anyone was going to have to miss my last family holiday, I would rather it had been her instead of James and his family.

My mother's sister with her family made their appearance shortly after her brother and his family showed. My Uncle Monte and Aunt Vivian arrived with their sons while my Uncle Nicholas and his clan were the last to show. Everyone snacked on the finger foods Sarah had prepared, lingering about discussing various subjects while the younger children ran around, filling the house with the familiar sounds of their laughter. The house was crowded, yet still felt strangely empty to me without the Chandlers. They had always shared all our holidays and all those present felt their absence although no one uttered a word on the subject.

The food was superb, and everyone gorged themselves to capacity. After dinner and dessert, I nervously stood next to the stair rail gripping it so tightly my knuckles turned white. I had spoken to my Uncle Monte countless times in my life though this time was entirely different. I watched him carefully standing next to Vivian with his arm draped loosely around her waist. He laughed whole-heartedly at something my brother Jonathon said. He seemed very happy. In all the years of my life, I could never recall a time when I had even the slightest inclination that he was unhappy or unsatisfied with his decision to leave his other plane of existence.

I knew in my heart that if I was ever going to have a chance to heal and become whole again, I was going to have to leave this plane forever. I could not live in a world where I was so close to Jackson—to see him someday fall in love with another, marry her and then father her children. I could not bear it. The pain would be overwhelming, and I knew I would eventually succumb to my grief and have no desire for any sort of existence. Therefore, it was now or never if I could ever hope to have any semblance of happiness.

I casually approached my uncle and stood next to my Aunt Vivian. "Excuse me, Uncle Monte, may I speak with you a moment alone please?"

"Certainly, Jocelyn." He turned towards my brother. "Please, excuse me." He nodded towards his wife. "I shall return shortly, my dear."

Placing a loving kiss on her cheek, he turned and followed me to the other end of the house to my father's study.

I quietly closed the door behind us, and my heart began racing so loudly I was positive he could hear it. Uncle Monte took a seat in the armchair next to the fire and warmed his hands over the flames.

"My goodness, I believe we are going to have a bad winter this year," he grinned slightly. "Now Jocelyn, come sit down and tell me what is on your mind."

I took the seat opposite his and tried to think of the right words to begin with. "It is most difficult to explain, I am afraid."

He looked at me inquisitively. "Well then, you have my full attention and curiosity."

"Did my father speak to you regarding my engagement to Jackson?" I shifted slightly, feeling uncomfortable.

He leaned over and gently placed his hands over mine in a fatherly gesture. "Yes, he informed me Sunday. I am so sorry that you ended the engagement."

"That is what I wanted to speak with you alone about."

He sat back in his seat and gave me a confused look.

"I ended our engagement because he could not be honest with me about *EVE*."

My Uncle nodded in understanding. "Has your barrier disintegrated?" he inquired.

"Not completely. Although there are holes, and they seem to be growing almost daily. I am experiencing feelings and emotions that I cannot explain, events that are out of chronological order, some very recent, some from my early childhood. None of which make a great deal of sense to me."

"I would imagine not," he laughed. "It can be very disturbing to say the least."

"Yes, very much so."

"Was Jackson not clarifying episodes for you?" He leaned forward in his chair. "The Chandlers promised me they would do everything possible to guide you through this difficult time of adjustment. And now, to hear this," he shook his head.

"As you can imagine, the ending of our engagement has greatly changed my circumstances."

"In what way?"

"You may not be aware of what events have been transpiring *there*, but I am afraid that my relationship with Jackson and the recent announcement of our engagement has caused a great deal of stress in my life and strain on my family," I began.

"Yes, Mr. Chandler has been kind enough to keep me updated on your progress and told me what had transpired," he leaned back again and relaxed. "And I must say that it is a relief that your barrier is finally coming down. I have been waiting anxiously to ask you so many questions about my brother, Shane. I miss him dearly. How is he doing?"

"He has been so wonderful about all of this. While he did not approve of my getting married so young, he was supportive, which is more than I can say for my mother, Amy, and Ethan," I sighed, but my uncle laughed.

"That is not surprising. Amy is a very career driven woman. Mr. Chandler told me she was being difficult. Honestly, I expected nothing less of her. Yet, I am surprised that Ethan was so hard on you." His eyebrows furled.

"Ethan can be very moody when he chooses to be," I half smiled.

"And how is Sydney?"

"She is doing well. She is attending Northwestern, pre-med of course," I said with pride. "She came home for my birthday, and I believe she will be home for Thanksgiving."

"Is she dating anyone seriously?" he inquired.

"Not that I am aware of. I honestly do not speak with her often," I lowered my eyes. "I believe we do not have much in common with one another."

"No, I suppose not. She was always more like your mother, and you favored my side of the family more." He patted my knee and laughed. "But are you happy *there*?"

"Yes, I believe so. It really is such a different world, and I am still trying to absorb it all. I never would have imagined some of the things that I have learned about it and even seen for myself."

"Yes, it must be quite a shock for you."

"But I really have some amazing friends *there*. I am very active in sports. I play volleyball, basketball, and softball. I am a very good student. In fact, I will be going to college next fall, but I am not sure yet what I am going to major in." Those words felt so foreign coming out of my mouth.

"Good, good. I am happy to hear that," he nodded in acknowledgment.

I got up and wandered over to the window collecting my thoughts for a moment. "However, this situation with Jackson has caused me more grief in both my lives than I ever thought possible."

"What is on your mind, Jocelyn?" Uncle Monte leaned forward in his chair again.

"Since the Chandlers only came *there* looking for me because of our engagement *here* and that no longer being an issue, I asked Jackson to return to Boston and his studies at law school for the spring semester."

I hated myself for the tears that drifted down my cheeks. I hastily brushed them aside before I continued. "There simply was no point for us to continue our relationship or to go ahead with our wedding next summer *there*." I smiled grimly and brushed the tears away once more then returned to my chair across from him at the hearth.

"My dear, you cannot be serious. I know you are very upset with his recent behavior. Are you sure there is no possibility of you two mending your relationship?"

His eyes were full of sympathy and understanding like no other I had spoken to in weeks. It was like a weight being lifted just being able to speak with someone other than the Chandlers who I could be honest with and who understood every aspect of what I was enduring.

"I believe it is too far gone for that now." I hated myself for the endless run of tears.

"It is never too late for someone you love," my uncle added softly, taking my hands in his.

"If only that were true, I would fight for him."

"Then fight for him. Tell him that you love him. Tell him you forgive him. Do not allow the one you love to slip through your fingers, my darling. If you do you will regret it for the rest of your life." He looked deep into my eyes.

"Uncle Monte," I brushed the tears aside. "I read your journals."

"I see." He sat back in his chair and shifted his eyes towards the fire. "You must understand Jocelyn, I never intended for you or anyone to see those."

"Shane found them and showed them to me." My uncle nodded but remained silent. "He thought you were an amazing writer. He said it made him feel like you had actually experienced it all firsthand."

"I did," he muttered softly, still staring at the fire. "I should have destroyed them before I left."

He looked back towards me, but his eyes looked sad.

"Left? Don't you mean died?" The memory of being at his grave came rushing through me.

"Jocelyn,"

"I know you made the conscious decision twelve years ago to leave your life *there* and live solely on this plane." His eyes widened, and he slowly nodded. "As you could not live in a world where your wife did not exist, I cannot live in a world where Jackson does. Please I beg of you, Uncle Monte, if you love me and ever want to see me happy, tell me how to leave this plane so that I may attempt to rebuild a life *there* without him."

"Jocelyn, have you thought about this? I mean, really thought about this. What you are asking is not something that you can change your mind about later. You cannot take it back and this would devastate your family *here*. Do you realize that?"

"Yes, I know, and it is not something I would think of doing irrationally. Besides, is it so very different from what you did to us *there*? I remember what your death did to my father — our family. Shane still goes through it even now. He just now went through your stuff. That is how he came across your journals." I shook my head in frustration. "He barely talks about you and that is saying nothing of what it did to your parents. I was young, but I do remember it." Strange as it was, I honestly did. "How is my situation any different than yours?" I pleaded.

"I was not running away when I made my decision. I could not imagine ever loving someone else the way I love Vivian. I never wanted to be with another woman, *there* or *here*. What I did was selfish. I know that, and a lot of people were hurt because of it. You will move on with your life in time, my dear. I know it does not feel like it, but I promise you, it is true," he explained.

I shook my head in despair. "No. No. You are wrong. There is no moving forward. Not *here*, but perhaps I can *there*. Perhaps I can find a way before the barrier is demolished. I can believe that this has all been a dream, some horrible nightmare that I can finally awaken from. I can find a way to believe that it never really happened. That he was not real."

"Tell me something honestly." He got up and walked over beside me. "Did you also find the photo albums?"

I turned back towards the window and stared at the black evening sky. The thick cloud cover allowed no penetration by the sparkling stars. I couldn't see even the smallest bit of light breaking into the darkness. Nothing but black hovered over the outside world.

I wanted desperately to deny discovering the albums, but I knew he would see straight through me. I had admitted to reading the journals and they were packed in the same trunk as the albums so there was no getting around it. I nodded my head slowly without turning towards him.

"And you looked through them?"

"Yes."

"You saw your family — the family you and Jackson have?"

Tears rolled gently down my face. "*Were* going to have. But not now." I brushed the tears aside and turned back to my uncle. "How does that work exactly, Uncle Monte? What happens when things change events that in one era have already happened?"

"To be honest, I have not the slightest inkling." His eyes drifted towards the window as if he was lost in his own thoughts for a moment while considering the possibilities. "The entire concept of *EVE* was always very baffling to me. There were so many questions I wanted answers to but never found."

We returned to our seats by the hearth.

"I know. Imagine how I felt when I was told the me *there* was even named after the me *here*!" I shook my head with dismay.

"Yes," Monte chuckled a bit. "I always thought that was rather ironic when Shane and Amy told me about it. Of course, I could not say anything to them."

I leaned over running my fingers through my hair. A low laugh from my uncle caused me to look back up at him. "You realize that Shane does the same thing when he gets upset about something."

"Excuse me?"

"The gesture you just made. Your father, Shane does the same thing when he is upset."

"Really?"

"Yes, your *other* self is really starting to shine through," he smiled softly.

"And what will the impact be on my family line now that Jackson and I are not going to get married and have children? What will happen now that I have chosen to leave *here*?"

My uncle shook his head slowly. "I just don't know, Jocelyn. I wish I did but I really don't."

"Then I will have to risk it," I stated firmly.

"You cannot risk something we know so little about. Your decision could end your family line *there* and then you may not have a life to lead *there*," he tried to reason. "If you are set on only living on one plane of existence then you should leave your life *there*, not *here*."

"Are you serious?" I stared at him with disbelief. "You have to be kidding?"

"Not at all. You cannot risk so much. The consequences could be disastrous."

"Let's not be melodramatic, Uncle Monte," I huffed. "I have four brothers to carry on the family line. And if you think I would give up everything I have *there* for the life I have *here*...well then, you have forgotten all the amazing changes the world has made in the last century. If I was still going to marry Jackson on both planes, then I know I would have been able to find a happy medium." My eyes drifted towards the flames for a moment. "All right, so perhaps I am exaggerating a bit. I know I would have been happy no matter where I was as long as I had Jackson. But you are forgetting the bigger picture here. Our engagement is off."

"You can change that if you want. Besides, it is not your brothers whom your father, Shane, me and the *other* you are directly descended from. It is from your daughter...your and Jackson's daughter," he stated pointedly.

"But Alyssa Nichole, along with Gavin and Ethan are never going to exist," I shot back a little more quickly than I had intended. "I am sorry, Uncle Monte." I dropped my head back down in my hands. "This is so unfair," I complained. "I have given this a great deal of thought, and my mind is set. This dual existence is not what I want. I just want to be normal."

"Jocelyn, please."

"Uncle Monte, I know you understand how I am feeling. I read your journals. I know you have felt this sense of loss. Please help me. I cannot live like this. I must leave to move forward. If I do not, I know I will forever be unhappy," I begged with all my heart.

My Uncle stared at me for a long while with endearing love and empathy. I leaned forward a tad anxiously waiting with bated breath for Uncle Monte to speak the words I longed to hear to finally put an end to all my pain and torment. I knew I could never survive the pain of a life without Jackson and the very thought of watching him move on and eventually be with another was completely unbearable.

Suddenly a loud commotion outside the study drew both our attention towards the door. "I do not care if she wants to see me or not!" My heart stopped. "William, please...step aside!" Jackson's voice pleaded very loudly.

The office door swung open and there stood Jackson with William gripping his arm. The mere sight of him took my breath away and sent a blazing dagger straight into my heart.

"Jackson, leave her alone," William said through gritted teeth.

"She has to hear what I have to say," Jackson responded without taking his eyes off me.

"It is all right, William," I forced the words out. I couldn't breathe.

"I will leave you two alone. Excuse me." Uncle Monte leaned down with a slight smile and kissed the top of my head before he left the room, closing the door behind him.

Jackson stood there for several minutes staring at me without uttering a word. The silence was worse than the yelling.

"I thought you had something to say to me?" I forced myself to remain seated and not run into his arms like every ounce of me wanted to.

"Jocelyn," he softly began. "Please, do not do this." He crossed over and knelt beside my chair. "I am begging you."

"Jackson…"

"Please, do not leave this plane, leave me, leave us." His emerald, green eyes were surrounded by dark circles and looked mournful, dark, like he hadn't slept in days and his face was scruffy.

"You flatter yourself," I got up and crossed back over to the window. "I would have to still care about you in order for me to consider doing something of that nature."

He walked up behind me and wrapped his arms around me. I closed my eyes and told myself not to break down. "I love you, Jocelyn. I have always loved you and I always will. Nothing in either world will ever change my feelings for you," he whispered, leaning into my ear. "I only want to spend my lives with you." I could feel his hot breath on my neck.

"Jackson, please," I hated myself for the tears that returned. "It will never be over between us because I will never stop loving you."

"Nor I you."

He turned me around, but I refused to look up at him. I knew it would render me powerless and I was already quickly losing that battle.

"I was stupid and childish. I am so sorry I did not tell you the whole truth. I should have trusted you, trusted us. I never meant to deceive you. Please forgive me," he begged in a soft tone.

I stared down at the floor afraid to meet his eyes. I felt so ashamed for my recent behavior—on both planes. I was the one who had overreacted and behaved like a child. Not him.

"I am so sorry, for everything," I whispered. "Can you ever forgive me for the horrible things I said and the way that I behaved?"

"Marry me," he lifted my chin with his fingertips forcing me to look into his beautiful brilliant green eyes. "I love you sweetheart, please say you will."

I nodded stupidly lost in his eyes. A slow grin spread across his shapely lips. "Are you serious?"

Again, I nodded.

He pressed his lips firmly upon mine and I melted into him feeling the passionate fire soar through me instantly. Jackson picked me up and twirled me around in his arms.

"Oh, I love you so much, baby!"

"I love you too." I laughed. "I am so sorry for everything."

"No, it was all my fault. I am sorry for all the pain I caused you. I never meant to hurt you; I promise."

We held each other tightly in front of the fire, savoring the moment and never wanting it to end. I could hear the commotion outside the office door and knew it wouldn't be long before we were interrupted.

"Are you alright?" he asked with my favorite lop-sided grin.

"Never better." I rested my head against his chest, inhaling the smell of his cologne. I couldn't imagine ever feeling better than I did at that moment.

"We should probably open the door before your brothers kick it in," he laughed, giving me a tight squeeze.

"Let them. I do not care. I never want to let you go." I tightened my grip around him. "I missed you so much."

Jackson leaned down and kissed the top of my head. "I missed you too, my love. I have been so miserable without you."

"Me too."

"Never again."

"Never," I happily agreed.

My family was crunched up against the door eavesdropping to the point they practically fell in when Jackson finally opened it moments later.

"Oh….um, sorry," William stammered with Olivia and my mother leaning right over him.

"We were just… well…um," my mother looked embarrassed. "Would you like some dessert, Mr. Jackson? Sarah has made the best pumpkin pie, and we also have some whipped cream chocolate cake. It is Sarah's specialty," she attempted to recompose herself.

Both of us couldn't help but laugh at them. "That would be wonderful," Jackson glowed.

He took my hand, and we walked back into the front room when there was another knock at the front door. Eddie hurried to answer it while the others smothered us, congratulating us on our reunification.

"I am glad to see the two of you together," Emily's voice rang out as she approached us. She wrapped her arms tightly around me and then her son. "This is wonderful. I am guessing that the wedding is back on?"

I smiled and nodded. I could not seem to stop smiling. Everyone was suddenly talking all at once, but the only thing I could concentrate on was the fact that I was standing beside Jackson and his arms were wrapped tightly around me.

His parents and siblings and their families had all followed Jackson back from Boston. From what I could gather from the numerous conversations that were taking place simultaneously was that they had left shortly after they had realized he was missing. It seems they were unsure as to what kind of reception he was going to receive upon his intrusion on our holiday. The bits and pieces I had heard told me that my brothers were more protective of me than I had ever realized.

As the evening settled in and Jackson and I snuggled up on the lounge by the hearth surrounded by our family and loved ones, I found my peace and solace. This is exactly where I belonged. It really did not matter which plane we were on, if I had Jackson beside me, I knew I would be happy.

Appendix

2015

The Timmons'
- Shane Douglas, VP Compliance of Chicago General
- Amy Marie, Pediatrician at Chicago General
- Sidney Harper, Sophomore at Northwestern University
- Jocelyn Alyssa, Senior in high school
- Ethan Jude, Junior in high school

The Chandler's
- Robert Abraham, Corporate Attorney
- Emily Jade, Novelist
- Alexander Nolan, Divorce Attorney in Boston
  - Leslie, Alexander's wife
  - Lucinda, Alexander & Leslie's six-year-old daughter
  - Charlie, Alexander & Leslie's four-year-old son
- Phoebe Rochelle, Criminal Attorney in Boston
  - Carson Adler, Phoebe's husband
  - Wallace, Phoebe and Carson's one-year-old son
- Jackson Wyatt, Senior in high school/Studying law at Boston University

The Burk's
- Craig, Jenna's father
- Melinda, Jenna's mother
- Jenna, Jocelyn's best friend/Dating Kyle/Volleyball, Basketball player

The Clausen's
- Brett, Kyle's father
- Sonya, Kyle's mother
- Kyle, Jenna's boyfriend/Senior in high school
- Brandon, Kyle's brother/Freshman in high school

Friends

- Caitlyn Buchanan, Zac's girlfriend/Volleyball, Basketball, Softball player/Senior
- Zak Engling, Caitlyn's boyfriend/Quarterback, Point Guard/Senior
- Hilary Wade, Cody's girlfriend/Volleyball, Basketball player/Senior
- Cody Porter, Hilary's boyfriend/Wide receiver, small forward/Senior
- Mariah Jones, Ethan's ex-girlfriend/Junior
- Corbin Stewart, Hailey's boyfriend, Ethan's best friend/Junior
- Hailey Collins, Corbin's girlfriend/Junior
- Taylor Perry, Jocelyn's nemesis/Cheerleader/Senior
- Dakota Anderson, Taylor's sidekick/Cheerleader/Senior

Coaches/Teachers

- Coach Smith, Volleyball & Girls Basketball Coach/teaches English Lit 9
- Coach Shelburne, Football Coach/teaches computer programing
- Coach Minnick, Boys Basketball Coach/ teaches algebra
- Coach Kane, Girls Softball Coach/teaches PE
- Mr. Rand, teaches AP psychology
- Mrs. Neal-Beliveau, teaches AP biology
- Mrs. Killian, teaches Jocelyn's English Lit 12
- Mrs. Runyon, teaches Jackson's English Lit 12
- Mr. Dunn, teaches chemistry
- Mrs. Ulbright, teaches history
- Principal Julia Cosgrove

1878

The Timmons

- Patrick Michael, Physician
- Annabelle Nichole, Married to Patrick/Jocelyn's mother
- Patrick Michael II, Physician
  - Katherine, Patrick II's wife
- Jonathon Niles, Physician
  - Lizette, Jonathon's wife
  - Isaac, Jonathon & Lizette's nine-year-old son
  - Louisa, Jonathon & Lizette's eight-year-old daughter
  - Derek, Jonathon & Lizette's four-year-old son
- James Henry, Attorney
  - Rachael, James' wife
  - Abbigail, James & Rachael's five-year-old daughter

- Aiden, James & Rachael's three-year-old son
- Hannah, Housekeeper/Nanny
- William Arthur, Married to Olivia Adams/first year at Northwestern University
- Jocelyn Alyssa, Engaged to Jackson Chandler

The Timmons' Household
- Eddie, Stableman/Married to Mimi/Cora's dad
- Mimi, Manages the household/Married to Eddie/Cora's mom
- Cora, Housekeeper/Daughter of Eddie and Mimi
- Sarah, Cook
- Missy, Housekeeper

The Chandler's
- Robert Abraham, Attorney
- Emily Jade, Married to Robert/Jackson's mother
- Alexander Nolan, Attorney
  - Veronica, Alexander's wife
  - Casper, Alexander & Veronica's six-year-old son
  - Wyatt, Alexander & Veronica's five-year-old son
  - Kyra, Alexander & Veronica's three-year-old daughter
- Phoebe Rochelle
  - Silas Monroe, Phoebe's husband/School teacher
  - Wallace, Phoebe & Silas' one-year-old son
  - Katie, The Monroe's housekeeper/Nanny
- Jackson Wyatt, Law School at Northwestern University

The Chandler Household
- Barnaby, Stableman/Married to Carly
- Susan, Housekeeper
- Carly, Cook/Married to Barnaby
- Norma, Housekeeper

The Adams'
- Benjamin, Banker/Married to Harriett
- Harriett, Married to Benjamin
- Olivia, Jocelyn's best friend/Married to William
- Kincade, Olivia's seven-year-old brother
- Oscar, Olivia's four-year-old brother
  - Grady, The Adams' stableman

The Cain's

- Henry, Owns the mercantile
- Molly, Married to Henry
- Laurie, Friend of Jocelyn's/Theodore's girlfriend
- Quintin, Laurie's five-year-old brother
    - Gracie, The Cain's housekeeper

The Maddox's

- Elmer, Elizabeth's father
- Ester, Elizabeth's mother
- Easton, Elizabeth's twenty-year-old brother
- Elizabeth, Jocelyn's friend/Lee's girlfriend
- Edwin, Elizabeth's sixteen-year-old brother
- Elijah, Elizabeth's fourteen-year-old brother
- Elisa, Elizabeth's eight-year-old sister
    - Sabina, The Maddox's housekeeper

The Donaldson's

- George, Carpenter/Married to Corrine
- Corrine, Married to George
- Josiah, Dimitri's twenty-five-year-old brother
- Dimitri, formerly engaged to Maryanne
- Calliope, Dimitri's sixteen-year-old sister
- Ingrid, Dimitri's fourteen-year-old sister

Friends

- Christina Bowden, Jocelyn's friend/Thomas' girlfriend
- Thomas Reynolds, Christina's boyfriend
- Theodore Norris, Laurie's boyfriend
- Maryanne Kendrick, Formerly engaged to Dimitri/Jocelyn's nemesis
- Sean Preston, Dimitri's best friend/Died of pneumonia in Spring 2015/Formerly engaged to Olivia Adams
- Lee Miller, Elizabeth Maddox's boyfriend/Architect
- Mr. Grahame, History teacher

AUTHOR BIO

A. L. Waddington has her master's in military psychology and is currently working on her doctorate. She is an avid reader and researcher, has a slight coffee addiction and when she is not lost in a world of her own creation, she enjoys spending time gardening, hiking, and traveling with her family. A. L. and her husband, Eric, live in East Texas with their daughters and three spoiled puppies.

ILLUMINATION, BOOK 4

Can time predict the future?

In the gripping conclusion of the bestselling *EVE* series, Jocelyn and Jackson come face to face with the challenges of living combined lives on both planes. While Jackson struggles under the demands of his chosen profession, Jocelyn discovers hidden branches in the family tree. But the more she uncovers, the deeper she finds herself and her family in an uncharted realm that no one considered possible. Can EVE not only skip around with family members but also switch branches?

The happy couple soon learns that a branch, like time, has the tendency to bend in the most unexpected direction and occasionally break. When that happens, lives are forever changed, the forces of destinies altered, and fates derailed. The fluidity of time begins to take on an obscure meaning as the barrier between the two worlds fades into darkness.

DISHEARTENED, BOOK 2

THE SPIRIT QUEST SERIES

"I do not know which is worse — sitting on the edge of a Civil War you know is coming or watching your country implode from within on the verge of another that could happen at any time."
~ Sidney Timmons-Marshall

Gifted or cursed with the inherited ability of E.V.E., Sidney is forced into the inconceivable — her 1860 self-watches on the eve of the American Civil War as the Northerners and Southerners dismantle the fabric of the nation. Whereas her present-day self-witnesses the extreme Progressives and Liberals shred away the decency of the American Culture on a world-wide stage and make the USA the laughingstock of the globe.

Sidney is heartbroken watching everything her loved ones and countrymen from her other life fought to preserve be undone by a minuet mindless minority of entitled fanatics and a political party so hell-bent on spreading hate, they would rather burn the nation to the ground than relinquish power.

But what can she do? Can one small voice change the mind of millions with hate in their heart? Can she find her way back to the solace she once treasured in both her lives?

Alwaddington.com
ScarlettInkPublishing.com